WINDSWEPT

Windswept

Copyright © 2019 by Lynwood Shiva Sawyer

Book design by D. Bass
Original cover painting by Nad Wolinska (All rights reserved)
Cover design by Richard Amari
Photo of New York Skyline by Reynaldo #brigworkz Brigantty from Pexels
Photo enhancement by Becque Olson

ISBN: 978-1-7331750-0-5

Library of Congress Control Number: 2019905426

Catalogue-in-Publication Data

Windswept / Lynwood Shiva Sawyer

1. Fiction – Thriller 2. Fiction – Mystery 3. Fiction – Romance

For further information contact: hpb@exuspat.com

Hidden Pearl Books is an imprint of Pigtown Books.

Watch the Windswept Teaser on youtube.com, starring Kara Gilligan and noted
British actor Jonathan Hansler. Directed by Linzy Attenborough. Search on:
windswept - teaser - sawyer - novel

To the memories of

My mentors:
Adi S. Irani (the "Old Tiger"),
Bhau Kalchuri ("Meher Baba's Lion")
[Brother and Disciple, respectively, of
the silent Indian Master, Meher Baba]
Norman Rosten (Poet Laureate of Brooklyn)
Frances Witlin (Columbia Pictures East-
Story Department) and Sam Robins
(the "Mayor of Brooklyn Heights").
Their unstinting wisdom, expertise and love
shaped me into the writer I am today.

The ever-patient and incredibly courageous
lovely jubbly Jill Irene Maddox
(Mother Manonash
[Qutub-e-Irshad/Parvati])

PROLOGUE

Goa

Randall Yearwood opened the door with his foot.

The action saved his life.

Five slugs from a silenced .22 tore through the wooden slats. Splinters blasted from the doorframe hurtled past him into the Indian night, the air moist from an onshore breeze.

He dove to the ground with agility surprising for a man nearing fifty.

In the split second he'd eased the door open, Yearwood glimpsed smoke curling from the closet at the back. Still prone, he fired his own weapon, an odd pistol the color of goldenrod and made of a Celazole, a space-age material. The weapon discharged with a loud CHUFF. Acrid smoke, smelling more like a welder's torch than gunpowder, unfurled from the barrel like bluish spider silk.

Yearwood slithered toward the door with the caution of an aging athlete. His weight was close to two hundred pounds, mostly muscle, held in check by exercise and discipline. He pressed his body flat, grimacing as the damp sand ground into his tailored linen suit.

With a surgeon's meticulousness, he extended his gun hand onto the cement stoop.

He fired three more times. CHUFF. CHUFF. CHUFF.

Wheezing grunts followed a sharp yelp. His bullets had struck their target.

Yearwood cautiously eased the door open with his pistol barrel.

A simple room. A bare incandescent bulb jittered from the uncertain electricity, illuminating an iron-frame bed draped with mosquito netting. Crude teak furniture.

His foe, still concealed behind the half-opened closet door, made no response other than the rasping grunts.

Yearwood wriggled backward on his stomach, dirt working its way into his salt-and-pepper beard.

The murmur of the surf blurred into the buzz of insects and faint strains of a celebration wafting from the outskirts of nearby Panjimi. The night was astonishingly dark, penetrated only by streaks of distant lightning and the glow from waves lit by phosphorescent plankton. The air was dense, redolent with the fragrance of night-blooming jasmine.

Yearwood's breath came easily as he slowly rose, unhastened by either exertion or fear. Mugginess, not sweat, brought a sheen to his espresso-colored skin.

Something crashed through the underbrush behind him.

Yearwood dropped into a crouch, his pistol tracking the commotion.

A smile split his fierce concentration as a wild sow and three piglets broke through the bushes. They scurried back into the darkness,

Relieved, he brushed the sand from his beard and suit.

He circled stealthily around the stucco building, searching for an open window.

No movement nor even a sound from his adversary.

Yearwood paused. He resembled a philosopher, contemplating some obscure and perhaps frivolous problem rather than a professional assassin pursuing a man who wanted to kill him.

Only insects and bats stirred in the scattering of one-storey buildings – the staff and remaining guests had all gone into town for the festival.

He stooped beneath the far window, then jiggled the screen sash just enough to ensure the man inside would notice.

Leaping away, he awaited another hail of bullets.

Nothing.

He wiggled a log loose from its garden-border mooring, hefted it to his shoulder, then hurled it through the screen.

In the gap made through the curtains, Yearwood spotted his quarry, doubled up in the closet. He returned to the front of the bungalow and eased himself through the door.

●

Yearwood sprinted around the edge of the room, pistol at the ready. Taking a deep breath, he flung open the closet door and jammed his pistol into his victim's temple.

Groaning softly, arms clutched around his middle, the man did not reach for the suppressor-equipped .22 that lay beside him.

Exit wounds had flared into a large crimson blossom on the back shoulder of his camouflage tunic. The man was darker-skinned than Yearwood, though his features had a distinctly Oriental cast. His coal-black hair lay in thick waves across his head. His face was full, the lips plump, and even in agony his eyes had a soft languor. His features made his age ambiguous. He might have been in his early thirties. Or maybe late forties. He certainly did not fit the image of a hardened guerrilla leader who had spent the last decade slogging through jungles evading helicopters and native trackers.

Though that was indeed who he was.

The man's eyes flickered as he struggled to work his expression into a smirk. Agony won, forcing him to settle on a grimace.

"It do not matter," the man wheezed. "Money you people give bullshit government . . ."

A slug had punctured one of his lungs. Maybe it had collapsed.

Yearwood's expression softened, sympathetic in the knowledge that his enemy's suffering was genuine. Nevertheless, he kept his pistol tightly aimed.

The man's voice was barely louder than a whisper and his thick accent made his speech almost unintelligible.

Yearwood froze. "What money, Jobim?"

He drew closer, his face tensing. He drilled the pistol into Jobim's temple.

"General Maningrat seventeen million dollar. You company pay to kill our people. You piss it away. General never get it." The man chuckled hoarsely, the sound rattling in his chest. "Never never never."

The blood-spumed coughing fit that followed was a small price to pay for the malice he derived from taunting Yearwood. Around Jobim's neck was a knotted leather thong with some sort of ivory amulet. Obviously, the talisman's protective power was bogus.

"What are you talking about? How do you know who I work for?"

Yearwood could no longer resist. He shoved his pistol into his belt and grabbed Jobim by the lapels. Blood from entrance wounds converged like crimson anemones across Jobim's front.

Yearwood dragged him into the middle of the room.

"Where is our money?" he demanded.

Jobim's head lolled in the collar of his tunic, He flinched in pain and refused to answer, biting his rich, full lips.

"Tell me and I'll save your life. I'll get you to a hospital." Yearwood's well-modulated voice grew ragged, echoes of a Brooklyn accent coarsened from the strain of unkeepable promises.

He crouched and ripped Jobim's tunic open. Buttons skittered across the pale flagstones. Distress puckered Yearwood's expression at the quantity of blood soaking his victim's undervest.

"We rebel . . . also . . . have most good friend in you company. Not son-bitch like you." Jobim was forced to gasp for breath, at first between his words and finally between each syllable. "Most . . . good friend to . . . my people . . . help us get our country back . . . drive . . . drive . . ."

"Someone inside the company? A traitor? Who?" he shouted at the dying man. Tell me!"

Yearwood was an individual who loathed surprises and rarely encountered them because he micromanaged away all uncertainty before embarking on any mission. Jobim's revelation provoked him into a state approaching recklessness.

"I'll see you get a decent burial. Provide for your family. Please, please. Give me his name. Her name. A clue. Just one initial."

Jobim's lips contorted into a wobbly gash of triumph. His eyes slid upwards in their sockets.

Yearwood dropped to his knees and cradled Jobim's head between them.

Jobim coughed hoarsely, sighed.

Oblivious to the blood staining his fine linen suit, Yearwood straddled the unbreathing man and forced his own breath through Jobim's now pliant lips. Pressed the motionless chest.

To no avail.

He knew a hundred ways to terminate someone's life but was a complete amateur at prolonging it.

After several minutes he rose, breathing heavily, disgusted by his own now bloody face and clothes.

He pulled a pair of latex gloves from his pocket, he donned them and searched the room in an organized frenzy.

Jobim traveled light; Yearwood discovered little.

Camouflage clothes hanging in the closet. A cheap canvas bag under the bed. Nothing in it nor even space for secret compartments. A nylon shaving kit with Indonesian toiletries. A carton of clove cigarettes.

Yearwood stood in the center of the room, contemplating.

The light bulb continued to flicker with a dozen different shades of brightness. It animated Jobim's cooling corpse with a peculiar ersatz simulation of life.

Suddenly inspired, Yearwood crossed to the bed and started to unroll the mosquito netting.

There was indeed a lump in the upper left hand corner. He withdrew a Damascus Laguiole knife from his pocket and slashed the netting away. A string-tied bundle fell out.

Yearwood cut the string with the knife and carefully separated the items.

Jobim's billfold, fat with rupees. An Australian passport made out to Joseph Ng. An around-the-world plane ticket, originating in Port Moresby, and continuing through Goa, Frankfurt, London, New York, San Francisco and Honolulu.

One-half of a torn Asahi beer coaster.

It had to be the token Jobim would have presented to his contact. The traitor inside Yearwood's firm who would possess the matching half.

Two Swiss passports in the names of Caspar and Judith Schütz.

So the traitor had an accomplice. According to the documents, Caspar was forty-one and his wife thirty-two. The passports were already colorful with visas and entry permits, but lacked photographs. There were also two plane tickets for Mr. and Mrs. Schütz, one-way from JFK to Dominica the following Wednesday evening. The same Wednesday Jobim had been scheduled to land in New York.

Yearwood returned to the passports and studied the blank spaces where the photographs were to go. He tried to visualize the faces the gaps might contain. His brow furrowed, his lips tightened from withheld curses.

At last, he broke away.

He took a plastic bag filled with grey clay-like material from his jacket pocket and removed it. He kneaded the mass until it was pliable. He then coated Jobim's motionless face with oil from a small vial, rubbing it carefully from the fallen man's brow to chin.

With an artist's delicacy, Yearwood applied the grey substance to Jobim's unbreathing features, shaping the material until an even layer spread from chin to scalp.

As Yearwood waited for the substance to harden into a striking death mask, he again studied the Schütz passports, the minimal clues to the turncoat or turncoats inside his organization.

His concentration was so intense that a dozen mosquitoes landed on his exposed flesh and, unmolested, feasted on his blood.

CHAPTER 1.

Lady Liberty

"Bring a passport photograph but not your passport," Thomas Catherton Lockhart had instructed Meghan Joyce the previous week.

Which was easy because, like so many Americans, she never had one.

"And a small carry-on with a few clean knickers and your favorite cosmetics," he continued. "We'll buy you a complete new wardrobe and whatever it is in all those bottles when we get there. We should be gone for three weeks."

He smiled the wry smile that so endeared him to her. "Let us see how many shades of wonderful we can attain."

She had spent several days in a cycle of excitement. Of speculative eagerness as his words attenuated into feeling, then yet other bursts of happiness as she mentally replayed his instructions.

•

"You have gorgeous red hair," a young banker proclaimed.

His smug voice disrupted Meghan's reverie, and she tried to bring her surroundings back in focus: the grand ballroom of the Lady Liberty, a triple-decked party ship that plied the waters around Manhattan. On a seemingly endless circuit upon the Hudson and East Rivers, the vessel catered singles dances and corporate office parties. Although the Lady Liberty had all the charm of a chain motel, the tightly-knit crew was the closest Meghan had ever come to a family.

She turned her attention to the banker, finding it difficult to tell where the storm-aggravated yaw of the ship ended and his drunkenness began. Filaments of scotch sloshed from his glass onto his crimson stirrup tie.

He took her disorientation to mean that she had not heard the compliment and repeated it loudly. "You have the most gorgeous red hair."

"I'm afraid it's tawny," Meghan corrected him.

Though its shade was closer to strawberry blonde, she had a redhead's temper, especially when called one. Nevertheless, storms brought out forgiveness in her, and delicious anticipation of her impending rendezvous with Thomas rendered her giddily immune from suggestive overtures, even insults.

"What?" asked the banker, befuddled by her response.

"Haven't you ever heard the word 'tawny'?"

"Like a lion?" The banker could not have been older than twenty-five, but he ogled Meghan as if she were eighteen, a more than dozen years younger than she really was.

"Exactly," she replied. "But thanks for the compliment anyway."

When she spoke slowly, it was hard to tell that she had been born and spent most of her life in Queens. She wondered why it was that, until recently, the only men who ever seemed to find her attractive were either very drunk or very desperate.

With a swirl of black taffeta, she hurried away.

The banker called out half-coherent entreaties, his drink-flushed face turning a deeper pink.

Meghan resumed her hostess duties, smiling appropriately at the queasy guests, but her thoughts immediately returned to Thomas. Never in her life had she had anything to anticipate, neither holidays nor honors or anniversaries.

Until now.

Meghan was thirty-five years old and ground down by grim experience. By meeting so many jerks. By meeting seemingly nice men who later turned out to be jerks. By futilely pursuing secret jerks who did not wish to be pursued and remaining oblivious to their rebuffs. The more she tried to deny her desperation, the more desperate she had become.

Her outlook had not been improved by her happily married cousin Moira's warning: if Meghan were not careful, she would soon reach the age when an unmarried woman was more likely to be struck by a meteor than find a sane and healthy unattached male.

Meghan had dismissed her cousin's prophecy with an uneasy laugh.

Then suddenly Meghan was twenty-nine. Though she finally had a job that did not fill her with self-loathing, she had arrived at a drab plateau, filled with millions of other women, all searching for the same elusive Prince Charming. Women who had far more to offer, with whom she claimed no kinship beyond gender but who nevertheless provided a troubling projection of her own future. In a number of women several generations above her, she saw a trajectory of loneliness laid out before her. A life not uncomfortable, but fulfilling nothing in particular, until she passed into oblivion, isolated and unnoticed except for perhaps a pet cat or twenty.

As she shielded herself from the drunken revelry around her, Meghan realized her tolerance for solitude was now far greater than her tolerance for masculine idiocy. Fending for herself instilled an exhilarating independence. The gnawing and nagging doubt ceased, replaced by freedom to work on all the neglected aspects of herself. She felt as if she had been Mrs. Marley's ghost, suddenly shedding massive iron chains of doubt and depression.

Life in Manhattan, cleansed of desperation, became joyous instead.

Her exalted state lasted only a few weeks, not to collapse, but instead to be elevated to a higher level.

Another banker, mojito in hand, staggering more from alcohol than from the sway of the boat, approached her.

Sensing his presence, she stared even more intently through the sliding glass doors onto the afterdeck.

Exactly one year ago, during a similar dinner cruise, she had met Thomas.

•

After three years working for the cruise line, Meghan had already been promoted to hostess.

The previous July, Captain Hofmeister, a ruddy man in his fifties, professionally crusty and personally warm, had informed her that the cruise that evening was for their most important Wall Street client.

To her, the cruise evening seemed like any other corporate event, the clientele wealthy, jejune, completely interchangeable, especially in their dismissal of the enormous effort the crew exerted into ensuring they enjoyed their affair.

Through the glass doors leading to the afterdeck, she had spotted Thomas, in tuxedo and cummerbund, perched absurdly atop the taffrail.

An impending storm was already spattering the deck. The breeze was light and the swell moderate, not enough to be dangerous, but enough to make his position precarious.

She had rushed out onto the stern. "Listen, sweetheart," she cried out. "Whatever you're planning to do, you sure as hell aren't going to do it on my ship, on my watch."

Thomas's concentration made him oblivious to Meghan as he declaimed into the night. "'My spirit's bark is driven, far from the shore, far from the trembling throng, whose sails –'"

His rich English baritone enchanted Meghan. Nevertheless, she grabbed his damp tuxedo coattails.

"I can't very well topple gracefully into the river," he protested, "if you won't let go of my tuxedo,".

Meghan refused to release her grip.

"You are not going to –"

She yanked him back onto the deck with the force of an angry schoolmistress.

Thomas allowed himself to teeter back onto the deck. He stumbled and righted himself. Brushing his coat back into smoothness, he stared down, nearly a foot taller than she.

The George Washington Bridge, glowing behind him like a misty Gothic vision, granted his profile a chiseled jauntiness. Raindrops bejeweled his curly black hair.

"– screw it up," Meghan managed to finish, her reprimand reduced to a mumble, her breath taken away by Thomas's classic features.

He turned again to the Hudson.

"'– were never to the tempest given. The massy earth . . . '" and then to Meghan. "Shelley, you know."

Meghan swayed, unable to take her eyes off his face.

He paused, placing his hand on her arm. She felt her body tingle, as if some exotic electricity were coursing through her.

"Are you unwell?"

He seemed oblivious to her concern for his own safety.

"I don't know," Meghan mumbled.

Their roles reversed; she was now the tongue-tied schoolgirl.

"There now. Relax," he reassured her. "The wind's calming."

"Were you trying to commit suicide?"

Even in the darkness she could see his wry, rueful smile, the mischievous sadness that would later so enthrall her.

"Actually, no. But who's to say the storm might not do it for me?" he replied. "Isn't that what we all search for and never find? Blamelessness?"

"Why?" She held his arm tightly and not merely to prevent him from climbing back up on the taffrail.

"Drowning has such cachet and noble precedent – John Jacob Astor. Ophelia. The Gadarene Swine. Darling Clementine. My fellow country-woman, Virginia Woolf. Succored by the waters of oblivion. Honorably. Romantically. And especially our own dear Percy Bysshe."

"Why would someone who looks like they stepped off *Gentleman's Quarterly* want to kill himself?"

Thomas glanced back through the sliding glass doors where his col-leagues, oblivious, partied joyously.

He focused momentarily on someone inside – a tallish man with salt-and-pepper hair. But so many of the men at the party had the same description. Thomas's face soured with a ripple of self-disgust.

"One day you discover you have become one of those whom you despise and realize you'll never be able to forgive yourself."

Anguished vulnerability eclipsed his height, his muscular frame, his sar-donic assurance. She wondered what events could have driven him to the bleak precipice upon which she found him. Every nurturing impulse, every instinctive pulse of sympathy she felt for those who had been wounded and rejected by life swelled up within her, prompting a burst of speech.

"Don't. Please reconsider. I mean – I don't know why. Not just because suicide is a cardinal sin. But . . ."

She suddenly felt unsure of herself, confused between her instinct to protect this obviously vulnerable man and the surge of desire for someone so obviously comfortable to be with yet sophisticated.

"I – I mean, New York would be a much worse – an emptier place without you," she declared, aware even as she spoke that the statement had no basis, and so she trailed off. "At least to me it would,"

Meghan was rarely effusive, and blushed whenever her emotions tricked her into volubility. She was grateful darkness concealed her embarrassment.

Thomas's bearing softened as the Lady Liberty proceeded south. He sensed her concern and seemed quite struck that someone should be anxious about his well-being, as if it were a phenomenon that had never before occurred. He studied her in the faint glimmer of the lower Manhattan skyline, then said, "Shall we go back inside, my dear?"

Gallantly, he offered her his arm.

The wind rose, teasing whitecaps out of the roiling water as Thomas led her back through the sliding doors into the raucous party.

•

Meghan could not believe that the encounter had taken place exactly a year ago. She reached the forward sliding doors and stared out at the rainswept bow. If not for duties, decorum, and her rendezvous with Thomas in a few hours, she would shed her clothes and stand naked on the rail itself. A breathing Celtic figurehead, she would have invited the rain to pummel her until her spirit achieved union with the gale.

The Lady Liberty had threaded the tricky currents at Spuyten Duyvil and was steaming south, toward the George Washington Bridge, towards the spot of the first encounter with Thomas. Manhattan had disappeared in the squall. Not even the lightning sporadically fracturing the darkness could resurrect the island from its shroud of rain and fog.

She had never seen the Hudson this turbulent, nor whitecaps like the ones now surging over the gunwales. The possibilities of danger added a feral note to her reticent demeanor.

The singer and the bass player were seasick. The remaining three musicians were playing a valiant, lopsided rendition of "Begin the Beguine," but the wind, shrieking through the outside railings, almost drowned it out. The dance floor was empty. Most of the bank employees huddled around their tables. A few of the braver ones ambled jerkily towards the bar, trying to outguess the roll of the ship as it listed from side to side.

Behind a stanchion huddled three secretaries, their arms intertwined in terror. An elderly woman nearing retirement, her gray hair clipped with bullet precision, and a tall woman in her twenties, with bright pink lipstick, gripped the African-American woman between them. The latter's stoicism barely concealed her dread.

Meghan planted herself, legs apart, before them. She flung back her head, inhaling deeply. "Smell the air! Feel the waves! Doesn't this make you feel glorious?"

"I'm scared sick," quavered the elderly woman.

A flash of lightning blanched the faces of the fearful trio. A thunderclap made the ship shudder.

The young secretary yelped and clung even more tightly to her friend. "It's going to be okay, isn't it?" asked the woman in the middle.

As if it were the most intriguing fabric she had ever seen, Meghan scrutinized the sleeve of the young secretary's gown. Patting the shoulder pad, she looked up triumphantly, "Nori Tremayne!"

"Huh?" asked the young woman.

"You know. The designer."

The elderly woman, despite herself, volunteered, "Is that a real Nori Tremayne?"

"No . . . I . . . ," the young secretary stammered. "Do you like it?"

"I wouldn't have guessed it was anything but," affirmed the woman in the middle, winking to Meghan as the latter slipped away.

"I actually bought it at Bloomies."

As Meghan headed towards the musicians, she beamed at the uneasy passengers.

A tall man with commanding jowls, like the wattles of a turkey, pontificated to a subordinate whose face was tinted a dispirited green. "Who knows if this damned scow's even seaworthy?"

Another wave slammed against the boat; wineglasses slid off tables and shattered. The underling appeared ready to bolt until Meghan patted his queasy shoulders.

"Sure, it's safer than Noah's ark," Meghan reassured him.

"The ark wasn't built by union labor," the executive retorted.

"That's why it survived and was never found." Growing up surrounded by several generations of union men, she smiled her gracious, well-trained smile at him. "Enjoy the storm. It's going to be over soon."

Another flash of lightning, another thunderclap.

The jowled man gave her a chastened salute. "Aye-aye, Ma'am."

The band was keeping one eye on their instruments and another on the tilting deck. It gave their music an intriguingly choppy rhythm.

"Do you play "The Anniversary Waltz"?" she asked the guitarist.

"Of course." In deference to the night's clientele, his usual blond dreadlocks had been unraveled and clipped back. "Whose anniversary is it?"

"Mine," she replied over her shoulder, with a gentleness that felt almost gushy, but she could not help herself.

"Didn't even think you had a boyfriend."

She smiled enigmatically, pleased that she had managed to shield her private life from scrutiny and gossip. Thomas had not exactly proposed to her during their recent conversations, but he had hinted that very soon they might be in a position to spend a great deal of time together.

The band had played only three chords when an enormous wave slammed against the vessel.

The boat shuddered.

The engines sputtered.

Died.

Lights flickered.

They, too, died.

Only the last beats of the drummer could be heard. Then these also were drowned by panicked cries as the passengers realized the diesels had ceased. Silhouetted by winks of lightning, the western pier of the George Washington Bridge loomed closer and closer to the foundering vessel.

•

On the bridge, Captain Hofmeister, futilely spun the suddenly unresponsive wheel. "Rudder's not responding at all," he exclaimed.

The chief engineer, short, red-haired, with a Winston Churchill countenance and temperament, furiously manipulated levers and buttons on the frozen console.

"Going to auxiliary power," he muttered.

The lights flickered, then came back on, though dimmer.

The massive concrete pier of the George Washington Bridge seemed to be accelerating toward the Lady Liberty. The engines sputtered and died.

Hofmeister reached for the microphone.

"Your attention please. Your attention please," Hofmeister barked from the squawk box. "Would the crew please assist all passengers to the foredeck and stand by for further instructions. Over."

Galvanized, Meghan leapt onto a table, maintaining her balance as wave after wave slammed against the vessel.

The perfect hostess was unobtrusive, deferential and reticent, which meshed well with her wish to be unobserved. Still, in contradiction to, or perhaps because of her aversion to display, within her simmered a yearning to be uninhibited, daring and extreme. Many safety drills had prepared her for this moment. Now the possibilities of danger thrilled her.

"Quiet!"

When few people obeyed, she stamped her foot with adrenaline-charged fury. "I said 'Quiet!'"

As the frantic talk died down, she continued. "In an orderly fashion we are going up on the upper deck. There we will await further instructions from our captain, who has been piloting this ship for twenty years. You will remain calm. You will let the person ahead of you go up without interference."

The engines sputtered hopefully, then failed again, their death mourned by the crowd's wail.

Through the mist, Meghan could see an occasional wink of car headlights on the bridge high above them. "No one panics. No one gets hurt."

Beside the table, the imperious man barked in a voice icy with command, "You heard her. Do it."

People froze and immediately stopped talking as they jostled towards the companionway.

The man gave her his hand to assist her down from the table. "Hurry, Mademoiselle Courageous. You go on up. For me it would be a dignified end."

"That's the one thing they never told me," she mused as she rushed over to join the crowd. "Whether the hostess was supposed to go down with the ship."

The man smiled paternally and waved her onward.

The massive abutments of the bridge suddenly loomed through the mist in the ballroom windows. They seemed like movie sets, not monstrous structures of concrete and steel capable of smashing a fatal gash in the ship's hull. Meghan had sailed near them over a hundred times, never noticing how solidly they'd been constructed.

She trembled with a flash of dread. If she drowned, how would Thomas know? Though he might consider drowning a noble exit, she could not help thinking it was an ignominious end. What reason would he have not to suspect that she had stood him up?

The crowd resumed murmuring as it surged up the companionway, an uneasiness that might easily grow into a panicked stampede.

"Everything will be all right," Meghan shouted, keeping her attention on the young secretary on the step above her. When the woman spotted the abutments, she started to scream. Meghan hastily leapt up and cupped the woman's mouth.

Suddenly the engines coughed into life. The vessel jerked toward starboard.

With inches to spare, the Lady Liberty steamed awkwardly beneath the high span. The passengers whooped and cheered. Their upward movement ceased. As they drifted down the companionway back into the ballroom, they, the men especially, assumed tones of sheepish nonchalance, as if they had never been frightened in the slightest.

When the Lady Liberty pulled into the dock at the end of West 41st, Meghan was so eager to see Thomas that she was barely able to linger by the gangplank to say her mechanical good-byes to the disembarking guests.

As the last guest, the wattle-jowled man passed by, he saluted her, "Well, done, ma'am. Carry on."

He sauntered off to the waiting black car.

With a smile, Meghan collected her carry-on.

•

"I heard you did an excellent job when we lost power," said Hofmeister as Meghan approached the gangplank.

She smiled at him. "Thank you."

She took two steps before the meaning of his words dawned on her, then turned in surprise. "Was that a compliment? Hey, you just paid me a compliment."

"Have a nice vacation." The smile seemed out of place on his ruddy, craggy face. "And be sure to come back."

CHAPTER 2.

Restaurant X

The cab dropped Meghan off at the corner of Park and East 46th, under the watchful gilt-rimmed clock of the Helmsley Building.

As the cabbie pulled away, she tried to count all the horizons that Thomas Lockhart had opened for her. He had appeared in her life the first time she had ever felt content, and on top of independence, she felt as if she had been granted her girlhood again – not the frivolity or the childishness, but the sense of wonder and possibility, of experiences colorful and impractical to be enjoyed for the sheer merriment of the enterprise. She had almost forgotten those realms mentioned by her foster father but dismissed by her mother as "that vast dreaming uselessness."

Thomas's wisdom was like a freshly discovered continent, full of mystery and hidden understandings that would astonish her whenever she came upon them. Music. (She had never attended an opera until she met him.) Theatre. Art. His appreciation of the myriad architectural styles of Manhattan had seeped into her previous unawareness. She could now recognize an egg-and-dart border from a hundred yards. The delicate artisanship of century-old terracotta suddenly intrigued her.

And especially food.

Before she met him, she'd considered oregano and paprika exotic. Now, although she was still not a gourmand, her tongue could discern when fresh ginger was used in a dish or when it was from a jar, freshly prepared curry powder from the commercial kind.

His interests and observations revived a hunger in her for knowledge that had lain dormant for decades.

And yet Thomas never lorded the depth of his knowledge and diversity of his experience over her. She never detected any condescension in him. He was reluctant to mention things and seemed surprised when she seemed surprised.

Though she had been raised side by side with a cousin who received an abundance of praise and adoration, Meghan had never been praised or adored. Almost inevitably she reacted with stiffening suspicion to anyone who thought well of her. Indeed, in the first few months of her relationship with Thomas, she had been extremely wary. Not only because the compliments flowed in an endless and seemingly spontaneous stream, but also because of his other inexplicable quirks.

He would not tell her what company he worked for nor what his job was, though he did say it was down on Wall Street and had something to do with international finance. He would not allow her to call him at the office. He would cancel or postpone dates, and whenever he arrived late, he would be grim and tight-lipped, taking hours to resume his usual jovial wryness.

At first she suspected that he might be married or involved with other women, but though the signs were there, her intuition (which was almost never wrong) told her that she was the only woman in his life.

He would tell her little of his past, beyond the fact that he grew up in Kenya, went to Oxford and had worked in Singapore. All the belongings in his apartment were relatively new and somewhat impersonal, as if he had sprung into the world full-grown several years ago and immediately acquired rather than accumulated his possessions. Indeed, she'd often teased him that this proved that he was an alien from another galaxy.

Initially she had other fears. That one day he would grow tired of her or find her too American or too Irish or not pretty enough for his refined British tastes. Or she would do something so gauche that even his expansive heart would be unable to forgive her. But nothing she said or did, other than insisting that he not swear, seemed to annoy him.

Thomas had started off merely fond of her, and though Meghan accepted the fact that she was far more invested in the blossoming relationship than he was, she sensed that his initial affection had deepened into something much more profound. As her apprehension subsided, she was able to open up to him as she had to no one else, and no longer fretted about where their relationship might be headed.

•

Suddenly, when it no longer seemed important, Thomas and Meghan found themselves shyly undressing each other on the bed in his Fifth Avenue apartment. Not in desperation, not in conquest, not even in desire, but in supreme appropriateness. The full moon cast shadows made by the air conditioner, falling upon the carpet that turned them almost cobalt blue,

Thomas nestled his head on her stomach, tickling her breast with his wavy locks. "Has anyone ever told you how gamine gorgeous you are?"

Instead of swooning at the sweetest reassurance she'd ever been given, Meghan stiffened with apprehension.

"Yeah," she replied, "all the guys trying to get me into the sack. You've already succeeded, No need to flatter me."

The words of Sister Mary Alberta, her elementary school teacher, revered as a thoroughbred because she actually was Irish, came back to haunt her.

"Of all corruptions of the spirit challenging a woman, pride in her physical beauty is the most heinous sin in the eyes of our Lord and Creator."

Even at Meghan's young age she observed that Sister Mary Alberta, with her square jaw, wrestler's wrists and ingrained scowl, had been spared the challenge of this particular corruption. Young Meghan suffered such guilt for having these wicked thoughts that her feeling of sinfulness could never be confessed away.

Even worse, the Sister's warning penetrated so deeply into Meghan's conscience that she never was able to fully accept the fact that she was indeed a natural beauty, a self-doubt that only made her that much more alluring to others.

Thomas had taken her words as a rebuke, his eyes knitting in perplexity, as he studied her pale silhouette in the moonlight.

Worried that she had spoiled one of the most poignant moments of her life, she hastily tousled his hair. "Never mind."

Relaxing, Thomas smiled, his concern ebbing. He laughed and nibbled on her ear. Then, with tiny sweeps of his lips he proceeded down her shoulder and crossed to her breast.

And Meghan succumbed.

The past and the future collapsed into the present. Meghan found herself unleashed as never before. Swept away by a passion that had not been so much suppressed as absent from her deepest being, a glorious powerlessness she could have never anticipated. Suddenly, her breath spilled relentlessly from her, a stream of stuttering hisses that she was powerless to control. Finally then she lay gasping, engulfed, disoriented, spinning in a tumult of unaccustomed feelings. This storm rendered all previous intimacies and longings as perfunctory and mechanical.

She sensed that Thomas had unbuttoned her blouse with a sense of sport, adventure even, but her unexpected shyness and pale slopes and valleys of her flesh had drawn his soul deeper toward somewhere he had never expected to be. She was astonished that his cultivated thoughtfulness and melancholy dissolved in a single flash to unleash thrusts of primal power, as if he felt oblivion were just around the corner.

As delicious pleasure subsided within her, the guilt that would never cease to accompany her gradually took control. She felt tears welling up, her cheeks moistening.

He studied her in the moonlight, then touched his finger to a tear. "Your tears are like water squeezed by your soul."

"No," she protested, embarrassed at her obvious vulnerability to him and the magic he brought her. "It's –"

"Shhh!" he whispered. He placed the fingertip on the tear and then licked it. "I will treasure this forever."

She grasped him with all her strength, snuggled as close as she could, annoyed that the barriers of flesh would not allow them to truly merge.

In the morning, without the need to discuss the previous night, they realized that each had unlocked a realm of passion in the other that had lain forever untouched in his vast and her limited experience.

●

For the last few months, inspired by one of his whims, they had been alphabetically eating their way around the world. "A" for Armenian, "B" for Brazilian, etc.

Since they could find no Qatari restaurants in New York, Thomas remarked, "'Q' was for 'Quandary'."

Fortunately, they agreed the newly revived Quilted Giraffe was sufficient to qualify (whether the food was up to the former QG standards, they did not know – the bill certainly was). And although not really a country, the restaurant was close enough for their lighthearted game to continue.

Tonight was their first anniversary, and they were already up to "X."

She had been worried that their culinary journey would end at Welsh, but he assured her that there was indeed a restaurant named X. There was a Yemeni restaurant on 13th that had been around for years, and if the Zambian restaurant in Queens remained open, they would complete the alphabet within the week after they returned from vacation.

X for Ten? X for Unknown?

The restaurant was small, nestled in the lee of the Helmsley Building in an obscure walkway between East 45th and East 46th. No more than fifteen candlelit tables with a scattering of diners. The menus were hand-lettered, filled with items that Meghan imagined even Thomas would find obscure: *karela* gourds, *huitlacoche*, *msawu* fruit. Despite the pompous maitre d' with his inauthentic German accent, the anthracite-colored tiles and black-and-white china that gave the room the stark austerity of an obituary notice, the restaurant was imbued with offbeat charm. Perhaps the waiters, who were young and enthusiastic, did not quite leave their twenty-something irreverence at the door.

Thomas sat at a table in the corner, swirling a tumbler of scotch in his hand, a plate of exotic fruits and nuts before him.

Ten years older than Meghan, he had the looks of a man who had lived the good life to the hilt. Of someone who achieved easily yet could not be bothered to chronicle his own achievements. He was muscular; his body, once hardened by the tumult of rugby scrums, had been softened by the comforts of a sedentary life. Though his face had a cast of British good-old-boy jollity, underneath lay weighty seriousness, of secrets concealed, of private aches that would go to the grave unshared and unhealed.

He was wearing a fawn-colored twilled-silk suit and blue shirt with white French cuffs, fastened with lapis-lazuli links. His yellow necktie, crisscrossed with white, had been tied in a strange fashion she had learned was called an Eldredge knot. Usually, after a day at the office, he would retie it into something simpler and loosened it around his throat.

She gave him a light kiss, set her carry-on under the table and, shedding her raincoat, said, "Happy anniversary, darling."

She eyed the glass.

"Is that a triple?" she asked.

"It's the Distiller's Edition," he replied, as if that somehow excused the excess.

Her eyes widened but she said nothing further and opened her Chloe Drew handbag (another of his offhand gifts) and rummaged in it. "Anyway, you would not believe tonight. Lady Liberty almost slammed against the G.W. Bridge. We nearly ended up at the bottom of the Hudson. And you know my biggest fear? Not of drowning but the chance you would think I stood you up."

At last, she found the envelope with the passport photographs and slid out a sheet of four. She blinked as she tried to study them, grateful that the dim light would not allow him to see how the flash brought out her freckles and delineated the lines beginning to form around the corners of her eyes. The photos made her eyes a soft green, though in actual fact their color was blue-green, appearing one or way the other depending on the light.

She handed the pictures over. "Don't look too closely."

As she grew accustomed to the dimness, she noticed that his fawn-colored jacket was still buttoned, and his yellow tie with its striking Eldredge knot had remained almost chokingly tight at his throat. His dark curls spilled over the back of his collar, but somehow they seemed more tangled than usual.

He set the photographs beside his drink without looking at them.

She reached across the table and lay her hand upon his. "Thomas, it's our anniversary. Cheer up."

He peered deeply into her puzzled eyes. His own remained mysterious, blue with the unsolved eddies of the ocean. He spoke softly, but his accent granted his voice an authoritative resonance. "Meghan, dearest, stop."

"Thomas?"

"There's been a change in plans. The trip has fallen through. We must cancel."

"Do you know the hoops I had to jump through to get three weeks off?"

Caught off guard, she studied his face to see if he were teasing. She detected no humor, only a forcibly concealed distress.

"Why don't I book us on an Alaska cruise?" she suggested. "Go see the whales. August in New York is like two or three equators south of Hades."

"I'm leaving New York immediately. I won't be coming back."

Meghan looked helplessly around. Her lips fluttered as she searched for speech. "So? I'll visit. I get discount flights through my job."

She tried to keep her voice contralto, to prevent the disbelief seeping into her face. She was not succeeding.

"You can't. Nor telephone. Let's just enjoy our dinner and bid farewell," said Thomas.

She felt as if she were toppling from reality into nightmare without ever falling asleep and with zero chance of waking up. "Thomas," she managed to mumble. "It's . . . it's our anniversary."

"It has to be over, Meghan. Don't you realize?"

His placid demeanor upset her far more than brutal rejection.

"What about our vacation together? Remember?" She pointed at her carry-on. "And this? My summer clothes? I've been lugging it around all day. You said we would be spending a lot of time together."

"Then I apologize."

"Maybe our entire lives."

"I didn't intend to mislead you."

"Oh, god," Meghan exclaimed. "Give me a moment to get my head around this."

"It's quite straightforward actually."

"Straightforward? As in like 'I'm being dumped'?"

"It's simply that we can't see each other any more."

"Then what is it then? You're gay or something?"

"Hardly."

"Then why am I losing you?"

"The women I work with on Wall Street are basking sharks circling their prey. They shut me down swifter than an ice cold shower. But you are so . . . refreshing. Tender." He paused. "Authentic."

"And yet you want to end this? Why didn't you do this over the phone?"

"Not coward enough."

"At least I could have hung up on you."

"I'm sorry part of me must remain a mystery. Not to deceive you, but to protect you."

"Right. To protect your own guilty conscience. I never expected you to marry me or anything outlandish like that, just not string me along then dump me without warning."

The impact of his words was particularly devastating because his unspoken commitment had managed to penetrate her carefully constructed barricades. Every tender gesture lulled her deeper into a comfortable serenity and only doubled the rejection she now felt.

"I trusted you. It took me months and months. I never trust anyone because they always end up hurting me. But you were so sincere, so gentle. Of course I had to trust you."

There had been no warning signs whatsoever. No unreturned phone calls. No lapses of attention on his part to indicate the intrusion of other women or waning interest in her.

"That's what's so unbelievable, I actually trusted you, and now . . ."

"I'm sorry, Meghan. I didn't string you along intentionally."

"If you just wanted me for a fling or some sort of trophy, to drape on your arm, you should have gone on one of those sugar daddy websites. I'm sure you could have scored somebody a lot glitzier than me."

Suddenly, irrationally, Meghan realized Thomas had never actually paraded her anywhere. Nor had she ever met any of his friends or vice-versa. Even more implausibly, why had it taken a year for her to realize this?

"I was committed to you. I mean I am committed to you."

Thomas glanced around uncomfortably, troubled by his inborn dread of public scenes. She knew that he knew that she loathed them also and suspected that was exactly his strategy, to lure her into a public place to intimidate her into silence.

"What did I do to drive you away? I'm sorry I mentioned children. We don't have to have any. I don't know what came over me that day. I was feeling weepy and . . . I've gotten over it. Whatever you decide will make me happy."

He looked at her puzzled, her statement dragging him from whatever thoughts festered within him.

"What?"

Meghan could see that he was having trouble recalling the outburst that she had been brooding over for weeks.

"Remember? Outside the Plaza? When I was going on and on about wanting to have children some day."

He made a gesture of dismissal with his elegant hand. "Children with you would have been lovely, Meghan. But now that's totally out of the question."

Apprehension had fanned itself into fear, which was fanning itself into a terrified outburst she was helpless to prevent. "What is within me that scares off everyone I try to get close to?"

"Nothing. You've been exemplary," said Thomas.

He was growing agonizingly desirable with each new obstinate statement.

"Or were you planning to discard me at the first opportunity?"

The situation was dissolving her self-control, plunging her into the irrationality she dreaded. She felt herself becoming the old Meghan, the desperate Meghan.

Their waiter approached, a red-haired boy in his late twenties, who did not look much older than his teens. When he saw the intensity of the exchange between Thomas and Meghan, he retreated to the safety of the kitchen.

Never had she been a whiner, but she felt plaintiveness making her sound like one. She could feel her Queens accent growing sharper and coarser. She prayed for a meteor to strike her and release her from the sensation that her carefully woven life was unraveling without warning.

"Was I too clutchy?" Meghan resumed.

"Which I appreciate," continued Thomas.

"Then why are you just throwing me aside? What are you looking for that we can't have together?"

She took a swallow of water, to give herself enough breath to ask, "Another woman? Did a wife you forgot to mention return unexpectedly from her shopping spree at Harrods?"

"There is no other woman, Meghan," Thomas replied softly and, as far as she could tell, with genuine feeling. "You were uncontested. Uncontestable."

"Were-were-were. Why do you insist on talking about me in the past tense? Because you're bloody English?"

He opened his mouth, but she did not give him the chance to speak.

"I'm still refreshing. I'm still innocent, though I'm getting less so every second. Or are you rationalizing that I've lost whatever you found attractive?"

"Please, Meghan. Don't act so emotional. That's not the way I want to remember you."

"I wish the Lady Liberty HAD rammed the bridge, and I HAD drowned. If I had known this is what you'd planned, I'd have gone ahead and jumped myself."

"'Suicide is a sin. New York would be much emptier'," he quoted softly.

She flinched bitterly, hearing her own words aimed back at her, made doubly infuriating by his pious tone. And perhaps even scarier that somehow he had been paying attention to and recording in his memory her every word. A sickening feeling of disappointment was beginning to replace her sense of unreality.

"Perhaps I am a coward," Thomas continued. "But not enough of a one to end it that way."

"What is this, Thomas? If you insist on calling it quits, can't you at least give me the courtesy of telling me exactly why? I don't wanna be lying in bed, twenty years from now, wondering, 'What in hell was that all about?' I always thought you confided in me more than anyone else, but now I realize, you only APPEARED to confide in me. I don't really know you any more than I know the Man-in-the-Moon."

"I assure you, Meghan, no one else has ever got this close or spent as much time with me. No one else has ever participated in my life the way you have. I'm sorry if there remain parts of my life that must remain a mystery, but it must be that way. Not to deceive you, but to protect you."

"You men have such a wonderful way of phrasing things. Say the cruelest things claiming that you say them not to hurt me, but really it's to comfort your own guilty conscience."

If she had felt him slipping away, perhaps she could have coaxed him back. But his heart had bolted in the few moments she had relaxed her guard, and she had no inkling of how to retrieve it.

"My cousin Moira is constantly yelling at me that I'm a pathological rescuer, always trying to save people from themselves. Sure enough. Put me in a room with one hundred of the most desirable bachelors in New York. I'd make a beeline for the one guy planning to kill himself and try to talk him out of it. I guess that's exactly what I did."

The statement startled Thomas into speechlessness, but with an almost imperceptible gulp he recovered. "If it hadn't been for your enthusiasm, your optimism, I would have been gone long ago. Think of our time together as a gift to both our lives, a gift that perhaps should never have been granted."

"You admit it yourself. Our time together is such a gift. And you've given me so much, Thomas. You don't know how much you've expanded my life."

He smiled sadly, a curl of his lips indicating resignation more than levity. Despite what Meghan's mind and Thomas himself were telling her, she felt that she was indeed peering into his soul.

"It's amazing when you sum up, how very little we actually accomplish in our allotted decades," he mused. "But somehow, I feel that that satisfaction I've brought you, even if brief, is somehow my crowning achievement. You're the one glory I have to my credit, that I introduced you to a few things and perhaps contributed a little to your believing in yourself."

"Isn't that nice? I know I was your lover. I thought perhaps I was your friend. I'm glad to find out at long last that I was actually your science project. I hope you make it to the national finals and win a blue ribbon or something."

He shook his head, beshrouding his features in pensiveness, but he did not contradict her.

Her lips parting slightly, she again slipped under the spell of his brooding silence and strove to resurrect her emotional shields.

"Just do one thing. Don't lie to me about what's going on. The way you're acting is crazy. Okay, you're right. I DON'T sense another woman. But there's absolutely no other explanation."

She allowed him to take her hand in his, but she did not respond, her fingers remaining rigid.

"Just remember all the wonderful times we had together," he suggested.

"I don't mind being plugged back into my monotonous, stale old life. I'd actually learned to enjoy it just before I met you. But I don't want to spend who knows how much more of my life grieving."

"You might believe this," Thomas interrupted. "But know well, I myself will spend the entire rest of my life grieving."

Meghan was on a roll, and besides, she did not believe him. "Dealing with heartbreak is like driving on snow. Do it often enough, you become adept enough not to crash into a tree. Heartbreak's exactly the same. The more it's broken, the easier repairing it should become. I just despise having to go through it all over again because it seems identical."

"Meghan, please –"

"You know what makes it so much worse? I had this beautiful picture of what the future could have been with each other. With just a tiny bit of commitment on your part. That's what going take the longest to erase from my soul."

Her intensity did not affect him; he remained in his state of wistful melancholy, inhaling her fragrance.

"I have no such picture," he said. "So please, let me remember you the way I always knew you. Sweet and vulnerable. The smell of lilacs that always seems to linger about you. The way you look so preoccupied when you sleep. The way your tawny hair swirls on the pillow."

For a moment she managed to harden herself to the words and accents that once so enthralled her.

"Thomas, just once, please. Don't retreat behind your poetry."

She retrieved her hand.

"What chance does a near-orphan from Woodside have of winning a prize like you? Me? After all, you DID go to Oxford. And you DO have an apartment on Fifth Avenue. And I'm just the hostess on some cockamamie dinner cruise line. But Hofmeister did compliment me on the way I handled things during tonight's crisis."

"Meghan, this doesn't have to turn ugly."

"Why should this relationship end any different from ugly? So many guys come on as Mr. Compassion. Then one month later, two, you find out what jerks they really are. How did you keep up the kind caring sensitive act for an entire year?"

"Because I was falling in love with you," he replied. "And because I wanted to make this pleasant."

For a flicker of an instant his longing smile almost made her believe him.

"You want to make it pleasant? Let me help you out."

She dropped the sun block on the table.

"Just tell me you're busy this weekend."

She stumbled to her feet and ripped up the passport photos.

"Then tell me you're busy next weekend."

She flung the scraps at him.

"Then tell me you're busy the rest of your entire fucking life!"

He grabbed her wrist.

"Dammit, you bloody woman." His tone was low but so forceful that everyone in the restaurant turned. "You're the most precious thing that ever came into my life. I just don't want you destroyed like I will be.

"Liar!"

She slapped him; his flinch was almost imperceptible, a flicker across lips that quickly resumed their crooked curl.

He kept his expression coolly unperturbed, as much for the other patrons who watched the argument, forks poised, Meghan thought, as for herself. With true New York aplomb, the diners at the next table, an elegant silver-haired couple, placidly continued their meal as if there were no commotion at all.

Meghan reeled away, stifling tears, sorrowing, not because she was bereft, but because she had violated every one of her own precautions in allowing herself to become so vulnerable. She teetered toward the bathroom.

Thomas sighed, downed his drink, and stood. At last the silver-haired couple turned to watch the proceedings.

"Meghan!" Thomas called after her.

In the relative sanctuary of the restroom alcove, Meghan fumbled with the door to the women's room,

Locked.

She leaned against the wall, trying to blot from her mind the grim future that this man she trusted had suddenly thrust upon her. The future a bitter echo of her past, poisoned by all happiness she had tasted.

She felt a hand upon her shoulder and found herself softening despite unwillingness to risk being brutalized all over again.

"Excuse me," a voice now so tender as to be almost inaudible.

She wanted to give him no leeway in which to appease his conscience.

Nevertheless, she took the hand, cupping it to her cheek. Her moist lashes brushed against his fingers.

"I'm sorry, I'm sorry," she murmured, waiting for him to again cradle her in his sheltering arms. "Thomas, I didn't mean to slap you, but –"

"Ma'am?" said a voice that did not belong to Thomas.

She dropped the arm and whirled. Through the blur of her tears she saw a face remarkably similar to Thomas's. Longish black hair (though straight), blue eyes, a mouth that seemed capable of flexing into a smile that would distract anyone from noticing his underlying seriousness.

But the man whose hand she held was much younger than Thomas, in his mid-twenties, and dressed in a chef's uniform, neckerchief and toque. Behind him, the men's room door slowly closed.

"Sorry. I thought you were someone else," Meghan apologized. "You even look . . ."

"I wish I were," said the man. "My name is Gil. DeLeo."

He extended his hand, but Meghan ignored it as she stared around the restaurant.

The front door was closing. She thought she saw a vanishing flicker of Thomas's coat tails. She was about to step forward when Gil swung around in front of her.

"I'm not trying to interfere, but are you okay?"

Concern creased his innocent features as he studied her. His dark blue eyes glistened with a sudden enchanted longing.

"Yes. I mean no. Excuse me."

He gripped her wrist, gently, but with a plaintive firmness. "I don't know how to say this – it sounds like what a million other slobs must have told you. But for me it's true."

Even in the dim light of the restroom alcove she could see him flushing. Despite her wrath at Thomas, something in the young man's sincerity made her hesitate.

"It's just that I feel like somehow I've known you before. I mean, not that we've ever met, because I know we haven't. But there's something so familiar," Gil continued. "It's not like I want to get to know you better. But like I want to catch up with an old acquaintance. I'm sorry. I know it sounds stupid. Something about you . . ."

He released her and turned away to hide his embarrassment, mumbling protests that he never behaved like this toward anyone.

Softened momentarily by his earnestness, she squeezed his shoulder sympathetically and rushed back into the dining area. She snatched the scraps of the passport photographs from the table. Shoved them into the envelope and the envelope into her bag, then grabbed her raincoat and carry-on. She detested being stared at, but could feel every eye, even those of the elderly couple, locked upon her.

Toque in hand, the young chef approached and hovered, as uncertain as Meghan herself. The stares of the patrons kept his voice to a whisper. "Anything I could do to cheer you up, no matter what, I would do in a heartbeat. Any sacrifice, you name it."

She raised her tortured gaze to his face, and despite herself, was drawn into his deep and puzzled compassion. At last she forced herself to break their exchange.

Meghan dashed out. The instant she was out the door, she called out to Thomas, who was nowhere to be seen, "Stop!"

Gil trailed behind her, then halted, visibly moved.

CHAPTER 3.

Park Avenue

There was no sign of Thomas in the small walkway. Raindrops drummed on the mullioned-glass canopy. Meghan looked south, towards East 45th, and seeing no one, took a chance and ran north, through a pair of trees, their gauntness compensated somewhat by the lights spangling them.

The wind had again risen with fitful gusts when Meghan bounded down the shallow flight of steps and emerged on East 46th. She rubbed particles of rain from her eyes as she peered up and down. No sign of Thomas.

Looking back over her shoulder, she saw that Gil had come out of the restaurant and stood transfixed. She managed to smile weakly at him.

He gave her a sad, courtly nod, and called out, "Please come back. Soon."

She wondered if Thomas had gone back out the other side of the Helmsley Building passageway. Then she spotted him on Park Avenue, just beyond the sculpture that resembled enormous coupling black worms. He was hurrying uptown, covering the ground with brisk, wary strides. Despite his muscles, his pace gave him a gangly, almost adolescent aspect.

She dashed across East 46th and ran after him. The instant he heard her clattering steps behind him, he increased his speed, coat-tails flapping behind him.

"Thomas! Thomas!" she called out, her wail quickly dissipating in the windy canyon of Park Avenue. She felt weighted down by her carry-on and was tempted to jettison it. Her pleas only encouraged him to run faster.

In the middle of East 47th, he hesitated – construction scaffolding surrounded the building on the next block. If he stepped into the walkway, Meghan would have him trapped.

Desperately, he hailed a passing cab, which screeched over to a stop.

He was opening the door when Meghan grabbed the handle and slammed the door shut.

"Thomas!" she let his name escape between gasps for breath.

He stood silently, head bowed, his hand covering his eyes.

The cab driver was grumbling in Russian with increasing irritation.

"Let's go someplace," Meghan said. "Straighten this out. Just so I can be clear about what really happened."

Never in her life had Meghan begged for anything from any man. She did not want Thomas to see her in this distressed state, but protective barricades she'd allowed to harden around her like a caterpillar's chrysalis had been almost completely dissolved by his gentleness. She wasn't sure how long it would take to rebuild them. She certainly had no illusions that she would ever turn into any sort of butterfly.

With a final spew of Russian curses, the driver stepped on the gas. The cab accelerated off, dragging Meghan with it for a step until she released the handle.

Thomas turned to Meghan, irritation making him even more towering. Annoyance coursing through his face transformed him into someone she did not recognize. "For your own sake, stop following me. Now!"

"Why?"

"Because, dammit, you're the most precious thing in the world to me. When I'm destroyed, I don't want you to be destroyed, too."

"What is this crap, Thomas?"

She trapped him in her stare, her eyes flashing with a Celtic fury that pinned him to the spot.

"The truth is what you are hearing now. Everything I told you before was crap. Growing up in Kenya. I never even played rugby. I've been to Singapore, but I didn't work there. Lies, Meghan. Cruel, deliberate lies. Go away. Forget you ever knew me."

"So you exaggerated your past a little. I didn't go to NYU not because I couldn't afford it, but because I was never accepted. I was never accepted because I never applied. There. I was wrong to embellish, I know it. I'm sorry. That doesn't mean that I stopped caring for you. And even if you lied with a few words you didn't lie with your feelings. I would have known. So what could possibly have happened in just a few days?"

He sighed, his face, his whole being sagging with the exhalation.

"Shall we walk? Listen carefully to everything I say. Look cheerful. Act like we are two sweethearts having a rapturous conversation. Do not raise your voice or say anything that could be eavesdropped, even from a distance."

"I won't be acting."

She put her handbag in her left hand, on the same side as the carry-on, and took his arm with her right hand. He guided her across Park Avenue.

The Helmsley clock indicated that it was quarter till eleven.

The traffic, mostly taxis and livery cars, droned steadily along. Taillight red mingled with skyscraper twinkle in puddle reflections. Mist spiraled up from the asphalt, the residue of the storm rejoining the clouds that scurried restlessly above the glass towers. Cheap umbrellas, purchased a few hours earlier from street vendors and now shredded, flapped in trashcans like pterodactyl carcasses.

Thomas took her cheeks into his hands and lifted the edges of her mouth into a smile.

"So what is all this cloak-and-dagger nonsense?" she asked through her grimace.

Surveying the street for anyone who did not have an obvious purpose, Thomas maintained his expression of tender concentration. Meghan's apprehension prevented her from savoring the pleasure of renewed contact. Satisfied that no one was observing them, he relaxed his grip.

"Well?" she whispered.

Thomas put his arm in the small of her back and eased her forward. He did not speak until they had passed a homeless person with a ragged green hood concealing his face. The specter pushed a laundry cart stuffed with soggy cardboard.

His expression still a mask of blissful infatuation, Thomas said softly, "Something has gone horribly wrong. I am about to be killed."

"What?" snapped Meghan, in a voice loud enough to echo off the walls of the corporate buildings flanking the avenue. She stopped and faced him obdurately. "Come off it, Thomas."

"Shh!" he ordered, dragging her again to his side.

He glanced quickly around. The homeless person continued to guide his cart downtown, oblivious to her outburst.

"I don't know if they've found out yet, but they will. I estimate I have roughly twelve hours before the jig is up."

"Who?" said Meghan. "Thomas, you're not drunk are you? If you want to call it off, you don't have to fantasize some imaginary plot –"

"I don't want you to be murdered also. By mistake or because someone thinks killing you will send a clearer message than calling Western Union. The old days are gone, Meghan. They don't spare you simply because you're a woman or a child. And since you don't have artificial knees or breast implants, it would be difficult to identify your body."

Her mouth moved up and down, but no words came out.

Thomas headed onto East 50th, towards Madison Avenue. "Now I must go and make what few preparations I can and protect those who still have a chance. Don't wait to read about me in the newspapers or watch for my story on the news. These people tend to be very meticulous. Pray that they are in haste and not feeling particularly creative for my appointment."

He hailed a cab, then kissed her on the cheek.

"Farewell," said Thomas with a rumpled smile.

He quickly got into the cab. Before it could pull away Meghan opened the door and jumped in beside him.

"Have you gone completely crazy? Nobody's going to kill you. Nobody's going to kill me. Now, stop being melodramatic. If you're in trouble, I'll help you. Tossing me out of your life will only make the situation worse."

She took his hand, trying to traverse the cruel distance at which he was keeping himself.

"I've never been a burden to anyone. I won't be a nuisance to you. Thomas, I've had to struggle for everything I have. Why won't you let me help you now? I'll battle whoever wants to hurt you with everything I have, until my dying breath. Simply because you're worth it."

"Meghan, there's a lot I'm regretting about my life right now."

He leaned forward to speak to the cabbie. "84th and Fifth. No, make that 79th." Then back to Meghan. "And more than anything else in my life I regret involving you in my folly. I wanted to believe my harebrained scheme would succeed. Are you familiar with the Charge of the Light Brigade? During the Crimean War?"

"What could that possibly have to do with why you're so intent on wrecking my life?"

"It was folly from the beginning. The officers in command knew it. The cavalry knew it. Yet they went ahead with their mission anyway when any reasonable person, with only a trace of objectivity, could see it was doomed from the outset. What made them proceed? Did destiny blind them? My plan never had even the most slender chance of success. Yet I went ahead obliviously, thoroughly convinced that I could pull it off and not only that, escape all consequence."

"What, pray tell, are you talking about, Thomas?"

He slumped in the seat, succumbing to the isolation he had been trying to impose on himself. The rain had cleansed Madison Avenue and denuded the street of pedestrians. She nestled close to him, offering more than herself, offering her very soul for support. But she could not make a connection between his lecture and the sudden cessation of his affection.

"Tell me the details. Don't lecture me about some irrelevant historical tragedy, please. The Irish are far better at those than you English."

He studied her, her naive stubbornness coaxing a sad smile from him. He sighed again, with the weariness of someone who had experienced almost all the world has to offer.

"There's 'a green isle in the sea love,'" he began. "A Pacific paradise with vast reserves of what are known as 'rare earths'. It's a tiny little group of islands, a backwater presided over by clan chiefs. Shunned by tourists. Except for the jungle, a whole lot like Kuwait must have been at the turn of the century. So just like Iraq, the greedy country invaded poor little Islandia. Drove the government into exile. Killed the native chiefs. To enable my company to demolish a mountain and loot these obscure little metals without which our modern world would collapse."

"Come on. You promised not to talk politics," Meghan said, though she herself knew it was her wish, not his promise.

"Not one country raised its voice to protest the invasion. Instead, to get its hands on these rare earths, the West made itself an accomplice in the subjugation. Your government was sending some funds through my company to the invading government to wipe out the last bit of local resistance. I simply diverted the money. I was planning to forward it to the rebels and to give them a fighting chance."

He turned to her for his sad finale. "Now the people I work for have discovered their money is missing. Jobim, the guerilla leader who was to meet me and collect the loot, then help us both escape, has been assassinated. Everyone who helped in the diversion is now in jeopardy."

He leaned forward. "Driver, I've changed my mind. 180 Water Street."

"Downtown? That's the opposite other direction entirely," the driver grumbled in a melodious West Indian accent.

"I'll make it worth your while." Thomas settled grimly back into the seat.

Meghan squeezed his hand, studying him questioningly. When he remained mute, she asked, "Why are we going down there, Thomas? At this hour?"

CHAPTER 4.

Consolidated Resources

The taxi had stopped in front of a monolithic black skyscraper. As Thomas paid the driver, Meghan craned her neck to stare at the cloud-shrouded upper stories. The edifice filled her with an inarticulable dread.

"Grim, isn't it," said Thomas.

"It looks like a sky-high tombstone."

"Close, very close," he murmured.

The wind whipped off the East River, fluttering the pennants at Seaport Plaza. A hide-and-seek moon, occasionally peeking from behind the racing clouds, seemed suspended over Governor's Island.

"Shall we go in?"

Meghan shook her head. She looked hopefully back toward the cab; it was already out of hailing distance. "Why don't we just go back to your apartment?"

"Why are you so hesitant?" Thomas asked. "I thought you wanted to be included in every facet of my life."

"You said you worked in an investment bank. This doesn't look like an investment bank to me. They have signs. This-or-That Bank. Thus-and-So Brothers. How come you don't have a sign?"

"Weren't you listening to me? I told you that I was lying. I do deal in financial matters, but I am not an investment banker."

"What is this place?"

"Consolidated Resources."

"What do they do?"

"Keep track of things."

"What sort of things?" Meghan demanded.

"Whatever sort of things that need to be kept track of. Mostly goodies that come out of the ground. Especially things that will be in short supply in the future." Softening, he added, "And sometimes your government gives us astronomical sums of money to implement policy without the messiness of policymakers and even better, immunity to the Freedom of Information Act. Now promise me one thing."

She tilted her head questioningly.

"Promise?

She nodded.

"Always keep your head bowed down and your hand over your face, like you're suffering from a cold. Okay."

She nodded uncertainly.

"Shall we go in?"

Meghan allowed herself to be dragged along. She, who had earlier that night stared down a gale, found herself terrified by a tranquil skyscraper lobby.

Black marble. Huge. Dim in the glow of the security console. She was conscious of the clatter of her heels on the slick floor and resorted to a sliding gait to minimize her presence. She hung back, head bowed down, peering at her surroundings through gaps in her fingers.

From his pocket, Thomas took a pass with his picture on a chain. He hung it around his neck.

"Hell of a storm, wasn't it, your Lordship?" the elderly guard greeted him. "I mean, Mr. Lockhart," he added hastily.

"It's okay, Harry. At the moment, my nickname is the least of my concerns," said Thomas. "I also need a pass for my friend. Sorry, she has a terrible cold, and I don't want you to catch it."

Meghan coughed helpfully.

Struck shy by Meghan's feminine presence, Harry handed Thomas a red security pass, marked "Visitor", also on a chain. After he draped it around her neck, Harry waved them through the chromium security gate.

●

Thomas punched an unmarked button between those for the 41st and 43rd floors. He and Meghan, never looking up, stood apart in the elevator, as if they were strangers, meeting for the first time. At last she held up one forefinger. He did likewise, then extended it to touch hers. She slowly rotated her hand, simultaneously lowering her thumb and bowing her finger.

Their fingers had made the outline of a heart.

"Have you ever wanted to make love in an elevator?" she asked.

"Always," Thomas replied. Before she could respond, he added with an upward point, "Preferably one without a camera."

She pulled her hand away. "You see, I knew someday you would break my heart."

When they arrived at their floor, the elevator stopped but the doors did not open. Thomas again pressed his pass against the card reader and the doors opened to a featureless hall, even the few doors almost invisible in an overwhelming whiteness.

Meghan was about to exit when Thomas pressed her head back down. Striving not to let her trepidation take charge, Meghan, face covered by her fingers, followed Thomas. He inserted his pass into a reader beside a glass door. Next to it was a sign:

CONTROLLED AREA
ID BADGES MUST BE DISPLAYED AT ALL TIMES OR
ALARM WILL SOUND.
NO FOOD OR DRINK PERMITTED.
PLEASE TURN OFF PHONES
SENSITIVE BURN: 0900, 1200, 1500, 1800

"What's a Sensitive Burn?" Meghan asked as the buzzer sounded in the door lock.

"Voila," said Thomas, taking her by the arm.

He led her into an immense white room, populated by coffin-sized computers. The black devices were almost featureless, only bands of blinking lights on their front panels. At the back of the room, in front of an opaque window, stood a bank of squat power units.

"This is very weird," Meghan whispered, unnaturally loud, to be heard above the pulsing hum. "What is this place?"

"Cloud Cuckoo Land." He smiled to himself.

"I don't get it."

"Welcome to the Sanctum Sanctorum, the Holy of Holies."

"'This is the way we wash our cash, wash our cash, this is the way we wash' . . ." he sang with off-key melancholy.

He typed a few words into a terminal. "Read this."

"'Islandia Turnaround. Code Black. Priority Red?'"

Thomas pressed a key and scenes of a tropical island appeared in a monitor window.

"If all had gone as planned it would have appeared that an aide-de-camp of Maningrat, the invading general, had embezzled the money," Thomas explained. "The ADC would have been terminated with extreme prejudice, and we'd – you and me – would have been home, scot-free."

"Which general?" Meghan asked.

The images on the computer – beaches so white they were almost blinding, virgin palm trees – enthralled her.

"From the greedy country that invaded Islandia," said Thomas. "We were going to meet Jobim tomorrow afternoon. I would turn the money, bearer bonds actually, over to him. He would give us fresh passports and plane tickets. The world would have been our oyster. But unfortunately Jobim had to cancel. Because my boss had him killed."

"Was he the guy you were staring at the night I saved your life?"

Thomas nodded.

"Thomas, this is . . ." said Meghan.

"Jobim was a soldier's soldier. To die on the battlefield would have befitted him, but at the hands of Murdock's thugs . . ." Thomas shuddered. "I only hope he didn't suffer. At least he hadn't gotten the money yet. Otherwise it would have gone right back to the invading bastards."

"Where is the money, the bonds?" said Meghan.

"It's safe." He avoided the question and changed the subject. "This world is a snare, and only if you're fortunate can you drum your way out of it."

"How much money is it?" said Meghan.

"When you're in my apartment, remember those words."

Meghan could not be dissuaded. "How much is it?"

"Gobs and gobs. Not gobs and gobs and gobs, since this was to be a Marks-and-Sparks clean-up operation, but enough that Murdock will be very upset."

"Okay, so you'll get arrested. I know some dynamite attorneys. They'll bail you out," said Meghan. "What did that junk bond guy get? Six months? And he absconded with several hundred million. I know this is well out of the range of your expertise, but haven't you ever heard of the term 'Plea Bargain'. Listen, we'll –"

"Mr. Murdock favors assassins. Within a few days, I shall be at the top of his hit parade," said Thomas.

"Okay, so you stole some money. People don't kill you for that these days." At his rueful smile she added in a small voice, "Do they?"

He turned aside, shaking his head.

Meghan grabbed the lapels of his jacket. "Damn it, Thomas! Get hold of yourself. We'll think of something. Two resourceful adults like us. I survived growing up an orphan, well, almost an orphan, in Queens. I don't know what you survived, but it's bound to be much worse than this situation."

"If you had but a week to live, how would you spend it?" he asked suddenly.

"With you. And you?"

He undid the top button of her blouse. The edges slowly separated, the black seams emphasizing the blue feathering of her veins, the milky whiteness of her skin, a legacy of endless generations of her Irish forbears. She clung to him unquestioningly, her finger looped around his tie.

"Doing what?" The huskiness in her voice was beyond her control.

He released her but she did not release him.

"Make love every place I've always fancied and never dared."

Atop the power units were manuals and a few cables. Thomas swept them aside.

"Is it safe?" she asked, as she began to unknot his tie.

"Nothing's safe near me," said Thomas. "Especially now."

He leaned his arms backward to allow her to slide his jacket off.

"I'm a tiger," Meghan assured him. "Well, maybe a tiger in training. But what about security cameras?"

"None inside. Proximity detectors but no cameras."

He kissed her tenderly, undid several more buttons, then gently eased the straps of her slip down her pale shoulders. She shivered. "If you're scared . . ." he offered.

"Oh, no. It's just so cold."

Her dress rippled to the clinically white floor in black taffeta folds. She started to remove her Visitor's pass, but he stayed her hand.

"Have to keep these on," said Thomas. She undid the French cuffs of his blue shirt, dropping the lapis cufflinks into his pocket. They were her birthday present to him the preceding April. Then she slid the tongue of his belt from its loop.

After he was undressed, he went to the window and pressed a button. The window's opacity faded to translucency and then to transparency. Brooklyn twinkled through the mist across the East River, knitted to Manhattan by the Brooklyn and Manhattan Bridges.

Thomas led the awed Meghan to the power units, an electronic altar in a futuristic shrine. He removed his watch, which Meghan had never examined very carefully, but which she knew by a glance was extremely expensive.

The chill air had stiffened her breasts into erectness. Embarrassed, she crossed her arms above her chest. He smiled when he noticed, then eased her into position. She could feel the plastic casing, as grainy as the skin of a dinosaur, embossing her shoulder blades and bottom. He tenderly unhooked her arms to kiss the crook of her neck.

Gradually he slid his head downward until his left ear warmed one breast and his probing lips stimulated the other. She twirled the base of his hair.

As he grew more passionate, she simply clutched the back of his head, pulling him into her with greater force as his ministrations aroused her.

She lay receptive, beyond enticements, relieved that he had agreed to remain in her life as they sought the sanctuary of each other's bodies. The impress of lips against lips, the rhythm of flesh against flesh, the confirmation and consummation that they were hiding in the dormant shadow of those who sought to harm them. Thomas was skillful, imaginative, energized with rage at the organization that had nurtured him and would soon want to kill him.

Meghan, beyond technique, was swept away, relieved that decades of abandonment crushing her had finally been dissipated by Thomas's passionate intensity. She ached to prolong their closeness forever. Hanging over the edge of the power unit, the chains of their entangled IDs vibrated from their passion.

Afterwards they rested, their need for fusion overcoming the discomfort of the power units.

Neither realized how late they had been out.

Like tendrils from a pink vine, filaments of dawn began to sprout through the deep blue canopy overhanging Long Island. The last black clouds of the storm scudded towards the Atlantic.

Reclining, Meghan watched him for a few minutes before she rose, still naked, and crossed to him.

With a wry smile, he traced the crocodile-skin pattern that had been embossed into her buttocks. She peered over her shoulder and rubbed her now mottled skin into a pink flush.

When he noticed her shivering, he draped his jacket over her shoulders.

"Finding love isn't enough, you know," she whispered. "You've got to recognize it, too. The only man who really loved me, after you that is, was my father. But then he died when I was six and a half. He was an inventor. Not really. Just called himself one. He was obsessed with inventing a filter to take the gold out of seawater – we were always going to Broad Channel on the stormiest days of winter. A scheme that would make us rich as Midas. He loved to read to me. As soon as I learned to read myself, he bought me a picture book called *The Triumph of Budica*. About this Irish princess who went to England and became a queen."

"I'm not sure that she was Irish. Celtic maybe. And I believe that she later poisoned her daughters, then committed suicide while the Romans slaughtered a hundred thousand of her followers. I would hardly call that a triumph."

"I suppose it was, in an Irish sort of way."

"Sorry," Thomas said. "I don't mean to be flippant, especially now."

"Budica had tawny hair, so my father always called me his 'tawny-haired princess.' That's why I always get upset when someone calls me a redhead. My mother used to complain whenever I read the book – she had been born in a carnival wagon in England and was terrified she might die in one in America. She'd shout at my father 'Liam, you're ruining the girl, keeping her nose buried in a book. You'll poison her mind with your ridiculous ideas. She'll stop going to mass; she'll start believing that you should do nothing but enjoy life. Then she won't be a fit wife nor mother, and not even the nuns will have her'."

Thomas had heard fragments of her history, but never in a continuum and never unadorned with self-deprecatory asides or humorous flourishes.

He drew her close, and indeed it seemed to her that he was attempting to shoulder some of her own burdens.

"My Da had this stomachache, and they took him to North Shore hospital, and they sent him home. It was a massive heart attack, and they gave him Tums."

Her voice fell, trembling slightly as she neared the unrevealed parts of her life.

"Somehow I managed to convince myself that if I hadn't always had my nose buried in that book, my father would still be alive."

"That's ludicrous." Gripping her by the shoulders, he turned her to look into his eyes. "The two had nothing to do with each other."

She looked up at him with a faint uncomfortable smile. "I know it's absurd, but what does logic have to do with a six-year old? My father's death was my fault. I'm genetically programmed to be guilty about something, so it might as well be for a genuine tragedy."

"Bloody priests," Thomas muttered. "The whole bloody culture of guilt."

"I suppose my father's death was a blessing for my mother. Allowed her to dump me with my father's sister, who shared my mother's low opinion of him. So my mother could move down to Florida and marry a guy who owned a laundromat. She bailed. Sentenced me to a lifetime in Cinderellaville. Wash the clothes! Scrub the floor! While my cousins were treated like princesses. Decked out in Gloria Vanderbilt jeans. Moira was my only ally."

Her gaze drifted to the increasingly dawn-gold Brooklyn. "When I escaped, I moved to the Bronx. You have no idea what the neighborhood I got stuck in was like. Rat infested, addict infested, infested with losers who spend their lives pregnant with dreams that winners like you laugh at because they're so trivial. Dreams like having a job with insurance or actually buying a dress from Laura Ashley. As pitiful as they were, every single one of those dreams were doomed to end up stillborn. But even when my tiny life was collapsing, one aborted fantasy at a time, I was determined my dreams would grow up strong and healthy into something I could be proud of."

"Don't make presumptions, Meghan. My own life might not have been what you expect."

Wrapped in her own painful memories, she was not listening. "My uncle was the one who took the prize."

She pursed her lips as if to spit and cleanse her mouth of his mention.

"Actually my aunt's husband. Small time hot shot in his union local. The only thing bigger than his ego was his beer belly. Raped me when I was twelve. I really didn't know what was happening."

Her uncle never knew what a staunch ally he had in Sister Mary Alberta about the perils of attractiveness. "Managed to convince me that it was all my fault. That I was a wicked woman who killed my father by my reading and tempted my uncle, that saintly man, into the paths of sin. I've been damned ever since. I'm sorry, Thomas."

She turned her sorrowful face upwards to him.

"It's not my habit to confide anything to anybody, not even to my priest, but somehow you bring out confession in me. I know you're in deep trouble, and here I'm blubbering away about my talk-show childhood."

She paused, composing herself. "But it all worked out, 'cause he got in trouble with the shys. They broke a couple of his fingers, one of which got infected and for a couple of months he looked like he was wearing sausage gloves. So Aunt Wicked Witch of the West took it out on me."

"Ah, the glories of democracy. Fifty years ago, only a small percentage of children could enjoy the pleasures of poverty and abuse. Now deprivation is available to almost all."

"Why do you always get like this? I try to talk about us, and you change the subject to politics. It's . . . it's . . . inappropriate."

"Because, dearest Meghan, politics is about to separate us with 'the vale no man can cross'."

"What does that mean?"

He peered down at her, her weariness making a visible thin fretwork of lines at the corners of her eyes. "I want to protect you from suffering. Or maybe myself. Wit is all I have to make me feel worthy of your love. Don't you see?"

She laughed sharply, a sound of release, not mirth. "How the hell would I know what love looks like, what it feels like? I've probably had a dozen guys who said they loved me. But I just wasn't aware of it. I simply sent them packing. Until I met you, Thomas, I never recognized it."

"Love is not what we have while it's happening," he observed softly, bathing her in the soft sharpness of his gaze. "Love is what we take away after everything's over. If you leave now, you'll have enough happy memories to last a lifetime. You'll have enough faith in yourself and humanity to persevere and not end up as cynical and doomed as me."

"Love is recklessness. Love is contradiction," she declared, uncertain what prompted her statement and feeling somehow that she was trying to compete with Thomas on his own turf. "I'm not going to lose you. I'm sticking around. We can't surrender. Not now. Why don't you give the money back?"

"Too late," Thomas answered.

"Or how about . . . let's run away together."

"Their success rate is one hundred percent. No one has ever escaped them."

"There must be someplace to hide."

Her flushed intensity heightened the band of light freckles across her cheeks and brow.

"Where?" With a sweep of his hand, Thomas indicated the ranks of humming storage units. "With all this tracking us down, they find us. Even on Mars."

"Oh yeah? Let's wreck these damn machines. What would a pint of Crazy Glue do?"

His hearty laugh echoed off the window. Thomas threw his head back and hugged her. "Not much. A bucket of water on the power units, however, might bugger up things royally. At least for a week or –"

"Then that's it."

Thomas sighed, the severity of his features easing. "That's why I love you. Like you said, 'love is contradiction.' You seem to have more street smarts than any woman I've ever met. At the same time I cannot believe the naïveté of some of the things coming out of your mouth."

"Or listen." Stubbornness stiffened her posture. "I'll persuade Mr. Murdock to spare your life. He can't be all that tough."

"Oh, he can indeed," Thomas replied.

"Let's kill him first. Self defense," said Meghan.

"You have no idea how absurd you sound."

When he saw the first hints of a pout curl the corners of her mouth, he crushed her in his embrace. "Have you ever actually killed anyone?"

"Of course not."

"Or caused anyone 'grievous bodily harm'?"

"Well, no. But if it meant saving your life, I would do it instantly. Without even thinking about the consequences."

"It's not in your nature, Meghan."

"It could be," she insisted. "I'd make it part of my nature. You've no idea how strong I can be, especially when my back is against the wall."

"It's madness for you to even consider getting involved."

"Nothing that saves your life can be called madness. I am not about to become one of those holy widows, always wearing black and cackling about death and mayhem. Why don't you destroy the people intending to hurt you? My whole life I had to fight for every morsel of food, every scrap of recognition. Giving up just wasn't an option."

"Ah, but sometimes when you consider the alternatives." He shuddered. And not from the chill of the air-conditioned room.

"How did you get involved with these monsters anyway? Why didn't you just quit?"

Thomas looked sadly towards the sun-roseate towers of the Brooklyn Bridge, at the steady stream of delivery of trucks bustling into Manhattan.

"There are as many ways to seduce people as there are human beings, or as the Russians say, 'as many minds as heads'. Doesn't have to be flattery. It can be a whisper to your longings, a false honoring of what you are deluded into believing is your own uniqueness. A complexity that convinces you you're the only person who can accomplish some Sisyphean task."

"Thomas," she said softly, "I'm not quite sure what you just said, but I can sense that it's something you desperately want to believe, but it isn't the truth. When are you going to tell me what really happened?"

Though his face was turned toward her, his eyes remained locked eastward, towards Brooklyn and Long Island and the far Atlantic and perhaps his own former island home.

His voice grew subdued. "Meghan, you just told me yourself that you grew up desperate. Wanting things that you'll never have in your lifetime."

"Why would you, of all people, ever be desperate?" she interrupted him.

"To watch people you know aren't as clever as you or conscientious as you, being rewarded for virtues they don't have. You know Wall Street is like a jungle? Not because it's brutal. But because despite the flamboyant greenery, the soil is very thin. One year you're pulling down a hundred thousand dollars. The next six you're out of work simply because of market whims. Murdock made me an offer that meant I would never be desperate again."

"It meant that most certainly you would be desperate and maybe even assassinated."

"You have no idea how smitten I was by Murdock. He was so worldly. So certain and unafraid and seemingly benign. He has a marvelously sardonic sense of humor. I felt I could learn so much about dealing with heavy hitters. I started off doing some interesting economic analysis, about precious metals, their needs by the electronic industry in the future. Then Murdock offered me a few tantalizing tidbits about a television network about to be taken over, insider information. I took the bait, made a tidy sum, though I knew I was committing a felony. Arranged some financial dealings with a few dictators that were violations of your country's foreign policy, though not necessarily against what you call your executive branch. Before long I was arranging to send money to brutal military regimes to murder people they didn't like."

He at last turned his gaze away from the rising sun, his face lined with regret. Meghan was struck, having believed it to be one emotion of which he was incapable.

"People think you plummet into the abyss. You don't. You stroll gently down this grassy incline. From unethical to immoral to illegal to amoral. And at some moment you look up, and all the justification in the universe will not convince you that you have not become the evil person you formerly despised. That night we met, when I was standing on the stern of your boat, I was half-hoping that I would get swept overboard. Passive-aggressive repentance. That was the night Murdock cheerfully informed me I had become one of them. That there was no way I could ever leave his organization without being killed or imprisoned. He found it comforting. So I've been biding my time, awaiting a chance to perform some decisive act of atonement. If Jobim had lived long enough to get his money, I would have succeeded."

"Thomas, would you stop thinking only of yourself? We may not be married, but I'm committed to you. So whatever mess you've gotten into, I've gotten into it with you."

"You have not. I pray you do not."

She stared up at his bowed melancholy head. She squeezed him, hoping to wring enough despondency out for him to absorb her reassurance. When he did not respond, she rubbed against him with catlike expansion and contraction.

"What are you doing?" Thomas asked.

"Staking out my territory."

He held her aside to press the wall switch. Brooklyn gradually disappeared in the window's increasing opacity.

Copiously, recklessly, she covered his chest with kisses.

He could not help but respond to her fervor. As if drawn by some irresistible gravity, still linked, they drifted back toward the power units and resumed their embrace.

●

As they stepped from the elevator into the lobby, Meghan still careful to keep her features concealed, the orange light of sunrise cast a hellish glow upon the black marble.

"Good night, Mr. Lockhart. Miss. Or good morning. Get what you need?" Harry asked.

"Something for which Jason searched many years," replied Thomas.

"That would be the Golden Fleece," Harry innocently chuckled.

"It would indeed," Thomas replied.

Meghan elbowed him in the ribs.

He walked her toward the entrance. When they were at a suitably discreet distance, she entwined her fingers in his. "I'll go back to my apartment and pack –" she said.

"Noon. The Oak Room at the Plaza. We'll make our getaway plans."

He turned toward the lobby.

Stunned, she was barely able to utter, "You're not going back up there, are you?"

"If I don't clean out my files, dozens of innocent people will be killed," said Thomas. "I have a four-hour window."

"Just forget it," said Meghan. "Save yourself. Save us."

He kissed her deeply, then broke apart. He hurried back to the security console.

"Thomas!" Her plea echoed off the lobby walls.

She watched, distraught, until he disappeared into the elevator bank. At last she dragged herself into the Wall Street reveille of the graveyard shift cleaners in their company uniforms leaving early and bankers coming in their uniforms of dark suits and silk ties.

•

Disoriented, bereft, determined, Meghan had wandered out onto Water Street. Never had the deserted canyons of the Wall Street district seemed more forbidding. She remembered something Thomas had once told her.

She halted, realizing that she could recall almost everything he had ever said to her and the circumstance of its utterance. The entire city of New York had been imprinted with his observations, and she had begun to observe it through the refraction of his interpretation:

"Inside those bland buildings cities are devastated or lifted up, nations brought to their knees or granted reprieve. Bloody marvelous, isn't it?"

At the time she had merely replied, "Nah, it's spooky. Let's go someplace friendly."

Now, in dread of her lover's life, overwhelmed and impotent, she understood the brutal might lurking in the sleek buildings, the depth of Thomas's insight.

It WAS bloody marvelous.

She wished the Old Fulton Fish Market were still there. She loved going there as a child, enchanted rather than repulsed by the overwhelming odor of the day's catch. Somehow it had always struck her as being very REAL in the midst of the frenetic faux city of Manhattan, of which the current tourist-thick South Street Seaport was a perfect example.

And she could never get out of her mind her father's comment when he took her there for the first time, that it reminded him of "the dead-letter branch of the mafia post office."

An hour earlier, she had been exhausted, ready to succumb to a day-long slumber. But as soon as she stepped onto the wind-whipped streets, the dappled sunrise charged her with nervous energy, a vitality that could not be employed for any useful purpose but which nevertheless would prevent her from falling asleep.

She wanted to linger until Thomas himself emerged. But she dared not draw any attention to herself and thus to him. His assurances had not reassured her, and she doubted the earnestness of his instructions to meet at the Oak Room. Returning to her tiny Tenth Avenue apartment to wait until their meeting did not appeal to her.

At last she hailed a cab and instructed the driver to take her to Thomas's apartment.

CHAPTER 5.

Ethernet

Befitting a man of his position, Locke Murdock's corner office on the 48th floor of the Consolidated Resources building was furnished with handsome simplicity. A red granite table that served as a desk, a rosewood sideboard and several rosewood chairs. Despite the expanse of the table, the only items on it were a telephone, legal pad, walnut pen set and a few framed photographs. A light drizzle spackled the spacious windows, allowing glimpses of the mist-furled sprawl of Brooklyn across the East River. Dominating the room was a framed detail from Michelangelo's "The Last Judgment" showing the doomed being dragged into Hell.

In his mid-fifties, Murdock was a man of relentless and capricious authority. He was taller than average, though his aura of command arose more from his bearing than his height. He wore a Hong Kong-tailored suit. His hair was the requisite salt-and-pepper and impeccably coiffed, as if at any moment he expected a *Times* reporter to step into his office and interview him. His grey eyes had an inviting softness, and when combined with his quieter-than-normal voice, had the power to lull those in his presence into ingratiated confidence. His eyes harmonized well with his professionally jovial countenance, his aristocratic skin was tanned well in all the right watering holes in all the right seasons. Above all, he had the ability to conceal the ferocity always lurking beneath his poised surface.

As he stood behind the red granite table, Murdock was doing his best to sustain his air of paternal benevolence. Amodio "Mo" Spinelli, his amiable second-in-command, flanked him. He was shorter and younger than Murdock, with darker hair and complexion, and by any measure nowhere as adroit or polished as his boss. Nevertheless, he had an even more rare talent, that of being present without being a presence. Highly attuned to Murdock's wishes, Spinelli could instantly interpret the orders implicit in his boss's expressions and asides. As he watched the ongoing performance, Spinelli's true feelings – a grim amusement – occasionally rippled through his grave demeanor.

The unstylish glasses, ill-fitting suit and loud plaid tie worn by Larry Franklin made him seem much younger than his mid-thirties. Though the systems director had done nothing wrong, he fidgeted guiltily in one of the chairs, tilting his ear to make sure he caught every one of Murdock's almost whispered words. At the least sign of his superior's wrath, it seemed he might dive to the floor.

"What do you – your computers – know?" Murdock's anger muted his voice to near inaudibility.

"You mean about the missing money?" Franklin asked.

Resisting the compulsion to be sarcastic made the veins on Murdock's neck bulge. He allowed himself a slow nod.

"The funds went from Brunei into Switzerland. Then they popped up in a Nassau bank, where they were converted into Bearer Bonds only to disappear again."

"Granted. But who made the transfer?" asked Murdock.

"Good question," Franklin replied.

"And when will the nerd herd have the answer?"

"Soon, I hope. So far – So far –"

"So far what?"

Franklin's tilted head seemed to direct his gulped answer towards his shoes. "So far the audit trail seems to have disappeared in mid-transfer."

"You mean with a half a billion dollars' worth of computers at your beck and call, you can't track down some two-bit money transfer?" Murdock's suppressed anger hoarsened the edges of his voice.

"Sir, I'm doing my best. Whoever diverted the money –" Franklin looked as if he were about to cry.

"I'm not yelling at you, Franklin," sighed Murdock. "It's just –" He walked around the table and lay his arm on his subordinate's shoulders.

"Losing – I mean losing – seventeen million dollars – does not reflect well on the abilities of our organization."

"Thank you, sir," said Franklin.

He leapt to his feet and hastily backed out of the office, grateful at being released unharmed.

As soon as the systems director had exited, Murdock exploded, pacing behind the desk with sharp, furious strides. "What kind of bullshit organization am I running, Mo? Seventeen million dollars heads south, and no one informs me until Monday morning. We've got a traitor weaseling his or her way through our midst."

He paused to stare at Spinelli, leaving unsaid in his now hardened eyes the thinnest edge of accusation.

Spinelli returned the glare, his dark brown eyes unyielding until Murdock resumed his tirade.

"I kept warning people that this place had all the security of a sieve. That we better tighten up or catch it where the sun never shines. I want that traitor found, Mo. Immediately. I want him terminated without a shred of mercy. And I want his fate publicized in this organization so thoroughly that no one will ever try to cheat us again."

Murdock slumped in his chair, patting his hand on the table. His elegant gold cuff links made a series of clock-like ticks on the granite surface.

Spinelli pulled a checklist from his pocket. "The helicopter's waiting at Kennedy. The auditors should be here in an hour. We've got a sleeper in Jakarta that we're pulling in immediately. He's probably been in contact with Jobim. He might have flipped."

Just then, Randall Yearwood entered the office unannounced. He was wearing sunglasses, a tropical shirt printed with palm trees and flamboyant parrots, and carrying a briefcase. He stood somewhat insolently at one side.

"Bring me the latest update," Murdock instructed Spinelli. "Yank that son-of-bitch in Jakarta. Then get to Zurich ASAP and see if there's any sort of paper trail. I want to know where everybody – I mean everybody, especially anyone in Global Assets – has been in the last two weeks."

He took the list from his subordinate.

"Got it, Mr. Murdock," said Spinelli as he exited.

Without losing a beat, Murdock barked, "Randall, would you take off those sunglasses."

Yearwood held out his hand until Murdock gave it a grudging shake. Only then did he remove the glasses and flip open his briefcase. He lifted out the contents of Jobim's bundle and deposited them onto the granite table. "Now, it seems to me –"

"Do you have it?" Murdock's whole being had modulated. His voice, again soft, was husky with anticipation. His eyes moistened as they grew lidded as a serpent's.

"Have I ever let you down?" muttered Yearwood.

"Let me see." Murdock's eagerness was almost palpable, his anticipation choking his voice deep in his throat.

Yearwood removed an object wrapped in dark blue velvet and lay it on the table.

With a shy, almost adolescent eagerness, Murdock undid the velvet folds until he revealed a plaster cast of Jobim's death mask. The white replica accurately captured every curve of the guerilla leader's face, every whorl and indentation of his final anguish. Murdock studied it, exhaling deeply, transfixed.

He gently lifted the mask off the table and carried it to the window. He shifted to several angles to study it by the light shimmering through the fitful rain. The corners of his mouth trembled on the verge of ecstasy; he gave several exhalations of pleasure.

"Jobim was a handsome son-of-a-bitch, wasn't he? He might well be the pride of my collection," Murdock observed. "You know someday, Randall, I'd like to join you on one of your forays."

His words were barely audible, but Yearwood's hearing was acute, and he refused to be lured closer.

"Enjoy Jobim all you want," he snapped. "But later. We've got some crucial issues we better deal with right now."

With a reluctant sigh, Murdock returned the plaster cast to its velvet wrap. "Before we begin, do you have your expense report?"

"Oh, hell. With a situation this screwed up you're going to nickel-and-dime me –"

"Receipts then."

Yearwood reluctantly fished out a wad of stubs from the pouch of his briefcase. Murdock flicked through them, glowering when he came across a plane ticket. "Premium first class from Bahrain to London? The super premium from London to New York? I've warned you about pulling stunts like this without somebody signing off."

Yearwood's obstinacy emphasized his stocky muscularity.

"You want to get your money back? Or do you just want to kiss it good-bye?"

"If we don't recoup, we'll expect reimbursement."

Yearwood ignored his superior's threat and held up the Schütz passports. "It seems to me that the key to finding the traitor is here."

He flipped open to the page where the picture would have gone. "He who has access to the money also speaks German. An old Vietnamese saying."

The two men studied the page, as behind them, unnoticed, a woman in her fifties entered. Her grey hair was cropped close in an executive cut. Her blue off-the-rack suit was tight at the seams. Her face was full, with the look of someone who had recently quit smoking and gained a few pounds.

"The key would have been for you to have gotten more information out of Jobim," Murdock snapped.

"Listen, boss. I told you, he plotzed before I could get any details. Once I give someone their exit interview, they EXIT."

Murdock lifted an approving hand towards the woman, as if noticing her for the first time. "Why didn't I send Ilsa? She could get a stone to talk and give her useful information to boot."

Ilsa accepted Murdock's praise almost timidly.

"I don't like curry," she said with a shy tremor.

Even her voice was nondescript.

"So who the hell was the wiseass who blew Islandia?"

Murdock pulled a folder from the sideboard and flipped it open. Memoranda, photocopies, aerial maps.

"What's gnawing my guts is that it's someone we know very well. Or thought we knew very well."

Spinelli rushed in and laid a typed list before Murdock. "Here's the shortlist."

Murdock snatched it and scrutinized it fiercely as Yearwood studied it over his shoulder.

"Thomas Lockhart's on it?" exclaimed Yearwood. "No way."

"We have to be sure," Spinelli said quietly. He was assimilating Murdock's ploy of the lowered voice.

"But there was a passport for a wife or a girlfriend, and as well as I think I know him," said Murdock, "frankly, I'm not even sure he likes women. I don't think he's been married. Never seen him with a girlfriend."

"Besides, he's English," added Ilsa.

Yearwood slid into one of the rosewood chairs. "You know, boss, I spent a lot of time thinking about it. We automatically assume that the traitor is a man and the other passport is for his wife. Stop. Just for a moment. Maybe the traitor is a woman, and the other passport is for her main squeeze. That could be why she flipped. To keep hold of him. You know there are some ladies in Global Assets –"

The phone rang and Murdock answered grimly. "Send them in, Mrs. Carr." He hung up and turned to Spinelli and Ilsa. "I'm sorry, folks. Will you excuse me?"

Three men entered: Judd, a Marine colonel in full regalia. Alistair Hagan, a chunky businessman. He had an edge of menace, which was immediately blunted by Murdock's scowl. And Mr. Marwari, a distinguished, grey-haired Indian in a silk and linen suit.

"Have fun, sir," Yearwood said with a veiled smile.

He graciously took Ilsa's arm. Together with Spinelli they exited between the crossfire of icy stares.

"Colonel Judd. I thought our meeting wasn't till next week," said Murdock, glancing uneasily at his watch.

•

Franklin, waving a lengthy printout, rushed into the outer office where Mrs. Carr, nearing fifty, her haired tied back in a severe bun, typed primly at her computer. "Where's Mr. Murdock?"

Before Mrs. Carr could intercept him, he had dashed into the office.

"Stop!" Mrs. Carr shouted ineffectually, her sharp features aghast at the breach.

The three visitors stiffened apprehensively when Franklin entered. Murdock had been standing and hurried around the table to head him off.

"It's his Lordship!" shouted Franklin.

Murdock's flinch was barely noticeable, and he instantly recovered. "Wait outside, Franklin," he ordered.

Franklin suddenly felt the pressure of three brutally suspicious stares from Murdock's visitors.

"Uh, sure," he said as he backed out.

"Who's his Lordship?" said Judd.

"Code name for an AI analyst," Murdock replied. "You know these computer people. High on enthusiasm but a little low on discretion. Too much Red Bull."

"I believe you know Alistair Hagan," Judd cut Murdock off.

"Bohemian Grove. Last year," said Murdock. He extended his hand.

"We've met," said Hagan, initially ignoring the hand, but under the weight of Murdock's cold stare, finally accepted it.

"Mr. Marwari, who's been helping us with the Islandia operation," said Judd.

"Islandia fuckup," said Hagan.

"Gentlemen, from now on kindly refer to it as Country B," Marwari said in accented English.

"I'm aware there's been some slippage in the cash flow to the neutralization operation. I've got my top people on it," Murdock began.

"The money. Where is it?" said Hagan.

"We are well aware that somebody has blown open the project," said Judd. His voice was as lean and inflectionless as his face.

"It appears to be an electronic glitch, Colonel Judd. I can put two million on stream immediately," Murdock promised.

"Meanwhile the patriot forces are in a world of shit," Judd retorted.

"Money is the mother's milk of democracy," added Marwari.

"Sixteen million nine hundred and seventy-two thousand dollars," repeated Hagan. "Where is it?"

"Why do all these problems seem to have occurred on your watch?" demanded Judd.

"I told you. I promise two million in your account by this afternoon. If that's not acceptable –"

"The balance by Friday." Hagan cut Murdock off as he rose.

Judd and Marwari followed suit. Judd and Hagan nodded curtly; Marwari bowed politely.

Murdock watched them depart, then retreated to the solace offered by contemplation of the painting. Uncertainty had a disconcerting effect upon the features of a man who rarely felt it.

"Come in!" he roared to the outer office.

Franklin crept in, ready to flee. He had attempted to straighten his tie and had buttoned one button of his jacket. "I'm sorry, sir. It is indeed his Lordship. Prince Charming."

Disbelief burgeoned across Murdock's face. He lay one of the framed pictures face up on his desk. Last year's office party on the Lady Liberty. Inebriated men, their arms on each other's shoulders, mugged at the camera. He and Thomas, the latter's expression ironic and melancholy, next to each other at the center of the photograph.

Regret and a sense of betrayal fluttered beneath Murdock's stoic expression. He almost appeared more vulnerable than Franklin. "I really went out on a limb to hire him. And the times I stuck my neck out. I would have trusted him with anything in this organization."

He flipped the picture face down.

Oblivious to his superior's distress, Franklin brightened up. "Really ingenious the way we smoked him out. Managed to write a rollback on one of his phone calls and then the whole web unraveled."

With a decisive exhale, his face hardening once again, Murdock picked up the phone and dialed. "Randall there? . . . He did? How long ago?"

"At 4:40 this morning, someone tried to access it," Franklin continued.

"Security? . . . Randall Yearwood? Gone through yet? No? Don't let him! Have him call my office. Immediately."

Murdock slammed the phone down.

"We checked the queue, voila, there was Thomas Lockhart's name in black-and-white . . . cyan and magenta, actually. I know that's a weird color scheme, but –"

"I'll see you get a bonus. Now if you'll excuse me." He motioned towards the door.

"I've had a lot of experience with GUIs. Once –"

"Out!" Murdock shouted. "Mrs. Carr!"

Franklin unbuttoned his jacket in a gesture of attempted informality. He exited, still chattering pleased technical endearments to himself, as Mrs. Carr entered.

"Call around the building," Murdock ordered Mrs. Carr. "Get Randall Yearwood in here. Pronto."

"Yes, Mr. Murdock." The question in her voice narrowed her already slim face.

"Book a black van in the basement. Then phone Thomas. Tell him to get his ass – bring himself – up here."

"Has he been naughty again?" Mrs. Carr asked.

"Don't let him know he's in trouble," cautioned Murdock.

He dialed a Washington number as the secretary exited. "Listen, Scooter," he said into the phone, "I hate to disturb you with bad news. Your door closed?" He summoned the fortitude to utter the distasteful words. "Thomas Catherton Lockhart. He's turned."

"Not my fair-haired boy!" A shocked senatorial voice came over the speakerphone.

"I need an enormous favor, Scooter. Judd was here today. With Alistair Hagan no less. And some Hindu wheeler-dealer. Can you cover me with them?"

"Judd, yes. Hagan, I'll do my best . . . You're absolutely certain that Thomas has flipped?"

"In black-and-white. Or cyan and magenta."

"What?" said Scooter.

"Never mind."

"Too bad," The fuzziness of the speaker could not diminish Scooter's magisterial tones. "He had a hell of a future."

"It's Lawn-Gro now," said Murdock. "Can you spread the word to the appropriate agencies?"

"No problem. If he tries to get out by land, sea or air, he's yours."

Murdock hung up.

He opened a lower desk drawer and withdrew a plastic drop cloth.

He crossed to his private elevator. The control panel had only three buttons: Penthouse, Lobby and Basement. When the door opened, he stepped inside and he pulled the Emergency STOP knob. With grim delicacy, he unfolded the drop cloth and spread it carefully on the elevator floor.

•

The view from Thomas's 30th floor office was pedestrian, the featureless flank of an adjacent skyscraper. The only personal touches in the office were two pictures on the wall, an etching of Keats and a photograph of Charlie Watts, the drummer from the Rolling Stones. Frantically feeding papers from his desk into a paper shredder, Thomas was reciting over the whine of the blades. "'Into the jaws of Death, into the mouth of Hell' –"

Someone knocked.

He started visibly, then cautiously opened the door, blocking the view of Mrs. Carr into his office.

"'– rode the six hundred'. Mrs. Carr, what a pleasure."

"Oh, Mr. Lordship. I mean Mr. Lockhart." She grew as flustered as a schoolgirl. Her sharp features softened. "I just stopped by. Mr. Murdock –"

"– wants to see me?" Thomas was suddenly wary.

"As soon as you can." She looked up and down the corridor, then lowered her voice. "I shouldn't tell you this, but I think he's somewhat upset."

"'Cannon to the right of me, cannon to the left of me . . . '" Thomas recited offhandedly. "I have an appointment. Or rather a rendezvous."

"You'll have to cancel it."

"I'm afraid that will be impossible."

Mrs. Carr sighed. "Do you want me to tell him you've gone out?"

Thomas pushed the shredder to the wall and put a few documents from his desk into his briefcase. He slid into his jacket.

"You are most gracious," said Thomas, kissing her hand.

A smidgen of his charm seeped through Mrs. Carr's impervious demeanor, and she smiled despite herself. Her inherent firmness immediately reasserted itself. "Five minutes and you better be in his office."

"Give me two seconds and I'll be right up."

He shooed her out of the office.

He crushed the remaining papers into a pile on his desk. Searching through the drawers, he found a pack of matches. Three left. The first two failed to light.

He paused to consider the third one, then once again rummaged through the drawers.

No luck.

With a silent prayer he struck the third match. It wavered uncertainly, then flickered into stubborn flame. He held it under the pile of papers until a yellow legal sheet started smoldering. A rind of smoking black expanded concentrically, then burst into flame. The other papers ignited. With a few judicious breaths, he coaxed the pile into blaze.

He positioned the desk directly under the smoke detector and hurried out the door.

●

Yearwood and Ilsa were chatting inside the elevator when Thomas entered.

"Bradykinin. Even has a lovely sound. Strongest pain-inducing substance known to science. Inject less than one hundredth of a microgram under the skin –" Ilsa sounded like a teenager in her giggling enthusiasm.

Yearwood pulled two tickets from his shirt pocket. "Thomas! Got an extra ticket to the Mets. Saturday. Wanna join me? I'm telling you, it's a hell of a lot more interesting than that damn cricket."

"What do you Americans say? I'll take a rain –" Thomas caught himself. He tensed imperceptibly, sensing something deeper in Yearwood's question. "I'd love to," he finished with a thoroughly bogus smile.

"Great!"

"But you have to promise to explain to me exactly what is happening out on the pitch," Thomas tried to banter.

"First off, it's called the 'diamond'," Yearwood replied, smiling broadly. Thomas's reply seemed to cheer him up more than the acceptance would warrant. "Meet me at my usual watering hole, in Brooklyn under the Manhattan Bridge. Saturday night at six."

Yearwood turned back to Ilsa, who resumed her chirruping. "It feels like their entire arm has been shoved into a sausage grinder. Now, when I was having my discussion with Adolfo, I taped his eyelids open. Anytime he told me something I already knew, he could watch as I turned the valve on the i.v. bag. Let me tell you, Randall, I was just flabbergasted at what a chatterbox Mr. Stoneface Buttonlip Adolfo became thanks to a few squirts of bradykinin."

She chuckled.

"Oh, Ilsa," sighed Yearwood. "People like you give our profession a bad name."

Thomas's efforts to mask his apprehension fortunately went unnoticed by the other two.

"You really should have borrowed my ambulance," Ilsa continued to Yearwood, "I just had it re-outfitted. Jobim would have told you everything you could possibly want to know. Whomever the traitor is wouldn't even be history by now."

"How would I have gotten it to India? Driven it across the Himalayas?"

"Like Hannibal," Thomas managed to utter.

"Lector?" Yearwood asked, brow furrowed.

Ilsa noticed Thomas's uneasiness and with some embarrassment said, "Sorry, Mr. Lockhart, we don't mean to talk shop."

•

"Morning, your Lordship," said Harry as Thomas bolted through the security gate. The latter barely nodded in reply.

Yearwood and Ilsa had only gone a few steps past the gate when Harry called out, "Mr. Yearwood!"

He turned, as did everyone else in the lobby. When Harry spoke quietly to him, a hard expression crossed his face. He shrugged to Thomas and turned back to the elevator bank. With a shudder, Thomas hurried out onto the bustling sidewalk.

He paused at the ATM in the wall of the bank whose headquarters were in the skyscraper adjacent to the Consolidated Resources building.

He withdrew the maximum amount he was allowed on his card – $2,000.

•

Murdock fumed behind his desk, drumming his fingers on the passports as Yearwood paced in front of him.

"Can't you let Thomas repay the money?" Yearwood asked.

"Encourage jerk-offs like him and Jobim?"

"Then give Ilsa the job," Yearwood pleaded.

"That butcher?"

"You know there's going to be mourning in the admin section," observed Yearwood.

"There's going to be lamentation in this very office. But it will not delay what needs to be done," Murdock said sharply. "Nail him, Randall. Nail him fast. Nail him hard."

"Damnation and double damnation," sighed Randall. "But you're the boss. Last known location?"

"1032 Fifth Avenue. Four-R," said Murdock.

"Aye aye, sir," said Yearwood. His face was distraught, his pace leaden as he went out.

"Yearwood!" Murdock called.

His subordinate turned in the doorway.

"Don't speak to him. Do him, and don't open your mouth. Don't even let him open his. If his words start worming their way into your brain, you might flip yourself. We wouldn't want that, would we?"

"No, we wouldn't."

Yearwood nodded to his boss and stepped into Mrs. Carr's domain.

"One more thing." Murdock spoke in his disarmingly gentle voice. "You don't have any second thoughts, do you?" He smiled, a gentle flux of lips, his eyes as softly hypnotic as a cobra's.

Yearwood hesitated for the thinnest fraction of a second. "No, sir," he answered.

"And don't do anything to damage my trophy. I thought Jobim was going to be the pride of my collection. But I've just changed my mind."

Murdock gestured him away, then swiveled in his chair to study the wall's painting. He focused on two demons dragging one of the damned off to hell. The unfortunate soul covered one eye with his hand, his expression a blend of curiosity, terror and anticipation.

Murdock was able to savor the scene only for a moment when the fire alarms went off.

A panic-stricken Mrs. Carr rushed in as he was leaping to his feet.

CHAPTER 6.

A Day However Glorious

The treetops danced in Central Park as storm clouds and sun battled to possess the sky.

The canopy at the entrance of Thomas's building flapped like the sail on a clipper ship.

Across Fifth Avenue in the Metropolitan Museum piazza, vendors were serving customers with one hand and holding down their cart umbrellas with the other. Visitors scurried up the steps of the museum, gripping their clothes and bags as tightly as they could to protect themselves from the wind.

Meghan was relieved when she discovered Julio, the super, was on break. She entered the elevator unobserved.

Though she had possessed a key to Thomas's apartment for several months, this was the first day she had been there by herself. She tiptoed in, uncomfortable at violating an unspoken covenant.

His living room was furnished with the whimsy of a man unconcerned about resources. A large Turkish carpet. Cherry wood writing desk. Marble chess table. Well-stocked bookcases. A Victorian sofa, upholstered in green velvet. A leather recliner. Above the ornate mahogany fireplace was a large white space in which hung a small painting by Turner.

Incongruously, in another corner of Thomas's living room stood a gleaming drum set, and beside that, a digital camera on a tripod with a cable running to his computer.

On the computer monitor, a flight simulator flew an endless loop around electronic simulacrums of Big Ben and the Houses of Parliament. Many of the games stacked around the computer were still in their original shrink-wrap. Others Thomas had purchased, played once or twice, and then set aside.

She felt a twinge at his casual attitude toward money. Almost all of his purchases were made on impulse. Her entire life she had been forced to spend cautiously, to scrimp for months to purchase dresses she liked and wear until they frayed.

When she and Thomas had first started seeing one another, anything she mentioned that struck her fancy, from offbeat tennis shoes to a lapis necklace, he would immediately purchase. His nature was to act spontaneously, without expectation of reward, and even with annoyance if her thanks were too effusive.

She had to watch her speech, lest she praise any object too highly. Otherwise, a few weeks later, having forgotten the item, he would give it to her with his self-deprecating generosity, clumsily wrapped in a page torn from a magazine.

Or at least until the incident with the velvet suit.

●

The preceding year Thomas had two tickets to the Lincoln Center premier of an opera based on the life of Marilyn Monroe.

Believing that she had nothing suitable to wear for such a grand occasion, she and Thomas had gone shopping. The September day had been perfect, cloudless but not hot, with a mild breeze that could be enjoyed without ever being felt. The twin of that other perfect day in May, when for a few magic hours even New Yorkers halt their unstoppable grumbling about the city that they will only confess to loving when they are far away from it. The crystalline weather somehow seduces them into shy courtesy and even into the extremes of smiling at each other. Any strangers happening to visit them immediately fall in love with Gotham (not realizing those few magic days occur only twice a year and sometimes not even that) often return to breathlessly inform their friends that everything they had heard about the incivility of New Yorkers was untrue.

Thomas and Meghan had drifted from store to store, mostly basking in each other's presence, unworried that closing time was approaching or that they were no closer to finding her a dress than when they started.

In one of those Upper East Side boutiques, with only two clothing rails and probably no more than forty items for sale in the entire shop, twinges of anxiety afflicted her the instant she crossed the threshold.

A tall, sleek Scandinavian woman, who seemed to have been sent over by central casting, pretended to study invoices at the counter in the back. She had the carefully cultivated languor of a whippet, apparently soporific but in actuality hyperalert, waiting until she scented a sale to sprint up to her quarry.

A black velvet suit by James Galanos seemed to be signaling Meghan that it was indeed the evening dress especially for her. She took the jacket from the hangar and started to slide her hand into the sleeve when she glanced at the price tag. $4,000!

Appalled, she was about to return it to the rack when Thomas asked, "What's the matter?"

Meghan could only point at the price tag.

He held up another tag attached to a sleeve button: $1,800. "More than half off. We're getting it wholesale."

Reluctantly, she tried it on. And when it did indeed enhance her slender figure, they purchased it (although the slightest trace of a smirk in the whippet's face confirmed Meghan's suspicions of the clerk's suspicions of her relationship with Thomas.)

She brooded about the suit all week and was careful that nothing would affect the price tag. Until she realized she dreaded her revulsion at spending so much on clothing far more than her fear of Thomas's reaction.

The day before the premier, she returned the skirt and jacket to the shop and used her own money to buy a simple linen dress on sale at Bergdorf's.

Thomas had been pressing her to have her hair done in the style of Botticelli (like so many of his references, her first exposure to even the name of the painter). Armed with a picture of the portrait of Simonettta Vespucci she downloaded from the Internet, she went to several salons to see if they could recreate it. Most of the hairdressers were booked for weeks, but in a trendy boutique salon on East 57th, the sleek young man with the Italian accent accepted the challenge.

Several hours later and several hundred dollars (a large chunk of her savings) poorer she emerged, trailed by admiring stares all the way back to her apartment on West 10th.

•

In the crisp dusk that night, Meghan crossed Lincoln Center Plaza, filled with a mixture of apprehension, defiance and resignation, oblivious to the gazes of wonderment that seemed to follow her and did not cease until she was out of sight.

Thomas stood by the fountain, his hair glistening from the spray.

As she mounted the stairs from Columbus, she saw him glance in her direction, then dismissed her as not the one he expected, recognizing neither her new dress nor new hairstyle.

When she approached, she could see the question forming in his face as he scrutinized her with a gaze that ran from her head to foot like some science-fiction robot.

Meghan had planned a calm but firm explanation of her motives, but when she saw Thomas's stern expression, she blurted, "I had to take the suit back. No way I'm going to let you spend that much money on a bunch of fabric. Don't worry, they're crediting your card."

In his unexpected way, Thomas burst into laughter. He drew her close while she remained stiff, dreading his wrath.

"You're not angry?" she asked.

"Not at all."

He was about to tousle her Renaissance hairdo, but afraid of mussing it, withdrew his hand instead. "You look radiant, like you just stepped out of Boticelli's studio."

"You recognize it?" she said softly.

"Of course, I do. It would have been bloody ridiculous, wouldn't it? To spend that much on a suit you'll wear a few times a year."

"And not on a hairdo that will only last a few weeks?"

"How much was it?"

When she refused to answer, Thomas said, "I'll cover your coiffure out of the return money. Now come on. Let's enjoy the opera."

Although the libretto was wonderful, powerfully moving and heart-breaking, the score sounded to them like three hours of Stravinsky outtakes.

●

Meghan smiled; the incident seemed so simple and innocent long ago.

A black Burmese kitten rubbed against her.

Thomas claimed that it had followed him home, but she found that highly implausible. Nevertheless, he smilingly stuck to his story.

Meghan set her handbag and carry-on down, then lifted the creature up so that it could peer out the window.

The rain had resumed. Drops splattering against the window transformed the Metropolitan Museum into an Impressionist postcard. The glass-enclosed Temple of Dendur was only intermittently visible. Umbrellas sprouted like mushrooms on the sidewalks.

"Oh, Kitty Kitty Bang Bang, what are we going to do about Thomas? We must rescue him from this mess."

She rubbed her face against the kitten's fur; it purred with deep feline contentment.

"Purr all you like. But remember. He's mine."

The cat's unconcerned indolence was contagious; she suddenly felt exhaustion crushing her like a cloud avalanche. She was starving, realizing that she had eaten nothing since lunch the previous day, but not even appetite was powerful enough to drive her to the kitchen.

Shedding her raincoat, she stumbled into Thomas's bedroom. Usually she was obsessively meticulous about her clothes, especially in his apartment, but once she removed her taffeta dress and slip, she simply dropped them between the four-poster canopy bed and the wall.

She put on one of Thomas's shirts from a carved walnut wardrobe and crawled under the bed sheets. The cuffs were so stiff with starch they scratched her wrists. She slipped out of the shirt again. In the process she glimpsed herself in the mirror, her complexion pale with stress, her hair turning dark and stringy. She felt old and incapable; her last thought before she fell asleep was that she hoped Thomas did not see her in this dire state.

His shirt still dangled from her hand when she closed her eyes.

•

She did not hear Thomas enter, fling off his jacket and remove a pill bottle from the writing desk.

With care and regret, he examined his whisky shelf until he settled on a bottle of twenty-five-year-old Lagavulin. He poured himself a tumblerful and after a medicinal gulp, adjusted the settings on the computer monitor, which quickly filled with an image of the living room.

He dragged the chair in front of the video camera, settled in and studied his image on the monitor. Displeased, he dashed to the mirror to straighten his tie and comb his unruly locks. He rubbed his beard-stubbled face with distaste and glanced towards the hall to the bathroom. He almost entered, but with an impatient shrug, instead returned to the chair.

From his jacket pocket he withdrew one-half of a torn Asahi beer coaster and spun it sorrowfully between his thumb and forefinger. He laid it aside, then slid a fresh memory chip into the camera.

For a few minutes he sat, grim sadness darkening his expression. He exhaled deeply, then switched the camera to record.

"Meghan, I'm furious at you," he began, unable to suppress the twinge of love in his voice. "Why not part like civilized adults, darling? Why did you drag yourself into this? Here I was, all set to cash in my chips, and you came and almost convinced me there was hope that we could somehow beat the house. But the house, at least the one that so recently employed me, never loses. There is so much that you think about me, Meghan. So much I wanted you to think about me. And so much that we both thought about me that is not only false but folly. Earlier this morning, you –"

Suddenly, Spike Jones's wild version of the William Tell Overture filled the room. Thomas nearly jumped from his seat. After a few bars, his recorded voice said, "As you can see, there's too much going on at Casa Lockhart for me to speak. Leave your name and number, and I'll call you back."

The machine beeped. There was only the sound of the caller's breathing followed by a click and a synthesized voice: "This message was received at 10:17 a.m."

The announcement startled Meghan into confused wakefulness; only the presence of the kitten curling into her reminded her of where she was. She rolled over, and closing her eyes, instantly surrendered to oblivion.

•

In the bedroom Meghan remained curled in sleep, her breath shallow; no other muscles moved. The kitten nestled into her stomach.

With a grimace, Thomas deleted the file and started over.

"Meghan, my tawny-haired warrior princess, after you reprimanded me for thinking of nothing but myself, I tried to rectify it by spending the entire morning contemplating you. Your profile against the sunrise, your rousing touch, your Boticellian coloration, your courage, your scent somehow my own. The way you rubbed yourself against me, marking your territory. But that territory is lethal. I'm not going to let you suffer trying to protect it.

"Meghan, death is so immense that all clichés wither in its presence. Though death itself may be simple, the decision to die is not. It must be made, not out of cowardice but out of the gravest fortitude, when every decision tree has been torn up by its roots, when all the branches of your life are destined for the bonfire. So I accomplish what I am about to, not because I am afraid of Murdock and his murderers, but because death is the most viable option. I will not allow him the pleasure of hunting me down. We had our fun, Meghan, moments in the sport of love, but the innings are over, and we will never make our century. But for a few hours, I actually saw us on the powdery white beaches of Islandia."

Thomas took a long slow drink of the single malt as he reflected.

"No, not there. My company, in cahoots with Western governments, will insure that an innocent paradise is soon destroyed. But somewhere like there. Where I could play my drums, and you could 'wash your linen and keep your body white / In rainfall at morning and dewfall at night'."

He took another gulp of the whiskey.

"You must understand that I cannot subject you to that fear also. Not knowing when to expect the bullet in the back, the quick shove off the subway platform. I'm sparing all of us – Murdock, his underlings, and especially you, my dearest – the poisonous aggravation of uncertainty. Of the possibility of making personal contact with the innocently named but terrifying substance bradykinin. Of you being forced to depart this world in the same manner as your beloved Budica.

"Meghan, I say goodbye now not to reject you, but to include you. You encompass all the women in the world to me. Jobim is dead. His contacts are dead also. No way can I get the money to my friends in the rebel forces. So it's all for you, dearest. As far as its location, remember those words I recited in the computer room, the only way out of this world. You'll find what I've left you there. Be sure to pay the restaurant where late we did our dine-and-dash. Though I doubt that you'll ever have the chance, should it arise, could you do my tiny legacy one favor? Dump a bucket of water on those computers and watch Murdock squirm. Oh, and send some lilies-of-the-valley to Mrs. Hildegard Carr, care of my office. With a card, 'To a gracious lady'."

"Thanks, darling. Now. Please erase this file once you've watched it, but not the next one."

He leaned forward, switched off the Record button, and extracted the memory chip, which he slid into his shirt pocket, and replaced it with a fresh one.

●

The kitten sat on Meghan's chest and laid its paw upon her nose. The sleeping woman at last stretched; the shirt fell to the floor.

"Hey there, Randall," Thomas recited into the new file. "Can you believe it? Here I am. Dead. Hope it's you that's watching this and not that cretinous harridan, Ilsa. Sorry I can't make it to the game, rendezvous with death. I know pills are rather bah-NAL. Or is it BAY-nal. Never quite sure. But as you know, I haven't the time for artistry. Anyway, I win. Murdock loses. I bite my thumb at him. You can warn him that Islandia will be no piece of cake. I've seen to that. And the odds are now quite even."

Meghan opened her eyes and smiled at the kitten. She still had not crossed the border back from the land of dreams; the threat of imminent death and separation seemed far away and insubstantial.

She languorously eased out of the bed and retrieved the shirt from the floor.

●

Thomas poured the pills into his hand and raised his glass in a toast: "Here's to you, Randall, old killer. This video is for your trophy case. Souvenir of the one that got away."

He took a swig of whisky. With a flourish, he unstoppered the pill bottle and dumped the contents into his hand. He stirred the pills with his finger, examining them, morosely but coldly calculating their effect.

He steeled himself and raised his arm to swallow the drugs when Meghan's hand swooped down and grabbed his wrist.

The pills cascaded to the floor.

The whisky spilled.

"Bloody hell!" Thomas exclaimed.

"Thomas! Stop!"

Meghan kicked over the camera, which toppled. The display now focused on their legs.

"Don't you dare!"

"You promised to meet me at the Plaza," Thomas exclaimed. "Why aren't you there?"

"Why aren't you?"

She switched off the camera.

"It's over. Once to my rescue is drama. Twice is cliché."

"When? How?" she managed to utter. "Why does it have to be over?"

"What does it matter. I am found out. Food for the worms. The bravest thing I could do in my life is bow out of it gracefully. Won't you at least grant me that one last dignity?"

"Shut up! You don't want to die."

She shook him with the fury of a fed-up mother shaking an obstinate child.

"Stop being such a schoolmistress. What I want is not what I must do."

"Thomas, we are going to escape."

"Even in Antarctica they'd track us down," he reminded her.

"Then we'll go somewhere else."

"We all die. I intend to do it in my own time, in a way of my own choosing. With flash and dash and dignity, not as an item on some hit man's to-do list, damn it. Don't you understand, Meghan? I am doomed. If you get mixed up with me, you're doomed, too."

"Enough of this suicide crap. I will not let them kill you."

She embraced him roughly.

He resisted but did not try to escape. As her grip grew even firmer, his resistance broke. His shoulders softened, his face merged into the folds of the shirt. She stroked his dark hair over and over, the cuffs scratching her arms with their stiffness.

They rocked back and forth, Meghan murmuring reassurances.

"There now. I'll take care of you. I won't let them kill you."

"You are one persistent woman, aren't you, my tawny-haired warrior queen," said Thomas. "Cry havoc! – and let loose the dogs of Murdock. Catch me, catch me, if you can."

They kissed passionately.

He slowly flowed her onto the floor until they lay face-to-face on the thick carpet.

"How much time do we have?" Meghan asked.

"Not enough," said Thomas, ruefully, resuming their passionate clinch.

Someone knocked discreetly at the door.

They froze.

Meghan recovered first, leapt up and pulled Thomas to his feet. The knocking stopped, and the person in the hall began to pick the lock. She scooped up the glass and pills, and shoved Thomas towards the bedroom. She righted the camera,

•

At last the door swung open and Yearwood, tools in hand, entered. Now dressed in a blue seersucker suit, he peered silently around, his eyes settling on the painting by Turner.

"All style and a mile wide," he said to himself.

Hand concealed in his jacket, he stalked down the hall.

Meghan had managed to slip into her taffeta dress and scoot into the spacious kitchen. The room was almost as big as her studio apartment. Gourmet cooking utensils hung from ceiling hooks, wine was stacked in an iron trellis.

She was calmly opening a can of cat food as Yearwood entered. When she spotted him, she dropped the can onto the counter and shrieked.

Grabbing a paring knife, she wielded it threateningly.

The kitten ignored the commotion to mew at Meghan's ankles.

"Who are you? What do you want?"

Yearwood quickly slid his hand from his jacket: it held a wallet. "It's okay. I'm the building inspector."

"I leave the door open? Why didn't you knock?"

"I did. Nobody answered. Mr. Lockhart around?"

"Went to California," Meghan responded.

"Hmm, California. You a neighbor?"

"Yeah. He asked me to feed his kitty cat. Now look what you made me do."

Yearwood scooped up the cat food off the counter with a paper towel and threw it away. He appeared casual, but every sense was alert.

"And you are?"

"Uh . . . Shelley Clementine. And you?"

Yearwood flashed a card from his wallet. "Cecil Teach, Building Inspector."

He pocketed his wallet, and pulled out an electronic device.

"Gotta check for radon gas."

"Radon?" said Meghan.

"There's been leaks. In the air conditioners," Yearwood said, as he leaned over to the wall unit.

He made a convincing show of checking the controls.

"This one looks fine."

With no indication he was about to move, Yearwood was suddenly in the living room. Meghan trailed behind him, noticing that Yearwood was carefully scrutinizing Thomas's briefcase.

"Can you believe this stormy weather?" said Meghan.

"I'm really glad it's raining, it keeps things cool. But then when it heats up, it's twice as muggy as it was before it rained."

She remained intrusively close to him, mumbling any thought that came into her mind. She could tell by the tightening of his lips that her attempts to distract and annoy him were succeeding.

Yearwood wheeled, retracing his steps back to the hall. Meghan dogged him, unshakable. "So tell me, what do you think?"

He was unable to ignore her as they stepped into the dining room.

"Or are you one of those people who really like it when the humidity's off the scale?" Meghan persisted.

Though she neither heard nor glimpsed Thomas, she had sensed him hastening down the hall.

Yearwood cocked his head, listening intently, forcing Meghan to speak even louder. "Tell me, what sort of air conditioner would you recommend for this rainy weather?"

"GE," Yearwood replied without thinking. "Guess that's about it."

He feinted a move towards the door.

Deceived, Meghan was unable to block his way when he decisively strode into the bedroom.

Instead, she managed to cross and lean against the wardrobe as he headed toward the air conditioning unit.

"I almost forgot," he said blandly.

His eye never left the wardrobe. Remaining at her station, Meghan's eyes tracked every movement. Yearwood mumbled quietly, as if asking her a question. Meghan instinctively bent closer to observe.

The device beeped.

Yearwood yelped, leapt backward, pushing Meghan away. He pretended to grab the wardrobe door handle for balance. Falling to the floor, and then raising himself by the door, he stared deep into its recesses.

Meghan gasped; her hand flew to her mouth.

Nothing in the wardrobe but clothes. Even Meghan was surprised. She, too, peered carefully inside.

"Sorry," said Yearwood. "How dreadfully clumsy of me."

"No kidding."

Meghan snatched the device from Yearwood. "Let me see that."

She scrutinized the small device. It resembled a beeper with several additional buttons.

"Doesn't look like a radon detector to me," she snapped, having no idea what a radon detector might actually look like.

Yearwood retrieved the device and shook it near his ear. "Readings were sky high. Must be some kind of short."

"Inspection over?" Meghan asked.

"Seems okay. Miss Clementine, was it?"

"That's me. Bye now."

She urged Yearwood to the door and pushed him out.

Frantically, she ran from room to room, whispering out Thomas's name as loud as she dared. She did not see him, visible through the window at the end of the hall, pulling himself up over the fire escape railing.

He quietly slipped in through the window.

When he put his arms around Meghan, she shrieked in surprise and spun out of his grasp.

"Why did you scare me so?" she demanded, her anger merely an expression of her relief.

"You were splendid."

His face broadened with pleasure at her subterfuge; his grim eyes brightened to a twinkle.

"Who was that thug? Temperature dropped thirty degrees when he slithered in."

"His name's Randall Yearwood. A baseball buddy from work."

Meghan was beginning to learn to read between the lines of his casual remarks. Yearwood's ominous presence, Thomas's feigned levity, told her all she needed to know. She dared not ask him to confirm the unspoken knowledge that had brought her to the edge of panic.

In the bedroom, Thomas carefully examined the suits in his wardrobe.

"We've got to get out of here," Meghan said as she paced at the foot of the bed. "If this is what things are going to be like, I'd rather go back to Cinderellaville."

"Absolutely right." He removed two suits from the wardrobe. "Should I take the tweed or the herringbone?"

Meghan flung them aside. "If we don't get the lead out, the undertaker will decide." She picked up the kitten. "What about Kitty Kitty Bang Bang?"

Thomas lifted the kitten from her arms, stroked it briefly, then gently set it down. "Marushka upstairs will be glad to play foster mum."

He turned to his bureau and started pocketing loose change.

"Were you two ever an item?" Meghan demanded.

Thomas peered innocently at the kitten, "No, she's too young."

Grimly he held up his credit cards. "A one-hundred- thousand-dollar line of credit. But if we buy a single hamburger with these, we might as well just phone up and say, 'Here we are. Come and get us'."

They returned to the living room. He lay on his back to wriggle under his drum kit.

"Thomas, this is not the time for aerobics," Meghan scolded.

Reaching up into his snare drum, Thomas extracted a small manila envelope from the springs.

"'This world is a snare, and the only way out . . .' I would have figured it out," Meghan insisted as she suddenly realized the meaning of his cryptic comment.

Though she was not sure she would have.

Thomas did not even have enough time for a single triumphant wave before she yanked him to his feet.

"Get a move on, would you?"

With a regretful glance at his drums, Thomas opened his briefcase and slid the envelope inside.

•

Both in their raincoats, Thomas clasping his briefcase, Meghan her handbag and carry-on, they tiptoed down the fire stairs.

Meghan was about to open the door to the lobby when Thomas intervened. He carefully cracked it.

Yearwood and Julio, the superintendent, stood by the lobby elevator. Julio was middle-aged Hispanic, with a furrowed brow that rose up into his thinning grey hair. His utilitarian blue uniform, his name embroidered above the pocket, was starched to a military crispness.

" . . . that we contact Mr. Lockhart immediately," Yearwood was saying.

"Mister, it's like you heard it. He went up. He didn't come down," said Julio. He removed his glasses and angrily started polishing them.

"Very curious." Yearwood stepped into the elevator.

The instant the doors shut Meghan and Thomas emerged.

Julio put on his glasses and peered in their direction. "Mr. Lockhart!" he exclaimed with some surprise. "Guy from the management looking for you."

"Tell him to ring my office, Julio."

Thomas urged Meghan towards the entrance. "We're going to California for a few days."

As they went through the revolving brass door he called over his shoulder. "Would you ask Mademoiselle Dolgoff to feed my cat?"

"No *problema, amigo*. Want me to call you a cab?"

"Quite all right."

"When you coming back?"

"'When the hurly-burly's done. When the battle's lost and won.'"

Julio shook his head, grinning.

Thomas summoned a cab. He pounded on the trunk with his fist. When the driver popped it, Thomas placed Meghan's carry-on in the back. Meghan slid in with a flounce of raincoat and taffeta.

"*Linda*," Julio whispered to himself. Then with even more emphasis, "*Muy linda*." And finally, "*Lindísima*."

"Kennedy Airport," Thomas said as they settled in.

The dark-haired driver nodded and eased out into the southbound Fifth Avenue traffic.

Thomas studied the driver's card and when he saw the driver's name was Sayed Khan, he asked "*Kassay ho?*"

"You speak Urdu, sir?" the driver responded.

Meghan looked at Thomas, surprised at yet another one of his inadvertent revelations.

The rear window shattered. Meghan screamed.

Khan cursed.

The cab jumped the curb. The driver slammed on the brakes, screeching to a stop just behind a bus discharging Japanese tourists.

Pedestrians scattered. Fortunately, none had been in the path of the erratic vehicle.

Thomas cupped a flesh wound at the base of his neck as he opened the door and dragged Meghan through the panicking crowd.

Another cab had stopped in front of the bus and an elegant middle-aged woman was in the process of paying the driver.

Thomas shoved Meghan past the woman into the second cab then hopped in himself.

"I'll get it, Madam," Thomas snapped. "Here." He handed a wad of bills to the Slavic driver. "Kennedy Airport. Quickly."

"Yes, sir," said the driver.

Thomas held Meghan down in the seat, below the sight line of the window. The driver leisurely nosed the taxi out into traffic.

"A hundred-fifty dollars if you can make it in forty minutes," Thomas offered.

The driver joyously hit the accelerator.

"Thomas! You're bleeding!" Meghan exclaimed, peeling back his collar to examine the wound more closely.

Thomas gently pried her fingers away and pulled his collar up. "It's only a crease."

He cradled her, murmuring reassurances, shielding her from his bottomless dread.

Pistol hand suspended through a shattered window, Yearwood tracked the second cab as it headed down Fifth Avenue. He held his fire, then at last retracted his arm.

He brushed fragments of glass from his hand and sucked the blood from a series of small cuts.

CHAPTER 7.

JFK

Within twenty minutes Yearwood had completed his preliminary search of Thomas's apartment, the only sign of intrusion the dismantled drum kit laid upon the Turkish carpet.

Frustrated, he sat on the sofa, joining and separating half of the beer coaster left by Thomas, now soaked by spilled scotch, with the half he had retrieved from Jobim.

He righted the camera, then played the video clip.

He watched it once.

Twice.

A third time.

"A souvenir of the one that got away . . ." Thomas was saying on the display.

He took the swig of whiskey. The bottom of Meghan's torso came into frame as she jarred his hand.

"Bloody hell. What are you doing here?"

Then Meghan's voice: "Thomas! Stop!"

Her bare leg enlarged to fill the frame and a second later only their lower legs were visible.

"Lady, lady, you shoulda let him. He'd be better off," Yearwood muttered.

The kitten approached, mewing.

"Okay. Where's that briefcase?" he demanded of the small animal.

The kitten's only response was to rub against Yearwood's leg.

"What's going to happen to you now?" Disgruntled, he deposited the coaster halves into his pocket.

He shut off the television, swept the kitten into his arm and went into the kitchen.

For an ominous moment he held the kitten up to the open window, then said, "It's a rotten lousy world out there, so be careful."

He set the kitten down and spooned the cat food into the dish. He licked the spoon himself, and swallowed. "Not bad. Better than McDonald's anyway."

Holding the dish tantalizingly close to the kitten, he asked, "Now tell me, where did his Lordship go?"

The kitten mewed more plaintively.

"Nobody in this city speaks English any more, do they? And I sure as hell don't speak Feline."

He set the dish down, and the creature greedily gulped its dinner.

•

Yearwood sat on the living room sofa, reflecting. Several times he swiped his phone open, glanced at his watch, and switched off the display.

At last with a sigh he dialed straight through to Murdock's private line.

"Hate to bother you in the car, boss, but his Lordship's skipped. Is the city sealed? . . . Bus stations too? . . . Okay. Just checking," said Yearwood. "I winged him. Flesh wound on his left shoulder."

He held the phone from his ear as Murdock swore at what he assumed was either Yearwood's incompetence or a deliberate act of traitorous mercy.

Yearwood was unable to utter a single word in his own defense before Murdock embarked on a rant about the disruption caused by the fire Thomas had set.

•

Meghan sat open-mouthed beside Thomas, fixated by the line of blood at the base of Thomas's neck.

"There, there," Thomas murmured, patting her hand.

She squeezed his hand, unable to speak, tears starting to well in her eyes.

"Now, do you believe me?"

Meghan wrapped herself around him. She gulped, nodded. "They . . . really . . . do mean . . . to kill you, don't they?"

"We're not going to let them, are we?"

She rubbed her hands in the tears on her cheeks and used them to wipe the blood from his wound.

"We got away," he consoled her. "We're alive."

"For now," she managed to say.

"I'm not in any peril of going to the Great Beyond."

"We need to get you to a hospital."

"I'm only creased," Thomas consoled her. "A hospital would only make us sitting ducks."

He unknotted her scarf and tied it around his own neck.

"Now relax. Allow me to wear the colors of my Lady Meghan Budica as I sally forth into combat."

Meghan forced herself to smile while every other particle of her expression put a lie to any optimism she tried to display. She threaded her fingers through Thomas's.

"I know you don't have a driver's license, but do you have your New York ID?"

She nodded.

•

The taxi dropped Thomas and Meghan off at the American Airlines terminal, where they joined the queue for first class passengers, Meghan's fingers still firmly entwined in his. Except to get out of the cab, she had refused to release her grip.

" . . . Puerto Rico. I have a very dear friend. He'll get us passports. Dominica definitely is out of the question, though I was quite looking forward to it," said Thomas. "Since we can now go anywhere in the world, where do you fancy?"

They reached the head of the line. The airline representative, a buxom young woman with a middle European accent, was directing them towards an available agent when Thomas spotted two city policeman near the entrance door. Their eyes met for the briefest instant.

The taller policeman pulled his radio out of its holster.

"You sure you're well enough to travel? You haven't lost too much blood?" Meghan whispered.

"Sir, the agent at the end is available," prompted the airline clerk.

Thomas dragged Meghan from the line. "Sorry. Change in itinerary."

"Thomas, what are –"

Meghan spotted the approaching policemen. The taller one was sliding his radio back into its holster.

"Bollocks! Murdock must've tipped them off," said Thomas.

Thomas and Meghan moved faster, easing themselves between passengers, trying to hustle as quickly as possible without drawing attention to themselves. By the time they reached the stairs to baggage claim, they were racing, heedless of propriety.

They jostled through a family returning from Disneyworld, sunburnt parents and three tow-headed children, all clad in Mickey Mouse regalia.

"Watch it, buddy," snapped the father, who had obviously made the transition from the jovial Magic Kingdom to the less-than-jovial Big Apple the instant he had landed.

The policemen picked up speed as they, too, raced towards the stairs.

The arrivals lounge was crowded with passengers greeting their families, businessmen collecting their luggage, and a phalanx of drivers. Without pausing to reflect, Meghan and Thomas rushed over to a freckle-faced older driver with thinning red hair. He held a sign: "Walsh."

"Ah, driver, there you are. I'm Mr. Walsh," said Thomas.

"Thought Walsh was a woman," the young man replied in a thick brogue.

"I am. He's my husband," Meghan immediately, said. She lifted up the scarf to show the driver the bloody groove on Thomas's neck. "Mr. Walsh is a hemophiliac. Need to get him to a hospital. Quickly."

Thomas could not help but look at her with fulfilled appreciation and respect. "Suitcase fell on me from the overhead," he added, already urging the driver towards the door.

"Any luggage?" the driver managed to ask as his passengers rushed him to his limousine.

Thomas shook his head, then squeezed Meghan's hand. "I always knew you were a quick study," he whispered.

"Like I keep telling you, I'm a tigress," she replied.

•

JFK

The limousine driver had already merged his vehicle into the flow of traffic when the two policemen emerged from the terminal.

Meghan could see them approaching the dispatcher at his little booth, and the dispatcher shrugging his shoulders as the officers questioned him.

The traffic on the Van Wyck had slowed to a crawl. Far behind them Meghan heard the wail of a police car.

"Which hospital?" the driver asked through the partition. "I can take to you Jamaica Hospital or maybe Kings County in Brooklyn."

He punched the GPS button to Navigation.

"Back to Manhattan. Lenox Hill on 68th and Madison," said Thomas.

"Are you sure we want to go back to Manhattan?" Meghan whispered.

"It will give me a chance to think."

The siren was growing louder.

"Pull over. He's going to be sick," Meghan commanded.

The driver maneuvered the limousine to the expressway shoulder just before the Metropolitan Avenue exit.

"Should I call an ambulance?"

Across the highway in the Maple Grove Cemetery, a funeral was wending its somber way through the acres of tombstones. A few of the black-clad mourners held umbrellas above them as protection against the threatening clouds.

Meghan prayed that the cortege was not an omen.

"That won't be necessary," she told the driver as she gathered Thomas's briefcase to her along with her handbag and carry-on. She hopped out, dragging Thomas with her.

Thomas shrugged and smiled at the driver. "Won't be but a jif."

Meghan and Thomas scrambled up the embankment. Their driver had emerged from limousine and shouted up at them, his irritation and bafflement deepening his accent. "Hey, where do you two wallies think you're going?"

They reached Metropolitan Avenue and frantically waved their arms to flag a cab. None slowed; their gestures only goaded the taxi drivers to accelerate even faster past.

"It's been a long time since anybody called me a wally," Thomas managed to say. The thought seemed to please him.

Windswept

The flashing lights of the police car were visible down the Van Wyck; motorists were squeezing dangerously close together to allow it to pass. The driver stood at the rear of the limousine, uncertain whether to pursue his passengers, stand guard over his vehicle until they returned, or simply proceed.

Thomas paused to watch the pursuit until Meghan decisively yanked him toward Main Street.

"Thomas, do I have to keep reminding you our lives are in danger?"

"Yours isn't," said Thomas. "At least not yet."

Before they rounded the corner to Main Street, Thomas took one last look towards the expressway. The police cruiser had pulled up beside the limousine and the policemen were getting out, guns drawn.

"Murdock has his antennae everywhere. It's going to be a rough ride, Meghan."

"So I see," she replied.

She squeezed his hand. When she released it, he held up a Metro card.

"What is this?" he demanded.

"You know what that is."

"Only secondhand," he replied. "You don't actually expect me to ride in a subway, do you? I don't have many rules to live by, but there is one I follow to the letter: in Queens, the only vehicle in which I ride is a Cadillac. Be it a limousine or be it a hearse. I don't care, as long –"

"Your Lordship –"

"That might be acceptable for a security guard to address me that way. It is not all right for –"

"– there are a whole lot of things you are going to have to get used to. Millions of people ride the subway every day, including me, and we're none the worse for wear."

"Don't you know the Army conducts its biological warfare tests on the subways? All the latest plagues and pestilences made their debut courtesy of the Metropolitan Transit Authority."

"Dammit, Thomas, this is one hell of a time to hop on your high horse. This is MY borough. I know the rules. I know the escape routes. If we're going to survive, you're gonna have to listen to me."

"I vowed to myself I would never ride another underground in my life," he muttered as he followed along.

They reached the Van Wyck Boulevard station. Meghan marched resolutely inside and swiped herself through the turnstile.

A chastened Thomas followed. "And where exactly do you intend to go?" he asked.

After they stepped off the escalator, Thomas drew her into a corner of the mezzanine. He eyed the passers-by who ignored the couple and anything else not in their immediate line of sight.

"Ah, New York. Easiest place in the world to be a hermit," he said. "Unless you do something truly outrageous, and often not even then, you are totally invisible."

He took Meghan by the shoulders and looked into her eyes with an intensity as hard as granite.

"Meghan, you can leave me now and resume your life. It might not be quite as lush as the life we've been living, but you'll sleep at night and never worry about getting unexplained phone calls, looking over your shoulder or finding some heavily armed stranger in your bedroom at three a.m."

"Thomas, ever since I met you, I knew at some point you'd rationalize some way to dump me. I thought this assassination malarkey was a made up way for you to slide, but now that I see you're serious, I'm even more determined to stay by your side."

She drew herself up to her full height, like one of those creatures who puff themselves up to make themselves more intimidating. Even so, she was no match for his height and obduracy.

"I'll never have another decent night's sleep if I desert you in your utmost hour of need."

"Meghan, ever since we've been born, we both have lived for the moment, and somehow it's always worked out. But those moments are drawing to a close. If you come with me, you're never again be able to contact your friends or family."

"What friends or family?"

"You will have to disappear from social media."

"Are you kidding me? I can't remember the last time I checked my Facebook page. I'm not even sure I still HAVE a Facebook page."

"Do you want to prove it?"

"I AM proving it."

"Give me your phone."

Puzzled, Meghan reached into her handbag, retrieved her phone and handed it to him.

He removed the SIM card.

Her emerald eyes widened almost out of their sockets as he bit the SIM the card in half and swallowed the two halves.

Before she could utter a word, Thomas dropped the phone to the concrete platform and ground it underneath his heel.

Passersby barely turned their heads.

•

The forensics team, white Tyvek suits rendering their genders indeterminate, finished their sweep of Thomas's apartment. No hidden safes. No sign of the seventeen-million dollars. The DVDs had been boxed. His camera and computer had been dismantled and wrapped in bubble wrap and now lay by the door. The carpets and sofa were still damp with luminol; finger-print dust smudges were everywhere, particularly in the kitchen.

The taller of the figures had already run scans of the fingerprints they'd discovered through AFIS, the Federal Fingerprint Identification system. The majority were Thomas's, the rest a smattering of the building superintendent's, a maid who was working on a Green Card, and an unknown party, probably the woman Yearwood had encountered, Shelley Clementine.

Whoever she was, she had never been arrested nor had she ever worked in the financial services industry, which would provide Murdock some relief knowing that Thomas's female collaborator was not part of his organization.

•

Franklin's office resembled the lair of a phosphorescent octopus, illuminated only by monitor glow. Cables draped from the ceiling or rose up from the floor tiles to run indiscriminately to CPUs, keyboards and scanners.

JFK

Swiveling in his taped-together chair, Franklin hung up the phone. The telecommunications expert had determined that other than the one incriminating phone call, Thomas had not used his corporate phone for anything but business.

He pinged the number, and finding that the last known location was the Van Wyck Boulevard subway station, scrolled out on the monitor until almost all of western Queens was visible as a series of blinking lights.

Franklin hurried out of his office, and speed-dialed Yearwood.

"Get yourself to Queens," Franklin ordered, his voice tightly wound. "Track the E line to Van Wyck Boulevard station and await further instructions."

"Has Murdock authorized this?" asked Yearwood.

"He will. Trust me."

Franklin hung up, then dialed Mrs. Carr. "Patch me through to Murdock. Now!"

•

The E train was relatively clean, though the riders themselves were in dire need of maintenance, dulled by fatigue, debilitated by the struggle of earning their crust in the ever more Darwinian metropolis (or necropolis, as Thomas often called it) that New York had become.

His face crisscrossed by an odd distress, Thomas scrutinized the passengers, who, slumped in their private woes, didn't bother to scrutinize him back.

A derelict, snoring contentedly, sprawled across three seats. At the far end of the car, a beggar gave up on the passengers who were stonily ignoring him, and proceeded into the next car.

Meghan tried to peer under the scarf at the wound, but Thomas swatted her hand. "I'm quite all right," he snapped. "Where are we going anyway?"

"Woodside. To my cousin Moira's house."

"I wouldn't be caught dead in Queens," Thomas muttered.

"Exactly my point."

"Well," he conceded, "maybe to watch the West Indian cricket matches. I have done that. And I promised –" he hesitated for a fraction of a second, but Meghan still noticed – "that I'd go with him to a Mets game with him one day."

The train braked to a stop, and a street prophet entered the car in mid-rant. ". . . and in those days shall men seek death and shall not find it."

He wore a battered slouch hat and an Army jacket with frayed thread outlines where insignia had been ripped off. The jacket was several sizes too large and stained with food flecks, some of which remained in his bedraggled beard. His gray eyes were sunken in their sockets, retreating from witnessing the world to focusing on one that only he could see.

Wincing, Thomas rose and stood irritably beside the engineer's compartment.

"They shall desire to die, and death shall flee from them," continued the man, wild-eyed in rapture at his own stridency.

Meghan shot the intruder an angry glance, but he was beyond all reproach. She rose to stand protectively behind Thomas.

The train stalled. The overhead lights went out. The emergency lights flickered. The riders groaned in unison.

"O, city of iniquity who art to be destroyed," intoned the street prophet.

The engineer was adjusting knobs as he communicated to the command center.

At last Thomas could stand it no longer. He pounded on the engineer's window before Meghan could stop him. "How bloody long are we going to be bloody stuck in this bloody tip?"

"You're not claustrophobic are you?"

He glowered at her without speaking.

The engineer looked up, frowned at the disturbance, then resumed fiddling with the controls.

Thomas sighed and leaned his brow against the front window. He turned into the corner, and Meghan could witness him moving his hands up and down in front of him.

Meghan pressed herself against him, trying to communicate her assurance. "Don't take it personally, Thomas. This happens every time it storms."

"I'm claustrophobic, and I'm going crazy." He turned sadly to her, "Had I known that you went through this on a regular basis –"

"It's not so bad since I moved into the City."

"– I would have a hired a chauffeur to be at your beck and call."

"You have fouled the waters and laid waste the land," the street prophet cackled happily. "Verily, verily shall ye be swept away."

The engineer swore and jerked the tiller back. The lights at last came on.

The train lurched forward, slamming Thomas into the street prophet. They stared momentarily at each other then Thomas grabbed him by the shoulders.

"I say, dear chap, is that really a United States Army field jacket?"

"Huh?" The never disconcerted street prophet was thoroughly disconcerted.

"Pip, pip. Hurry up now."

"Uh, I guess so. Got it from a surplus store on 42nd Street."

"Splendid!" Thomas exclaimed.

The man eyed him narrowly.

"You septics – sorry – Yanks saved my grandfather's life in the World War, and ever since, my heart's desire has been to own a genuine U.S. army field jacket."

Suspicion not only oozed but flooded from the man. He folded his arms tightly around himself. "Not selling it," he muttered.

"I would never dream of sullying an exchange with cash," Thomas said. "But I would trade this Dormeuil silk jacket for it. Got it custom made in Hong Kong. Any pawnshop will give you a thousand quid – dollars – for it."

"Thomas!" Meghan snapped.

"Shh!" he hissed sharply as he slid out of his jacket and held it out before the man. "Feel the material."

The man took a bit of sleeve between his fingers and tried to suppress his inadvertent admiration.

"What happened here?" the man indicated the rip in the fabric made by Yearwood's bullet.

"Caught on some construction wire," Thomas replied. "Any tailor can sew it up for a few bob."

With a whir of electric motors, the subway crept forward.

"This offer will expire by the time we reach the next station."

Thomas put his left arm back into a sleeve.

The man stayed his hand. "Wait."

He slid out of field jacket and held it out, refusing to release it until he had secured Thomas's jacket for himself.

Thomas embraced the jacket between his crossed arms, "Somewhere in heaven, my grandfather is sending his blessings."

Thomas's jacket had rendered the street prophet speechless. He tried to see his reflection in the polished metal of the subway car.

"Cheerio, old chap," smiled Thomas. "Be careful not to get swept away."

The man turned, trying to register Thomas's intentions, but irony was not part of his emotional toolkit. He backed away, opening and shutting his mouth, the momentum of his tirade disrupted, and then huddled against the front of the compartment, glaring in puzzlement.

Taking Thomas's hand, Meghan, said, "Come on."

"Just a sec." With an enigmatic smile, he slid into the field jacket.

After limping along at half-speed, the train braked at last as it pulled into the 65th Street subway station.

"Let's go," Meghan said, urging Thomas towards the door.

The street prophet was about to get off himself, but when Thomas glowered, he slunk back into the corner of the car.

Meghan led the disoriented Thomas up the steps to the mezzanine.

Three beefy men lurched upwards by them, the smell of alcohol floating pungently in their wake. Thomas was riveted to the step, refusing to ascend until Meghan snapped, "Thomas, would you come on? You look like a target."

He remained frozen to spot, an expression of peculiar dismay on his face, one that she had never seen before.

"What's the matter?" she asked, seizing his wrist. "When we were getting shot at, chased by police, you were fine. Now a bunch of cheesy shops are scaring you?"

"It . . . reminds me of things," he mumbled.

The force of her hand on his arm at last provoked him into motion and he moved downward into bustling Woodside. His steps were forced and obviously distasteful; his expression resembled that of one of the doomed sinners from Murdock's office mural.

●

Yearwood was steering his old Buick through the thicket of Jackson Heights traffic when Franklin's call came through.

"He's surfaced!" the IT director said, zooming in on a street grid with an orange icon moving in stops and starts.

"Location?"

"He's just come out of the Queen's Plaza station. Hold on," Franklin instructed. "I'm going to overlay you."

He clicked a few buttons and a turquoise circle icon appeared inches away from the orange one.

"He's on Queens Plaza North between 28th and 29th."

"Okay. I'm two blocks away."

Franklin flinched from the screech of the accelerating Buick on the phone as the two icons converged.

"Zooming to street view now. It's not real time so I can only tell you roughly where he is."

"Give me what you have."

"There's a nail salon. A coffee shop. Then there's a bookstore with racks of books outside. He might be studying those."

The turquoise icon stopped, fractions of an inch away from the orange one.

"It looks like you're on a few feet away. On your left."

Yearwood glanced out the passenger window to see a man in Thomas's jacket bending over the racks of books, fingering each title as he did.

Engine running, he jumped out the passenger door and jammed his ceramic pistol into the man's jacket.

"Okay, Thomas," whispered. "The jig is up. You're coming with me."

The man whirled.

The street prophet!

His wild-eyed look even wilder as he cried out to the heavens.

"O Lord, please forgive him, for he knows not what he does."

Yearwood had seen too much his career to be startled by anything, but the fact that the man wasn't Thomas coupled with his histrionic reaction had definitely caught the assassin off guard.

The shop clerk, an attractive young woman with long brown hair and horn-rimmed glasses who seemed to deliberately affect a bookish affect, appeared in the door.

Yearwood hastily slid his pistol into his pants.

"Take all my money," shouted the street prophet. "You damned doomed sinner!"

He reached into his pants pocket and flung a handful of pennies and nickels at Yearwood.

This did catch the attention of passersby but, being New Yorkers, only for a moment before they hurried on.

The street prophet reached into a jacket pocket.

"And take my –"

He withdrew Thomas's burner phone.

"–phone?"

"Thank you, I will," Yearwood replied.

Before he could remove the phone from the man's hands, the street prophet had jammed it into his pocket and backed into the bookstore entrance. "It's a miracle!" he shouted. "Hallelujah! It's a miracle! Thank you, Lord,"

Yearwood didn't even pause before he smoothly yanked the man's arm behind his back and eased the phone out of his hand.

"Stop, thief!" the man cried as the clerk looked on in alarm from behind the counter. She grabbed the phone and dialed 911.

Yearwood shoved the phone into his jacket, removed a hundred dollar bill from his wallet and flung it at the man.

"Uh, never mind," the clerk said into her phone as Yearwood scrambled back into his Buick.

"Yearwood! Yearwood!" came Fanklin's excitable voice over Yearwood's Blue Tooth. "What's happening? You get in?"

"Chalk up one for his Lordship," sighed Yearwood as he slid the car into gear.

CHAPTER 8.

Queens Takes Pawns

Thomas remained in his state of silent disbelief as they crept down Roosevelt Avenue. All the possibilities regarding the path on which they had embarked, most with dire outcomes, traced deeper fissures in his brow.

"Keep your head down," Meghan ordered when she noticed him staring, neighborhood familiarity granting her a slight modicum of confidence.

They turned down 57th and stopped in the middle of the block, before a small, quaint house, decades old, with dark brown clapboard siding.

As was the case with many other houses on the block, a black wrought-iron fence fronted the tiny yard, most of which was taken up by a fieldstone grotto. A painted statue of the Virgin Mary resided in its blue niche, a rosary draped over her crude plaster fingers. Meghan studied the statue, simultaneously fearful and grateful to see the familiar figurine. But she could determine nothing from the Virgin Mary's expression, neither welcome nor rebuff.

Thomas scanned the empty sidewalk, starting when Meghan creaked the gate open.

He eased it shut behind them, sheltering her as she unlocked the front door.

They entered a foyer, lined with coats on racks and a row of shoes and boots. Thomas yanked off the field jacket and flipped it into the corner.

"Anywhere around here I can get decontaminated?"

"Thought you'd been looking for a field jacket forever?"

"That quest is now officially over."

"What was that all about?"

"I'll explain later."

Meghan set down her carry-on and flipped on the living room light.

They entered the living room. Thomas stared in wondrous awe at the chock-a-block pinball machines, antique arcade games. A glass-enclosed bubble with a manipulable scoop. In the bottom lay small stuffed animals and stamped tin toys. A bowling alley no more than six feet long, the pins cut in half vertically and suspended by wires from a wooden cage.

"This is very weird," said Thomas.

"Moira's husband, Steve. He collects this pinball stuff."

"Are those two discreet?"

"Absolutely. He's a union guy and gets about six weeks vacation. They're working a carnival downna shore. Till Labor Day."

Hanging on the walls and resting on flat surfaces were photos of JFK and the Pope and much green and white bric-a-brac – ceramic shamrocks, a plaque reading "It's Great to Be Irish," a tea towel with a map of County Kerry. Dried fronds from some long-ago Palm Sunday wilted in a vase as well as plates with illustrations of Italian landmarks. The artifacts only contributed to Thomas's sense of ironic amusement.

Meghan turned him around to face her. "Thomas, you had this beautiful scam, why didn't you let me in on it?"

"You honestly think this was a scam?"

He broke free, his eyes bearing fiercely down upon her.

"Well, I –"

"You still don't understand, do you?"

She chewed on her lower lip, sheepish but defiant.

"Had my plan succeeded, the innocent people on an island paradise would have live happily ever after. They would have had several years of sanctuary anyway."

"Then what? Kill yourself?"

"Meghan, you can walk at any time, I'll ensure they leave you alone. I won't think any the less of you. In truth, I might find myself admiring your fortitude."

She embraced him with a sigh, her head buried in his coat, shaking her head, "No."

Thomas kissed her on the forehead, then from a corner shelf, removed a framed picture, cut from a company newsletter. An executive was shaking a stocky Meghan's hand, a similar but slender woman at her side.

> Robert Sabatier, Division Manager, welcomes cousins Meghan Joyce, 20, and Moira LaRussa, 22, to our Fiber Optics Splicer Training Program.

He set the picture aside and reached for a framed newspaper snapshot. "Oh, no!" Meghan exclaimed.

She tried to snatch it away before he could pick it up, but did not succeed. He held the picture up as she pleaded with him.

"Don't look at that picture, please. I hate it. I look so ugly."

Thomas, puzzled by her reaction, studied the photo: a young Meghan, and someone who could have been her skinnier, darker-complexioned twin, both wearing bikinis, headlined:

SUMMER'S HERE

And captioned:

> Cousins Meghan Joyce, 16, and Moira Dennehy, 17, come to Atlantic City to gambol in the Surf.

"*Sancta simplicita*," said Thomas.

He grinned and kissed the photo.

She took the opportunity to seize the picture from him and put it face down on the shelf.

"You look lovely," he protested

"Don't you see how fat I was? A real pudgette. I was as clumsy as the Goodyear blimp. And that picture makes my nose look as crooked as a hillbilly highway."

Through some ironic seesawing of nature, Moira was now the plump cousin and Meghan the slender one, but Meghan could not shake a perception of her own unattractiveness that had been ingrained in her since childhood.

Thomas gently took Meghan's face in his hands. "Why do you always insist on undervaluing yourself? Even if you were an ugly duckling or a late-bloomer, which you weren't, now you're a swan. You're soaring into the sky with wide white wings."

"Let me take care of your wound," she said as she undid the lapis lazuli cufflinks and slid off his shirt.

●

Although Meghan entered Moira's bedroom with an easy familiarity, Thomas paused in the doorway, mouth open as he took in the undistinguished furniture. The crucifix over the bed. A porcelain statue of St. Francis on the dresser, a dove perched in his bleeding palm. Nothing approaching the casual luxury of his apartment or the Spartan simplicity of Meghan's on West 10th, nor even the garish mechanical clutter of the living room. Meghan opened the windows as Thomas removed his shirt.

He sat on the edge of the bed as Meghan applied antiseptic to his wound. He winced more from the sting of the medicine than he had when the bullet grazed him.

She placed a bandage over the wound and covered the area with kisses. "Anything else you forgot to mention."

"Well, there was this Chinese woman," Thomas said. "Actually, she was only half Chinese. In Singapore."

"You told me that stuff about Singapore was a lie. Where were you REALLY? And where was that Chinese woman anyway?"

He smiled mischievously and playfully seized her wrist, then used her own hand to hoist her chin. Their eyes locked as their separateness fused.

They clung together, desperate for each other, astonished at their own survival.

Thomas and Meghan looked into each others eyes; the sparks in them grew into twinkles that grew into smiles that grew into a face-wide grins that erupted into an outburst of simultaneous laughter.

They collapsed in the bed, shedding their clothes, seeking comfort with each other but simultaneously realizing they were both too exhausted, too drained for any sort of physical union.

They lay naked and entwined until nightfall. The net curtains billowed into the room, filling it with the bluish pink of sunset.

Outside on the sidewalk, girls jumped double Dutch, chanting as two of their number hopped between the twirling ropes:

I won't go to Macy's any more more more.

Got a big fat policeman at the door door door . . .

One of the girls stumbled, and amid a shower of giggles, fell entangled in the ropes.

•

Meghan did not wake but rather drifted into wakefulness around nine-thirty that evening.

She leaned into the spot where Thomas's flank had been. When he was not there, she gasped into alertness.

Draping herself in a sheet, she raced downstairs, catching her breath only when she found him in the kitchen. He stood in his shorts by the kitchen table.

With a pair of kitchen shears, he was carefully cutting the papers from his office into tiny random scraps. He seemed surprised at her agitation, and did not know how to respond when she flung her arms around him, awkwardly entangling him in the sheet.

She could not help but notice the stack of hundred dollar bills in his brief-case, beside the envelope he had removed from his drum kit.

He discretely closed the case.

"I can think of nothing more delightful than spending a week with the woman I love in beautiful Woodside, Queens. However –"

With delicate apprehension, he opened the aging refrigerator. Two pet-rified bagels. Catsup. Soy sauce. A cardboard can of parmesan cheese. He wrinkled his nose and shut the door.

"I'll get some takeaway."

"Are you really sure you want to abandon your life for me?" Thomas touched his bandaged shoulder. "You see what the stakes are for me. At this point you're still an innocent bystander."

"What a terrible loss," she said dryly. "Never be able to claw my way from job to job? Never be able to go down to the subway and ride a train carrying four times the people it was designed for? Give up being groped and clutched by the asylum dregs flushed out to live on the streets of Manhattan. Miss my mother's annual Christmas phone call from her new husband's place down in Florida? Why would I ever want to give any of that up?"

"You can't even go back to your apartment. Ever."

This rattled her, and he caught her momentary flinch.

"What is that you can't live without?"

"It's silly," she said, embarrassed, turning away.

"What?"

"You know what."

"Meghan, one thing I always respected you for was that you were never coy. Tell me what it is."

"My Budica picture book. It's all I have left from my father. And a rosary that belonged to my Grandmother. It's on my dresser."

Thomas lay his hand across her shoulder. "A picture book and rosary, no matter how cherished or sacred, is just not worth risking your life."

"I understand," she answered sadly, though deep down she did not.

"Anything I've ever done that may have aroused your suspicions, my evasiveness, was not to deceive you but to protect you. And us."

"We're both starving. I'll be back soon."

"Any chance Moira has black hair dye?" he suddenly asked.

"What? Has hiding a few gray hairs suddenly become a crime?"

"I want you to dye your hair."

"Lose the tawny tresses you love so much?"

He gripped her shoulders. Never before had she felt his gaze drilling through her, maybe even emerging from the back of her skull. He spoke so quietly she had to tilt her head towards him to pick out his words. "Maybe somewhere in the five boroughs. Maybe not even America, there is a room filled with what they call 'super spotters'."

•

In the basement of a generic skyscraper in Long Island City, thirty or so men and women of every age and ethnicity, with intent bordering on obsession, studied computer monitors in bland cubicles. Each monitor displayed a different image, mostly crowd scenes – Times Square, transportation hubs like the Port Authority or LaGuardia and subway stations, interspersed with shots of the few seedy areas remaining in Brooklyn and the Bronx. Jutting out of the corner of each cubicle was a pipe with a police-car style light atop it.

"Bingo!" shouted a young black woman in the room. She flung her hand up as everyone in the room paused and stared in her direction. Two clean-cut men in dark suits appeared as if out of nowhere to confer with her.

The men led the woman, now beaming, towards a side door. She looked back over her shoulder and gave her co-workers a thumbs up.

After a beat, the workers bent down as if one, conversation concealed behind cubicle panels.

Fifteen minutes later, a buzz-cut, stocky man escorted Franklin across the stage at the front. He clapped his hands with primal ferocity. "Listen up everyone."

As if awakened from a trance, the spotters turned their attention to the massive screen. On it appeared a far larger-than-life image of Thomas's face, lifted from his ID card.

"We have an Alpha Red Alert," the man continued, "Tier Three Bonus for a Locate. Tier Two for a Residence. Tier One for Apprehension."

The spotters resembled bloodhounds tugging at their leashes as they scrutinized Thomas's blown up portrait.

Images of Thomas – company photos from the Lady Liberty event, captured from the Consolidated Resources security CCTVs rippled across the screen and the recognizers' own monitors.

"Thomas Catherton Lockhart," the buzz-cut man continued. "Forty-eight. Six foot one. Hundred and seventy pounds. Last known sighting JFK, where he took a limousine to the Van Wyck. He jumped out and fled with his accomplice at Maple Grove Cemetery in Queens. He's been wounded on his left shoulder and might be wearing a bandage."

The man paused, waiting for the spotters to absorb this information. Images flashed sequentially on the screen.

Thomas and Megan in the Consolidated Resources lobby appeared. The screen zoomed in on Meghan's finger-concealed face.

"Although she calls herself Shelley Clementine, this is obviously an alias."

Meghan and Thomas at the airline counter.

"Miss Clementine is late twenties to mid-thirties, approximately five foot six, one-hundred and thirty pounds, wavy red or light blonde hair."

Getting into the limousine.

The man turned to Franklin. "Anything you care to add?"

Franklin cleared his throat, obviously unaccustomed to any form of public speaking. "Unfortunately, Mr. Lockhart –"

"Louder," the man said.

"Unfortunately outside of work, Mr. Lockhart appears to be a complete Luddite. A forensic examination of his computer showed no evidence of any social media profiles or email accounts. The only search engine entries we could locate were for high-end restaurants. He's obviously been in touch with insurgents in the South Pacific, but we've been unable to determine the channels he's using to communicate."

Franklin stepped back, glad to escape the focused attention of forty pairs of gimlet eyes boring into him.

"Anything else?"

"Lockhart fancies himself a bit of a gourmand," Franklin added. "If he's still in the city, there's a strong chance he might try to sneak into some trendy upscale restaurants."

He nodded to the man.

"All right ladies and gentlemen," the man boomed. "Let the search begin."

The spotters leaned forward, their eagerness palpable.

Fresh images of the five boroughs rippled across the recognizers' monitors, each one different from the one beside it.

•

"It will make their jobs more difficult if you dye your hair and eyebrows black."

Meghan's eyebrows rose questioningly.

"Yeah. THOSE eyebrows."

"Absolutely not."

"Not even to save my life?"

She pouted, conflicted, and glared at Thomas.

"Then buy a black wig. Made of human hair. So well made that not even your mother would suspect?"

"Wouldn't suspect? She wouldn't even notice. But the Hassidim have models so realistic not even YOU would suspect."

"And are you still being stubborn about your eyebrows?"

She hesitated, uttering a low growl of reluctance.

"One of the major things the spotters notice, even if they don't notice they're noticing it. Channel your inner lycanthrope."

"What?"

"Your inner werewolf. Make your eyebrows look like they go all the way across the bridge of your nose. Arch them and extend them far on the sides."

"Okay." Her shoulders sagged as she agreed.

"You also need work on your frumpiness. Pick up a pair of flat lens librarian glasses the next time you're out."

She rolled her eyes and shook her head.

He studied her intently. "What would you look like in a burka?"

With a stamp of her foot, Megan broke away. "No! Absolutely not."

"And you can't wear anything you've been wearing the last few days. Obviously, someone's gonna have to go out for supplies, and it can't be me. Can you wear Moira's clothes?"

"I suppose," Meghan replied. "I'll try my best to pull it off, but she's a Pastel Spring and I'm True Leaf Autumn."

"What?"

"We don't have a single color in common."

"What are you talking about."

"I suppose I could take in some of Moira's dresses."

"My promise is still good," Thomas said. "Once we get out of this mess, I'll buy you the complete new wardrobe I promised."

"As long as nothing costs more than hundred bucks. No more thousand-dollar dresses for me."

He embraced her. "Not to worry, the situation's only temporary."

They both froze at his use of the word in simultaneous realization of the terribly possible outcome that might render it so.

●

On the kitchen table Thomas laid a junk mail envelope face down, then drew a large number 1 at the top. He circled it over and over until it resembled a drawing of an electron spinning in its orbit.

Half an hour later, Meghan, in a pastel yellow sundress, two sizes too large for her, came down the steps, her newly thickened eyebrows extending across the bridge of her nose.

"How's this?"

Thomas turned to study her. "Splendid!" he exclaimed.

She gently rubbed the raven-colored eyebrows. "You know my skin is very sensitive. If I break out in a rash, I'm not gonna let you come near me until it heals."

"Soon we'll have all the time in the world."

She grabbed her handbag and a plastic carrier bag and headed for the door.

•

Forty-five minutes later, Meghan entered the living room, quiet as a stalking cat, the sharp tang of Chinese food preceding her.

Thomas stood at an antiquated pinball machine, hammering the flippers with focused ferocity as the bumpers rang and counter reels spun rapidly in the light box. He sniffed, then turned. The ball bumped down into the tray, the reels froze, the score a half of dozen points short of a free game..

"Not Chinese again," Thomas moaned. "We've already eaten Ceylon. Even if it's Szechuan, that's still S, and we've already eaten Singhalese."

"Better get used to it," she retorted. "Your other choices are Italian or Greek. Or another I for Irish. There's an infinite supply of corned beef and cabbage in Woodside, Come on, give me a hand."

As he set the plates and cutlery on the kitchen table. Megan opened the flaps on a carton. "When they asked me how I wanted the bean curd, I told them, 'weapons grade'."

Thomas's leaned over to sniff the cart. He sighed with deep contentment and straightened. "How do you remember so many details about me?"

"Maybe because you're so unforgettable."

"You didn't use your credit card, did you?"

"Cash," she replied. "Now come on. Lunch is ready."

He slid out a chair and motioned her to sit. She grabbed the back and seated herself. "You know I'm quite capable of seating myself."

"Instinct, I'm afraid, my dear. Gallantry is encoded in my DNA."

•

A feeling of temporary escape triggered ripples of exhaustion that crept upon them as they ate.

Meghan grasped a prawn in her chopsticks and popped it into her mouth. Until she'd met Thomas, she'd never used them. Now, she was as adroit as if she been using them her entire life.

"What are we going to do now."

"I'm considering alternatives."

"Moira's gonna be back in about two weeks. Then what?"

"Meghan, I assure you, if I am in Queens next week, I deserve to be shot."

"Thomas, stop it!" His words provoked such terrible apprehension within her that her voice's shrillness startled even herself."

"Sorry. "Thomas softened. "Some forms of wit just never crossed the Atlantic."

"Aren't you some kinda high level corporate person? Surely you must have Plan B, Plan C. Maybe beyond even Plan Z."

"Plan B is the bloke we were to meet in Puerto Rico. Robert Calvino. I saved his life once and now he owes me. We were planning to meet the day after tomorrow. But now I need to intercept him before he pops up on Murdock's radar."

"How?"

"He's even more of a gourmand than I am. He'll be in New York late tomorrow afternoon. Always dines at Soupçon in Red Hook."

At her askance look, Thomas said, "I forgot. Your borough is Queens. So you have no idea much Brooklyn has changed. Four-star restaurants built above Mafia body dumpsites. I was tempted to trek out there myself, but when we got around to French, I was too hungry for the trek out there."

"That's not why I am worried."

"If we can get a message to him, he might be able to get us over the Canadian border. Once we're across, we lay low long enough for the world, at least the one that's pursuing us, to forget us."

He held a piece of bean curd underneath his nose, inhaling its pungency, swallowed it and pushed his plate aside.

"And how do we contact him?"

"Let me sleep on it."

The sentence seemed to be a snowball that catalyzed an avalanche of weariness upon them both. They exchanged demi-glances, looks half thwarted by their droopy eyelids.

Thomas rose with some effort and helped Meghan to her feet.

They stumbled into the bedroom and shed their clothes. They collapsed onto the bed, not even bothering to pull the covers down.

Meghan placed her finger on the bandage on his shoulder.

"How –"

Thomas put his finger to her lips. "I'm fine."

He tugged her into an embrace. They nestled silently, seeking the shelter of each other's arms, their breath subsiding into a soft harmony.

Except for the fact that she was confined to her cousin's dowdy house in Queens and that a professional assassin, with unlimited resources and backed by the latest surveillance technology, intended to kill the only man who had ever loved her as she deserved to be loved, Meghan was approximately in heaven.

CHAPTER 9.

Teabag It

Wearing one of Moira's night dresses, Meghan was lying languorously in bed the following morning, adrift in the pleasant safety of her dreams when Thomas woke her up. "Lipton's! There's nothing in the house but Lipton's!" he railed.

She blinked groggily, trying to fathom the source of his distress.

He waved a tea bag at her.

"The ghastly stuff they serve in restaurants. I know there's no Fortnum's around the corner, but surely we can do better than this."

"All right, all right. I'll see if I can find some Lady Grey, but in this neighborhood, I doubt it."

She swung one leg over the edge of the bed, then the other, using them to hoist herself into unsteady verticality.

•

Thrashing and mumbling, Thomas was still somewhat asleep when she returned.

Meghan held a cup of freshly brewed Lady Grey tea under his nose. The fragrance somehow penetrated his restless his thoughts, growing pleasure somehow smoothing the troubled furrows grooving his face.

"Ummm," he murmured, blinking awake and sniffing the scented steam.

"The stars must be smiling on you today. First health food store I went into had it."

She could only laugh as his expression, his whole body revived, and his unspoken gratitude beamed over her like a ray of her own personal sunshine.

He took a sip, "Ah, that first sip in the –"

Only then did he notice her black glasses.

"They suit you very well. When we get out of this situation, you should apply for a librarian job."

"Hush," she said with a mock slap.

Meghan had purchased the morning papers, and together they scanned them for reports of their encounters the previous day.

"You see, it shows how unimportant we are," Meghan said.

"It shows how adroit Murdock is at getting news suppressed."

•

As Meghan fried some eggs in bacon grease, Thomas watched the small television on the kitchen counter, channel surfing the news. Again, nothing about their narrow escape.

•   .

All morning Thomas made a restless circuit between the kitchen table, where he would hesitantly write down a name, cross it off with a black line as fierce as sword slash, then stomp back to the pinball machine. Concentration whirred in face like the scoring reels of the device as he resumed play.

Meghan paced, pummeled by her own thoughts, not daring to interrupt Thomas's far more intense ones. Occasionally she eased the front curtain aside to scan the street for pursuers.

"What are we going to do?" she asked from the sofa.

Thomas hesitated, just a beat long enough to lose control of the ricocheting steel ball. With a series of mechanical thumps and clicks, the machine reset itself. He had earned himself seven free games.

"I've got to figure out a way for you to meet Calvino," he said.

"How?"

"I wish I had a photograph, but I don't. Or it would be nice if I could draw you a picture. But I can't. He's about forty-four, he's dark-skinned – actually he's half-Puerto Rican and half-Sicilian – and he's probably got a deep tan. Dark eyes. He looks younger, but he's going bald, sort of like a monk. What's left of his hair is fairly curly. He's got a stocky build, the athlete going downhill."

"Any clothes he might be wearing? Jewelry?"

"He loves calamari and scungilli."

"Uh-uh," said Meghan. "I gotta cast iron stomach, but squid . . ." She shuddered. "Just looking at little legs makes me want to throw up. He better order something else. You still didn't say anything about his clothes."

"Probably wearing snakeskin boots." Thomas thought hard for a moment. "Oh, he's five foot four."

Meghan almost laughed. "Why didn't you tell me that at the beginning?"

"I hadn't thought about it. Now this restaurant is on Van Brunt. Near Verona Street. It's not much to look at on the outside, but it has a posh clientele. You'll recognize it immediately. When you see Calvino say, 'Did you know moray eels can bite through air hoses?' That should get his attention. Mention that you're an emissary from his Lordship and explain that I need his help. Find out his hotel. Tell him I'll contact him. I don't know if Murdock's goons are even aware of Calvino. I pray they are not. But if you see anyone suspicious, don't even try to make contact. Come back immediately. Circuitously but immediately."

Meghan nodded as she absorbed Thomas's instructions. "Do you know what subway it's near?"

Thomas opened his briefcase and withdrew a $100 bill. "For heaven's sake," he said, "take a cab."

CHAPTER 10.

Soupçon

Meghan had not been to Brooklyn in ages and Thomas was once again correct - her impressions of Red Hook were obviously out of date. The hookers trolling for sailors from cargo ships and the rundown bars had disappeared, replaced by well-dressed power couples strolling past rehabbed houses and trendy restaurants. A Japanese steakhouse. A Lebanese restaurant. When Meghan studied the menu, she wondered if the food being served was as mouth-watering as the prices.

No wonder Thomas had considered the Soupçon for "S" as they had eaten their way around the world.

In the middle of a block on Van Brunt, a knot of people had collected, the women slim, well dressed, the men handsome in the youthful, intense way of the upwardly mobile.

A hostess in a sedate black cocktail dress periodically peered from the restaurant to summon the fortunate ones to their tables. Her hennaed hair captured the dregs of sunset as she spoke, her voice convivial with a tinkling French accent.

Meghan threaded through the waiting patrons, their leisured postures and confidence somehow excluding her, or even worse, ignoring her as if she did not exist. She looked carefully around, but saw no one who even vaguely resembled Calvino.

"I told someone that I might meet him here tonight," she said to the hostess. "May I see if he's arrived?"

Soupçon

The woman graciously led Meghan through the close-spaced tables and when they found no one resembling Calvino, offered to add Meghan's name to the list, but Meghan declined.

For two hours she stood in the recessed alcove of a medical office opposite the restaurant, desperately praying that her contact would appear.

At nine-thirty, two couples sauntered up. One of the men fit Calvino's general description, though he was neither as short nor as bald as Thomas had described. Meghan approached him despite her misgivings.

"Did you know moray eels can bite through scuba hoses," she whispered.

The man glanced at her quickly, then averted his gaze. His companions, two well-lacquered women and a companion with the impatience of a Park Avenue attorney, stared openly as he held out several quarters in her general direction. They clinked to the ground, contemptuously unheeded, as the group scuttled into the restaurant.

The hostess held the door for them, casting a puzzled stare at Meghan.

Embarrassed, Meghan retreated across the street, dodging a taxi that swerved to avoid her, the horn honking much longer than the near-miss warranted.

No more customers entered after quarter till eleven. At midnight she trudged out of the shadows to hail a taxi. No one even noticed her presence.

•

On the small kitchen television, the Hairy Gourmet bustled about his kitchen set as he held up a bowl. "*Et voila*! A tabouli salad that took minutes but tastes like hours. Tomorrow we'll make my delicious cauliflower curry. For that you will need four ounces of onions."

On the table lay an envelope with a shopping list. Beside it Thomas was transcribing the ingredients onto a pad from his briefcase when Meghan turned the key in the front door lock.

He had only had to look into her eyes to recognize the failure of her mission.

He took her into his arms.

"He's probably been delayed. Or decided to eat somewhere else. Our fallback position is to meet tomorrow at Grant's Tomb. Same drill as tonight if you are up to risking it."

Meghan raised her troubled face towards him. "And if Murdock's goons have it under surveillance? What will we do then?"

Thomas did not answer but instead tousled her now raven hair.

Her expression grew somber, her eyes darkening. Every plan she considered required evasion, concealment, deception, skills that she had never cultivated. Thomas's aristocratic bearing, which so appealed to her and allowed her to spot him in a crowd, would make him especially visible to those who sought him. And she understood intuitively how difficult it would be for him to debase himself merely for the sake of survival.

"Please don't brood," Thomas consoled her. That's an occupation for elderly chickens, not a courageous young lady like yourself."

She smiled a crumpled smile, unwilling to allow herself the luxury of hope.

"Come on," he said. "It's time for bed."

They undressed and lay entwined, neither coupling nor fully unconscious, as the hours crept towards daylight.

CHAPTER 11.

Grant's Tomb

When Meghan came down the steps into the kitchen, Thomas took the librarian glasses from the table, slid them onto her face and stepped back to admire her handiwork.

"Splendid," he said and clapped. "Two lovers for the price of one."

She mock-cuffed him. They both knew it was an attempt to add some levity to the life or death encounter upon which she was about to embark.

"Now, go! Go!" Thomas said. "You mustn't be late."

"Aren't you going to wish me Godspeed?"

He kissed her on the forehead. "Godspeed."

●

After Meghan left, Thomas eased the curtains aside and watched her get into the cab.

He went up into Moira's bedroom and thumbed through her husband's side of the closet. He removed a pipefitter's uniform and a Mets baseball cap.

He returned to the kitchen, thumbed through the aging, massive yellow pages and dialed a few numbers on the landline. The first three numbers had been disconnected, but he was lucky on the fourth.

"Do you deliver to Dumbo?" he asked.

●

Zaftig clouds drifted high above New Jersey, taking their time across the Hudson before they cast shapeless shadows on the grounds of Riverside Park.

Meghan shoved a few notes at the African cab driver, then hurried through the park towards Grant's Tomb.

A group of boys played soccer at the foot of the broad steps. They wore black pants and white shirts, with yarmulkes bobby-pinned to their hair. Two black-suited men with broad-brimmed black hats, probably the boys' coaches, watched from a bench.

When Meghan was only a few dozen feet away, she spotted a messenger dressed in green Spandex and cycling gloves dismounted from his bicycle. He leaned it against the wrought iron railing.

Their eyes locked for an instant as both questioned if they recognized the other.

Yearwood!

Meghan froze.

Yearwood, shrugging off the encounter, unbuckled his courier pack from his bike.

Averting her head, Meghan retreated behind a tree, terrified.

In elementary school, the boy in the desk behind her had pulled her pigtail, and when. she turned around and walloped him, Sister Mary Alberta immediately dragged her into the hall. "You may think you are tough, Meghan. But inside you are basically a vulnerable young woman. It's so very obvious, and if you do not behave, you're going to find yourself in dangerous situations from which it will be difficult to escape."

Had Sister Mary Alberta's abstinence granted her some sort of foresight into her destiny, Meghan wondered.

When at last her breath calmed down to normal, Meghan peered cautiously around the tree. She did not notice the ambulance parked behind her on Riverside Drive, nor the woman in it observing the scene with a pair of binoculars.

Yearwood casually mounted the steps, hand in his pack.

In the vaulted interior of the Tomb, Calvino, in his signature snakeskin boots, paced in a staccato rhythm from column to column, peering around each one. Hearing footsteps on the portico, he whispered, "Thomas?"

"Had to cancel," said Yearwood. "But he asked me to deliver a message."

Calvino glanced at Yearwood and spun around the column. "Yeah, right," he called out.

Yearwood rolled behind a column base at the entrance. He fired his goldenrod pistol three times, Swishing CHUFFS barely echoed off the portico as bluish-gray smoke wisped out of the silencer.

Meghan's eyes widened, uncertain how to respond.

The boys playing soccer looked up, then at each other, shrugged, and resumed their game.

Yearwood eased himself erect behind the pillar.

He fired once. Again the CHUFF. A chunk of granite splintered with a spray of rock dust away from a pillar.

"Calvino, I didn't come here to kill you. I came here to persuade you," Yearwood shouted into the geometric portico. "And to make you a very rich man. We know Lockhart is going to try to contact you. When he does, let us know. That's all."

He awaited a reply.

Silence.

He adjusted the Bluetooth in his ear. "Courier here. Over."

In the ambulance Ilsa lowered her binoculars. "Calvino's gone down. Might be a trick. But he's fallen on his pistol arm. Very peculiar."

"I know I didn't hit him," Yearwood muttered. "The slug ricocheted off a column. Over."

"It's your call. Over."

Yearwood tried to find a reflective surface to see if he could glimpse Calvino but without success.

Fraction of an inch by risky fraction of an inch, Yearwood peered around the column. At the least sound he was ready to whip back into protective cover.

When he saw Calvino's hand jutting just beyond the pillar base, Yearwood jerked his head back, then cautiously extended it to peer around the other side. Just as Ilsa described, he could see Calvino's boot, made of an elegant green snakehide, leaning against the wall.

"Throw the pistol out where I can see it," said Yearwood. "You might as well do it, Roberto. We've got your back. If you try to escape or pull any more of that pistol shit, I'll pluck you like a turkey."

Yearwood waited for a few moments.

Calvino's pistol still did not appear.

Three teenagers were slouching down Riverside towards the park. Punching each other in mock hostilities, they ignored both the paralyzed Meghan and the ambulance.

"Make one phone call and you'll be set for life," Yearwood called out. "You know we can do it."

He whispered, but loud enough for the Bluetooth to pick up, "He's still not moving. Can you do the tourist bit?"

Yearwood waited; Calvino's boot remained motionless. He watched the ballplayers in the plaza below, praying that none mounted the steps.

Behind Meghan, Ilsa, dowdy in a straw hat, print dress and sunglasses, over-sized straw bag and camera meandered through the players and up the steps. She paused to take the occasional snapshot.

"Hit him in the butt," the crouching Yearwood whispered to Ilsa. "Somewhere to shake him up a little. Don't hurt him."

She indicated that she understood by sliding her hand into the straw bag. She circled the columns, feigning interest in Upper Manhattan.

Yearwood could not see what his accomplice was doing but a moment later there was the sudden rip of tearing cloth, a soft thunk and clattering sound as a .22 slug bounced off the granite wall. He caught a whiff of acrid smoke.

"He isn't moving," said Ilsa. "Not even Olivier could play possum that well."

She headed towards Calvino as Yearwood emerged from behind the column base and joined her.

They both stared in dismay at the man sprawling facedown on the granite floor, pistol arm beneath him. A bloody gash ran across the seat of his pants.

Ilsa nodded.

Both kept their pistols trained on the fallen man as Yearwood tiptoed up him, ready to leap aside.

He prodded Calvino with his foot.

Nothing.

At last Yearwood gently turned Roberto over with his foot.

One eye was open, staring at nothing. The other eye was a bloody pulp, sprinkled with granite powder and slivers. Calvino's lips were half-open, his face still bearing an astonished expression.

With an open hand, Ilsa indicated the pit in a column where Yearwood's bullet had chipped out the sliver of granite that had killed Calvino.

"Damn!" shouted Yearwood. He kicked the base of a pillar. "Damn."

His outburst had caught the attention of the ballplayers, who paused in their game to stare upward.

"Let's get out of here," said Ilsa.

With a perky, touristy bearing, she nudged Yearwood towards the steps. They separated to allow a group of three giggling Japanese girls to pass.

Meghan looked down as Yearwood and Ilsa passed. The pair ignored her.

"Look at it this way." Ilsa patted Yearwood on the arm. "We've cut off his Lordship's most promising escape route."

Meghan's entire being froze, with the exception of her lips, which moved silently in expressions of despair, disbelief and prayer.

Out of the corner of her eye she glimpsed Yearwood loading his bike into the back of the ambulance, but she did not dare look up until the vehicle pulled away.

In the portico, the giggles of the Japanese girls turned to screams.

•

Cringing from the sight of the stainless steel instruments hanging in prim ranks above the twin gurneys – some of whose purpose he knew and some he did not wish to know, Yearwood squeezed through the opening to the driver's compartment.

Ilsa drove. Sitting in the passenger seat, monitoring communication traffic, was Abe Shirazi, a dyspeptic man in his early forties, a worrier and a perfectionist.

"So what happened?" Abe asked. "He's no good to us dead."

"No kidding," Yearwood answered.

"Why didn't you just scare him a little? Not losing your edge, are you?"

"Dammit, Abe. I'm a better shot than I was twenty years ago. The slug didn't come anywhere near him. As far as I can tell, the column splintered. A chunk went right through his eye and into his brain."

Ilsa's grave spinster's face seamed with maternal sympathy. "Things like that happen, Abe."

Her remark did not console Yearwood. "I've just had a bad luck streak," he said with guttural annoyance. "It'll shift."

Ilsa braked sharply and some of the instruments clanked against each other.

Yearwood shuddered.

Meghan was barely able to tell the cab driver Moira's address and could not react to his attempts at conversation with anything but curt monosyllables.

Ilsa's sentence about cutting off "his Lordship's chance of escape" played over and over in her thoughts like some horribly inescapable song lyric. She tried to think what she would say to Thomas but could not summon the slightest shred of optimism to frame her report in anything but the most desperate foreshadowing.

CHAPTER 12.

Ring O'Kerry

As factories fled Brooklyn for South Carolina and Georgia, the workers fled with them. One by one the bars that served the welders and pipefitters also closed, until only a few remained open to serve their aging clientele. The Ring O'Kerry, beneath the riveted Gothic sweep of the Manhattan Bridge in the Brooklyn neighborhood nicknamed Dumbo, had comforted generations of workers from the nearby Navy Yard. When that facility was decommissioned, Ring O'Kerry's customers had dwindled to a few forklift drivers from the recycling yard nearby, punch press operators from the bindery and grizzled men of no definite occupation who nevertheless always seemed flush enough to run a tab all night.

One lobe of the neon shamrock in the window had gone dark. Worn spots pockmarked the linoleum, some grown deep enough to reveal the pine flooring underneath. The grey vinyl upholstery in the booths was held together with duct tape. The bar stocked nothing more exotic than Dewars.

Though the decommissioned facility was being renovated with all sorts of modern facilities and amenities, the bar still had a gritty ambience that scared away all but the most intrepid of the young up-and-comers that were starting to flood the neighborhood. But all the clientele could see the incoming wave, counting the days until bearded hipsters and astronomically paid geeks would replace the fading old-timers.

In a booth at the back, Yearwood nursed a beer. Across from him sat Beryl, a middle-aged woman whose designer glasses accentuated her high cheekbones and walnut-colored skin. When the front door opened, he instinctively tensed and eased his hand under his jacket.

But when he saw that it was only a deliveryman, in a uniform two sizes too small, hunched over a beer keg, Yearwood relaxed and returned his attention to his friend. The deliveryman stumbled and the keg went spinning towards Yearwood's booth.

"Watch out!" cried the deliveryman. Yearwood instinctively rose, his arm reaching towards his jacket.

But Thomas was quicker. He instantly slid into the booth and slammed Yearwood against the wall, disarming him as he did so.

"Son-of-a-bitch!" said Yearwood.

"Mr. Yearwood," Beryl snapped.

Out of sight beneath the table Thomas kept Yearwood's own gun pressed into his adversary's side.

The patrons stared at the commotion, glasses poised in mid-lift.

"My fault. Bartender, the keg is on me!" Thomas called out.

Customers cheered. Two men hopped down from their bar stools and joyfully wheeled the keg toward the bar.

"Don't tell me. You've changed your mind about the tickets to the Mets game," said Yearwood.

"Hands on the table and away from your boots."

"Randall, do you actually know this man?" Beryl demanded.

"He's a friend from work," Yearwood muttered as he complied. "Thomas, meet Beryl. She works in the Mayor's office."

"Pleased to meet you, mademoiselle."

"Listen, honey, don't you have to go the powder room?" Yearwood urged.

Beryl was about to protest, but the edge of command in Yearwood's suggestion made her think better of it. She rose, and with a graceful nod headed towards the rear. She stood outside the restroom, studying Thomas suspiciously, until Yearwood glared at her.

Her lips tight in protest, Beryl went into the hall leading to the toilets.

"Nice lick with your phone," Yearwood said as soon as Beryl had disappeared. "That street crazy almost bought the ranch because of you."

"Oh, I knew you were too much of humanitarian to snuff some poor down-and-outer."

"Whack me and somebody without my world class compassion will whack you," Yearwood warned.

"Not my intention at all. Since I know that you deliberately grazed me. Right?"

A tightening of his cheek muscles was Yearwood's only response.

"If you had wanted to, that slug would have gone right through my skull. Was it because of my lady friend? Or were you afraid of hitting the cab driver?"

Yearwood shrugged. "Some days, my aim is lousy."

Thomas raised a skeptical eyebrow, and before he could speak, Yearwood said, "Oh, and that fire in your office was a brilliant touch. Murdock is still in an uproar."

"'Has his knickers in a twist' is the correct expression. But why did you have to do Calvino? He wasn't involved in the slightest."

"We're all involved, Thomas."

"I suppose you're right," Thomas admitted mournfully. "I'm afraid civilians went extinct a few decades ago."

"I only wanted to talk to him," Yearwood continued. "First three shots didn't do anything. So I fired another warning shot. A rock splinter hit his eye socket. One chance in a damn million."

"He didn't suffer?"

"Never knew what happened. I NEVER knew what happened."

"And Ilsa didn't get her hands on him."

"Word of honor," Yearwood assured him.

"Was he thinking that I planned to meet him?"

Yearwood did not answer.

"Why the hell did you have to do that? He might have died thinking I was in on it."

"No," said Yearwood, uncomfortable under Thomas's fierce stare. "Maybe at first. But when he died, he knew the truth. Now, may I have a sip of my beer?"

"As long as it doesn't end up on my face or the glass on my head."

"Promise."

Yearwood took a deep draught. He cradled the glass in his hands, studying the swirl of suds for signs and omens.

"Thomas, you weren't on the fast track; you were on the rocket to the roof. Bide your time, and you could have become Murdock himself."

"I know. A thought that nauseates my very being."

"Yeah, mine too," Yearwood concurred.

"Which is why I had to redeem myself. But someone . . . something's changed. Tell him to call off the dogs. I'll return his bloody money."

"Why did you do it?" Yearwood persisted. "You probably were earning ten times what I make. Wasn't that enough?"

"You know, Randall, you Americans confound me. I understand everything there is to know, or perhaps everything worth understanding, about Homer or Thucydides. I can tell you anything you need to know about a corporation. How its cash flow relates to EBITDA and how currency swaps impact management buyouts. Jargon, buzzwords, I can bandy with the best of them. But I will never figure out Americans. Not in several lifetimes. Since I've always been game for a challenge, here I am."

"American's aren't very complicated. We're the simplest, most straightforward people in the world. Gullible. Idealistic."

"You might have a point," Thomas conceded. "There really wasn't any reason your country had to send its sons to die on European soil. Not once but twice. Of course we're all very grateful. If you hadn't intervened, I'd be greeting with you '*Güten abend*,' instead of 'Good evening'."

"Or '*Das vedanya*'," Yearwood added pointedly.

"I didn't know you spoke Russian."

"A few words," he admitted. "Just in case."

"I always admired Americans for their energy. Do you think it was an accident that Winston Churchill's mother was half-American? I love your willingness, your openness. You don't know what it's like in England. If your father was a bricklayer, you'll be a bricklayer, and your son will be a bricklayer. No matter how unqualified you are or whatever other talents you might have."

"Tommy, boy, there are a helluva lot worse situations to be stuck in than bricklayer. Trust me. Always was. Always will be."

"At least here you can aspire. Over there, if you try to be anything other than a bricklayer, your mates and the system conspire to beat it out of you at a very early age. Yet with all that Americans have, why are you so sad?"

"What do you mean?" Yearwood's eyes narrowed.

"Like your music, for instance. Country. Blues. Listen to a few songs, and you want to slit your wrists. Every other word is 'lonesome'. Every song is about losing someone you once had or wanting someone you never will obtain. Why?"

"That one's easy." Yearwood smiled. "Because all American music is based on stuff my people brought over from Africa. After all we been through and still are going through, no wonder the music is called 'the blues'."

"If you only knew how much you had to be happy about," sighed Thomas.

"Murdock warned me that you could be the most convincing son-of-a-bitch he knew. So stop all this highfalutin' talk, Thomas. Just tell me, why did you steal the money?"

"I suppose I was turning into an American myself. I had this sudden insatiable urge to lend a helping hand to those poor sods in Islandia against the likes of Marwari and Judd. I know I should have been on my guard against aiding the poor and downtrodden, but I guest I just got swept away by that old American enthusiasm."

"Damndest excuse I've ever heard. Hell of a lot more creative than claiming that your father gave you the strap –"

"Pater and I had problems; that wasn't one of them."

"– or your mother never fed you enough ice cream."

Beryl poked her head through the swinging door. One glare from Yearwood sent her scurrying back to the ladies' room.

"Tell me about Jobim," Thomas said.

Yearwood studied his one-time friend and now adversary, his wary brown eyes taking in every line in Thomas's face and incongruous uniform.

"No," Yearwood answer softly. "Better you don't ask. But I'll tell you this, at the end I did try to save his life. Be thankful I couldn't, or you wouldn't be sitting here now."

"He was a hero," Thomas observed, "not just to his own people, not just to me, but in every aspect."

"He was indeed," Yearwood concurred. "You would have been very proud of him."

"How did you end up in this business anyway?" Thomas asked.

"Do you know how difficult it is to actually kill somebody? On paper, TV and film, it's a piece of cake. But ninety-nine out of a hundred people have circuits wired into their brain not to harm each other. If they didn't, the human race would have gone extinct the day after they invented bows and arrows. I'm not saying that wouldn't have been such a bad idea."

"It certainly would have simplified my life," Thomas muttered.

"Like in the World Wars. Most of the dudes lugging those old Enfields and M-1s never squeezed off a single round. Even when garbage was raining in on them from all sides. So for Vietnam, these genius Army shrinks upgraded combat training. They'd turn those Iowa hicks, who'd never even been in a fist-fight, into lean mean killing machines. Know something?"

"They succeeded?"

"Beyond their wildest imagination. 'course the eggheads never worked out how to turn off these killing machines once they got back to Iowa, and there weren't any VC within six thousand miles."

"Implying you're one of those brain-tampered psychopaths yourself?"

"Not at all. Only saying that I got the best on-the-job training the United States government could offer. With my MOS – 11B Sniper – what else could I be? Certainly couldn't wash dishes in McDonald's the rest of my life."

"Doesn't it ever give you second thoughts? You know what the Muslims say? That we all wear a book around our neck in which our deeds are inscribed. On the Day of Judgment the angels will read the list of what is written and tally up everything we have done. Do you ever lay awake at night wondering what has been inscribed in your book?"

"Come on, Thomas. You know I've never taken out anyone who didn't deserve it. Not only that, no one who didn't expect it. Ever think about lions and their prey? What happens when a lion brings down a gazelle? You think the gazelle shrieks? Starts complaining that out of the millions of gazelles on the earth, why did it get picked out to suffer? Wallows in self-pity as the lion eats it? No. It faces the lion calmly, because it knows its destiny as a gazelle. None of the people on my list ever whined. They knew what would be their end, as losers or fools or double-crossers."

Then with a pointed look at Thomas, he added. "And sometimes all three."

When Thomas did not react, Yearwood continued. "And something else, know how the other gazelles behave? Rush to the aid of their unfortunate brother? Paint up gazelle protest signs and picket the lion? Hell no. They just celebrate the fact it ain't them getting eaten."

"That's a lovely metaphor, being compared to a gazelle. Although I suppose since it makes you the lion, you're coming out ahead."

A smile approximated itself on Yearwood's lips.

"For someone in your line of work, you certainly have put a lot of thought into it," Thomas observed.

"I spend most of my life sitting on stumps and in parked vans in weird locations in hostile foreign countries. With nothing to do but think about stuff. Amount of time I've spent meditating, I could have become a Buddhist monk. Probably gotten enlightened by now."

"Listen, Randall, you probably guessed, but I'm here to ask you an enormous favor."

"Thomas, old buddy, you're not going to start whimpering on me, are you?"

"Not in my nature, I'm afraid. But, alas, now I'm in love with a lovely lassie. I mean colleen. What's even far, far worse, she's in love with me."

"The one on the video clip?"

"Have you been stalking me?"

"Only professionally."

"You know, for someone who has read as much of the Romantic poets as I have, you'd think I'd believe in the magical protectiveness of love. That romance would trump adversity. That her great heart-wrenching prayers on my behalf would somehow confer an advantage to my survival."

Yearwood grimaced as Thomas permitted himself a smile.

"I don't believe it either. But she's surviving on these dreams, wisps of hope and ignorance of Murdock's true reach."

"You know what I am to my family?" Yearwood asked suddenly, his dark face furrowing, trying to shed the attention suddenly focused upon him.

"The first one to go to college?"

"Too simple. I'd have thought you had more insight than that. My sister, a whole slew of cousins have college degrees. Some even have Masters. They got their token entry-level jobs in the big corporations, worked a couple years until the first downsizing, then got the axe. Nope. I'm the first person in my family to get vested with a pension. You don't want me to cancel your contract and risk that, do you?"

"I wouldn't ask that of you, Randall."

"Then what?"

"I will return every cent of the money, but tell Murdock my terms. They are not negotiable. One. That all overt and covert actions in Islandia sponsored by Consolidated Resources or any of its subsidiaries cease immediately. Two, that he call off his assassins, hit men of whatever job description and make no attempt to track down either me or my lady friend."

"What's her name? I'll be sure –"

Thomas wagged an admonishing finger at him. "Now, now. Nice try, Randall old sport. You do deserve your pension. Murdock must unequivocally guarantee the safety of myself and my friend in perpetuity. I don't want to spend the rest of my life wondering if you're going to pop up somewhere and put a bullet in my back."

"That's not my style," said Yearwood.

"Three, that he pay for a suitable memorial stone for Calvino. It's the least he can do."

"Anything else?"

Thomas sighed and stared deep into the curves of Yearwood's face. "If the old bugger doesn't accept, when the time comes, would you look me in the eye?"

Yearwood stared down at the table, unsettled.

"Would you?" persisted Thomas.

The other's lips separated several times but no words emerged.

"For old times' sake."

Yearwood's gaze remain embedded in the tabletop, until at last he nodded.

"You will speak to Murdock? If not for me, for my beloved."

Yearwood swallowed hard the dregs of his beer. He held the mug hopefully up to the light and tilted it. A few languorous drops dripped onto his tongue. The bar had grown more boisterous with the tapping of the keg. The stoolies were singing an enthusiastic, disjointed version of "The Rising of the Moon."

Thomas listened carefully, the refrain of rebellion evoking a deeply bitter-sweet expression.

Yearwood at last spoke, his words sticking in his throat, breaking free only at the end of his sentence. "Okay, Thomas, I'll ask him."

"How will I know his answer?"

"The usual feed. One o'clock tomorrow afternoon. 'Coast's clear' means exactly that. Now, may I have my pistol back?"

"Why don't you give this up, Randall? Retire. Play some golf. I'm sure you have more hobbies than helping Murdock's enemies slough the mortal coil. Treachery's a game for Peter Pan boyos. Not old and honorable men like ourselves."

"Actually been considering it, especially now that you won't be there to brighten the place up. My weapon please."

"What is this pistol anyway? Feels like it's made out of a flower pot or something."

"Might well be. It's some sort of ceramic that slides right through what-ever security scans they have so far. I'm field-testing it for the government. All kinds of trouble's gonna come down on my punkin' head if I lose it."

"I didn't mean to interrupt your beer. Go ahead, just don't try any-thing crafty."

Thomas slid the pistol under the table and Yearwood eased it back under his jacket.

"How am I supposed to have contacted you?"

"Pay some idiot off the street to leave a bullshit message on my voice mail. Make it plausible."

"Done," Thomas replied.

"You're safe till I speak to Murdock. But if he says 'No', the party's over."

"Misericordia. Isn't that what friends are for?" Thomas said, then added, "Remember, you promised not to look away."

They sadly shook hands, and Thomas rose.

The barflies were shouting and saluting Thomas. For a moment, he wasn't sure why but then saw the beer kegs and looked down at his pipefit-ter's uniform.

A few of the regulars tried to pump his hand, but he shrugged them off. He doffed his cap, bowed and opened the door

"Oh, and Thomas," Yearwood called.

Thomas turned, expecting the worst for a fraction of a second. A slight flush of shame reddened his face for even considering the possibility of betrayal. "If by any chance you ever meet us again," Yearwood whispered, "will you tell Beryl I work for Post Office security? She's a little bit naïve about these things."

Thomas nodded and called out to the bartender, "Keg deposit's on me."

And he stepped out into the uncertain night.

•

When Beryl saw Yearwood refilling his glass at the keg, she cautiously crept out of the hallway. "Who was that hoodlum?"

"Most shit-lucked hero I've ever known." Yearwood shook his head sadly. "By the way, you want to see the Mets on Saturday? Seems I just got an extra ticket."

CHAPTER 13.

The Gloomy Gloaming

"Thomas!" Meghan called out even before she had fully opened the door. She froze and called out more softly, "Thomas?"

Apprehension clutched her when she received no response. Meghan crept into the kitchen. There she found a note on the back of a junk mail envelope.

"My dearest darlingest lovely jubbly Meghan, I heard about Grant's Tomb on the news. Be brave, and please don't worry. I have a plan that will buy us time at least."

She paced. She switched on the television on the kitchen counter and channel-surfed. She boiled a bowl of potatoes preparatory to making a shepherd's pie. Though she had enough concentration to slice them, she did not have enough to mash them.

Unbearably restless, she went upstairs in the bedroom. Thomas's pants and shirt lay draped on the bed. She stood motionless, completely baffled as to where he had gone and what he might have worn. She clutched the shirt to herself as she collapsed.

Her mind would not stop misbehaving, thoughts whirling uncontrollably as she wondered whom she might contact. She could never phone the police. She didn't want Moira to even know that she had been staying at her house – that could wait till later.

Horrible speculation about Thomas's fate alternated between even more disturbing conjectures that he had seized the opportunity to abandon her. She was too frightened to consider the future, not even the immediate future, because she knew she would fall apart.

She did not know how long she huddled on the bed as despair throbbed within in her. Suddenly, Thomas spoke behind her, "Am I being snubbed? No tea? No slippers?"

She leapt to her feet. Her cry barely escaped her throat as a croak. Relief and rage swept over her as she rose to embrace him. Preoccupied, he barely registered her distress.

"I came home and couldn't find you. I was sure Murdock's men had kidnapped you, and that then they had –"

She shuddered, afraid to utter any of the possibilities.

"Why did you desert me?" she babbled, "That note could have meant anything."

He murmured reassurances, unyielding to the desperation that caused her to press against him.

At last she calmed enough to notice his dark green uniform. The cuffs rose far up his wrists, and she stroked his exposed flesh. She traced the white oval on his chest, embroidered with the name "Steve" embroidered in green. "Why are you wearing Moira's husband's uniform?"

"Plan B," Thomas replied with a lopsided smile.

"Thank the lord," Meghan sighed. "I think."

"How much did you see at Grant's Tomb?" he asked

She shook her head. "Not much."

But she dared not say what she had overheard Ilsa say. The words played relentlessly in her brain like some demented song lyric. "We've cut off his Lordship's most promising escape route. We've cut off his Lordship's most promising escape route. . . ."

"Were you tempted not to return after seeing Yearwood in action?" Thomas asked. "I wouldn't blame you in the slightest if you didn't."

Outside, a motorcycle gang roared past. They both froze, listening as the rumble died down. They sank upon the bed, not as a prelude to making love, not even considering the idea, but nestling side-by-side, the only sanctuary of self-protection that either could offer.

●

The following morning, Thomas was restless, alternating between reading the papers Meghan had brought, nibbling his breakfast and playing a few desultory games on the living room pinball machines.

He again wore the delivery uniform, refusing to put on any of Moira's husband's other clothes. Only towards lunchtime did he settle down. He had been clipping the diminishing articles about Calvino from the newspapers, when he came across a small article in The Times headlined "Guerilla Leader Slain in India."

His expression grew more somber as he read it. Meghan glanced at it, glanced away, at last could resist no longer and snatched it off the table.

"Murdock's handiwork," said Thomas. "Or rather, I suppose, Yearwood's. If Ilsa had done Jobim, you wouldn't be able to read about it in a family newspaper."

"What's so special about Ilsa?"

Thomas was about to answer but Meghan's apprehensive expression halted him. "I'll tell you later."

"Why do you keep saying that? When we get out of this mess, promise to spend our first month together going through all the things you've promised to tell me later."

He looked at his watch with a start, then turned on the television set to a noontime call-in show. A long-faced emcee in a wide-lapelled suit sat in a small, cheap studio, a single phone on the desk before him.

"Thomas, what don't you want to tell me about that woman, Ilsa?"

"Shh," he admonished her, concentrating on the television.

"Why do you want to watch this crap?"

"Because my company subsidizes it. A good way to get announcements across the airwaves without raising suspicion."

"That sleazebag works for you?" she said in surprise.

He took her hand, restlessly threading his fingers into hers.

"Our first call is from a Mr. Yearwood. Stuart Crosby here," the emcee said. "How are you today, sir?"

"Not very well," Yearwood's mellifluous voice came over the broadcast phone.

Meghan gasped. Thomas covered her mouth.

"So, what are your feelings about the Palestinian situation, Mr. Yearwood?"

"I just wanted to say . . ." Only Yearwood could not say; his voice was breaking over the air. "That . . . that the party's over."

Thomas took the announcement as if he'd been struck in the solar plexus. Meghan put her arms around him protectively as he deflated.

"Okay, that's definitely a different viewpoint. Anything you wish to add, Mr. Yearwood?"

"I tried, Lord knows I tried my best, to change fate but. . . ." Yearwood did not even bother to try to conceal the distress in his voice.

The line broke off to the dial tone.

Unfazed, the emcee picked up the phone. "Stuart Crosby here –"

Thomas swept the television off the table. It crashed onto the floor, the screen going dark outward as the pixels died.

"Damn. Damn. Damn."

Thomas lowered his head into his hands.

Meghan knelt beside him. "That's the end of Plan B?"

"I'm the one who is the coward." Thomas spoke into the tablecloth. "I capitulated. I offered to return his bloody money. I was justifying sparing myself to spare you, Meghan, but it was the most craven thing I could do."

"Please, Thomas. Let me talk to Murdock. I'll convince him to take the money back and let you go."

Her plea jolted Thomas upright. He slammed both fists upon the table.

"No! You have no concept of that man's ruthlessness. His perversion. His cunning. He sits on his throne in his Spider's Club, spinning his evil web. Everyone who comes into contact with him gets wrapped tighter and tighter in the strands. Until he bites them and they die or else go mad waiting for his strike."

"The Spider Club? Where is that?"

"On Pine, near Broadway. Where he can slip in and out during his lunch break."

"Never heard of it."

"Of course you haven't heard of it. If you had, we wouldn't even be in the same room together."

"Why?"

"Because the only way to get past the bouncers is to belong to the crème-de-la-crème of perversion. Or maybe the scum-de-la-scum."

"That's why Murdock's a member?"

"No one dares defy him. I'm the first person in donkey's years."

"That Jobim guy stood up to him. And Calvino."

"Totally inapposite."

"I've sold dinner cruises to seasick ninety-year-olds," Meghan said, her accent growing more pronounced as she herself grew more strident. "Believe me, I'm sure I could persuade Mr. Whatever."

"No."

Meghan sighed and forced herself to relax so as seem as casual as possible. She knew the order in which she asked her questions and presented her request would be crucial, if she were to obtain his permission without arousing his suspicions.

"You know, we never paid Restaurant X."

"So?"

"Thomas, maybe because I'm superstitious, but I don't want to jinx our escape simply because we didn't pay a simple bill."

He scrutinized her sternly. She tried to simplify the angles of her face, to make herself appear as ingenuous as possible.

"You're wearing an awful lot of make up to pay a bill," he muttered.

"I'm in disguise, remember? It was your idea."

His narrowed eyes widened slightly, and she knew he would probably give her the go-ahead, if only to humor her.

"Hmmph."

"I'll be all right."

"It still seems awfully risky."

"Only if you're one who goes there."

"Do you promise not to do anything rash? You're not going to try to go by your apartment, are you?"

"You know that I'm even more paranoid than you are."

"Hmmph," he grunted, a response by which she knew he would agree.

"Be very, very careful," he muttered as she took out one of Moira's rain-coats, a sea-green calf-length model with toggle buttons.

CHAPTER 14.

Gil

In the kitchen of Restaurant X, Gil DeLeo and Joel Slater, the owner, were heatedly arguing. Slater was in his fifties, his off-blonde hair coming to a sharp widow's peak. His mail-order clothes granted his pudgy frame a false note of rugged authority. He was a lawyer and spoke with a lawyer's preemptory assurance. Defiantly against all regulations, he had removed the battery from the smoke detector, and now let his fat cigar smolder in a saucer (there being no ashtrays in the restaurant).

Gil was wearing his chef's toque, white apron and red neckerchief. He twirled a scallop die that resembled an irregular cookie-cutter. "I'll go along with it if we call it shark scampi."

"Sharks, scallops. Who can tell the difference?" asked Slater.

"Me," Gil replied.

"It falls within the legal definition. Scallop means to cut."

The sous chef, Barbara Anderson, watched the argument, anxiety flickering over her features. She had just turned twenty, and even after a decade, was still not yet accustomed to being as tallish as she had become. Her awkward earnestness endowed her with an endearing charm. Over her ragged blue jeans and a torn t-shirt she wore an apron from beneath which poked a pair of expensive running shoes.

"You want to serve sharks? Bring me one gross of lawyers."

Gil pounded it into the cutting block. "I'll personally turn them all into scallops."

He removed his apron, neckerchief and hat and flung them on the counter.

"Okay," Slater conceded. "We won't serve scallop scampi."

"I told you a year ago. Six months ago. If you didn't stop stiffing the customers, I was gone."

He stalked out of the kitchen, pushing aside the swinging doors aside with such ferocity that it took several oscillations before they settled.

"Gil, be practical," pleaded Barbara, and then to Slater. "I'll talk to him."

She hurried through the swinging doors.

"Remind him I didn't fire him. He's still on the payroll," Slater called out.

With a grimace he plucked up his cigar and hungrily sucked it in. He irritably exhaled pungent black smoke that provided him no relief.

Barbara trailed Gil as he stormed through the restaurant. Diners watched out of the corners of their eyes, straight-faced, but secretly relishing the conflict as if it were scheduled entertainment. Only a few looked askance, hoping that the strife did not compromise the quality of their own meals.

"Try to understand Slater's point of view," Barbara urged.

"It's totally understandable. It's the only one left in this city. Cut corners. Me me me and the hell with you you you. I'm going back to Seattle where there are a few traces of honesty left in the way people treat their customers."

"Enjoy your meal and pray that actually you got what you ordered," Gil announced as he stepped out.

He smiled with angry triumph when several of the diners stopped eating to stare down at their plates.

Outside, the wind was gusting, flipping Gil's long black locks from side to side, tugging Barbara's hair from beneath a red kerchief. The sky was a sickly emerald, boding windstorms or nervous rain.

"You're letting one little argument –" said Barbara.

"I've been thinking about this a year, Barbara. It's high time I got out."

"You can't leave."

She had him by the arm, her dark brown eyes looking up at him with piteous plaint.

"Why?"

"Because I'm here. I like New York."

The forlorn softness in her voice made her sound almost like a teenager. "You're young. Enjoy."

"And even more importantly, I want you."

"Barbara, I am sorry. But I just don't have time."

"Don't you find me at all attractive?"

"You're a peach. Hundreds of guys would sleep at the chance to jump with . . . I mean jump – you know what I mean," he trailed off.

"Great. We'll line up all the contestants and have the Barbara Olympics. Won't you at least try out? There's nobody more qualified."

"Barbara, understand. Refusing you takes every bit of willpower I have. You're terribly kissable, *et cetera*."

"Here comes the 'but'."

"But you know I've promised myself. No involvements. Not for now."

His oratory rendered his idealistic features even more earnest.

"I know. 'The New Revolutionary Gourmet Health Cuisine'." She spoke the slogan as mournfully as a dirge.

"Exactly. And I'm helping create it. Not only nutritious and delicious, it might even feed the world.

" . . . it might even feed the world," Barbara said simultaneously, her chin moving identically to Gil's as she emphasized each word. "Meantime, why starve for love? Sex is healthy. Health is holy, like you always say."

"Relationships are so distracting," said Gil.

"We're two of a kind. We'll share love and work. I'll help with your experiments."

"You're already a help."

"What about your acting career? Isn't that why you came to New York? You're not going to give up on that tremendous talent of yours, are you?"

"When was the last time I had a callback? When was the last time I even went on an audition? I mean I'd heard the term 'cattle call', but till I came here, I'd never actually experienced one. Peasants in India have easier lives than New York actors."

Meghan watched the exchange from the shadows, mesmerized by Gil's height, his coloration, his staccato movements. His grave but ironic responses reminded her so much of Thomas.

She empathized with Barbara's futile affection, knowing how shattered she would be if Thomas had rejected her. In Barbara she saw herself reflected at an earlier age, squandering her youth, her eagerness, on men who viewed her at best a diversion, at worst an impediment.

As the exchange between Gil and Barbara unfolded, a plan that had arisen a few days ago, as nebulous as mist, gradually firmed up in Meghan's mind, the same way spider silk is merely liquid until it strikes the air.

And like a spider's web, from most angles invisible, until dew condenses upon the strands to be refracted in the morning sunlight.

She shuddered with an intake of breath, a sound she feared was audible enough to give her presence away.

The young couple, intent upon their personal impasse, did not notice.

Recoiling from the idea, she dismissed it, chastising herself for even contemplating such a scheme. But the scheme's ingeniousness gave it an adamantine persistence that she could not shake away.

Only Gil's cruel and casual dismissal of Barbara's passion softened the blameworthiness of her idea.

She stepped into visibility and exchanged a look with Gil that Barbara could not help but notice.

Gil looked at her, puzzled, "Do I know you?"

Meghan handed several bills to Gil. "The other night, my friend didn't pay for his scotch."

"Okay," Gil replied uncertainly.

"You know, the guy that had the triple Lagavulin Distillers."

Recognition fluttered across Gil's face. "Why'd you dye your hair? It was beautiful." At Barbara's sharp look. "I mean, it was sort of nice."

"I hate to wear the same dress two days in a row," Meghan replied. "Why should I wear the same color hair every day of my life?"

"You weren't a redhead were you?" Barbara asked.

Meghan froze. "Even redheads get tired of being stereotyped."

"It wasn't red," said Gil. "Maybe more like strawberry blonde."

"Why – Why would you say that?" Meghan asked Barbara.

"My friend here is doomed to fall in love with one redhead after another."

"Barbara, don't be rude," Gil snapped.

"Actually, it was 'tawny'," said Meghan managed to utter.

"Hmmph." Barbara snatched the bills from Gil's hand and counted them. "You're thirty dollars short."

Meghan fished the last thirty dollars out of her purse.

"Would you give that to Slater?" Gil asked Barbara, and then to Meghan. "I just quit."

"You shouldn't have," said Meghan.

"See?" said Barbara.

She laid her hand on Gil's wrist and tried to coax him back into the building. Barbara's tender concern made Meghan feel more despicable.

"I'm sorry." Meghan studied him a moment, then mumbled, "I don't want to intrude."

She backed away, relieved that her plan had been thwarted before its inception.

"Forget it," Barbara snapped with a tone more command than concession.

Gil gently laid his hand on Meghan's wrist.

Barbara tried to divert Gil's attention from her sudden rival, but the young man's gaze remained affixed to Meghan.

"I don't know why I even bother," Barbara sighed irritably. "Whatever color you pick, I guarantee it will be big trouble for you, Mr. DeLeo. Night."

Muttering, Barbara went back into Restaurant X.

"So long." Gil's eyes still did not veer from Meghan.

Meghan was grimly pleased with both the young chef's immediate attraction to her and his tactlessness.

She took a deep breath and peered deeply into his eyes.

"The other night. I was in such a state."

"I know. I saw it all over your face. I wanted to reach out and hug you. Let you know that whatever it was, you'd be okay. Of course that wouldn't have been proper."

"Wish you had," said Meghan. "I sure needed it."

"Just another one of my many missed opportunities."

Barbara turned to watch the exchange from the restaurant. She tried to maintain a stoic expression, but longing far overwhelmed her determination. Her youthful features sagged like those of a mournful puppy.

"Now, where do you live?" Gil asked. "I'll see you home."

"You're so kind. But I don't really want to go home. That guy – the one from the other night – might call."

"Then where?"

"Can we just walk?" said Meghan. She tilted her head north, toward the Helmsley Building walkway.

Gil shyly followed.

They strolled up Park Avenue in near silence, and without even realizing it, soon reached West 57th.

Each simultaneously began sentences but only managed a few overlapping words until, with sheepish, sideways glances, they slid off into silence.

As they rounded the corner on West 59th at the foot of Central Park, Meghan asked, "Where did you go to college? How did you end up in New York?"

"Went to the University of Washington, the most beautiful campus in the world. Built to line up with Mt. Ranier. Most of the time it was too cloudy to see it. But on some afternoons the sky would clear. Gradually, gradually the peak would emerge from the clouds, as if it were levitating above the earth. So massive and white. Like you could walk across the campus and touch it, even though was actually sixty miles away. When the sun set, even though everything else was dark, the snowcap was brilliant red. Made it seem the whole mountain was on fire."

Gil's nostalgia evoked a twinge of anguish within Meghan, and she asked, "What did you study?"

"Theatre. Out there, I guess I was a star. Got all the leads. I loved being on stage, getting bowled over by applause. I was so deluded I thought it was the big time. Then when I got to New York I saw how penny-ante it really was. Never realized that talent only counts for one percent of success. Unfortunately, if you don't pick the right set of parents who are already well established in the business, you'll never get a foot in the door. My folks were very supportive, but my Dad owned a lumberyard. Mom stayed at home raising me."

"Actually, you sound very lucky."

"But I hadn't a clue about realizing when agents were jerking me around or taking a cut on yet another workshop. My professors could deconstruct the most complicated play ever written. They could analyze, blog their erudite criticisms in posts that no one but other people like them ever read. But I don't think any of them had ever been on a single audition in their life, especially one with 10,000 other actors, most of whom joined Equity when they were five-year-olds."

Gil pursed his lips. "So I ended up working in restaurants. Discovered I really loved food more than the performance jungle, and decided to become a revolutionary chef."

When they reached Columbus Circle, they stopped for a traffic light, halting to stare up at the skyscrapers surrounding it, the lights in the windows, confined like fragments of stars, the uppermost stories half concealed by mist. A coquettish wind conducted food wrappers and old newspapers in a leisurely waltz.

The light changed, and Gil gallantly took Meghan's arm.

"Manners! Your good parts go on and on," she exclaimed as they crossed the street.

"Where I grew up –" said Gil.

"You really know how I can tell you're from out of town?"

"My accent?"

"No. The way you walk. Sort of hung back."

She mimicked Gil's restrained walk with such accuracy that he chuckled.

"Now if you were a real New Yorker, you'd walk like this."

She took a few confident strides à la Thomas. Gil watched, amused by her intensity.

"Now you try."

He took a few tentative steps. Meghan pushed him forward. "Come on. Strut!"

He swaggered forward.

"Too much. The swagger part's right. But you can't let go of your caution at the same time."

She resumed her rendition of Thomas's gait. Gil followed, imitating.

"Once you show your confidence, just watch the girls come after you."

"Wouldn't you be jealous?"

"Me? Nah. I'm not the jealous type."

He took a few more steps with stiff determination.

"Better, better. But keep your hips straight."

Meghan placed her hands on his hips, keeping up with him until he looked back over his shoulder, deep into her eyes. They slowed. Tenderly Meghan turned his face around and urged him forward.

They continued up Columbus, past the storefronts and sidewalk cafés, tables emptied by the fretful wind.

Gil's walk grew progressively accurate. By the time they reached West 61st, he had it down perfectly. He loped up to Meghan in triumph. She clapped and kissed him on the cheek.

"And this is the best spot to watch Manhattan Henge, when the sun set perfectly between the buildings. Happens every July. I'd been waiting all year to see it for myself, but the entire week was nothing but frog stranglers."

"What?"

"It rained." He pointed down the street, "I live between Amsterdam and West End."

"Is that where you're leading me?" Meghan teased.

"Won't you come into my apartment, said the fighter to the spy?"

Meghan flinched, but quickly covered her uneasiness by joining Gil in his laugh.

She nodded.

Splatters of increasing rain accelerated their pace.

•

Gil's flipped the broken light switch in his apartment. It immediately flipped back down into the OFF position.

Meghan reached over to give him an assist.

When her fingers brushed against his, she sensed him tingle. At last the light remained on to reveal a cross between a kitchen laboratory and a studio apartment, pine floors worn smooth by generations of feet. The only furniture was a found dresser, overpainted a hideous green, a ratty chair and typing table that held a chopping block. Plants sprouted in jars. A large tank in the window, bubbling with dark green algae. Onions and cheeses hung from the ceiling. On the wall a U.N. Green Revolution poster. A blackboard with the nutritional analysis of Maine vs. Idaho potatoes. The walls gleamed with pots and implements.

The simplicity of the room itself and the complexity of all the items crammed into it did not jar, but complemented each other in an atmosphere of comfort.

"Have a thing for utensils, don't you?" Meghan managed to utter.

"I'm a gastronomic revolutionary. How do you like my hideout?" Gil said enthusiastically. "Come on. Let me give you the grand tour." He pointed to the tank. "Here's where I grow my. . . ."

"How interesting." She did not feign interest very well.

Gil hastily cut himself off. "I'll tell you about it sometime."

"Is that your bed?" said Meghan, indicating the futon on the floor beside the algae tank.

"It represents an intention. Or it did."

"Honorable, I hope."

"Too honorable, I'm afraid," said Gil.

His guileless face, his innocent blue eyes, filling with chagrin, entranced her.

"For you, that would be impossible," she reassured him. "You're very cute. You know that."

"Cute as, say, a button?" said Gil.

"Maybe. But you'd be a lot cuter if your hair were curly." She allowed him to help her out of her raincoat.

"Come into my parlor and let me show you how cute I really am."

Their gaze grew more intense. Powerless to resist, he crossed the slight gap between them. Questioningly, he touched his lips to hers.

Even though the success of her strategy would result in the sparing of Thomas's life, she wondered if she had the courage to sacrifice herself to the degree required. She was in agony, feeling soiled and sordid, as if she were betraying Thomas. Deep down (though not at the core of her soul), she knew the masquerade was necessary. Gil interpreted her turmoil as acquiescence and pressed against her. She started, as she tasted strange lips upon hers. She dared not feel any pleasure at the sensation.

"No, we can't. I mean, I can't. I shouldn't have done this."

She broke from their clinch, keeping her face averted.

"Are you afraid of . . . Would you like to see my blood donor card?"

"No. I know you're wholesome," said Meghan.

Her expression grew increasingly troubled as doubt and regret roiled within her.

"Then what?"

"Holding you. I can feel how . . . sincere . . . you are. But. . . ."

Her uncertainty granted her a roseate allure. Instead of repelling him, her withdrawal only increased her magnetism. She backed away, towards the wall

He followed, embracing her from behind. "I want so much to stop your hurting."

He gently unknotted her kerchief.

"I don't know what I was thinking. I don't know what made me come here."

"Isn't it obvious?" Gil asked.

"You're so handsome."

She ran her fingers through his hair almost clinically, examining its color and texture.

"You're just so perfect," she whispered to herself.

"Then why don't you like me?"

"You have no idea how complicated this situation is," Meghan sighed.

"What is it? Disease? Pregnancy?"

"I wish it were that simple."

"Weren't you just saying –"

"Oh, you are so cute, cuter than any button I've ever seen, but. . . ."

"Afraid I'll fall in love with you, then turn out to be like that jerk the other night?" Gil released her. "You seem like the kind of woman men fall in love with."

She laughed a small bitter laugh. "Not in the slightest. Unless they're very driven or very desperate. I'm sorry. I didn't mean that. I just. . . ." Then, after a sorrowful pause, "But I'm even more terrified of the opposite – that I might fall in love with you."

"Don't be afraid," said Gil. "I'll be gentle."

"It's wrong –"

"Why are you suddenly acting so guilty? Sex is healthy, health is holy. Why starve yourself for love?"

His face almost resembled Barbara's in its plaintiveness.

"Maybe this is the biggest mistake I ever made in my life," she protested, making no movement toward the door.

"Let me hold you, just for a few minutes."

Gil gratefully slid himself around her.

Torn between implementing her plan or abandoning it, she neither resisted nor acquiesced. He moved his hands in slow arcs from the top of her shoulders to the top of her hips.

She sighed, and clasping his wrists, unhooked herself.

"I better go."

"You've already decided you don't like me?" Gil asked desperately.

"I think you're a wonderful human being. That's why I've got to leave immediately."

Gil tried to hold her out at arm's length but she twisted in his grasp, turning towards the door.

He spun her around to face him.

"When will I see you?"

"I don't know. Soon. Later. Sometime when fate brings us together."

She felt trapped and ashamed; her tongue was failing her. She tried to keep her humiliation concealed, but her expression betrayed her.

"Why?"

His faced loomed above her. Even his scent reminded her of Thomas.

"I heard you say you didn't want any involvements. I don't want to be the one responsible for your giving up your projects. If the whole world starves to death, then it will be my fault."

"How can I get in touch with you? I barely know your name," said Gil.

"It's Meghan."

"Your last name."

"Why do you have to keep asking me all these questions?"

"What if I go back to Seattle?"

"Leave this nice apartment? You won't."

"You don't know. Maybe I will. Everyone knows what a happening place Seattle is."

"Then it would be for the best. New York is the most brutal city in the world. Full of treacherous self-centered people who have absolutely no consideration for anyone but themselves. You'll be a lot safer if you leave."

"But you'll be here."

"I'll write," said Meghan.

"Are you married?"

"No."

"Some rich man's wife?"

"No!"

"Playing some little game of teasing hicks from the sticks?"

"No," Meghan replied miserably. "No! No."

"Where do you work? Who are you, Meghan?" Gil demanded.

"I didn't think you were the type to pry. I can't stand men who want to . . . Promise me you won't pry. I would hate for you to – Just so we can at least be friends."

"Okay, I promise," he muttered without a trace of sincerity.

"I knew you were a person with a lot of heart. Maybe I'll call you."

She kissed him brusquely. He was uncertain whether or not to accept. She grabbed her raincoat and rushed through the door.

"Meghan!" he called helplessly after her.

But she was gone.

Gil retrieved her kerchief from the chair. Bringing it to his nostrils, he sorrowfully, deeply, inhaled Meghan's lingering essence. He slowly lowered the scarf.

Steeling his resolve, he took several books from the top of the hideous dresser and placed them in a cardboard box.

CHAPTER 15.

Return

When Meghan reached Queensborough Plaza, there was flooding in the tunnel, and the 7 Line was out of service. She was forced to go all the way back into Manhattan and take the R. She settled into a moody reverie along with the other disgruntled commuters.

When she first encountered Thomas on that storm-racked cruise upon the Lady Liberty, her intuition must have gone on strike. She could not believe that magical prelude foreshadowed the plight in which she found herself exactly one year later.

He had allowed himself to be led back through the sliding doors from the afterdeck back into the main cabin. She still gripped his arm, her trance-like state overwhelming the normal propriety that always restrained her. It was all she could do not to wrap her arms around him and smother him with kisses.

Her wonderstruck fervor astonished and dismayed her. Her life had taught her never to have impulses, and whatever ones did arise, she had learned to control.

She and Thomas had separated with a clandestine smile.

Like a robot, she had performed her hostess duties, aware of his every movement, tracking him as he drifted from conversational clump to conversational clump. The only time she actually dared to glance at him was when she thought no one else was looking.

As the band was playing their usual limp version of 'You Light Up My Life,' Thomas interrupted the lead singer. "If music be the food of love, doesn't this schmaltz make you want to chunder?"

The band raggedly came to a halt.

"Pays the rent," muttered the singer.

Thomas snatched the sticks out of the hands of the startled drummer and nudged him off the stool. Some partygoers watched the exchange with annoyance, most with amusement.

"Do you do 'Paint It Black'?" Thomas asked.

When the musicians hesitantly nodded, he banged recklessly on the drums. The band uneasily commenced, but after a refrain or two, cut loose with the most rousing number they had played all evening. The partygoers danced enthusiastically.

Meghan could only smile at Thomas's audacity.

She hurried into the ladies' head. Although, she felt at that moment she needed every advantage she could muster. Her hand trembled as she brushed a hint of liner underneath her eye. The pulsing beat of the Stones song made the door vibrate.

"What is happening to me?" she whispered to her reflection. "So this is how it feels. And I don't even know your name."

She shivered, pressed her bare shoulders against the mirror.

"Who are you? Where did you come from?"

She searched her handbag for her lipstick, a soft rose that echoed her pale skin. As she applied it, she whispered to her image. "You know that we're on board a ship. If you propose to me tonight, Captain Hofmeister can marry us at sea."

She flexed her lips to scrutinize her handiwork, then wrinkled her nose at her own presumption.

The song was coming to an end, accompanied by raucous applause as Meghan emerged.

A frighteningly grim man, the one Thomas had glanced at through the afterdeck doors and whom Meghan later knew to be Murdock, stepped up to the microphone.

"All right folks, time for our light show. Please cross to the starboard window." His voice was soft but firm with authority.

The partygoers did as instructed. As they drifted towards the window, from the shadows she eavesdropped on Murdock and the sudden object of her affection.

"Nimble fingers, Thomas," said Murdock.

So his name was Thomas.

She whispered "Thomas" several times to herself, savoring its resonant delicacy upon her tongue. Wondering how the man would reflect the Doubting Disciple.

"All ten of them," Thomas replied.

"Let's hope not too nimble."

Although Murdock's tone was cheerfully innocuous, something about his inflection chilled Meghan. She felt her chest constrict, her nerves grow numb. All reactions seemed at odds with the older man's overtly cheerful demeanor. Nevertheless, she could not shed the feeling of creepiness Thomas's boss evoked within her, and wondered whether she was simply imagining a predatory glint in the man's eye.

The Lady Liberty had rounded Battery Park and was heading towards Seaport Plaza.

Meghan crept up beside Thomas. He winked at her, then kept his gaze dutifully ahead.

"*Son-et-lumière*," he whispered. "*Mais sans son.* Catchy. Sounds like a composer."

Across the water, the bottom-floor lights of a 50-storey skyscraper came on. Then the lights on the floor above. The next floor. All the way to the trapezoidal top, which rippled with ever-changing spotlights.

The passengers applauded appreciatively.

"That's cool," Meghan whispered, stepping back to an impersonal distance.

The skyscraper blinked once, like a faulty sign in Times Square, and went dark.

Murdock returned to the microphone. "Dancing will now resume."

"When you save a man from drowning –" Thomas whispered to Meghan, and when she turned, "– Don't look at me."

She instantly averted her gaze and nodded to the guests with her practiced hostess smile.

"The Chinese say, that when you rescue a man from drowning –"

"I know, I know." Her teeth were clenched, like a ventriloquist's. "You get to take care of him all your life."

"Empire Diner, 10th Avenue. Friday night at eight?"

"I work Friday nights."

"Sunday?"

Meghan nodded shyly, while pretending to smile at someone in the opposite direction.

Only a year ago, but centuries apart in circumstance.

•

Back in Queens, she trudged along Roosevelt Avenue, at long last fathoming the basis of Thomas's peculiarities. He never allowed her to call him at his office. He introduced her to the peripheral people in his life – Julio, the superintendent, the Jamaican couple who ran the laundry near his apartment – but never his close friends. She wondered if he even dared have any. Nor had she ever met any of his relatives, though if they were all living in the U.K. or Kenya, it might be difficult for them to travel.

As she walked along, she realized she was slouching like a cleaning woman and straightened up.

She had always moved with the guardedness of someone who believed herself unwanted, aware of every slight and snub, especially the unconscious ones. At social gatherings, no matter how welcomed she was, she felt like an impostor. Yet without any overt effort, Thomas had almost cured her of her pervasive doubts, nourishing many possibilities she'd never realized were latent within her. Meghan had never been praised, never been adored, and even worse, had been raised side by side with a cousin who had been praised and adored, despite the fact that Moira hardly deserved the approval showered upon her. Mercifully and perhaps miraculously, Moira had never lorded it over Meghan, unlike Moira's two older sisters.

She shook her head, trying to figure out why the most dazzling relationship in her life was collapsing in such a grisly fashion. Until she reminded herself, "Why should I have expected any other outcome?"

She should have accepted the sour wisdom of her black-clad aunts. Their relish for tragedy, their unshakable faith in the triumph of suffering, their glee at the martyrdom misery offered. The highest pinnacle any woman could achieve would be death during labor giving birth to a son.

Rain drummed against the windows of the rundown apartments; cardboard boxes piled by the curb subsided into soggy masses.

As she was crossing 54th, a gypsy cab sped by, hurling gutter water onto her raincoat and fringes of her dress. She whirled angrily and shook her fist at the departing vehicle.

●

The following morning Meghan sat by the breakfast nook window, ripping out the seam of an amber sundress of Moira's. She pinched out an inch-and-a-half of fabric, then sewed the two sides together with unconscious deftness, her fingers so practiced she barely glanced at her handiwork.

Thomas glided up behind her, staring hungrily out at the rear garden. The forsythia had not been pruned in years; the grass was nearly knee high after the recent downpours. Meghan studied him, recognizing the dangerous gaze of the prisoner staring at freedom.

"I promised not to do anything rash," she said. "Now you must promise me the same."

Thomas forced himself to look away from the sunshine and inviting verdancy to break their spell.

"That's only fair," he replied sadly.

"Now, what's your shirt size?" Meghan asked with forced enthusiasm. "And your collar."

"What was that?"

"What size shirt do you wear?"

"Why do you need to know?"

"Skip the catechism. Just give me the numbers," said Meghan.

"Forty long, collar 17."

"Thank you," she said, holding up the sundress. "How do you like this?"

"Unfit for public consumption."

She drew her hand along his cheek. "Are you actually jealous?"

"No," he replied, trying to rise to her teasing mood. "I told you. I'm not the jealous type."

●

RETURN

Cries of "Hey, beautiful" were followed by a series of wolf-whistles as Meghan hurried down Roosevelt Avenue. A hard-hatted construction crew eyed her happily from scaffolding high above.

She barely registered the shrill approval and automatically assumed it was meant for someone else. Even an appreciative glance from a man in a suit, who could have been an attorney, went unnoticed. Her grim concentration completely blocked any awareness of the attention her outfit caused.

Her first stop was Patrick's, a religious-goods store large enough to be a department store. She went immediately to the jewelry counter, where she purchased a miraculous medal of the Blessed Virgin Mary.

She took neither box nor bag, but wore the jewelry out of the store. The small gold medallion with the Virgin's countenance glistened against the skin of her upper chest. She did not know any of the deeper nuances of what the medal meant, nor whether it would protect her or prevent her from going through with her plan. Still, its beatific representation comforted her.

At the Pathmark supermarket she bought a home permanent kit. Next she went to Gottesmann's, a men's clothing boutique. The clerk, a bookish young man with shoulder-length hair, showed her various shirts. None appealed to her until he brought out a green and white and black dashiki block-printed with foraging elephants.

"These are our exclusive. Just got 'em in from Ghana."

"Very suave," Meghan said. "Okay, I'll take two. Extra large."

At a newsstand she bought a copy of *Backstage* and in a stationery shop a small box of linen paper.

•

She studied the *Backstage* classifieds as she took the subway into Manhattan, eventually getting off at the East 51st Street station.

In the nearby Terence Cardinal Cook Library, she sat at a study table to hand letter a notice. Beside her, a chubby bag lady, in a frayed woolen coat that might have originally been a light blue but was now weathered to a dingy gray rhythmically turned the pages of a recent *Vogue*. She seemed aware of neither Meghan nor the magazine.

•

Guided by an ad torn from her *Backstage*, Meghan crossed Manhattan to a rehearsal studio at 55th and Eighth Avenue.

Uncertainly, she approached the reception desk, actually a walk-in closet from the which the doors had been removed and a small desk installed. Behind it sat a receptionist in her early twenties.

Every light on her phone, at least seven or eight, was blinking on Hold. The rest of the desk was buried beneath a blizzard of paper: rehearsal schedules, resumes, headshots, minutiae, memoranda. The glossily attractive, excessively dramatic woman was frantically switching back and forth between multiple phone conversations and searching through the paper for crucial scraps. Stacks of scripts filled the shelf behind her. Even the doorway was almost invisible between the notes and photographs Scotch taped to it.

Meghan flinched enviously when a young blonde actress emerged from the classroom area, sauntering with the insouciance Meghan always wished she had possessed. The actress wore baggy Oshkosh coveralls, which made her nubile figure only that much more enticing. A muscular actor in a T-shirt, a would-be James Dean, trailed her.

"Need anything? I'm popping out for a minute," said the actress.

"Nothing for me," the secretary replied, and then to Meghan, "May I help you?"

"Popping out of what?" The actor leered. "Your jeans?"

"I apologize," said the secretary to Meghan. "Everyone's a comedian around here."

Meghan forced herself to smile.

"I'm certainly not popping out of these." The actress tugged the straps. "There's room enough for two in here."

"Can I be second?" the James Dean look-alike promptly interjected.

"May I put up a notice for a commercial audition?" Meghan asked the secretary.

"Ignore him. He's jealous because I got a callback on a five-figure booking," sniffed the actress.

"Don't forget there's a decimal point in the middle of those five figures," the actor retorted as they both stepped into the elevator.

"Of course not, sweetheart." The secretary beamed at Meghan. "Our students need every bit of work they can get."

As Meghan was putting up the notice, another young actor approached and read over her shoulder. He resembled both Thomas and Gil, but his guttural Brooklyn accent rendered his words almost unintelligible.

"That's me you're looking for, to a T," said the onlooker. "But I don't think I could sound like I was from Seattle in a million years."

"It's okay," Meghan reassured him. "They'll dub you."

He seemed eager to prolong their encounter, but Meghan hastened away, mumbling, "I'll see you at the auditions."

CHAPTER 16.

A Shot of Rye

Murdock's house in Rye, on Long Island Sound, had its own dock at which an eighty-foot Chrysanthe yacht was moored.

Along the seafront, boats with reefed sails rode nervously in the darkening water.

Murdock's house managed to be simultaneously medieval and post-modern. A chunky assemblage of concrete on a slim peninsula, several bunkers banded by a clerestory were joined together by a central concrete tower. Vertical black windows striped it like gun slits. It seemed a perfect habitat for brutal secrets, for torture and debased ceremony.

The overcast sunset, with muted gray clouds and rare bursts of scarlet sun, seemed to transport the edifice to a different continent, a different time, a different reality.

The topiary-precise shrubbery surrounding the structure barely acknowledged the increasing wind, as if it were waiting for the owner's permission to tremble.

Yearwood, in casual clothes, sat in a lawn chair, trying to savor the salt tang blown in off the Sound. Murdock, in a silk robe, his appetites too complex for such simple pleasures, paced behind him.

"You know me, Yearwood, tough but tolerant. Leather hide but an old softie's heart. Which is why people try to take advantage of me."

Murdock spoke softly, with the soppy conviction of a murderer convinced that in his soul of souls, he was the world's foremost humanitarian.

The slight shudder that passed through Yearwood's body could be attributed to the sudden shift in the breeze.

"The only sacred thing left in this world is public trust. Lockhart violated the trust you and I and everyone else put in him. I'm one of the most forgiving people in the world. I'll turn a blind eye to incompetence. I'll tolerate a son-of-a-bitch. But deceive me and you sign your own death warrant. What's the latest?"

"He's slippery, all right," admitted Yearwood. "Other than the fact that he did graduate from Oxford when he said he did, the General Records Office in Clerkenwell can't find a single trace of him. I'm afraid the minute he made it to Oxford, he wanted to put his background as far behind him as he could. Ever since then, everybody loves him. Nobody knows him."

"Making the rest of us eat worms," Murdock muttered.

In this private setting, with no possibility of public scrutiny, Murdock's pleasant façade hardened into immutable and vicious resolve, far more natural than his seemingly forthright corporate one.

"Think he might be from Australia? South Africa?"

"Or New Zealand or Gibraltar or the Virgin Islands, not to mention Rhodesia, Kenya, Uganda or who knows how many other countries there were in the Commonwealth."

"Okay," sighed Yearwood. "This Clementine he took off with," said Yearwood. "Late twenties, early thirties. Redhead. Working class. I would guess New York upbringing, outer boroughs, most likely. Clementine –"

"– is a pseudonym. That much we figured out even before we began our search. Franklin's working round the clock."

"How about other women?" Yearwood asked.

"I don't know any, but according to our Oxford sources, double digits, that sneaky son-of-a-bitch." Murdock muttered. "They're as hot to grab him as you are. For entirely different reasons. Any luck with his neighbors?"

"Woman taking care of his cat. She doesn't know shit," said Yearwood, then offered hopefully, "Maybe the police will nab him. They're in our pocket."

"Nobody but nobody screws me over like this. I want his hide."

"Why don't you have someone –" Yearwood began, and then, reconsidering, said, "What about the seventeen million?"

"We'll cover it somehow."

"Don't you want to try to get it out of him?"

Murdock studied the assassin thoughtfully in the cloud-dimmed dusk. "Even if we get our hands on his Lordship, we'll never find the money. He may look like some faggot Limey, but I guarantee you that not even Ilsa would be able to get a single word out of him."

"She just upgraded her torturemobile," persisted Yearwood. "She could probably convince me to flip on my own mother."

"Didn't you watch the video clip? That money has evaporated."

"You really don't care what happens to all that cash?" Yearwood asked, obviously still not believing that Murdock would write off his loss so easily.

"Forget about the money. I have. Nail him fast. Nail him hard. Nail him in such a way that wannabe traitors a hundred years from now will think twice about crossing me, even in my grave. I want his visage on my trophy wall before the week is out. I've already ordered the plaque."

"I got to locate him first," Yearwood insisted.

"Unless they've been hiding in a cave, someone's bound to have seen them. All we've got to do is contact that someone. And make damn sure that no warning shots ricochet off any nearby stonework."

"If the super spotters can't locate him, what chance do I have?"

A vehicle was navigating the access road, pausing and starting. Yearwood tensed when he saw it, but Murdock, unworried, allowed himself an even smile. "I have a secret weapon."

"And what if your secret weapon doesn't find him?"

Swarms of insects traced the sweep of headlights as the vehicle, an SUV, reached the end of the causeway and turned onto it. Murdock rose to greet the driver as he stepped out.

"Yearwood, I would like you to meet Miles O'Leary."

O'Leary's face was unlined, too youthful a mismatch for his silvery hair. Whether he was young and his hair prematurely grey, or older and the beneficiary of cosmetic surgery, was difficult to tell in the faltering light. His safari suit appeared custom-tailored, hanging with an easy authority on his slender but muscular frame.

Yearwood ignored O'Leary's proffered hand to look dubiously from his boss to the newcomer.

Before Yearwood could speak, O'Leary spoke hastily, the way most of Murdock's underlings did in his presence. "There's no way we can do it in that timeframe, Mr. Murdock. Writing. Shooting the re-enactments. Cutting. Plus the slot you had in mind is already spoken for."

"By whom?"

Murdock smiled his television interview smile, and placed his arm across O'Leary's shoulder. The latter accepted it with trepidation, trying to keep from flinching as Murdock lectured him in his soft implacable voice. "Miles, you ought to know by now that everything is negotiable. I'll provide writers. How long are these segments? Ten minutes, fifteen minutes? We've made a copy of a very crucial videotape. Five minutes worth. We'll be glad to supply it. The last known sighting of Thomas Lockhart, guaranteed to whet the appetite of your audience and set them on the hunt. We'll offer, say, a fifty thousand dollar reward."

With a significant look at Yearwood, Murdock added, "I'll get you a piece by someone who knew Thomas Lockhart. The tiniest detail. Observations about the only known encounter with Lady Clementine."

"Isn't this awfully public?" protested Yearwood.

"I'm sure Mr. O'Leary is nothing if not discreet."

O'Leary slid from beneath Murdock's arm to face him. "I'm telling you, the slot is already filled by a horsey-set wife-on-the-lam after conspiring to kill her multi-millionaire husband. With this particular crime constellation, our weekly reach is always above 25% with at least two-and-a-half million archival online hits in the one-month follow-on.

"It's August. How much can ratings matter?" Murdock retorted. "Besides, I'll make it very worthwhile for your show."

When O'Leary remained reluctant, Murdock added with a serpentine smile, "I'll make it VERY much worth your while. Upstream," then more pointedly, "and downstream."

"I'd have to start immediately and work around the clock."

"I knew you'd come through."

Murdock handed a business card to O'Leary with a number penned on the back.

"Call my speech writer immediately and start blocking out the segment. You can do it on your way back to Manhattan. He has the clips and enough to get you rolling."

Murdock nodded peremptorily to them, then started stalking toward his fortress-like home. He paused to snap over his shoulder. "I want tangible results from both of you by early next week."

He entered and slammed the wrought-iron strapped door shut. The floodlights immediate snapped off.

"Nice meeting you," O'Leary mumbled to Yearwood as he hastily retreated back into his SUV.

He switched on the ignition and with a spurt of gravel, the vehicle shrieked back down the causeway.

Irritated at both his boss and the high-strung producer, Yearwood watched the SUV depart, and with a sigh, stalked towards his Buick.

CHAPTER 17.

Plankton Pudding

By three the following afternoon, Gil had packed almost everything in his apartment. Scattered among the cardboard boxes lay the flotsam and jetsam of belongings about which he could not decide: a Greek fisherman's cap he seldom wore; a marble statue base, the statue long since missing; mason jars filled with out-of-date spices. A few pans and utensils remained in the kitchen area, and several loaves of bread rose under cheesecloth. A bowl of onions. A frying pan of *mirepoix*, chopped carrots, onions and celery were sautéing in butter on the stove.

Gil threw a few pairs of underwear into a final box and sealed it with tape.

He surfed the web for flights to Seattle, but there weren't any cheap ones until after Labor Day. Shuddering with resignation, he looked at bus web sites.

Unfortunately, all the Chinatown buses ran north south. None of them ran west.

On the rooftop opposite, a woman emerged from the stair shaft, blinking as the sun struck her eyes. Her pink bathrobe emphasized her pale skin and the wisps of strawberry blonde hair protruding from beneath her scarf. An image of Meghan before she dyed her hair.

He clicked on the Greyhound website, growing ever more aware of the woman's presence.

With an evanescent desirability that reminded Gil of Meghan, the woman slid out of her bathrobe to reveal a modest bikini. She untied her scarf and shook her hair loose. A shaft of sunlight breaking through the clouds scattered glints among the strands, making her resemblance to Meghan even more pronounced.

He searched instead on "Meghan" and "New York."

A million hits on celebrity Meghans of varying stripes, and Gil had no other criteria upon which he could narrow down THAT Meghan in a city no doubt filled with tens of thousands of them.

Enchanted by Meghan's facsimile on the nearby rooftop, Gil stretched to peer out the window.

A bearded, muscled man in shorts and T-shirt joined the woman. They embraced with happy congeniality. Gil's jaw sagged in dismay; his body settled. When the pair separated the woman turned in Gil's direction – her face did not resemble Meghan's at all.

Gil smiled ruefully, doodling on a note pad, which despite his antipathy towards emoticons, turned into a smiley face and beside it a valentine heart.

Lips pursed, he again clicked on he Greyhound Bus site. Cringing at the thought of five days on a bus, he closed his laptop lid.

●

Gil added the already softened quinoa to a double boiler, then began chopping kale. The doorbell downstairs rang, and he pressed the buzzer.

He opened the door and peered down the hall.

Moments later, Barbara ambled up the steps, a foil-covered pie dish in her hand.

When she entered the apartment, disbelief crinkled her unwrinkled features. "What's this?" she wailed.

"My former apartment," said Gil.

"You aren't actually going to leave, are you?"

Instead of answering Gil handed her a small cleaver.

Uninstructed, Barbara took a tomato and chopped it into slices with a knife much larger than really necessary.

"It was her. Last night. Struck out, didn't you?"

"It had nothing to do with her. It's simply that I'm fed up with this city."

"For someone so dedicated to his culinary crusade he can't even look at a woman," Barbara remarked, "you were certainly hypnotized by that one."

"She had a rough time the other day. And I sense she's had a hard life. Strange – you know, I have this feeling that I've met her before. I mean, before she came into the restaurant."

"Haven't you noticed how much make-up she wore?" snapped Barbara. "I'm telling you she's a lot older than she pretends to be."

"I hadn't noticed."

"Of course you hadn't. That's the point," replied Barbara, unable to conceal her exasperation. But then, with a tinge of plaintiveness, "You planning to meet her again?"

"Don't worry. She doesn't want to see me. Wouldn't give me her phone number. Wouldn't even tell me her last name."

"Someone like me is really what you need. You have nobody. That one's obviously unavailable." Then Barbara added with some annoyance, "Though she is very beautiful."

"You noticed it too."

"She's dangerous, Gil, especially to an innocent lambkin like you. That woman might have a map of Ireland all over her face, but the capital city's not Dublin, it's Troublin'. T R O –"

"I can spell."

"She's jerking you around like some little puppy dog. How can someone that erratic possibly be good for you? And her shoes. Haven't you noticed? Pay attention to them sometime. Those are VERY expensive sandals she was wearing. You should be wondering why a woman who could afford shoes like that would be interested in you."

"There is a lot more to Meghan than her shoes."

"That's what worries me."

Barbara lay the knife down and faced him.

"Now, Gil, this is very hard for me to say. I haven't slept with anyone in over a year. But I have thought about it and thought about it, and you have to be the one. There's no alternative. Don't you feel honored?"

Gil looked at her, dumbfounded.

"Don't you feel honored?"

"I feel . . . weird."

"Aren't I attractive enough for you?"

"You've got great – you've got a marvelous . . . figure."

"You really think so?"

"I'm quoting," said Gil.

"Who?"

"Barbara, this is ridiculous."

"It's not ridiculous! It's illogical!" she snapped. "For you to refuse. You're right here, I'm right here. Or do you really find me that repulsive?"

"You're progressive. Charming. I love the way you think. All the things we have in common mean we make wonderful friends."

"Our kinship is much deeper than that, which you would notice immediately if you were paying better attention."

She extracted a note from her ragged jeans.

"Now let's go down the list. A. You don't want to sleep with me because you have a girlfriend. We both know you broke up with her when you moved to New York and that one last night doesn't count. B. You're afraid of disease, which is perfectly understandable. Well, I had myself tested for everything and I'm clean. So that's no excuse. C. Secretly you're gay. Not according to previously mentioned girlfriend. Unless you just had a relationship *blanc*."

She swallowed hard. "Gil, is there something you haven't told me?"

"I am not gay," he snapped.

"Are you sure you're not just in denial? You're awfully handsome, and I've noticed that all the really gorgeous looking dudes in New York seem to have boyfriends. Even if you see them accompanied by these drop-dead stunning chicks –"

"I'm not even going to dignify that."

"So what other reason could there be for you to turn me down?"

"The whole thing's too complicated," Gil spluttered. "All my life, even when I lucked out and got that job at DisasterCard, I dreamed about creating a whole new cuisine, first-world gustatory experience from third-world ingredients. Now I am finally doing what I've always dreamed about. I just don't have the concentration to get involved with anyone. I was beginning to think New York was the perfect place to carry out my experiments, but I was so far off the mark it's absurd."

"I'm not just anyone, I'm Barbara Anderson, your dearest friend in this cruel city. Besides, I'm not asking you to get involved with me, I'm just asking you to sleep with me."

He gently took her by the shoulders. "It's too clinical. It's too ridiculous. It's unnatural. I've told you. It's out of the question."

"The only thing unnatural about it is you suppressing your natural urges."

"Barbara, I feel like you're stalking me."

"Just because you're a man bewildered by his own sexual magnetism is no reason for you to bewilder me, too!"

Barbara smiled triumphantly, her reasoning unassailable.

"Barbara, don't you realize how special you are? Every waiter at X has a crush on you."

"They never mentioned it."

"Well, they do."

Barbara wrinkled her nose. "They're all so immature, so- so- secret young Republican at heart who want to be just like the people who dine there."

"Have you considered other guys? This town is full of men who would be a lot better for you than I would be. I'm not asking you to sign up on some dating app, but consider reasonable alternatives."

"I have. That's why it has to be you."

With a sigh, Gil gave up.

He sampled the bubbling sauce with a spoon, blowing on it to cool it down. Pleasure gradually replaced his irritation.

"I hate to say this," admitted Gil. "But adding tangerine peel to this was a stroke of genius on your part"

Barbara pushed him aside and had resumed chopping tomatoes with grumpy ferocity. and ignored his peace offering.

"You know, for a woman with such weird ideas, you certainly come up with wonderful insights."

He cooled another spoon and raised it in placation to her lips, which she resolutely kept sealed.

"It's the story of my life," she muttered. "Wasting my best recipes on relationships that go nowhere."

With a sigh, Gil turned to stir the soup.

The doorbell rang again.

"Would you mind buzzing them in?" he said.

Barbara pressed the buzzer, and waited a moment or so. When she opened the door, Meghan stood outside, surprised and ill at ease.

Barbara's face roiled with dismay at the sight of her rival She scanned Meghan up and down, beginning with her floppy sun hat, the cheap sunglasses, Moira's amber sundress. Her sandals. She paused at a brace of multicolored balloons bobbing from her wrist, then back down her legs to the expensive sandals.

"Is Gil –" said Meghan.

"He's going back to Seattle. Bye."

Barbara tried to shut the door, but Meghan had inserted her foot.

"Do you have his –"

"Who is it?" Gil called from the stove.

"Nobody important," Barbara answered, and then to Meghan under her breath. "Please!"

When Gil came up from behind Barbara, she sheepishly released the doorknob.

Meghan entered, in no way acknowledging her victory.

"Not at all interested, huh?" Barbara echoed Gil's words back to him.

"I'm sure she just came back for her scarf. Right?" offered Gil.

Meghan nodded.

Gil crossed the room to lift her scarf, lying on the pillow of the futon.

"And to bring you these." She plucked their strings and allowed them to rise.

Almost reluctantly, he exchanged the scarf for the balloons. Barbara's expression tightened as she watched the pair's lingering interaction.

"You two haven't actually been formally introduced, have you? Uh, Meghan, this is my ex-assistant – from the restaurant, Barbara. And Barbara, this is, uh, Meghan."

The two women eyed each other, each resolutely keeping their hands at their sides, then both turned to Gil, Meghan, uncertain and almost plaintive, Barbara with a penetrating determination.

Gil held up his hands, trying his cheerful best to defuse the hostilities. "Why don't we all have a seat on the futon? I have one bottle of vranac left. Barbara's quite an expert on wines from Mitteleuropa. If we get to know each other better –"

"I've got to get back to the restaurant," said Barbara, her efforts to conceal her annoyance only making her foul mood that much more apparent.

"Aren't you sticking around?" said Gil.

"Please, stay," Meghan spontaneously urged Barbara. "I don't want to drive you off."

Meghan saw so much of her former self in the younger woman – the inability to truly perceive situations, the chasing after men who were either not interested or unavailable. Even when her pursuit culminated in some sort of connection, the relationship was doomed to disappointment from the outset.

"You know I have to nursemaid the sous chef," Barbara muttered to Gil.

She took her pie dish from the counter and shoved it into the startled Meghan's hands.

"It's macadamia-pecan chiffon. So you don't come empty-handed. Don't run away this time; he's very concerned about you."

Barbara stomped out, running shoes squeaking.

She paused in the doorway to glare at Gil. "Don't let your life get too complicated."

Before he could respond, she shut the door.

•

Gil turned to Meghan and spoke with a troubled dignity. "Barbara's a wonderful person. Spontaneous. Creative. I'm really sorry you two can't be better friends. You could learn a lot from each other." Then, "What's with the balloons?"

"There were dozens of bunches tangled up in the bushes in front of one those new luxury condos down the block. It looked like a balloon orchard just before harvest time. So I harvested you a few."

Meghan set the pie on the counter and indicated the cardboard box-chocked room. "What's this?"

"My life's work?"

"You can't leave."

"You mean these balloons aren't a going away present?"

He released them and allowed them to rise to the ceiling, then yanked them back down by their ribbons. Something about their insistence on escape resonated within them both.

They looked at each other and laughed shyly.

"I got them to celebrate your audition. Maybe encourage you to stay."

"Don't you see I'm already packed?" He waved his arm around the room. "It's too late."

"Promise me you won't go until you read this."

She gave him a hand-lettered notice from her handbag.

"Open auditions? Beer commercial? Male, late twenties. Northwest U.S. accent. Dark and –" He returned the notice to Meghan "– curly hair. I'm out," said Gil.

Meghan removed the kit from her handbag. "So I'll give you a permanent."

"Meghan. Get real."

"You haven't totally given up on acting, have you?"

"Yep," said Gil, heading back to the stove to turn the heat down under the *mirepoix*.

"Gil, you can get anything you want in this city. Except a second chance. Most people don't even get the first. So grab it while you can."

"You think I can live in New York City on the residuals of one dinky beer commercial?"

"One beer commercial. And some director sees you and you get a part in a B movie. Then another. Another. Before you know it you're in Hollywood. Rome. Major supporting roles."

She framed an imaginary scene between her thumbs and forefingers.

"Can't you see the screen?"

She shivered with an intake of breath.

"And Starring Gil DeLeo," she said in announcer's voice.

For a moment, Gil was caught up. He shook himself free from her attempted spell.

"I've been on damn near one hundred auditions," Gil muttered. "I've gotten two callbacks and no roles."

"Don't you believe in coincidence?"

She gazed deeply into his eyes.

"I suppose."

"Take advantage of this one."

She took him by the wrist, her face pressed close to his.

"Why did you come back?"

"To get my scarf. To tell you about this audition."

Outside, without warning of thunder or lightning, it had started to rain. Not a great number of drops; nevertheless obese clots of water quickly coagulated into puddles.

The slight breeze that drifted in through the window above the sink, instead of being cooled by the rain, felt even warmer.

"There's still something else," Gil insisted. "Actually there are a lot of things you aren't telling me."

With a weary sigh, Meghan sat on the edge of the futon. "Okay, Gil, if you must know, I'm not heartfree."

"You're still with that guy?" Gil was crestfallen, but the bitter curl on the corners of his mouth indicated he was somehow relieved to hear his suspicions confirmed.

"Not exactly. The man that night –" She swallowed. "I don't really know him. But there was one once, who was so dear to me. He's gone, far, far away from the life he loved so much."

She struggled to stay upright on some thread-narrow path between truth and fiction.

"But I'd never met anybody like him."

"I'm so sorry." Gil perked up. "How did . . ."

Meghan remembered a somber young man from one of his dinner cruises. His girlfriend had been on a French plane that disappeared in the middle of the Atlantic on a flight from Brazil. He wore his sorrow like a suit that he'd never be able to take off.

"Do you remember that French plane that went down over the ocean?"

"Yeah," Gil nodded. "It was the pitot tubes."

"What?"

"Sorry to get technical. Comes from growing up in Boeing country."

Meghan sighed and nodded solemnly. "He was one of the Brits."

"It must be very hard on you," He gently lay his hand on her shoulder.

"Especially around the Fourth of July. And whenever there are storms."

"This month must have been hell on you."

She gave him a bittersweet smile. "Fortunately my grief comes now in wavelets instead of tsunamis."

"You haven't met anybody since?"

"Mostly creeps. Like the other night at the restaurant. That's why I went out with the guy. Reminded me so much of him. Maybe that's why you seem so familiar. You kinda remind me of him also."

Gil leaned against the stove, listening hopefully.

"When you fall in love with a person, do you think it must be all of him?" Meghan looked up into his eyes. "Or do you think it's possible to fall in love with just an aspect? Like the way he walks? Or how a curl falls on his forehead?"

"Obviously it isn't my hair or my walk or my occupation. My eyes?"

"No, with you, maybe more the back of your neck."

He hugged her, then questioningly touched his lips to hers. Meghan allowed him the briefest kindling of an instant, then broke away to cover her eyes with her hands.

"It's him, isn't it?" Gil whispered. "The one who died."

Meghan threaded her fingers through his hair. "For me, he's still alive. Or maybe I've never found anyone to replace him."

"How come you're already so . . . important to me?" Gil asked, half to himself. "I want you to want me, not somebody else, living or dead."

"I am trying to want you for yourself," said Meghan. "But I'm so confused lately. I'm getting old and haggard. See the wrinkles around my eyes? My job's okay, but everywhere I look in this city I see people struggling. One minor setback, and you're crushed. You never recover. I spent seven years in a relationship with this carpenter from County Mayo. Every Friday and Saturday night for seven years we went to this pub up in the Blond Bronx. He would sit at the bar with his mates, I would be stuck in a booth with three or four secretaries having conversations about their hairdos that would last all night. The only time he ever showed any interest in me was if some cute guy came up to the booth. Then he'd start patrolling back and forth, back and forth, like a shark, until the guy got the hint and took off. I suppose he expected me to marry him out of boredom, but –"

The doorbell rang, and they separated sheepishly for Gil to buzz the person in.

Gil went to the door to admit a woman in her mid-thirties. She wore a yellow raincoat, a wrinkled rain hat and carried a large salad bowl.

Oh, no," she said when she saw the apartment. "Say it ain't so."

When she handed the salad bowl to Gil, water spilled from her cuffs onto the floor. "Oh, dear, I'm sorry."

She and Gil simultaneously bent to assess the damage, and when they did, a torrent from her rain hat deluged Gil. She brushed it off him, embarrassed, but Gil merely laughed.

"Meghan, meet Nancy Barringer. She's a computer programmer by day and member of our revolutionary food collective by night."

Meghan studied the situation, dismayed and uncertain, wondering what unpredictable obstacle had suddenly been dropped into her path.

"Listen, I better come back later," Meghan said.

She backed away but Gil grasped her by the arm and pulled her back into Nancy's presence.

"You know the primary rule for survival in New York: 'When in danger or in doubt, run to the table and pig out'," Gil said mischievously.

"Please, Gilbo, you're not in the boondocks any more. This is New York. It's 'pigu' like 'ragout'," Nancy rejoined, then cheerfully turned to Meghan. "Isn't Gil a genius? I hope you're planning to take good care of him."

"Not much chance of that, is there? Since she's not coming out to Seattle. Anyway, Nancy, I'd like you to meet Meghan."

Meghan looked between the faces of the two friends, searching for indications of deeper affection between them and finding none.

"So are you sticking around for dinner?" Gil asked.

Meghan reluctantly nodded.

"Splendid!"

He clasped her shoulders happily as the door buzzer went off again.

Eventually a dozen people crowded Gil's small apartment. Their ethnicities varied, their ages ranged from twenties to seventies, but they chatted with a warmth and camaraderie that transcended whatever differences lay between them. Meghan brooded wanly in the corner, trying not to be noticed, trying to shut her ears to the amiable buzz of conversation.

Occasionally someone would offer an exotic treat. She would select the smallest portion and eat without tasting.

Nancy noticed her lack of appetite, and foisting some sort of croquette upon her, said with buxom *gemühtlichkeit,* "Eat, eat. For whatever is troubling you, the best therapy in the world is food."

Meghan's heart was pounding and the effort of concealing her anguish constricted her breath even further. Over and over she tried to convince herself that when Gil left New York he would not be missed beyond the warmth that his friends were demonstrating.

Around seven-thirty a UPS man came, a young African-American with a military bearing. All the male guests helped Gil carry his many boxes down. Meghan half-heartedly volunteered and was grateful when her offer was declined. The diminishing stack of boxes was excruciating, somehow reminding her of grains of sand sliding through the waist of an hourglass.

As Gil was filling in the final bits of paperwork, he admonished the UPS man, "Treat them carefully. My life's work is in those boxes."

"Trust me," the other replied. "They'll have a far safer trip than you will."

Once, when he saw Meghan by herself, Gil dragged her by the hand around the room and proudly introduced her to his friends: an elderly couple, Sam and Betty, from across the airwell; José, a gentle youth from Costa Rica; Wei-Yung, a middle-aged Chinese woman and her younger sister, Cherie.

The guests offered Meghan conversational gambits, which she deflected as graciously as she could.

As the evening progressed she realized she had never been welcomed so warmly anywhere, where everyone was so willing to accept her as the person she presented herself to be. The entire course of her life seemed so wasted as she realized that this level of friendly intimacy existed in the world but had always been withheld from her. Somehow she managed to endure the evening until she reached its aftermath of empty paper plates and crumb-filled dishes.

Betty and Sam were the last to leave. Sam carried a box with a mixer, which he tried to return to Gil. "This is really too much. If I give it back, will you stay?"

"No, but thanks for the offer."

Gil kissed Betty on the cheek. "Come visit me in Seattle."

He shut the door and suddenly the loudest sound in the apartment was the burbling of the algae tank.

He turned to Meghan. "Well?"

"Well?" Meghan echoed.

"Thank you for staying."

The wan smile returned to her face. Her stomach was in knots, trying to sustain Gil's affections without toying with them.

"Do you want to say good-bye?" he asked. "Or want to help me finish packing and then say it?"

"Why does it have to be good-bye?" Meghan asked; her voice wavered, unrestrained for the first time that evening.

"Weren't you paying attention? That was my farewell party. Even if I had to throw it myself."

"What about me?"

Gil was washing Barbara's pie dish when he turned to Meghan.

"You know, it's funny. Yesterday you might have been enough for me to stay. Then when you said you didn't want to see me, I realized my sentence here was up."

"What about your audition?" said Meghan.

"I'm sure the advertiser won't even notice if I don't show."

Suddenly he set the pie dish down to pick up a pen and piece of paper and jotted on it.

Meghan retrieved the pie dish and towel and dried it herself.

"What are you writing?"

"Number one," said Gil, "cut off the phone."

Meghan lay the pie dish and towel aside to stay his hand.

"When will you realize you're not serious?"

"I'm UPS serious."

"Everyone talks about leaving New York, but no one ever does."

"I will," said Gil.

"Please, can we go for a walk? To be together. And then if you want, I'll leave. I promise."

Her eyes softened with her plea.

"Look at this apartment, I have so much to do."

She removed his keys from their hook by the window and dangled them before him. They swung from side to side like a minuscule brass pendulum.

"I cannot be hypnotized."

She tilted her head, raising her eyes.

At last he softened and swept the balloons into his hand, twining them around his fingers. "Since there's not going to be any audition, I suppose we can set these free."

"Don't be too hasty," Meghan admonished him.

CHAPTER 18.

Tram

The moisture from the storm had blurred the silhouettes of the buildings across Central Park, softening their geometric brick edges. The night buzz of crickets harmonized with the sound of distant traffic as Gil and Meghan threaded their way through the joggers and skaters, skateboarders and people on scooters who seemed impervious to insects or humidity.

Meghan slumped deeper into her moody silence; despair that Gil was actually going and her stratagem would be thwarted struggling with the massive relief she would feel for the identical reason.

She reached out her fingers, but the instant they touched Gil's, he brusquely retracted his hand.

"What is this? Last night you didn't want me. Wouldn't even let me touch you. Now you're suddenly –"

"I must have been crazy. Or maybe my horoscope was out of whack," Meghan replied. "Maybe it's the night air. Something about you. Something about me. Maybe because I realized how special you were. My brain is making those pleasure chemicals. For some reason, I just can't keep my hands away."

"Yes, you can."

"Why are you acting so cold? I apologize for last night."

She again reached for his hand. Though he allowed her to retain it, his fingers did not soften or flex.

"It has to be the right person, the right place. Otherwise, I'm petrified. Last night, it wasn't right, maybe your apartment was the right place, but not the right time. I just have this acute sense of timing."

The boughs whipped back and forth overhead, goaded by the winds of an upcoming storm. The balloons tugged at their ribbon tethers.

"We need to talk about a whole lot of things, Meghan," said Gil. "And quickly."

"Don't we talk enough already? Can't we enjoy being with each other? Silently."

"We've got a problem. I need to know who you are –"

"Don't tell me. Here comes Bare-Our-Souls Unhappy Hour," Meghan complained. "Aren't we having fun being together? You don't think I'll make too many demands on you, do you?"

"It's nothing to do with demands," said Gil.

"You can pry and pry all you like and then you'll find you have pried me right out of your life. Is that what you want?"

"I'm not prying. But I do have a real problem with a woman who appears without warning. Acts like she's madly in love with me. Then suddenly doesn't want to touch me at all. She disappears. Reappears. And once again she's all over me."

"One day, very soon," said Meghan. "I promise to tell you everything."

"I've spent all day thinking about us. It's better for me to leave than to try and drag the truth out of you. Or keep waiting for a day that may never come."

"That sounds like an ultimatum to me. I despise ultimatums."

"That's not my problem."

Meghan nuzzled up to him. "You've found someone else, right? I'm not attractive enough for you. Barbara persuaded you of what a monster I am."

She stifled a sniffle.

"That won't work on me, Meghan."

"I can't help it. When I met you, you seemed unsure, indecisive, fearful. All I wanted to do was to give you confidence, Gil. You can buy damn near anything in this city but you can't buy confidence. Now you're taking that confidence and running away with it. Abandoning the person who gave it to you."

"I'm not abandoning you, I just want to know who you really are."

"Just another woman like so many," Meghan answered softly. "Adrift in the big city, struggling like everyone else."

"And I'm just another man. But why do you get such a kick out of being so mysterious? Are you a spy?"

"No, silly."

"Terminally ill? What are you hiding?"

"I'm not hiding anything," she answered, wondering if she spoke too quickly.

"Or was I right about you the first time? Stepping out on your husband."

"I'm not married," said Meghan. "Why are you concerned about what's going on when I'm not with you? When you're with me, would you be with me?"

"What does that have to do with whether you're married or not?" Gil snapped. "Then who is your other lover? A captain of industry? A Wall Street broker."

Meghan froze, unable to speak.

He took her by the wrist. "Like your sandals. I don't know the first thing about women's shoes, but I have a feeling they cost a lot."

She looked down at them – they were Italian, with small turquoise medallions embedded in a band across the strap. And indeed they been given to her by Thomas.

"Women don't wear stuff like that unless they are either working in the executive suite or sponsored by someone who is."

"Quit being so cruel," said Meghan, jerking her wrist back. Her feminine radar was unable to shake the suspicion that Barbara had been goading him.

"Quit being so damned evasive," said Gil. "Why are you so nervous? Someone like you, intriguing, magnetic, probably a lot of experience. What do you have to be nervous about?"

"I'm none of those things. I'm just an ordinary person. A little private. I go to work. I live by myself in a two-by-nothing apartment," said Meghan.

"Then let's go there. Right now."

"It's really messy right now." She hesitated, "I don't want anybody to see it."

"Why not? It can't be any messier than my place, which you've already seen."

"I promise. You can come over some afternoon."

"When?" Gil demanded.

"Soon, very soon," Meghan answered softly.

•

They reached the Great Lawn, now surrounded by a fence. With the ground resodded, the edges of the squares of turf were still visible. Like living creatures, the balloons struggled in the rising breeze.

"When I was living out in Queens, I used to dream about floating away again, just like these balloons. Settling down, very gently, in Manhattan."

She plucked the pink ribbons like strings of a harp.

"Now, sometimes, I dream about floating away, but I don't know where. Certainly not back to Queens."

Gil unwrapped the ribbons from his wrist and handed them to her, "Here. Let them go. Maybe they'll take your wishes to wherever they land. Somehow everything you wish will be granted."

With a sad smile, she released the balloons. They lifted into the cloud-obscured sky and almost immediately soared out of sight.

•

Somehow Meghan and Gil ended up at the base of the Roosevelt Island tram. He turned to her with his endearing enthusiasm and said, "Why don't we go for a ride? The whole time I've been in New York I've never once ridden in it. It's like the Statue of Liberty or the Empire State Building. I've only been to them once, and that was when my parents came into town."

The second time he mentioned his parents. The reference added an extra, unwanted dimension to him, when she was trying to keep his dimensions as flat as possible. Would his mother and father miss him? Or had the familial cord already been severed?

She dared not reflect on it as she allowed herself to be led into the gondola, where she and Gil were the only passengers.

"I sure hope this thing doesn't fall in," said Gil. "In that river you'd dissolve before you'd drown."

Meghan's attention remained focused on the black sliver of the Consolidated Resources skyscraper, barely visible far down the East River.

"What are you looking at?" Gil asked.

"The Consolidated Resources building."

"What's that?" Gil asked.

"A company," Meghan replied softly.

"Yeah? What do they do?"

"They keep track of things," said Meghan. "In the ground mostly."

Only then did she realize the other implication of Thomas's description of his former employer. The sight of the grim building filled her with a resolve that had been wavering ever since she had reached Gil's apartment.

She took a deep breath and sidled closer to him, but he backed away.

"Why do you keep withdrawing?" she asked.

"Because every alarm I have is going off."

He took her wrist.

"Feel your pulse. You're so nervous. I'm afraid you'll explode like an overwound clock. What are you up to, Meghan? Where do you work? What else are you hiding?"

She took his hand in hers. "I'm sorry, Gil. I'm not up to anything! I've been taken advantage of every way a woman can. By charming men who betray me in a heartbeat. And never regret it. By parents and stepfathers and bosses and whatever form men come in. Everything in my life begins so promising and ends in catastrophe. Of course I'm nervous."

"I'm sorry, Meghan. I don't mean to be so hard," said Gil. "But you have to understand my history. too. I've always been adrift when it came to women, and doomed to boot. I mean, aside from Barbara, most of –"

"She seems to be a really nice girl," Meghan observed morosely. "A trace of bitch in her perhaps, but . . . ."

"– the women I meet are unavailable. Women that are sort of married. Or maybe married. Or about to be married. Or just plain married."

"Cute guy like you? I don't believe it."

"No, really. I never picked up a girl in my life. Then all of a sudden, here's this wonderful woman interested in me. I get you home, and you act like every other woman I've met who was out for a fling. Hear the standard lines from someone thinking of checking out of a bad marriage or maybe a good one, but wanting to test the waters first, before she does anything drastic."

"Try to sympathize," said Meghan. "I hate telling people what my life has been like. It makes me sound like I'm begging for sympathy. But I'll tell you one thing. I'd rather you misunderstand me than feel sorry for me."

He sighed and turned his attention to the lowering clouds, threading themselves among the concrete pinnacles on the Manhattan shore. She sensed Gil drifting away, not into anger but into resignation, from which it would be impossible to retrieve him.

Just beyond the tip of Roosevelt Island, past the ruins of the abandoned TB hospital, she saw the Lady Liberty heading upstream.

Her plan on the brink of collapse, she plunged. "All right, Gil. I'm a hostess for a dinner cruise line. That's one of my ships, Lady Liberty, sailing towards us now. By now they've probably pushed the tables back, and the band's playing one of their infinite renditions of 'You Light up My Life'."

"What's so mysterious about that?"

"Nothing, I suppose. It's just . . . by this point I thought I'd be running the cruise line. Not just be a glorified waitress."

"There's nothing wrong with being a waitress. You should be proud of yourself."

"I'm not."

"It sounds very exciting," Gil continued.

"Usually the East River is about as exciting as Iowa." She laughed morosely. "From what I've been told Iowa is like."

"Why aren't you at work tonight?"

"I've . . . I've taken a few weeks off for –"

The tram came to a grinding halt. The gondola swayed from side to side. Gil pounded the glass and kicked the hull. "I hate this city!" he snapped. "This is why I'm leaving. If it isn't way overcrowded, it's falling apart. Or if it's the subways, it's both. And to add insult to injury, everything costs out the wazoo. What can possibly be so complicated about a cable car, for heaven's sake? Or subway trains. Why is it outrageous to want the things in your life to simply be maintained and to function the way they were designed?"

He turned aside. Meghan gently took his hand. He snapped it away. "Cut it out."

She tried to turn him around, but he remained obstinately facing away.

"What else do you want from me?"

Meghan felt her minutely acquired advantages dissipating in the stalled gondola.

"A favor," he replied.

"Of course. Whatever you need."

"When – if – we manage to get back to land, come with me to the Port Authority Bus Terminal. Say good-bye. Then take my keys over to Barbara."

She had been expecting anything but this. "No, Gil. I can't let –"

"Dammit, Meghan, my mind's made up," said Gil.

Feeling Murdock's net tightening around her and her one chance of evading it vanishing, she turned away. A tremor of fear made her shoulders quiver. Gil continued to glower out the window.

Then, with grave, misty eyes, she took his hand and brought it to her lips. He started to retract it but reconsidered and allowed her to retain it long enough to brush a kiss against it. He still did not respond. She raised herself to press her cheek against his neck.

"Won't you ever change your mind? This is an opportunity," she whispered.

"Humph," was all he muttered.

Meghan rotated her face to his and kissed him. Tentatively at first, then with a grimly forced passion that only aggravated her sense of betrayal, Meghan forced herself upon him.

At first her intensity startled Gil, then gradually enthralled him. His resistance ebbed. "Meghan?"

She embraced him tightly, caressing him, until at last his arms, instead of forcing her away, hungrily sought her. He rubbed his cheek against her pale neck. He nuzzled her so fiercely the strap of her sundress trapped his ear. He wriggled his head to free it. They both laughed, parting for a moment to smile at each other.

Supported by the gondola rail, against the glittering backdrop of Manhattan, they resumed her embrace. Meghan sensed Gil softening; felt all of his suspicions subside as the gondola jerked back into motion.

Annoyed at the lapse of his own defenses, he stiffened, and abruptly relinquished her.

Neither spoke until the gondola settled into its landing pad on Roosevelt Island.

Two uniformed workmen slid open the door. "Sorry about the delay. You folks okay?" asked the older one, a dour Hispanic.

"I suppose," Meghan smiled sadly as she stepped out onto the platform.

●

They walked along West 61st, at odds in the aftermath of embarrassment and desire. Meghan tried to retain her soft, vulnerable expression against her mounting doubts and the first twinges of self-loathing.

A few drops of rain pelted against them as they passed a construction site. Grey concrete pillars protruded like fossil ribs from the gaping excavation.

"Oh, hell," she muttered.

"All right. Come on, let's get out of the rain," said Gil. For the first time he voluntarily took her hand.

They dashed through the craggy skyscrapers as the downpour commenced, then darted into a pocket park lined with benches. Redundantly, a fountain in the center spouted a steady column of water. Meghan collapsed on the brick bench surrounding the fountain, Gil remaining some distance away.

"Let's sit, I'm out of breath," Meghan managed to say between pants.

"Not before we go someplace dry."

"Why are you standing so far away?" she asked him. "If you're determined to leave the city, and we aren't going to see each other any more, can't we at least make the last minutes memorable?"

"Whatever happens to me, Meghan, I'll always remember the moments I spent with you."

"You think I'm ugly now," said Meghan, "because my hair is soaking wet."

Gil looked down at her rain-smeared, vulnerable face, studying her slightly smeared make-up and dismissing his observation. "No, Meghan, you're as desirable as you ever were. Even more so."

He looked irritably away, allowing the raindrops to sluice through his fingers.

Mischievously, Meghan flicked a few fingers of water at him. He brushed his neck, then turned to look at her, but she was still sitting sullenly. When he turned away again, she repeated her trick.

The third time, Gil was waiting. He pounced to grab her arm. "What are you doing?"

"If you're going to be a wet blanket, a few more drops won't make a bit of difference."

He irritably released her arm, and, adding a little momentum of her own, she flung her arms backwards and toppled into the shallow water of the fountain. "Please, aren't you gentleman enough to save a damsel from drowning?"

Gil at last stretched his hand out. Meghan stood on the ledge, and as he was about to help her down, she instead shoved him into the pool. With a cry of triumph, she struggled atop him, and pressed his shoulders down.

"Okay, Meghan. Enough!"

"I'm not letting you up until I wash that poisonous mood out of your system."

He strove to rise, but she again held him down. They continued to wrestle until Gil clambered astride Meghan.

"Okay, you win stop, stop!" she pouted. "Oh, you make me so mad."

Gil stopped but did not release her. She thrashed her head from side to side, frothing the water into a corona of foam around her head. She halted, exhausted, and looked up him, her eyelids drooping, her lips drifting apart, her features magnified by drops of water. He extended his hands and gently lifted her to her feet. Their arms slowly linked and drew each other together.

Her hands slid up and down his back in long slow strokes, her nails tracing his muscles as he compressed his body against hers. Her head recoiled, her lips sought his until they linked irrevocably. He kissed her with a passion that astonished her. She broke away in surprise. "Meghan, what's wrong?"

"I – I didn't expect you to be so – You're so passionate. I need to repicture what I imagined you'd be like."

Thankfully, his reckless desire did help somewhat to lessen her increasing sense of guilt and foreboding.

CHAPTER 19.

Permanent

Once they had returned to Gil's apartment, she wasted no time setting up the home permanent kit on the counter: cotton balls, two plastic bottles, a saucer of waving lotion. She put on one of Gil's aprons, tying it primly behind her.

He watched her bustle about, dubious and somewhat intimidated. "What am I suppose to do?"

"Take off your shirt."

He did as instructed, then sat in the chair Meghan indicated. She draped a towel across his shoulders, wondering how she would be able to work within the range of Gil's charged arousal. She wound the pink and blue curlers into his hair with a distracted expertise.

"Close your eyes," she said, and began constructing a barrier of cotton balls around his neck.

She was dependent on the momentum of the night; if she hesitated for an instant, qualms would cut her down where she stood. She dared not consider the intermediate effects of her plan, only that if she carried it out, Thomas would live. His image burned in her brain like an icon, his safety guiding her like a beacon. Confession fluttered on the surface of her tongue. She prayed that impending remorse would not release it into the charged atmosphere.

She rapidly combed the waving lotion through Gil's hair.

"This is without a doubt the most ridiculous humiliation I've ever undergone," he said

"Break my heart."

"You promise these permanents are only temporary."

"Relax. It will only last a few weeks," said Meghan. She wrapped a section into curl paper, and twined it around a curler. She spun it tight.

"Ow," Gil cried out.

"I'm sorry. You've been a perfect lamb." Meghan put a plastic cap over the curlers and shaped it snugly with a clip.

"I can stand it. For you." He grimaced, suffering.

"Now that stays on fifteen minutes. Do you have a timer?"

"On its way to Seattle," Gil replied. She glanced at her watch, then caught a trickle of lotion on Gil's brow with a cotton ball. "What happens if this goop gets in your eyes?"

"Now, now. I won't let it." She started clearing up after the first stage.

"You're so good at this."

"I ought to be. I'm a pro," said Meghan, reaching past Gil's head to fill a pitcher. He exhaled pleasurably as her lovely bosom slid by his face.

"I just happened to see that ad in my neighborhood, and I thought, 'What a shame. You'd be perfect for the part except for your hair.'"

"Where is your neighborhood?"

"I can't get over it. Coincidence again. I apologize for the chemical smell."

"I feel my chromosomes crumbling."

"You think I enjoy ruining my nails through this slop?"

"More than I enjoy having it sloshed on my scalp?"

"I confess," said Meghan. "This is just an excuse for me to get my hands in that fabulous hair of yours."

"If I'd known, I'd have let you grab till I went bald."

"Listen, you want the part? Or you want to be just another unemployed actor?"

"I'm an unemployed chef."

"Yes or no?"

"I want the part," he conceded.

"Then don't piss off the makeup department."

When she finished the first phase, Gil asked, "Aren't you starving? You ate like a bird during my farewell dinner."

"I'm very sorry Gil, I know most health food tastes like the bottom of a birdcage and the stuff tonight was all very tasty, but I just wasn't hungry. I mean, do you actually eat that stuff?"

She indicated the tank filled with green sludge.

"Algae's great stuff. About as low on the food chain as you can go. You can grow it in labs, on rooftops, even on your windowsill."

"Looks like the scum that grows on the Central Park Lake every summer."

"Well, they are related," Gil admitted. "Do you spend a lot of time in there?"

"Not any more. For a while I was a trainee park ranger. Then the city had all these cutbacks. I got laid off."

"You strike me as someone who needs nature in her life."

"You see that?" she answered in surprise.

"I don't know why, I just have that feeling."

"It's true," she admitted. "I always loved nature, even when I was a kid. Kept lightning bugs and a praying mantis cocoon in a jar until it hatched, and I ended up with thousands of tiny praying mantises in my bedroom. So I was perfect for Central Park, especially in the winter. There was a red-tailed hawk that lived near 72nd. He always seemed to be perched in his tree whenever I came to work. We would greet each other. But how did you know that about me? You aren't psychic, are you?"

"No," he smiled, "or I would have a much better reading on you than I do. You just seem like an interesting person who's been misunderstood all her life."

She was touched that someone, essentially a stranger, recognized a secret and prized quality about herself, an aspect that no one else, no matter how much time they had spent with her, even Thomas, had seemed to notice. Even more, she was secretly thrilled to be called "interesting."

"Why don't you come with me to my garden some day? I need to say good-bye to it."

"I can't believe you actually eat that stuff," she said, avoiding his invitation.

"It's totally scrumptious when a gourmet chef prepares it. Here."

He took a hideously colored cracker, tiger-striped green and orange, the last one, from a plate on the counter. He thrust it towards her mouth, but she warded him off, laughing nervously. So he started tickling her.

"No, no!" she protested.

When her mouth opened, he popped the biscuit into it and squeezed her jaw closed. Her recoil of disgust balanced for a moment on a fulcrum of consideration, then tilted to the side of pleasure. "Hmmm."

She swallowed and took the remainder of the biscuit from him. With gusto she finished it off. For the first time that evening, she realized how ravenous she actually was. The nibbles earlier that evening had been nothing more than that.

"You are a genius! How did you get that ghastly stuff to taste like this?"

"Professional secret."

"Tell me." It was her turn to tickle him. "Tell me."

"Why do you have the right to be nothing but secrets, and I'm not allowed to have a single one?" Gil demanded.

"Women's prerogative."

"I'll tell you my secret if you tell me yours."

"Deal."

"The secret ingredients were papaya and –"

He rummaged among the few jars remaining on the counter, then turned back to her. "You have a lovely face, you know. I'm not very good with faces. I have to think of them in terms of smells. That's the only way I remember them."

"Mine?" said Meghan.

"Orange and cinnamon, maybe with a dash of cloves. Something exotic yet still familiar. A mixture that reminds you of the holidays, full of anticipation but at the same time reassuring."

"And yourself?"

"Never thought about it."

He reflected on her question, his lips fluctuating as he considered and discarded various options.

"Something earthy, black truffles perhaps," she suggested.

"How do you know about truffles?"

She froze, hoping that he could not read her memories about eating around the alphabet, especially the Quilted Giraffe eatalike, where Thomas had treated her to duck and truffles.

Fortunately, at that moment, Gil found what he was searching for and did not pursue the question. He opened up a small tube and removed a vanilla bean. He drew it underneath Meghan's nostrils.

"Voilà, the other secret ingredient. A bouquet that stirs your entire body, instead of merely your nostrils like the artificial stuff does. It's actually from a boutique orchid grower in Key West. I've always dreamed of going there."

Meghan looked at him in astonishment. "I cannot believe this, Gil. One coincidence right after another. I've always wanted to go there myself. But I've never been able – that's not true – I've never had an excuse to go. Why don't we just take off? Together."

"You mean it?"

"Of course."

"No way I could swing it. Especially since I quit my job," Gil answered with a trace of disappointment.

"Don't worry about money," Meghan encouraged him. "I get deals."

"How?"

"Anyway, through my job we're hooked up with a lot of different travel agencies. You could go for free."

"Really?" said Gil.

"Even if you get the part in the commercial, they wouldn't start immediately. We'd be back in plenty of time for you to do it."

"Let's leave tomorrow?"

His eagerness and disbelief at his sudden good fortune were palpable.

"Tomorrow's your audition. Wednesday?"

"Yeah! That would give me time to clean up the last bitsies and bobsies."

"I'll meet you. Wednesday morning at 8:30. Sinbad Travel, Madison and 84th. We'll pick up the tickets, then we fly!"

"This is really wonderful," Gil exclaimed. He drew the vanilla pod across her lips and cheek.

"Nothing like this ever happened to me."

Meghan glanced at her watch. "Come on, let me neutralize you."

She led him back to the sink and took the Greek fisherman's cap from the counter.

"But when you go out tomorrow, be sure to wear this and tuck your hair up under it."

"Won't that defeat the whole purpose?" Gil asked.

"The cap will protect it."

A towel on his shoulders, Gil leaned back into the sink as Meghan poured pitchers of water over his head.

His senses shrouded by the stream, Meghan crept across the room and removed his wallet from the nightstand by the futon. She slid it into her handbag.

She indicated the faucet and turned it on.

"Now shake your head to get the water out."

Gil obediently stuck his head under the faucet, and as he did Meghan crossed to her handbag and slipped the wallet into it.

When Gil finished wriggling his head under the faucet, she rubbed a few strands of his hair between her fingers.

"Time to take these out."

"So where do you live?" asked Gil, his head jerking as Meghan removed the curlers.

Meghan did not answer. "Go ahead, Meghan. You can tell me. Anything. You still owe me your secret."

Meghan took a deep breath. "As a matter of fact, I still stay most of the time in his apartment."

"You can't go on loving a dead man," said Gil. "You need to go for grief therapy or something."

"You're right. I keep telling myself." She looked at him hopefully. "Could I take you there some time? Maybe you'd exorcise his ghost."

"If you think it will help."

Meghan looked around for a wall mirror, and finding none, led him by the hand to the bathroom.

"Have a look."

Gil inspected his hairdo, disconcerted. He touched it dubiously.

"How do you like it, gorgeous?" said Meghan.

"I look like a damned pedigreed French poodle."

"In that case, it's high time we put you out to stud."

"Why not? I've always had a weakness for beautiful bitches."

"I hate that word," Meghan said sharply. "Maybe I do have a potty mouth on occasion and only when appropriate, but I hate the B word a lot more than I hate the C word."

"It's not a word I generally use," he conceded, embarrassment brightening his features. "It's just – I guess, you do look like you have good breeding lines."

"I'm just regular mutt American," said Meghan. "Now, look at yourself. Like for the first time. Forget what you looked like before."

Gil peered into the mirror, his lips and eyes crinkling, then simplifying as his reaction grew increasingly pleased. Suddenly, he crowed like a rooster.

"Not bad for a poodle. Do you like me now?"

He strutted out of the bathroom and proudly did his Thomas walk for her, threading his way through the remaining boxes.

Meghan clutched the wall for support. Her jaw dipped; her lips formed the name "Thomas."

Gil grandly scooped her up. She pressed her hands against his chest and looked away.

"No, Gil. I can't." She spoke with a sincerity wrenched from the depths of her soul.

"Meghan, you're the most wonderful creature ever to enter my life. I can't tell you how much I need you."

"I'm not wonderful," she whispered miserably. Conscience captured her tongue. "You don't know me. You don't want to have anything to do with a woman like me. You have no idea how monstrous I truly am."

"I want to have everything to do with you. I want to be as close to you as two human beings can possibly be."

"I'm feeling queasy," Meghan muttered. "I need to lie down."

"You can lie down here."

"I can't."

She opened the door to the hallway with its peeling paint and went down a few steps. "I'll see you Wednesday morning."

"Yeah. Okay," he said uncertainly.

She took a few more steps down, "I hope your audition goes well."

A few more steps, "And practice your walk. You'll intimidate the hell out of them when you go back to Seattle."

CHAPTER 20.

Yorkshire Pudding

When Meghan returned to Moira's house, the kitchen was a disaster, reeking with a thin pall of smoke. The radio was tuned to a news channel with a bulletin about a hurricane about to make landfall on Cuba.

Thomas lay with his head on the table, asleep. He wore an apron and a chef's toque he'd fashioned from a white paper bag.

In low spirits, wistful, she studied him from the doorway.

"How beautiful you are," she whispered. She removed the cap, examined it gingerly, then crumpled it and threw it on the counter.

"Hmmm, what a lovely dream." Thomas gradually, gratefully came awake. "I thought you'd never get here," he said.

He opened his arms in welcome.

She dropped her handbag and sat on his lap. "Poor creature. You look different. Sort of older."

"I've never been under house arrest before."

Meghan sniffed the smoke-tinged air. "What's burning?"

"Don't be alarmed. I put the fire out. But it's going to take more than a day to turn me into a chef."

"All you've got to do is say things like 'plankton pudding.' And walk like you're from out West."

"What?" Thomas exclaimed.

"It's part of my plan. All you have to do is talk like a chef. TSA's not going to ask you to make duck *à l'Orange*. Don't worry about it."

She tousled his hair, measuring against some standard of her own.

"Enough. I feel like I've been run over by a steam roller."

"How about a stiff gin and tonic," suggested Thomas as he rose.

"Sure, I'd sell my grandmother for a drink."

As Thomas mixed the drinks from the odd bits from the liquor cabinet, she examined the smoldering remains of Thomas's culinary efforts in the garbage pail – several scorched clumps and two charred pots. "What were they?"

"Yorkshire puddings."

"Well, you can't be a whiz at everything," Meghan consoled him.

"Right. Rome was not burned in a day. Like Nero, I'm more the musical sort."

He handed her a drink, and raised his glass to her.

"To the day we finally escape."

"As soon as we get out of this, I'll never let you near a kitchen again," she vowed.

"And how did it go tonight?"

"I think it went well," she turned away, refusing to meet his gaze.

"What happened to your make-up?"

"I got caught in the rain on the way home."

"From where?"

"I'm exhausted. Please, don't ask me any questions."

She struggled to keep her expression neutral. Unconsciously, she toyed with her miracle medal praying that his weariness, his preoccupation would render her soul so opaque he would be unable to discern her near infidelity.

Thomas was so adept at concealing his feelings that she could not tell that he was anything but casual. She remained silent, until the pressure of his question grew too great.

"You'll see tomorrow at three p.m. I think I we have an opening to help us escape." She lay her hand on Thomas's shoulder. "Stop worrying. I obeyed all of your instructions. Did nothing to jeopardize us. Not one slip-up that could possibly trigger Murdock's alarms."

•

When they returned to the bedroom, Thomas felt slyly amorous. Meghan was too worn out and filled with melancholy to reciprocate. He accepted her disinterest with a quiet thoughtfulness. She fell asleep immediately, but then woke an hour later.

He still lay awake studying the flicker of the moonlight through the curtains.

"Thomas?" She stared anxiously into his face; a tear rolled from her eye.

He traced its melancholy path with his forefinger.

"Today I made a list of the five people in the world who might have been able to help us. You know something? Two of them are dead. The other three are almost certainly under surveillance. That is, if Murdock hasn't terminated them out of spite, and we just haven't found out about it yet."

She squeezed his hand sympathetically. He'd always been so self-assured. Uncertain how to respond, she realized he suffered loss and grief with the same intensity that she herself did.

Enshrouded in the tender and unjudgmental moonlight, they settled to their separate worlds of speculation and apprehension.

Thomas had foreseen the worst outcome of his life and was close to acceptance; Meghan's dread, the remorse and apprehension kindling within her, stoked her guilt into insomnia. She lay adrift at the edge of appalling dreams, jerking herself awake when the torment grew too much. She clung to Thomas's sleeping body until his rhythmic breathing soothed her back into the abyss and the cycle of dozing and nightmares resumed.

•

It was not until the sparrows started chirping on the phone wires, and the sky was turning a smoky blue that exhaustion granted her the oblivion she needed.

Thomas was not beside her when she awoke, but she knew better than to be alarmed. She put on one of Moira's robes and retrieved her handbag.

Then she went out into the living room where Thomas, dressed in Steve's uniform, was draped over the pinball machine. The lightbox blinked furiously, illuminating a buxom redhead in a bikini struggling in the paws of a hairy alien. Pings and bells rang so rapidly they formed a continuous tone.

"Three hundred thousand! I knew I should never have forsaken pinball wizardry in favor of cookery."

"Good morning . . . Steve," she greeted him, giving him an affectionate tickle.

He wiggled away, never losing the rhythm of his game. She took a dashiki from her handbag and handed it to Thomas. He at last released the flippers in favor of the garment, allowing the silver ball to bounce harmlessly into the slot. He held out the brightly colored fabric and exclaimed appreciatively.

"Magnificent." He slipped it on over his uniform. "Must have cost a fortune."

"It will definitely be worth it," Meghan replied.

Thomas went into the kitchen and fetched his briefcase. "I've got about eighty thousand left. Which reminds me." He held up the small manila envelope he'd concealed in his snare drum.

"If anything happens to me . . ."

She fell across him, shaking her head, refusing to acknowledge each and every untoward outcome. Her handbag was crushed between them.

He twisted out of her grasp and held up the envelope to display its tiny meticulous writing.

1. Go to Daumier Frères @ Park and 48th.
2. Take the escalator to mezzanine.
3. Take elevator in second tower to Private Banking Department on 9th floor.
4. Ask to speak to my Relationship Manager, Sebastiano Briones – he's expecting a red-haired woman he's never met.

Meghan looked up. "I never was a redhead, especially now."

"So? Take off your wig in the elevator."

She resumed reading.

5. Give the instructions on the legal paper to him. He will give you instructions on how to collect the money.

"He'll transfer the money into an untraceable account. After that, my dear, you'll be a millionaires plus."

"All the money in the world wouldn't be worth it if something happened to you."

Meghan dropped her bag, and the other dashiki spilled out.

She took the envelope. "Do I have to keep reminding you. Forget dead.

We're going to survive this mess to have our time in the sun. Together!"

He smiled sadly, then lifted the other dashiki from the floor. "What's this?"

"Ah. My plan," she said with a hopeful smile. "What time is it?"

"Quarter to ten."

She carefully parted the curtain and peered outside. "In about three hours you'll see."

"But if your plan doesn't succeed, we'll simply have to make a run for it. Fingers crossed that the hurricane heads our way and we can slip through the net during the chaos."

"I need to go shopping," she said. "I'll be right back."

"And be right careful."

●

Fortunately, Moira was at least two sizes larger than Meghan, and the print dress she chose should be floppy enough to provide some measure of disguise, as would yet another sunhat, this one plain white with a blue ribbon that trailed after her like the tails of a butterfly.

In the supermarket, it seemed to her that more people than usual were staring at her. Not just men, but women also. She examined her clothing to insure that were no rips or no unusual stains, but everything appeared to be in order.

Several times it seemed people whom she could not possibly know were on the verge of recognizing her. Then with shakes of their heads, they would look away. She attributed the incidents to her imagination, the edginess caused by her plan as it headed toward fruition.

She bought another box of Lady Grey tea from the health food store, and then went to Key Food, where she purchased all the ingredients for eggplant parmesan.

Feeling very stared at and vulnerable, she paid quickly and fled the grocery.

●

New York harbor sprawled outside the windows of the Consolidated Resources cafeteria. Clouds scudded in from the southeast in glorious mounting billows; Governor's Island was surrounded by whitecaps that resembled tufts of cotton.

Ilsa sat by herself in the corner, her lunch finished, her tray pushed aside. The chattering secretaries and file clerks at the nearby tables registered neither her presence nor her isolation. She was knitting with deft strokes, a ball of dark green yarn in her lap, inured to the grand tableau visible through the windows.

Yearwood slid into a chair beside her, sitting back to front. She peered at him through her thick glasses. The needles did not lose a single beat of her rhythmic click-click.

"Don't you think Mr. Murdock went a bit overboard putting his Lordship on national television?" she murmured. "We were bound to have tracked him down on our own."

"I don't know about national television, but offering a reward was ridiculous," grumbled Yearwood. "People would have turned in those rascals –"

"Rascals?"

"– just to get themselves a few minutes exposure on the tube. Now, anybody who imagines that he suspects he might have glimpsed Lockhart and Clementine has been phoning in on the infinitesimal chance they'll get the reward money."

"So the response has been good?"

"Over a thousand sightings. From Nome, Alaska to Tierra del Fuego. Right now, the entire nerd herd is ranking them according to probability."

"That television show might have been Murdock's masterstroke."

"He should have used the building's CCTV if he wanted to track Clementine."

"He gave it to the spotters," said Ilsa. "If they can't find her, nobody can."

Hell," retorted Yearwood. "I'm almost certain those two are still in New York. I could have told Murdock that without dragging in outsiders. But that's not why I'm here, Ilsa. Tell me, are you discreet?"

The corners of her mouth curled down in a stubborn arc. "What do you mean by that comment, dear?"

"I'm considering a negotiation that might be worth a goodly sum of money. If you'll let me borrow your torturemobile –"

"Intelligence Enhancement Vehicle."

"– for a few hours."

"It comes with a chauffeur."

"Of course you can come along," Yearwood conceded. "I didn't expect anything but."

"You're not contemplating anything that might result in us getting a severe reprimand or even us losing our pensions, are you?"

"Of course there's risk. Otherwise it couldn't be so rewarding."

For a moment, a slight twinkle of anticipation flicked around Ilsa's narrow lips. "I've been innovating some of my techniques. Do you think I'll be able to try them out?"

"Possibly," sighed Yearwood. "I'll think about it."

"So will I." Ilsa smiled back at him.

As three o'clock approached, Meghan grew increasingly agitated. She vacuumed, scrubbed the bathroom, washed and ironed Moira's sundress even though it hadn't been wrinkled when she took it from the closet.

At five minutes till three she could stand it no longer. She beckoned Thomas and led him to the window.

She peered through the curtains and breathed with relief, then eased them apart so he could peek out. "How do you like him? Third one from the left. Study his moves."

Half-a-dozen men who resembled Thomas milled uncertainly on the opposite sidewalk, Gil, wearing jeans and his Greek fisherman's hat, in their midst.

"I don't understand." Thomas turned to her in puzzlement.

"Don't you see? That's the guy who's going to take your place when your friend Yearwood comes calling. The dashiki will confuse the murderers. It's like baseball. He'll be your pinch hitter," Meghan assured him. "I thought I might get the killers on your tail and work a switch. Now we don't have to. You can pack your dashiki to wear on the beach."

"What?" Thomas shouted with enough fury that she could feel the window rattle in its sash.

"Shh!" She grabbed him by the arm. "Do you want him to find out?"

"That is what you've been up to?!" Thomas seized her shoulders.

"Ow, you're hurting me."

He ignored her complaint. "Are you mad? Are you actually contemplating the indirect murder of some perfectly innocent stranger?"

"Thomas, they're not going to murder him. They'll follow him. Once they get close, they'll realize they have the wrong person and let him go. Isn't what giving that bum your coat was all about? It will give us enough time to escape."

"How can you possibly predict what they'll do?"

"They have to let him go," she persisted. "They couldn't possibly kill him."

"Do you honestly believe what you are saying?"

"Of course, I believe what I'm saying."

Thomas's anger, however, was ruthlessly magnifying whatever growing doubts she had managed to suppress.

"I mean, if I were Yearwood, I wouldn't waste my time hurting Gil. It might cause all sorts of problems. You told me yourself he wants to keep a low profile."

"Meghan, optimism is one thing. Blind self-delusion is altogether different."

"It's him or you. I've considered every possibility. You showed me yourself those guys are everywhere. There are no other options. This is absolutely the last way out."

"It's bad, mad and ultimately, terribly sad. I will not permit it."

"Thomas, suppose, just for the sake of argument, even though it won't happen, suppose Yearwood and all did accidentally hurt him. What would it matter? He's the perfect fall guy. Don't you understand? Far away from home. No close relatives. No friends. Well, maybe one woman that he treats terribly shabbily. Besides, he said he would make any sacrifice for me."

Thomas reached for the doorknob.

Meghan grabbed his hand. "Where are you going?" she demanded.

When she failed to dislodge his grip, she pulled down on his wrist with her weight as the doorknob continued inexorably to turn.

"Where do you think?"

Thomas managed to open the door slightly; Meghan released his arm to slam her body against the door.

"Don't! Just let him go, please. We'll think of something else."

"How could you?" said Thomas.

"Because you're the only thing that gives my life any meaning. I did it for us. If there had been any other way, any smidgen of an inkling of a chance for us, I would have pursued it. Remember? You claimed I would never have courage enough to do anything like this? I have to prove to you I'm not afraid –"

"It's brilliant. It's sick."

"I lied for you. Stuck my neck out for you. And all you do is call me sick," Meghan wailed. "You're the one I'm trying to save. Why do you keep rejecting me? Why am I the one that has to suffer? What else do you want from me?"

"To go and warn him," said Thomas.

He stared down at her, his visage as unforgiving as a 17th century preacher's.

"I'll do it tonight, Thomas, I promise."

He stalked back into the living room. Though he only went several feet, she felt as if he had crossed to the other side of the planet, leaving her adrift, bereft. She ran to him, studying every twitch and blink in his now iron-hard face.

•

Across the street, Gil detached himself from the knot of actors and crept down the gloomy passageway between the houses opposite Moira's. The windows on either side were curtained and dark; the space narrow and oppressive. He looked in alarm from side to side, then hastily backed out.

When he returned to the men, he informed them, "Nothing down there but a bicycle and some garbage cans." He double-checked his photocopy of the audition notice. "41-24?"

"That's what it says, but there's no such address," said a man who resembled Gil, only heavier set. "And no phone number."

The men stared uncertainly at each other. At last Gil broke away and headed up the sidewalk to the right-hand house, the heavier-set actor and the Brooklyn-born one who had read over Meghan's shoulder accompanying Gil.

They rang the doorbell.

An elderly man in a greasy bathrobe opened the inner door. "We're looking for 41-24," Gil explained.

When the man refused to open the outer door, Gil held up the photocopy for him to read through the screen. "This is the address. But there's no such audition."

The man slammed the door shut.

"Typical," snapped the actor from the studio. "Typical fucking New York."

"What do you expect?" sighed Gil. "I'm from Seattle."

"Really?" I'm Eric, from Spokane," said the heavyset man, offering his hand. And to the actor from the studio, "But you don't sound like you're from out that way."

"You'd be surprised how quickly hunger crosses state lines," the actor muttered.

"And I'm sure the rest of us have drunk enough Ranier beer to qualify as honorary citizens," Gil volunteered. "Why don't we go grab one of those brews I planned to get as a freebie? It's the least consolation we deserve for missing the audition."

"Whole situation is very peculiar," muttered Eric.

"Cheer up," Gil patted him on the shoulder. "So far I'm batting a thousand on these damn auditions. Wouldn't want to mess up my perfect record."

"Where will we go?" Eric asked.

"Gents, look around you. We're in Woodside. Don't you know the fundamental house rules around here?" the Brooklyn actor asked rhetorically. "Never eat the food in a New York Irish bar and never drink anyplace else."

Disgruntlement providing them an easy communion, the group drifted down the sidewalk toward the subway station.

●

As Thomas scrutinized Meghan's submission, realization struck him with the fury of a thunderclap. He roughly held her shoulders apart. "You slept with him, didn't you?"

"What sort of question is that?"

"A perfectly reasonable one."

"Thomas, are you doubting my love?" She met his piercing gaze with her own obduracy. "I did not sleep with him."

He took her chin in his hand and tilted it slightly before she jerked it away.

"Why are you suddenly so suspicious? Don't you trust me enough to believe that I'm trying to get us out of here?"

"What is so difficult about telling me whether or not you slept with that poor slob?"

"Because I'm shocked at your jealousy. I'm sure you've had dozens of girlfriends, maybe hundreds. And merely because I spent some platonic time with a stranger . . . ."

She tried to get close to him, but he remained as unapproachable as granite. His gaze, too, had the hardness and weight of stone. She broke away and looked him in the eyes.

"All right," she admitted, "We came close – "

"Damn!" He slammed his fist into the side of the pinball machine. The "TILT" alarm blinked on and off in reproving flashes. Bells gonged furiously. She was grateful for his display of wrath – she did not know how she would have dealt with his anger if he had remained cold and withdrawn.

She fell upon him, "Nothing happened. I swear."

He continued looking down at her, his lips pressed together, "I believe you," he said without much conviction.

CHAPTER 21.

Bellevue

Despite his profession, Yearwood was extremely uncomfortable in the New York City Morgue at Bellevue Hospital. The drab corridors, the attendants padding soundlessly and without expression. The grief-stricken visitors, their faces registering shock or resignation. Although there were wooden benches outside the administrative offices, Yearwood was incapable of sitting. He paced restlessly, trying to prevent his own vitality from being absorbed by the stillness of the tiled hall.

At last the diener, who prepared the bodies for autopsy, emerged from his office. He was of indeterminate age, though youngish. His skin was pale, with the translucence of someone who rarely went outdoors, his lips so colorless they almost vanished in his face. "I'm sorry I was delayed, but I had a child to do. They're always the hardest. Now, how may I help you?"

"I have a major favor to ask," said Yearwood. "As you know, all transactions with our organization are proprietary."

"We've always been absolutely discreet," the diener assured him.

"I need an unclaimed," said Yearwood. "Caucasian male, six-two, six-three. Black hair."

"That's a tough one. Thirty years ago we had over two thousand murders a year. Last year we barely broke three hundred. The decline's creating havoc with our organ donations, too. Can't you use an African-American? Or Hispanic. Those I could supply immediately."

Even though he conducted himself with a funeral director's pious solemnity, the diener projected a genuine warmth that seemed particularly extraordinary considering his clientele.

"Hispanic would do in a pinch," said Yearwood. "If they were light-skinned."

The diener interlaced his fingers as he considered Yearwood's request. "Cause of death?"

"Gunshot would be perfect. But I could run with an OD."

"When do you need the subject?"

"Within the next two or three days."

"I'll do my best," said the diener in his comforting tones.

He shook Yearwood's hand. The diener's grip was cool and oddly neutral, a hand seemingly devoid of bone or cartilage.

"It will be greatly appreciated. As usual, you'll be quietly and adequately compensated." Yearwood extracted his hand from the diener's as quickly as he could.

"Saving the city some money would be sufficient."

"I'm afraid you might be seeing this one again, though he might have a different name."

The diener tilted his head and studied Yearwood with a pale blue eye, but discretion kept him from speaking.

"I'll be in touch," said Yearwood.

He dashed outside, to lean against the brick wall of the morgue, sucking in great gulps of the life-affirming air, slanting his face up toward the benevolent echoes of sunlight managing to bounce through the clouds.

•

At the Metropolitan Museum, the ancient white stones of the Temple of Dendur glowed softly from the overhead lights. A sprinkling of raindrops bounced against the glass wall. A stocky woman sat on the benches beside the potted palms. With her horn-rimmed glasses and nondescript jeans, she could easily have been a student.

She had trained a pair of binoculars obliquely across Fifth Avenue, studying Thomas's building so intently she did not notice Yearwood creep up on her.

He pinched her bottom. She leapt up with a yelp. "Keep your hands to yourself, Yearwood."

"I know, I know, Greta. Sexual harassment. Any sign of him or the Clementine woman?"

"Negative," said Greta.

An indeterminate expression flickered across Yearwood's face, perhaps apprehension, perhaps relief. He quickly suppressed it. "Who got stuck with the back entrance this shift?"

"Abe."

"Poor bastard gets all the shit details, doesn't he?" Yearwood sympathized. "On the slim chance his Lordship shows, buzz me. If you see him leave, buzz Abe to tail him."

"Roger," said Greta.

•

When it came time to pay for the beers, Gil realized he'd left his wallet at home, and shamefaced, asked the others to cover him. Everyone, including Gil himself, knew they thought it was the starving actor's excuse to slip the tab.

With his mild sense of disgrace, eased by beer, and feeling renewed aggravation at the city and anticipation of the joy he would soon feel at leaving it, Gil went to his garden plot on Manhattan's west side. Before the area was named Clinton, it was known as Hell's Kitchen. Now the number of boarded buildings was shrinking; almost all the tenements were being converted into luxury co-ops. A few burned-out hulks had been demolished and their sites opened to local gardeners till developers could raise the financing to erect more high-rises.

Gil and others fortunate to obtain slots grew plants to suit their personal fancies: corn and peppers and nicotiniana redolent with white blossoms.

Tilting his fisherman's cap to shield his eyes from the late afternoon sun, Gil sadly surveyed his carefully-tended rows and the anti-drug mural painted on the wall of the adjacent building.

He punched in the combination on the communal toolbox, removed a trowel and hung up his shirt.

He knelt in his plot and began firming up the rain-loosened soil around his tomato plants. He yanked out weeds, carefully patting the earth back down after every extraction. With the trowel, he deepened the drainage trenches on either side.

He was working on his cucumbers when his nose suddenly wrinkled as he reacted to a sudden pungency. He turned. Barbara stood behind him, clutching a spiny football-sized fruit.

"Barbara!" said Gil, rising. "Sorry. I clean forgot."

"I waited two hours at your apartment. Then I gave up and schlepped down to Chinatown by myself."

"But you got the durian!" he exclaimed.

"What have you done to your hair?"

She lifted his cap to examine it more closely.

"It was for a beer commercial audition."

"You get the part?"

"The audition was bogus. I didn't even get to read for it."

"She did it to you, didn't she."

"Meghan." Gil savored the syllables.

"You know, whenever you say her name I want to smack you for being so damn gullible."

"It's okay. You worry too much. Anyway, my hair, how do you like it?"

Barbara grimaced and at last said, "Actually, I do. But why are you wearing the cap?"

"She told me I should wear it a few days to protect the permanent."

"That doesn't make any sense."

He took the durian from her and inhaled its odor, somewhere between rotting mango and rancid goat cheese. "This is really wonderful, Barbara. Thank you."

"It's your going-away present. I looked all over Chinatown until I found the smelliest one."

"I bet you had the subway to yourself." He returned the durian to her and slid into his shirt. "You haven't seen my wallet, have you?"

"You haven't lost it again, have you?" She looked at him with the earnestness of an elementary school teacher. "Or did you pack it in one those boxes you shipped to Seattle?"

Gil sheepishly averted his gaze, unable to deny the possibility. Laying a hand on his wrist, she reassured him, "It'll turn up."

He locked up the trowel and put on his shirt.

He paused at the gate, breathing in the fragrance of the blooming flowers, the scent of ripening vegetables, potent enough to triumph over the smell of car exhaust and piles of garbage by the curb, even the pungency of the durian itself.

"You know, of all the things I do like in New York, I'll miss my garden the most."

"What about me?"

"Next to you, of course," Gil replied. "Will you promise to look after it?"

"I'll take care of it for you until you realize you can't go home again and decide to come back," she offered. "I'll even turn the strawberries into strawberry-black-pepper-balsamic jam."

●

In the non-descript room in Queens, the spotters stared ceaselessly at ever-switching views on their display terminals.

With an audible gasp, a prim young black woman leaned forward and zoomed in on two figures on her screen. She flipped a switch and the red light above her cubicle started spinning around.

Almost instantly, two men in black suits, both wearing earpieces, appeared behind her.

She indicated the screen, and the taller of the two twisted his head to speak into his Bluetooth.

The man nodded to the woman, who rose. The trio walked out of the room, followed by an envious glance from every cubicle.

●

Gil practiced his Thomas walk as he and Barbara headed east on West 51st. A dark blue Ford with tinted windows passed them.

"What is this?" Barbara snapped. "Your hair? Your walk?"

"For my remaining days here I'm going to stride like a true New Yorker."

"That's the most ridiculous thing she's got you doing yet."

In the middle of the block, the car screeched to a stop, backed up and moved parallel to them as they strolled towards Tenth Avenue.

"If that one was really concerned about your welfare," said Barbara, "she would have convinced you to come back to work."

"No can do. Meghan and I are going away. Tomorrow. To Key West, where I've always wanted to go."

The Ford pulled to the curb a dozen yards in front of Gil and Barbara. Two men got out, one bullnecked in a herringbone jacket, and the other a young African-American in a navy suit. They loitered on the sidewalk as the couple approached.

Barbara put her arm across his shoulders. "I'm scared for you. Every time you say her name, my skin crawls."

"I'll take my chances," said Gil.

"If she were any good for you, you wouldn't forget your work," Barbara scolded him. "It's terrible. Irresponsible. I'll take care of your algae. Your garden. Settle your lease. Anything. As long as you promise me that instead of getting on a plane to Key West, you'll get one back to Seattle. It would be better than risking your neck with that bimbo."

"How do you know she's a bimbo? She's very sensitive. And just as I suspected, she did suffer an enormous tragedy. Her sweetheart died in that French jet that crashed in the Atlantic. Remember?"

"No."

The older man blocked Gil's way and flipped open his wallet to display a police badge and ID for Detective Hickey, assigned to the 18th Precinct. "Don't even breathe, buddy."

The younger man also flashed identification, but so briefly Gil did not even have a chance to glimpse a name or badge number.

Hickey compared Gil's face to Thomas's on a computer printout when Barbara inserted herself between them.

"Out of the way, lady," Hickey gently eased her aside, then asked Gil: "Name?"

Gil could not speak.

"He's Gilbert DeLeo. Why do you want to know?" Barbara demanded.

"Phew! Stinks, don't it?" The young detective held his nose and pointed at the durian.

"In Thailand, this is considered a delicacy," Barbara retorted.

"In New York, this is considered –" the young detective said.

"Let him speak, miss. Or can't he talk?" Hickey did not let his colleague finish his sentence. "May we see your ID, sir?"

"I was just working in my garden. Gil remained flustered, sliding his hand in and out of every pocket. "I've been looking for my wallet, officer. Sir, I think I might have accidentally packed it in some things I was shipping back home."

"Oh, Gil, you didn't lose it again, did you?" Barbara repeated helpfully. "It's probably under your futon like last time."

The two detectives gave each other a knowing glance. "Where d'ya live?" Hickey asked.

"A few blocks away, West 61st at West End, officer." Gil pointed uptown.

"And where d'ya work?" Hickey continued.

"At Restaurant X. Or I did until a few days ago."

Barbara nodded supportive affirmation of Gil's statements.

"That's no English accent," the young detective observed with much regret.

"Can'tcha hear the cornfields. Don't you have any sort of identification at all? Library card, voter registration?"

"Well, um," said Gil.

"I'll vouch for him," Barbara piped in.

Hickey carefully pulled Gil's shirt across his shoulder.

"What do you think you're doing?"

Barbara grasped the detective's wrist. The younger man removed her hand. "Calm down, miss."

"No holes in him," Hickey observed.

"And she sure as hell isn't pushing thirty."

"I'm twenty-five and a few months."

The younger detective peered at Barbara's hair. "Brunette to her roots. Got a mouth on her like a redhead though."

"Okay, Mr. Leon, walk," said Hickey. "Just don't leave your house without no ID."

"And throw your garbage in the garbage," the young detective added, thumbing at the durian.

The two men got back into their car and accelerated down the street.

"Fascist bastards!" Barbara shouted after them.

"Shh! I wonder who they're looking for?"

"I hope he gets away."

"Come on, help me finish packing," said Gil.

"Please, Gil. Don't go away with her. You can stay in my apartment."

"I promise to think about it," said Gil.

He started to step down the sidewalk, but Barbara took his hands and forced him to look at her.

"Forget my feelings for you. Pretend I'm a total stranger watching you from a distance. That whole thing with the audition. Where did you hear about it? From her. Why would they hold an audition in Queens, of all places. If you were a great big beer company, wouldn't you have your audition on Madison Avenue?"

"Maybe they're trying to save money. Or they want some local color."

"Don't try to explain it to me. I'm out at a distance, remember? Just think about it. What could that woman be up to?"

"Exactly," said Gil. "What could she be up to? I don't have any money. She can't want to marry me to get a Green Card because she's already an American. She can't be interested in subletting or grabbing my lease. She would have asked me about it. Have you considered she might just be lonely and need some companionship? Or are you so jealous you don't see that there actually might be some feeling between us?"

"You're in denial," Barbara said.

"I'm in demand."

"Yeah, right." Barbara blew through her lips like a dismissive mare.

Gil wagged his finger at her. "Ah, ah, you're at distance, remember?"

"I could be standing halfway across the universe, and I'd still see you were in denial. I wouldn't even need a telescope."

With a sigh he turned and hurried on. She caught up to him. "Well, now I'm Barbara-on-earth again. Up close I can see that denial has dropped your I.Q. by about 100 points."

"Are you sure jealousy isn't doing the same to you?" he asked. "Now come on, Barbara." He took her hand. This is the last time I'll see you for a while. Let's enjoy being with each other."

They headed north on Ninth Avenue and decided to stop at Lincoln Center, to cool themselves in the mist drifting off the fountain.

A tall auburn-haired woman in a designer dress and sunhat was observing them from the Alice Tully portico. Gil and Barbara lingered for a few minutes in the fountain's delicious droplets and then rose off the fountain parapet.

The woman stepped into the sunlight and gradually crossed the distance between her and Gil and Barbara.

"Why does that one want you curly? It makes you more handsome but it's not you," said Barbara, then added, "See what happened at that imaginary audition? All that effort for nothing."

The auburn-haired woman caught up to Gil and Barbara. She spun Gil around to embrace him and the durian. "My Tommykins! I've found you again."

"No, I'm not," said Gil, trying to fend her off.

"No, he's not," said Barbara, even more energetically trying to pry the interloper away.

"No, you're not," said the auburn-haired woman, staring determinedly at Gil's face.

Disconcerted, she shrank back from the spikes and stench of the fruit. "Pardon me, from a distance, you . . . ."

Embarrassed, the woman retreated, examining her dress to ensure none of the durian had smeared upon her.

Barbara pointed at the woman as she hurried away. "Does this happen often?"

"Never in all the years I've spent in New York."

"Gil, I just remembered some errands. I'll see you tonight. Ciao."

It took Gil a beat to recover, then he said, "I'll take the durian."

"I need it," said Barbara. She clutched it tighter and walked quickly across the plaza, turning south when she went down the steps.

As soon as Gil was out of sight, Barbara switched on her phone and searched for dinner cruises on a ship named the Lady Liberty.

•

The main office of Hofmeister Dinner Cruises at Chelsea Pier was a messy confluence of papers, posters and brochures. Barbara, armed with the durian, stood in front of the receptionist, a black woman wearing a jolly yellow dress who cringed from the stench of the giant fruit on the counter.

"See her cubicle?"

A tiny paper-cluttered space, the walls lined with pictures of kittens, puppies and baby rabbits.

"She's on vacation. She was going down to the Caribbean or some-where," said the receptionist.

Through the window, the Lady Liberty could be seen sliding out of the rain-soaked obscurity of the Hudson and into its berth.

"Could she be at her boyfriend's?" Barbara asked.

"Honey, I only been here six months. I don't even think she's got one. Now would you get that smelly thing outta here?"

Barbara turned and slowly trudged towards the door.

"But if she does, I feel downright sorry for him," the receptionist called after her.

Barbara paused long enough to concur. "Not half as much as I do."

CHAPTER 22.

Fugitives Most Foul

For Meghan and Thomas the day passed in a choreography of half-begun sentences, of silence taut with avoided recrimination, of a formal courtesy, a chill that neither Thomas nor Meghan had before experienced with each other. She padded restlessly about the house until she settled into the chair in front of Moira's dressing table, reflecting and reflecting.

Thomas sat at the kitchen table, collating names from his Filofax onto the back of an envelope. Once when she came down to see him, and leaned over to kiss him on the cheek, she saw that he had written down ten names. When she brought him his lunch – a corned beef sandwich – there were fifteen names on the list.

"So what are your plans now?" he asked absent-mindedly.

"To spend the day working through my guilt," she replied.

"I'm sorry. The last thing I wanted to do was make you feel guilty."

"No, it's twelve years of parochial school doing what it does best. I can't believe that when I was young, I thought if you went to see a movie that the Legion of Decency had condemned, you were doomed to hell. And, now, look at me . . . ." her voice trailed off.

As she scrubbed the bathroom, an alternative plan gradually formed in her mind. She returned to Moira's room, and re-settling on the dressing table bench, allowed her thoughts to engulf her.

"What do you want for dinner?" she asked him around five that afternoon.

The list of names had been ripped from his pad and at least a dozen pages had been filled with his meticulous writing. She was only able to glimpse the first phrase – "Courier to Singapore?" – before he pointedly turned the sheets over.

"Is it that time already?" he asked, glancing in surprise at his watch. "Whatever suits your fancy."

Meghan had few culinary specialties and even fewer that appealed to Thomas, but she did make an excellent eggplant parmesan. Her secret was to take the extra step of frying the thin slices of eggplant and baking them in bread crumbs BEFORE layering in the tomato sauce and cheese.

When she brought the casserole dish around to Thomas, his chilly distance had lifted to a state of undefended discouragement. On his list of fifteen or so names, all but one had been crossed out.

She lifted the glass lid; the smell of the dish steamed out. Thomas merely glanced at the dish, not even bothering to sniff the fragrant steam.

"That's nice," he said, his tone flat. She had never heard him so noncommittal, so defeated that no quip embellished his response.

"That's nice. Is that all you can say? I spent all afternoon –"

"If you were more alert," Thomas snapped, "you would appreciate how drastic our predicament is. Half-a-billion dollars worth of computer equipment. Millions of television viewers, all with only one goal: hunt us down. You and I are two bullets away from the grave. Four actually, as I'm sure Yearwood is a double-tapper. And unless I –"

"You think I would have gone through what I just went through if I didn't realize how serious it was?" she retorted.

He took her in his arms, their distance breached for the first time since Gil's appearance on the opposite sidewalk.

"I spoke too hastily. Heretofore I've triumphed over every situation. This is the first time a situation has triumphed over me. Now let's eat. Mmmmm."

He at last inhaled the aroma arising from the dish.

Unable to sustain his brief enthusiasm past a few forkfuls, he impatiently waited for her finish. After she removed the dishes, he immediately resumed his brooding toil. Around eight she sat adamantly in the chair opposite him. Thomas was flipping the pages of his Filofax, front to back, back to front.

"Thomas –"

It took him a few moments to focus.

"I've been thinking about the situation. And I have an idea."

He held up his finger to silence her. "Meghan, I'm sure it's a wonderful idea. It might even be a brilliant idea. I must admit your plan today was thoroughly ingenious. But remember, I warned you that I would give you one day to implement. Which I did. So now, I must –"

"Don't condescend," said Meghan.

"Anybody who hasn't dealt with these people is hopelessly outclassed. Now if you excuse me, I have to consider our options."

He abruptly returned to his sheets of paper, making it obvious that the conversation was over.

In a huff, Meghan plopped into the living room sofa, sandwiched between a baseball pinball game and one based on some sort of gangster/mafia shootout.

She flipped on the wall television, and irritably went up the channels, from talent contest shows, grotesque reality shows, network sitcoms, shopping channels. Absolutely nothing that held any interest.

Until she clicked to the next channel.

A picture of Thomas and Meghan, head bowed down in the Consolidated Resources lobby.

"Thomas . . . ." she uttered, her voice merely a croak.

"The next day," the off-screen narrator said, "they were spotted trying to buy a ticket at Kennedy Airport."

"Thomas!" she shrieked as the scene switched to one of Thomas and her at the ticket counter.

Thomas came running in as Miles O'Leary strolled across the studio set of *Fugitives Most Foul*, where a dozen associates with headsets worked at consoles, answering phones, entering data.

He yanked the remote control out of her hand.

"So this is good-night from me, Miles O'Leary. If you or any of your friends spot Thomas Catherton Lockhart or the woman who calls herself Shelley Clementine –"

He cut the television off, and sat down beside Meghan, cradling her, whispering, "It will be okay, it will be okay," like a mantra in a futile effort to thaw her out of her shock."

"We're doomed," she whispered to herself, but so softly she knew he would not hear her.

"Think about it, Meghan. I know Murdock. If he wasn't getting desperate, he would never have gone public. Obviously he has no idea where we are."

"Millions of people watch that show," she protested. "They're always capturing the fugitives they profile. No matter where they flee or change how they look. Even in places like the jungles of South America."

"All it means is that we have to change our strategy. Now leave me be."

"What are you going to do?

"I'm going to try and set up an anonymous email account on Moira's Jurassic computer and get in touch with a friend in Chicago, Maxter the Fixture. He has a few friends, who uh, shall we say politely, have never been north of Houston Street, and who for a small, or rather no doubt, exorbitant fee, can not only get us across Lake Michigan or even better, Lake Superior, maybe even to Thunder Bay."

"And in the meantime?"

"I need to work it out."

With a peremptoriness she had never before seen in him, he went to the antiquated computer, which still boasted a CRT monitor, and switched it on.

Fortunately, the system was not password protected.

She watched him watch it boot and went upstairs.

CHAPTER 23.

The Spider Club

At 10:30 p.m., a car horn honked.

Meghan at last came down the steps, wearing Moira's glossy raincoat, belt cinched. Her wig was severely drawn back, her eyes heavily made up, and a floppy hat was pulled down over her head.

Thomas, completely absorbed in his work, had not heard the car horn and was barely aware of Meghan passing through the living room.

He turned and looked vaguely in her direction as she rushed toward the door.

The sight of her startled him and he jumped. "Where are you going? Not to see that bloody chef again, are you?"

"I'll be back in a few hours. Don't worry. Bye," She mumbled, keeping her head bent down and her voice low.

She dashed out and shut the door.

He raced over and reopened it. "Where the bloody hell are you off to?"

She was already at the livery car; the door was opened and she had one leg inside.

"Get back!" she exclaimed, her tone midway between a shout and a whisper.

Thomas, oblivious to the danger of exposure, took a few steps down the sidewalk until he was parallel with the Virgin Mary Grotto. "Don't lie to me, Meghan. You're made up like that just to tell some poor slob to get a haircut?"

A pink Spalding ball (now officially rechristened "Spaldeen," which was what generations of young New Yorkers had always called it) bounced towards Thomas. A young boy seized it and hurled it to the older lad standing on the manhole lid that formed home plate.

The night was subdued and neighborly, with people visiting on their stoops, chatting on their sidewalks. A stocky woman seemed to be paying particular attention to Thomas and Meghan.

Meghan glimpsed the woman and waved Thomas back. "Get back inside," she hissed.

"What justification is there –"

"I'll see you in a few hours. I'll explain."

She hopped in the car and slammed the door.

With one last fleeting scrutiny of the street, Thomas retreated inside and slammed the door.

•

Back in his apartment, Gil put his last pan in a cardboard box for Barbara to seal. Except for a few fat garbage bags, the found furniture and an ice cream maker on the counter, the apartment was now barren.

Crossing to the counter, she switched off her ice cream maker. After it ground to a halt and the lid popped, she dished out two bowls of ice cream and handed one to Gil.

He lifted a spoonful to his nose, savoring its exotic scent. As he put the sample in his mouth, he smiled, an expression close to ecstasy crossing his face.

"Yum-ola! Go ahead," he told her. "You try it."

Barbara cautiously licked her spoon. "The best part is that you can barely smell the durian."

"You'll enjoy it more as your palate gets more sophisticated. I wonder if Meghan would like it?"

"Hopefully it would give her cramps." Barbara's eyes grew wide, and she looked around guiltily. "Oops. Is that me being catty?"

Gil shook his head and sighed, too infatuated with the ice cream and anticipation of his impending vacation to react to Barbara's sniping.

•

Meghan did not go to Gil's.

Instead, the livery car dropped her off the corner of Broadway and Pine. The area was almost deserted, the purposeful bankers with their pinstripes and briefcases replaced by weary men and women dressed in cleaners' uniforms.

A limousine was parked down the block in front of a Japanese restaurant, the driver lounging against the fender and reading *The Daily Racing Form*.

Exactly as Thomas described, two heavyset men sat on stools outside the opened doors. One wore shorts, a beeper on his pocket, the gold chain dangling over his t-shirt proclaimed him to be "Luca." Although there was nothing overtly intimidating about the man's demeanor, something about his presence made Meghan apprehensive. His friend was more casually dressed and wearing a Yankees cap. Meghan wondered why all the bouncers in New York seemed to be sent over by Central Casting.

She deliberately ignored the bouncers as she strode into the lobby.

Luca intercepted her. "Sorry, Ma'am. Restaurant's closed."

Meghan parted her raincoat just enough to reveal the black blouse underneath. She hesitated for a second, then proffered what she hoped was a wicked smile; her fine teeth glinted in the restaurant neon. Her throat was dry, her chest tight as she tried to speak. "Even for a saucy little Spiderwoman like myself?"

She felt only desperation, not the confidence that she hoped her words would indicate.

Luca gave her the brief glance of contempt he gave all the clientele and thumbed her through.

Meghan entered the lobby and got into the tiny stainless steel elevator. As the elevator settled into the basement, she tried to remember the speech she had been composing as she made herself up in the mirror. She wished she had written it down and rehearsed it, knowing that it would be the most important words she had ever uttered in her life. Now she could not even remember if she had some sort of coy preamble or whether she intended to launch right into her request. She unconsciously crossed herself and grasped her miracle medal, praying that her delivery would be passionate, Shakespearean and ultimately irresistible.

With a gulp, feeling amateurish and tainted, she undid her raincoat and flounced the black lace across her chest. "Mr. Murdock, you don't know me, but I want to ask you the biggest favor –"

The doors suddenly opened, startling Meghan out of her frantic reverie. A pall of cigarette smoke rolled in like a fog bank, propelled by pounding techno-pop. Meghan stepped tentatively out of the elevator. The lighting was minimal and red, except for the occasional glint that spiked off a mirror ball suspended over the dance floor. There was a brass bed in the center, with a naked couple performing upon each other. The shadows reduced them to a series of listless curves and planes. No one in the audience seemed to be paying them any attention. The room was crowded with people attired outlandishly; women with no hair, men slinking around in feather boas.

One woman, her clothes as studded with steel spikes as a porcupine with its quills, was leading a man on all fours around on a leash. He wore a dog collar and a jock strap. Some women wore leather clothes that resembled medieval armor; some men were dressed as French maids. There were even people dressed as giant plush toys – a panda, a giant rabbit, a penguin.

"Mother of saints!" exclaimed Meghan.

She stepped backwards but the elevator doors had already slammed shut. She feverishly punched the UP button. Nothing.

She did not consider herself particularly puritanical, but could not believe that anyone in the world would be behaving like the people she now observed. She hastily retied her raincoat, praying that the disgust she felt did not register on her face. Her pulse started racing, her chest tightened. She felt foolish and vulnerable.

Sister Mary Alberta had once shown Meghan's wide-eyed class slides of a diorama at Fatima, Portugal. It depicted Lucia's vision of the damned suffering the torments of hell. The scene before Meghan seemed a virtual duplicate of the saint's revelation.

She stumbled away from the elevator. The room was flanked with upholstered alcoves. Bits of apparel straddled the shadows into the public areas. Couples and threesomes and possibly larger configurations writhed inside the alcoves with grunts and occasional shrieks of ecstasy. The air was musty with unsatiated lust and cigarette smoke.

Across the dance floor, Locke Murdock, one of the few men still wearing business attire, his tie crisply knotted, was talking to a towering woman dressed in flamboyant red.

She recognized him immediately as the man that Thomas had glanced at with such loathing the night she saved him from suicide. With a deep gulp, she drifted uneasily closer.

A woman in a black sarong and knotted silk blouse with more cleavage than blouse sidled up to Meghan. Her bleached punk haircut was showing brown at the roots. The woman might have been in her well-preserved forties. She might have been in her severely burned-out twenties.

The woman gently spread Meghan's raincoat lapels. "You certainly are wearing an attractive outfit," she told Meghan. "You don't mind me saying that, do you? But why keep it hidden?"

The woman began to undo the raincoat belt.

"Uh, I'm sort of new to this."

Meghan tried to hurry away, always keeping her eye on Murdock, but the woman persisted. She laid a hand on Meghan's shoulder, her fingers groping and eager.

"I have a friend who would like to meet you. And of course I'd like to get to know you better myself. Why don't we do both at the same time?"

She reached for Meghan's hand, but Meghan had the foresight to keep it tucked out of range.

"I'll take a rain check," Meghan muttered, speeding away to escape the woman's predatory overtures.

She felt panic sweat seeping out of every pore of her flesh, and she prayed that the tell-tale sheen was not apparent in the dim light.

She finally stepped into Murdock's line of sight, a dozen feet away.

She saw him glancing in her direction, looked him quickly in the eye, then lowered her gaze. His attention, like that of an alpha predator sensing the fear scent of some nearby prey, chilled her to her core. She hoped that his unconcealed arousal would prevent him from noticing her trembling fingers as she undid her raincoat to reveal an allure that was all courtesy of Moira: black miniskirt, tight black silk blouse, high boots and a wide belt with a silver buckle.

Murdock was still staring at her. She covered her face in her hand, a gesture that she hoped he would interpret as shyness but which in actual fact arose from disgust.

Steeling herself, thoroughly irritated at his transparent desire, Meghan was encouraged that Murdock was so obvious. She had no contingency plan if he had been absent or otherwise engaged or been immune to her meticulously crafted appearance. Or what she would have done if he had been one of those men crawling around on all fours.

"Who is she?" Murdock whispered to the woman in flamboyant red.

"Don't know. Must be her first visit."

"Bring her over," Murdock ordered.

The woman nodded and crossed to Meghan. "Someone would like to meet you," she whispered.

Meghan allowed herself to be led over to him, and as soon as she faced him, Murdock said, "May I say three things about you?"

He spoke softly; she had to strain to hear his words over the pounding music. Now in his presence, she again felt the sense of intimidating creepiness he had given her in the Lady Liberty. She doubted that she could speak if she tried, and allowed him to take her acquiescence as a "yes."

"Yum, yum, yum," he exhaled with enormous relish.

"I bet you say that to all your food," Meghan finally managed to respond.

He twirled a few strands of her wig in his forefinger. She froze, knowing that in fractions of a second, her disguise might well be uncovered.

"Only to the more exotic morsels."

Meghan coughed, twisting her head aside as she attempted to regain her poise. Fortunately, the wig slipped from his forefinger without being dislodged. "You're out of luck. Irish here," she replied, somewhat relieved that he was saying things to which she could respond. "Strictly meat and potatoes."

"Then allow me to spice up your life," he said, taking her by the arm. "Shall we get something from the buffet? Or the spice rack if you prefer."

An ambiguous smile worthy of a vampire.

Meghan hesitated. "I don't even know your name."

"Locke Murdock."

"Have I heard of you? Somewhere?"

She was buying time; all the speeches she had mentally rehearsed now seemed as vanished as phrases she had heard only once as a child. She could not recall the specifics, only the gist, and that only vaguely.

"You shouldn't have," Murdock replied.

They threaded their way through grappling couples of every description. His eyes narrowed as he studied her in the dim red light, but it was obvious that he was not thinking of her as the Meghan that his organization sought.

"And your name."

"Uh, Brigitte," she replied. "Brigitte . . . Budica."

"Is that Italian?"

"Probably. A long time ago," Meghan replied. "Can we go somewhere and talk?"

Allowing herself to be led away, she felt a near-overwhelming urge to depart the depraved tableau before them. She studied Murdock, trying to determine which gambit might appeal to his vanity or whatever slender moral qualities he might possess.

•

Gil had almost finished packing. Whistling a football march, he juggled a can of insect repellent and bottle of sun block. He turned his back to his carry-on and flipped the containers over his shoulder. The sun block went wide but the repellent fell nicely into the bag's black canvas mouth. He froze, hearing footsteps creaking out on the landing. He tiptoed over to crack open the door. "Meghan?" he whispered hopefully.

The landing was deserted. But when he shut the door he heard another creak. He flung the door open. Suddenly someone stumbled into the room.

"Come on, Barbara. I thought you went home hours ago."

"Why do you want me to go there?" she asked morosely. "What's at home?"

"A good night's sleep."

"I sleep fine on your floor. In the morning I could help you finish packing."

"Barbara, Barbara, what we will do with you?" he said, giving her a platonic embrace.

"This is pretty good for starters," she responded happily.

"Don't you have any pride?"

"No."

She disentangled herself and took a man's handkerchief from her jeans pocket. She loudly blew her nose. Gil patted her sympathetically. She jerked away.

"Don't pat me! I'm not your puppy dog. How about it, what do you say? Let's wrestle."

She planted her feet in a challenging stance.

"You're nuts! I've got to get a good night's sleep," said Gil, half laughing, half-annoyed.

"Come on, you wimp."

She crouched, beckoning, furious.

They grappled. She flipped him to the floor, and he struggled up. They locked arms. Barbara managed once again to get him down. She was actually far more adroit than he and almost managed to pin him. But he was much stronger. Finally, energized by annoyance, Gil dragged her down. Grabbing her in a half nelson, he straddled her and pinned her.

"I could still teach you a trick or two," said Barbara, grinning, and despite her inferior position, undefeated.

"You made your point, champ. Now. Go home!"

He allowed her to rise.

"Okay, Gil. But I warn you. You're jumping off a cliff with your eyes closed."

"No. With my eyes open," he replied fervently.

"Then use them to look at me." She took his chin and drew his face close to her. She stared at him, unblinking, with a gravitas of which he did not think her capable, an unswerving intensity that forced him to pay attention.

"Totally forget about me." She lowered her voice, escalating his attentiveness. "But as a woman I can see that she is using your own masculinity to rob you of your manhood. Once she has sucked every bit of life force out of you, she's going to discard your husk, and you'll never revive. You end up a shriveled old man with a life gone to waste, struggling to get by in a rest home dreaming about the beautiful times you almost had with some Lorelei who had forgotten all about you two days after she leaves you in the gutter."

•

Meghan and Murdock were sitting in an alcove in the back of the Spider Club.

Before them the crowd cheered as a pony parade circled on the dance floor. Naked men and women, in leather harness, with ostrich-plumed brow bands and horsetail butt plugs pulled chariots driven by whip-wielding drivers. The "horses," on their hands and knees, whinnied and neighed, moving their heads up and down whenever they encountered people they knew. The flamboyant woman in red, pulled in a chariot by two black men and two black women, received the loudest cheers of all.

Meghan could not eat more than a few bites of her dinner. A half-eaten steak lay before her; Murdock had almost finished his. He was eating with good manners, but voraciously, eyeing Meghan with equally keen appetite.

"Tell me about yourself," said Murdock.

"Tough but tolerant. Leather hide and heart of precious stone, that's me," said Meghan.

"What a coincidence. I love tough people. Even people who take advantage of me –" said Murdock.

"Even enjoy it –"

"– because they only do it once," he interrupted her. "Trust me, trust no one."

"Love many, trust few, I suppose," said Meghan.

"Been with many? Ever been a working girl?"

"Since I was fifteen. Had dozens of jobs. I was never fired from any of them. I always quit."

"That's not what I meant."

"I know."

"That's where the money is."

Meghan shrugged, slipping out of her role as she tried to ascertain an appropriate instant to begin her plea. Though Murdock seemed overtly cordial, a forbidding undercurrent ran through him, diverting her from her mission. She dared not leap into her speech. Realizing she was losing the upper hand, Meghan suddenly sat more upright, tilting her face attentively towards the man. "But I do respect women in the trade."

"Are you going to eat that steak, young lady, or am I?"

When Meghan shook her head, Murdock helped himself to it and slid it over onto his own plate.

"Now what are you doing after dinner?"

"I was hoping we could go somewhere and talk," she said.

He smiled his politician's smile. "Nothing would make me happier. I have a private suite two floors up. Would you care to come up for a nightcap?" He noticed her stricken expression and gently patted her hand. "Don't worry, Brigitte. I won't hurt you. I won't touch you. I won't even ask you to remove any clothes. All I ask is that you join me for a half-hour or so."

CHAPTER 24.

An Unforgettable Oubliette

Murdock's suite was painted dark red. Dozens of flickering candles reflected off furniture carved in grim medieval fashion. There was an armoire. A throne-like Gothic chair. A collection of medieval torture instruments mounted on one wall. Below that was an eight-foot-high wooden rack. On another wall hung riding crops and other whips. Incongruously, on a corner shelf bracket sat a teddy bear. It seemed to be staring balefully down at the room. Meghan stared balefully back, then turned her attention to the strange shelf to the right of the teddy bear.

On either side of a golden base, draped in blue velvet with gold piping, were seven life-sized plaster casts of men's faces, all with eyes closed. There were Caucasians, Orientals and one black visage. The farthest one on the right seemed to Meghan to be vaguely Polynesian.

"How do you like my collection?" Murdock asked, pleased with the pride of ownership. Pointing to Jobim's simulacrum, he added, "That's my newest addition."

Something about the plaster casts' anguished expressions gave Meghan goose bumps, but she could not quite figure out why. "What are they?" she managed to ask at last.

"Plaster casts," he replied, though the faces obviously could have been nothing else.

"What about the space in the middle?"

Murdock irritably twirled the velvet drapery. "It's for the glory of my collection. Although, at the moment, it is, shall we say, a work in progress." Suddenly aware of Meghan's awkwardness, he said. "Here, let me take those."

He retrieved Meghan's raincoat and her floppy hat from beneath her arm and set them on a dark leather settee.

"Excuse me a second."

Meghan, wide-eyed, with her back to him, continued to examine the torture implements with the fascination of horror. She wished she had a gun, a knife, any sort of weapon to both protect herself and finish off the monster a few feet away. She studied strange iron implements on the wall. The only one that seemed like it had potential was an iron bar with a series of curved claws.

She frantically crossed herself, hoping that Murdock would not notice her trying to pry it free.

"Mother of saints protect me," she murmured.

But the clawed iron bar was too firmly affixed.

"What do you mean the sightings are still coming in?" Murdock growled into his phone. "There's only two of them. It's impossible that both his Lordship and Lady Clementine could be in Ottawa and Panama simultaneously. Shortlist them by likelihood and on my desk by tomorrow morning. And Yearwood, I want the whole business concluded by Monday."

Meghan thought her gasp was loud enough to reverberate around the room like an explosion, but Murdock did not seem to notice. Her blood could not run any colder and she gave up on the potential weapon. She tried to move towards the door, but found she could barely lift her feet. Her shoes seemed made of iron and the thick rug itself a powerful magnet.

As Murdock returned the phone to his briefcase, he spotted her trying to escape. In two strides he was upon her.

He whirled her back.

She slapped him with such force they both went reeling.

He staggered against the wall.

Terrified, Meghan grabbed the nearest device, a riding crop. She brandished it fiercely, well aware that if offered little protection if Murdock reacted with fury.

"Don't come near me!"

Instead of being enraged at the blow, Murdock was pleased.

She felt her brow sweating, the wig as obvious as a fluorescent neon sign. But lust had slackened his face and made him blind.

"When did you guess?" he asked hoarsely.

"Well, uh, I uh, you know."

Murdock encircled her and yanked the riding crop out of her hand.

"Mr. Murdock," she pleaded softly.

"That's not how you hold it," he told her.

He tenderly shaped her fingers around the handle, then lifted her arm and swung it from side to side, to engrossed with his lesson to notice any discrepancy in her hair.

"Loosen up."

She was relieved that he was too excited to notice that she was trembling. Then he led her reluctantly to the rack; he himself was having trouble speaking, his words came out in clumps between his eager breath. "Don't worry, I'm not going to tie you up."

He handed her two lengths of velvet rope.

"On the contrary."

He smiled upward at the plaster masks. "You wouldn't mind if my little figures watched our little pastime, would you? I think they might enjoy it."

He undid his belt, dropped his pants and expensive silk underwear and bent over the rack.

When Meghan stood there, staring at Murdock's exposed backside, he turned to her. "Well?"

"What am I supposed to do?"

"Isn't it obvious?"

He wriggled his wrists at her, and she glanced down at the velvet ropes.

He watched with some annoyance as she tied his wrists to the rack as best she could.

"That's not how you do it."

He slid his wrists out of the rope, "Now watch."

With swift dexterity he tied his left hand to the rack with his right hand. "Got it."

Meghan nodded without conviction, then imitated the configuration of the rope as best she could.

"Not bad for an amateur," said Murdock.

She continued to stare, motionless.

"Go ahead," Murdock said hoarsely. "Remember the safe word is 'Peaches'."

Meghan retrieved the riding crop and tentatively brought it down across his bare buttocks.

"You can do better than that," he snapped.

She whipped him a little more energetically.

"Harder!"

And with each increasingly forceful stroke, he repeated, "Harder."

When she brought the riding crop down as hard as she could, he sighed with pleasure, "Finally."

The single word unleashed every pent-up emotion within Meghan and she brought the whip down harder and harder, each moan of Murdock's pleasure only infuriating her further.

When his cheeks were virtually solid with red welts, Murdock gasped out the safe word, "Peaches."

Meghan ignored this and continued to vent her rage, her anguish, her terror.

"Peaches. Peaches! PEACHES." he repeated, which only caused her to strike more ferociously with the riding crop.

Somehow Murdock managed to release his wrists and whirled to face her. He grabbed the riding crop, "Don't you know this is a game?"

"I guess I'm really new at this."

Her fury was not yet spent, but she was exhausted and frightened by Murdock's hardened confrontation.

"You know for an amateur you got a lot of potential."

"What does your wife think about this?"

"She knows better than to ask."

Murdock drew up his underwear and pants and re-cinched his belt. He chafed his wrists together to restore their circulation and studied her face in the glow of the flickering candles.

"There's something that candlelight brings out in you. Heat? Consummation."

"Yes," said Meghan.

"Is that all? 'Yes'?"

"What do you want me to say?"

"'Thank you' would do. Or 'What a poetic turn of phrase'."

"Thank you," Meghan echoed. "What a poetic turn of phrase."

"You're not pining for someone else?" Murdock asked, pressing his sweaty face close to hers.

Meghan responded immediately. "No, there's nobody else. I don't think anyone else could compete with you."

"I hope you're keeping that in mind. Nobody else could compete with me. Now, about our return engagement. I'll give you three hundred an hour for repeat performances Tuesdays and Thursdays."

He tucked his shirt back inside.

"Not enough," said Meghan.

"Four hundred," he offered, but she shook her head. "Name your price."

"What I really want is . . . ." The moment came but the words hung in her throat. She could not finish what she intended to say " . . . is for you to spare the life of Thomas Catherton Lockhart. He's very sorry for what he did, and he'll give you back every penny he borrowed from you. With interest if you like."

Instead she mumbled, "What I really want is . . ."

She felt his stare penetrating her, violating her far more than if he had done something physical. At that instant she recognized the wisdom of Thomas's insight – Murdock would never spare her lover's life. It was stupidity, perhaps even much worse, perhaps the height of foolish vanity with which she had placed herself in the situation. ". . . is a job. In your big black building."

"How do you know what kind of building I work in?" he asked with surprise and caution.

"You're either an attorney or you work down on Wall Street. Every one of them I know works in a black skyscraper of some kind," she improvised.

"Don't you have a job?" said Murdock, with surprise and caution.

"I'm sick of it. I guess I want excitement."

"The jobs in my outfit are boring."

"I'm not talking file clerk. I mean up where the bodies are buried," said Meghan.

Murdock frowned. The smile slid from his face and was replaced by his domineering frown. He retrieved the riding crop and twirled the handle back and forth in his palms.

"I don't know what game you're playing, young lady. Or think you're playing. I'm fairly sure it's not blackmail. Or intelligence."

"No, I'm real dumb. I was just talking to a woman out there," said Meghan, genuinely frightened.

Her stomach was in upheaval; she realized that instead of extricating herself, she had only mired herself that much deeper.

"Whatever it is, keep it up and you'll find yourself in a body bag wearing a death mask yourself."

"I was kidding." She was on the verge of tears.

"Let's just hope you were."

She slid across the room, grabbed her raincoat, hat and clutch bag and tried to turn the door handle, but it was locked. She pounded on the door until Murdock dropped the riding crop and jerked her hand away.

"Don't run away, Brigitte. But you must understand, a man in my position must always be on his guard. Against strivers, opportunists, people that are jealous of my position or like I said, people who try to take advantage of me for the first time."

"I want to go home," wailed Meghan.

"I've been looking for you all my life."

"I've got to pee," she said.

Murdock pricked up his ears and cocked an eyebrow. Lust returned to his face.

Meghan laughed nervously. "Oh, no, not now. Maybe next time."

"Okay, then. Thursday it is." He pointed. "Bathroom's in there. I'll call you a car. Where do you live?"

"Uh, up in the Bronx. Don't worry about it. I'll get a cab," Meghan said as he crossed the room.

Murdock listened for the shutting of the bathroom door and pressed a speed dial button on his phone. "It's Murdock. Who's available? . . . No, not him. How about Abe? . . . Good. This is an emergency. He needs to use the Yellow Cab. Get him to the club and have him pick up a woman coming out. Blue rain coat, black miniskirt and a goofy hat. Immediately. And I want a full background done on a Brigitte Budica. She lives in the Bronx."

Once he heard the toilet flushing, he hastily flung the phone back into his briefcase and hurried over to a walnut liquor cabinet. He was pouring himself a shot of Jagermeister when Meghan re-entered.

"Don't you want to at least stick around for a drink?"

"I'll take a rain check. Next Thursday." She feigned a smile to mask her terror and disgust; praying that he could not see through her deception.

Murdock smiled back, the lines of his exquisite teeth visible through the narrow slit of his lips. He spoke in his feather-soft seductive voice, "You know where to find me."

CHAPTER 25.

To Escape from Escape

Thomas sat hunched over the ancient computer, head bowed. The life of Maxter the Fixture was more volatile and unreliable than his own. The email addresses he had for the last person who could somehow ease him out of his predicament were not longer valid. He transposed some of the letters, hoping that he was misremembering it.

Nothing worked.

He gave up. He turned to the home page of *Fugitives Most Foul* and went to the page with the night's program. He clicked on the link to "Thomas Catherton Lockhart & Shelley Clementine."

After a moment's buffering, Miles O'Leary strolled across the screen, the studio with the busily toiling clerks behind him. "Welcome to *Fugitives Most Foul.* I'm Miles O'Leary, and tonight we profile the story of Thomas Catherton Lockhart, a corporate high flyer who crossed to the dark side, and his accomplice, Shelley Clementine, although that's probably an alias. Lockhart had embezzled several million dollars from his company, which he intended to funnel to a terrorist organization in the South Pacific. The story starts —"

Furious, Thomas switched the computer off.

He sat there, head bowed, for maybe twenty minutes. The pinball dazzle, garish on the lightbox, was playful and pastel by the time it fell upon his resigned features.

At last, he rose.

He shaved and brushed his teeth with the razor and brush Meghan had purchased. Finally he involuntarily splashed some of his unsuspecting host's Old Spice on his cheeks.

●

> "Love is sacrifice and acceptance, but sacrifice of your-self, not of your beloved. I am not going to sacrifice you on the altar of my absurd folly. All I ask is your acceptance, that I must sacrifice myself, a husk I only temporary inhabit in order that you have a life devoid of fear. My love for you is eternal, and it shall endure, even if the one you love does not."

He wrote his farewell message on the back of another envelope, then taped it to the wall beside the door to the kitchen where Meghan would be sure to see it.

With a resolute exhale, he went out the door.

He walked down the few steps and out the wrought iron gates. A tentative moon did its best to intrude through the restless clouds, but a few seconds after contributing the most light of which it was capable, the clouds again engulfed it. Though there weren't many trees on the street, the wind was strong enough to sound as if it were blowing through a forest.

He had only a gone a few steps when he saw a woman with gray hair trimmed almost into a globe shape scrutinizing him. He looked back towards the door, torn, and then proceeded towards her.

Fear and uncertain recognition flickered across her face.

"Evening, ma'am," Thomas addressed her with a flawless, friendly Midwestern accent.

The woman listened carefully, her expression replaced with something verging on disappointment.

"As you can tell, I'm not from around here," Thomas continued cheerfully. "But I was wondering if New York is always so stormy this time of year."

"Well, um. Sometimes," the woman muttered. She scooted past Thomas as he saluted her.

"Thank you for the information," he called after her.

The boys, as always, were playing stickball, the youngest one now wielding the broomstick. He swung wildly as the ball spun past. The others guffawed wildly.

The girls continued skipping rope, darker echoes of adulthood seeping in their innocent verses.

> Daddy was a union man,
> Joined the strikers,
> Held up his sign,
> Got hauled to Rikers.
> How many months did he have to serve?
> One Two Three Four Five Six Seven.

Thomas strolled down the sidewalk towards Northern Boulevard, head up, inhaling the moist night air. He was now afraid of nothing but the fear that a decade from now Meghan would still be grieving, never having the fulfillment she mistakenly thought she had found in him.

He began to review the events starting from the realization that Jobim had been killed, the confrontation in Restaurant X, the consummation in the cloud storage room, but realized retrospection and speculation were futile.

When he stopped focusing on the events of the past few days, a hollow ache, as vast as a boulder of emptiness, afflicted him, the harsh realization that Meghan would never again be part of his ever-shortening life.

He trudged down the street towards Northern Boulevard, heading towards his personal appointment in Samara, knowing neither the time nor the place only its inevitability.

He stopped a few houses short of the end. A young couple stood beneath the yellowish sodium streetlight, not yet upgraded to more modern LED illumination.

The woman was slender and with dark hair banded into a ponytail that reached her shoulders. Her jeans seemed spray-painted on, and she wore a striped blue top that left her slender midriff exposed. The man was taller, with tattooed snakes and dragons that writhed their way up his heavily muscled arms to the sleeve of his Mets jersey.

The woman was in a half crouch, tugging on his arm as the man looked away with some annoyance.

"I took like halfway to forever to finally accept that I was your girl-friend," the woman said in half-sob, "and now you wanna just chuck me out into the gutter like some piece of garbage?"

"Shauna, you work in a diner for chrissakes," the man sighed. "Quit acting actin' like some damn soap-opera queen."

Thomas froze, an inadvertent eavesdropper to something he had no desire to witness. Humanitarian impulses surged within him, urging him to intervene as some sage, impartial counselor, but he knew that any words on his part would lead not to them reconciling but would present them with a fresh target upon which to deflect their anger. He barely breathed, not wanting to interrupt their argument by alerting them to his presence.

He could tell that from the couple's perspective, the entire universe had shrunk to the few square feet of sidewalk upon which they confronted each other.

"Sandro, I would go to the ends of the earth to be with you. Keep on living in this crummy rat hole that you seem to like. But it's like you're rippin' my heart right outta my chest, and you didn't even bother to knock me out first."

"What? You want I should hitch you?" he snapped. "That ain't me."

"I love you, Sandro," pleaded the woman. "You can't abandon me now."

"I ain't abandonin' you. I love you, too."

"Then why . . . ."

"I can prove I love you."

"Really?" Shauna lifted her face upwards, daring to catch the slightest intoxication of hope from Sandro's fixed expression.

"Ain't you ever heard? If you love someone, set them free."

"So?"

"So I ain't abandonin' you," Sandro replied, peeling her fingers away from his wrist. "I'm settin' you free."

He yanked his arm out of her grasp and wheeled away towards Northern Boulevard.

Shauna collapsed to her knees, sobbing, and making Thomas feel as if suddenly the entire world itself were bereft.

He crept backwards, head bowed.

The boys were still playing stickball – the Spaldeen swished before him and the smallest one dashed past Thomas, snatched it and spun around, hurling it at the player standing on the manhole cover, who triumphantly punched the boy running towards it. The runner tumbled.

Thomas paused, knowing what they did not, how these seemingly inconsequential moments in the tranquil nights were perhaps more precious and transient than any others that would ever follow.

He continued past the girls spinning twin ropes with apparently unending energy.

> When I get my Four-Two-Twenty,
> Gonna buy some Good and Plenty.
> Name the flavors in the box.
> Cherry and berry and chicken pox!

He continued back to Moira's house, carefully closing the gate and grateful that in his state of murky focus, he had neglected to lock the door.

He yanked his note off the wall, and ripping it into shreds, tossed it into the garbage can.

CHAPTER 26.

A Cab Ride Home

A taxi had just pulled up when Meghan dashed by the bouncers. They barely noticed her as she slid in to the back. The balding, paunchy cabby, however, was impressed and glanced through the partition appreciatively. "Queens. 57th between Northern Boulevard and Broadway," she said.

"You want I should take the Tunnel?" he asked as they pulled away.

"Whatever's fastest," she answered and then, under her breath, murmured, "By the skin of my teeth!"

She took her compact from her clutch bag and held it up to her face, peering over her shoulder at the traffic behind them as they pulled out onto Park Row. She froze when she became aware of headlights several cars back. The other vehicle seemed to be paralleling the cab's movements.

"I grew up in Queens. Nice place to raise a family. You married?"

"No," said Meghan.

The headlights followed them at an identical speed. Meghan could see the car had tinted windows.

"Stunner like you can get a guy easy. You live alone?"

"I got a boyfriend," said Meghan.

"Lucky fella. Planning to get married?"

They were approaching the entrance to the FDR when Meghan suddenly exclaimed, "Turn right! Now!" With a squeal of brakes, the cab veered up Centre Street. City Hall loomed gleaming and deserted; no one was working late. Behind them, a Pontiac low-rider continued out onto the FDR. Booming salsa music made the entire car shimmy. "Thank you. We'll pick it up at Grand Street."

"Whatever you say, lady."

The cabby tried to start several conversations until Meghan snapped, "Just drive, nosey. I got a lot of thinking to do."

"Hey, no offense meant," said Abe.

"None taken," she replied. They were driving by the New York County Court building, otherwise known as Central Booking, at 100 Centre Street, an Orwellian bloc of dull concrete and barred windows. Lights burned in many windows as the New York approximation of justice ground away. As she pondered the drab lives being pressed flat in the squat building, she wondered if there were a cell reserved for her. The thought horrified her.

She curled into the corner of the backseat, recoiling from the memories of the night, wondering how she had allowed herself to become so degraded. Although she considered herself a great sinner, she was horrified that she had been such a willing participant in her own moral breakdown. Activities, ideas in others that would have disgusted her beyond any possibility of forgiveness now controlled her. As the building lights flickered over her anguished face, she tried to justify her actions as required by the enormity of the circumstances in which she found herself.

She was not successful. She was forced to admit that the events of the past few days were so much larger than her own life. International killers, secretive multinational corporations headed by world-class degenerates, obscure intrigues – nothing had ever prepared her to deal with anything of this scope. Her job on the Lady Liberty, which had felt so confining and mundane, now seemed such a haven.

If she were ever able to return, she would settle back into it with such fierce gratitude and nothing short of the boat sinking would dislodge her from her thankfulness.

•

When the taxi arrived at Moira's house, light shone in the upstairs windows, the shades down. Meghan paid the cabby, taking no notice of the cabby's name on the hack license: Shirazi, Abraham.

As soon as she was inside, Abe speed dialed his phone. "This is 746-ABE. Dropped subject in Woodside," he said. "Says she's got a boyfriend. I'm staking out. I need the grey Chevy. Pronto." Thomas's silhouette crossed the window shades. "Hold on. I see his shadow."

When Meghan entered the house, Thomas rushed down the steps and swept her into his arms."

"What's that for?" she asked.

"Proof that I love you."

She smiled her crumpled smile.

Curious, he undid her raincoat to reveal her seductive black miniskirt and high boots.

"What is this?" he asked. "Have you turned Jezebel on me? You promised me you'd have nothing more to do – "

"No, Joan of Arc," protested Meghan.

"The one that was thrown to the dogs? Or the one burned at the stake? And that perfume? I hope our dear chef was enchanted. So you intend to make an ongoing affair out of your one-night stand."

"I didn't go see him," she said as she dropped her purse onto the sofa chair.

"Then where, pray tell, did you go?"

"The Spider Club."

She faced away, unable to look at him directly as she spoke.

"You what?" Thomas grabbed her.

"You heard."

Thomas held her at arm's length. "Of all the stupid, foolish idiocies. First you screwed that silly chef –"

"I didn't. And you promised you wouldn't mention it again."

"You actually thought you could seduce Murdock and get him to spare me? The idea of his bloody hands on you –"

"They never went near me." She lied, but only a little.

"The thought of you two even breathing the same air makes me physically ill. I would never have allowed it."

She removed her hat and flung it aside. "Don't you see?" she said as she undid her hair. "I knew it would be a long shot, but if it had worked . . . ."

"You pig-headed harpy. You have no concept of that man's ruthlessness. His sadism."

"Sadism is hardly the word for it," said Meghan.

"What did you do?"

"Nothing."

"Nothing?"

"I didn't even take my clothes off. Well, I did beat the crap out of him," Meghan admitted. "With a riding crop."

The image mollified Thomas somewhat. "Hope you left some welts."

"Striped him like a zebra," said Meghan. "But he didn't buy it."

"How much did you reveal about me?"

"I couldn't even bring up the situation," she answered softly. "He was incredibly suspicious. Thomas, I really intended to plead with him, offer him anything if he would let you live."

"What did you expect? It was insane to even try."

He again seized her by the shoulders.

"How did you get home? How do you know you weren't followed?"

"What do you think I am? An amateur?"

Meghan shook herself free.

"Compared to these guys."

"Murdock had these very peculiar plaster masks in his apartment. Do you know anything about them?"

Thomas went white and flipped off the light before Meghan could notice. "So they aren't simply a rumor."

"What do you mean?"

He shushed her, then crept to the window to cautiously peer out in the crack between the shade and sash. The street lay quiet in the moonlight. The only movement was the flutter of wind-tossed trees. A line of parked cars, the cab among them, though Abe was not visible, stretched out to Northern Boulevard.

"I might have been tailed, but I shook them. Stop being so edgy, Thomas. It was stupid and foolish and I was in way over my head. Okay?"

Her face glowed otherworldly from the lights of the pinball machines.

"But our fallback plan is Maxter the Fixture, right?"

Thomas bowed his head and said nothing.

"Thomas? Right?"

He shook his head, again without speaking.

"I take that to mean he's not coming to our rescue. Then what are the options now, Mr. High and Mighty? A bullet through your head?"

She tried to thread her fingers through his, but he kept his fist tightly clenched. "Thomas, our only hope is to go through with my plan."

"To butcher a perfectly innocent young chef?"

Thomas leaned against the Plexiglas scoop game. He clasped his hands and somberly studied the floor.

"No one's perfectly innocent!" snapped Meghan. "I told you. They'll figure it out. They're professionals, aren't they? No one's going to harm him," she said with amplified fervor that was as much to convince herself as Thomas. "Those few hours of confusion will give us just enough time to escape."

"Yearwood's losing his edge," Thomas said quickly. "Otherwise I would have been dead in a taxi cab outside the apartment. What if he doesn't recognize the substitution soon enough."

"Please, Thomas. You know even better than me, it's our only chance."

"And a slender one at that."

"Please, Thomas, please."

Trailed by a silent Thomas, she trudged up into the bedroom and shed her clothes with as little motion as possible. "Excuse me," she muttered as she went into the bathroom. She stood under the shower, washing her hair three times.

She turned up the shower as hot as she could stand, then scrubbed herself from head to foot. Again. And again. It was nearly an hour before she felt even partially cleansed.

As the sordidness she felt gradually trickled from her body and into the drain, another aspect of her situation struck her.

After so many years of either being snubbed by men or, more often, unconvinced by their attentions, Meghan had decided to exert her energy in other arenas. She had not been quite sure what she would accomplish, but the rewards would belong exclusively to her. Then suddenly, without warning or expectation, three men were in her thrall. Was it due to Thomas's benevolent influence, or had she acquired it earlier when she had decided to take herself off the market?

In either case, she was astonished to have this power and even more surprised to discover that she could use it.

How exactly to utilize the capability still eluded her, and she brooded about her plans for the following morning. Unable to come up with any alternatives, she tried to fathom how stacked the odds were against them. As the water sluiced over her, malleable, purifying, Meghan accepted the fact that she had no option but to go through with her initial scheme.

She wore Moira's pink robe when she emerged from the bathroom. Thomas lay on the bed, still dressed in the boiler suit, only the occasional flex of his mouth indicating how brutally alert he in fact was. His arms folded, he clutched his dashiki to his chest.

Meghan dragged her carry-on from underneath the bed and opened it beside him. She threw her few items of underwear into it.

"Not much choice, is there? So we're going through with the other plan, like it or not. Now listen up. I only have time to say it once. Tomorrow morning I'm meeting him. We're buying the tickets. Will they be watching your apartment?"

"Like vultures," said Thomas.

"That's what I thought." She selected a Laura Ashley dress and a pinafore from Moira's closet.

"You'll take him there."

"Yeah." Meghan began rummaging through Moira's shoes.

"Why the dashiki?" he asked.

"I'll pack it for you to wear on the beach."

She pulled out a pair of sandals.

"While the other will be dripping with his blood."

Thomas tucked the neck of the dashiki under his chin and held out the sleeve with his hands, sadly contemplating the fabric.

Meghan whirled on him, throwing a sandal at him with all her force. It went wide and fell harmlessly against a wall.

"Thomas, STOP THIS NEGATIVITY! You're going to jinx it. Something terrible WILL happen if you don't cut it out immediately."

Her whole being sagged. She crept slowly across the bedroom and knelt, laying her head on his lap. Her tresses fell in raven-colored waves across the dark green of the uniform. She tried not to whimper.

"I'm degraded. I'm lost. It's so hard, it's so hard."

"Meghan, Meghan. I'm sorry. How can you endure me? You're putting it all together, taking the risks for me, whilst here I sit, reproaching you."

He threaded and unthreaded his fingers in her hair. At last releasing it, he stroked her neck. "Tell me what's to be done. Shall I help you pack?"

"Clean up the kitchen maybe. Let's leave it nice. Would you write a note with money for pots and pans and the TV? Moira'd kill me."

"Consider it done," said Thomas.

Meghan tied the pink bathrobe more tightly around her as Thomas went downstairs.

She retrieved the fallen sandal, frowned at for a moment, then clasped it to its mate.

From the kitchen came the clatter of Thomas cleaning up as Meghan crossed to the dresser.

She held up the small manila envelope with the redemption instructions, kissed it, and set it beside the two wallets. Gil's was worn-out and thin; Thomas's slim, fattened with hundred dollar bills, made of well-sewn Italian suede.

She emptied the former: driver's license with Gil's hair close-cropped; dog-eared recipes; library card; insurance card with medical information; blood donor card, O Negative; membership cards, including one for Greenpeace; sixty-eight dollars. A recipe for quinoa bread.

Then she removed from the items from Thomas's: a platinum credit card, airline privilege cards, over a thousand dollars in hundreds

She sadly kissed the portrait of Gil on his driver's license and placed it in Thomas's wallet, then the rest of the items, and finally the recipe.

Then she put the credit card and airline privilege cards into Gil's wallet along with a few twenty-dollar bills.

She turned off the light and opened the curtains. Cheek against the window frame, she gazed into the unreassuring night. The wind soughed in the trees; the curtains ebbed and flattened in the cloud-speckled moonlight.

●

In the kitchen, Thomas hung up a final dishcloth. He picked up the impromptu chef's hat and set it on his head before he turned off the light.

"All tidy and shipshape," he said as he entered the bedroom. "Clean as a whistle. Neat as a pin. Kettle's scoured. Foodstuffs in the dustbin. 'Order is a lovely thing. On disarray it lays its wing'."

Meghan sat up in bed, hands clasped around her knees. "I have been thinking. It'll be suicide to try to go back into the city. So if we catch the LIRR at Mineola. We can get out to Montauk. From there we can catch the ferry to New London."

He looked at her, dubious.

"We should have six or seven hours for them to figure out what's going on. They'll never expect you to head away from the city, much less take buses rather than planes or trains."

"Well, I never expected myself to take buses."

"Please," she teetered on the edge of a bottomless precipice of weariness.

Thomas laid the chef's hat on the dresser and leaned against the headboard beside her. He turned her to face him; she looked blindly into his eyes. He kissed them closed.

"'And there I shut her wild, wild eyes / with kisses four'."

She clung to him. "Why do I want you more and more?"

"I, too. I never used to be insatiable."

"Me neither. If only we could make love forever," sighed Meghan, adding plaintively, "and never have to think."

"Oh, wouldn't that be the greatest blessing in the world? To be spared the misery of conjecture. To endure nothing but the delight of being together."

●

The street was deserted; no one saw the grey Chevy pull up beside Abe's cab. The passenger door on the cab and the driver's door on the Chevy opened simultaneously. The Chevy driver hopped into the cab as Abe circled around the front of the Chevy. "If they split up, stick with the guy," instructed the driver.

"Got it," Abe responded as he slid behind the wheel of the Chevy. The cab drove away, its lights off. Abe eased his new car into a slot a hundred feet from Moira's house and waited for the sun to rise.

CHAPTER 27.

Appointment in Gotham

At 7:45 the following morning, Meghan and Thomas were still asleep.

The increasing wind moaned through the telephone wires. The sounds of morning traffic came through the curtains. Dreams that nagged Meghan more than weariness finally forced her eyes open. She glanced at the clock and bounded out of bed.

"Shit! How could I forget to set the alarm?"

She slid gracelessly into her underwear and snapped on her bra.

Thomas, slowly coming awake, watched her performance. "I'll make coffee," he offered.

"No time," she replied as she stepped into her pantyhose.

Thomas rose, slid out of the borrowed pajamas and wrapped himself in a towel.

Meghan shimmied into the sundress and adjusted the straps. She put the small manila envelope into a zippered compartment in her handbag, then she flipped on the radio.

". . . high winds continue for the fourth day. The hurricane has stalled off the coast of Florida. Eighty percent chance of thunderstorms this afternoon. Z 100 drive time is ten minutes till eight. Now to Arlene Castro with Shadow Traffic," said the announcer.

At the dresser mirror, Meghan put the wig on and carefully adjusted it. She brushed out the few tangles and twirled it into a tight bun, onto which she pinned a tortoise shell clasp.

"Don't forget your wallet," she told him. "It's on the dresser."

"Thank you, Hal." The voice of Arlene Castro continued on the radio. "The winds overturned a tractor trailer on the Queensborough Bridge inbound lanes. No injuries. Ten minute delays which are expected to increase."

"Damn," said Meghan.

"One good wind and the city falls apart," Thomas muttered as he entered the bathroom.

"That means I'm stuck taking the subway."

"Be careful!" he called out.

"I'll buy a *Post* and bury my face in it all the way into the city."

In the bathroom, Thomas lathered his face and shaved haphazardly. Unable to meet his own gaze in the mirror, he lowered his razor, his eyes remaining focused on the sink.

"I'll call you as soon as . . . as it's – as soon as they're on his scent," Meghan called from the other room. "I'll ring once, hang up, and call back. Pick it up. The minute the coast is clear, you head out to LaGuardia. Don't pick up the phone, except for me. Don't answer the door. Keep clear of the windows. Did you hear that?"

"I heard," said Thomas.

Meghan put her raincoat on, picked up her handbag and carry-on and peered into the bathroom. "Bye," was all she could say.

She hurried across the room, but before she could reach the door, Thomas had intercepted her. He raised his hand in a STOP gesture.

Meghan skidded to a halt, dropping her carry-on.

"Not even a kiss?"

They clasped and rocked together.

"Can we actually go through with this?"

"Just a few little hours, and we'll be free. Together. For always," she said.

"You know you're risking death yourself."

"I'm a tigress. I've got nine lives. Kiss me. Now."

In the middle of their prolonged kiss, she broke away and hurried downstairs.

"'If 'twere done when 'tis done, then 'twere well / it were done quickly'," Thomas whispered to her departing back.

Downstairs, the door slammed. Through the gap in the curtain he watched as she hurried down the sidewalk, his expression filled with pride at her pluckiness and distaste at what he himself had provoked her into doing.

•

He was about to put on the French-cuffed shirt Meghan had bought him when he noticed the chef's hat on the dresser. He sadly smoothed it into shape and stood it upright on the dresser, either as a trophy or as a *memento mori*.

The image of himself in the mirror drew him inexorably. As he slid his arm into a sleeve, he tried to study his reflection but was unable to raise his eyes above the image of the towel.

He flung the shirt to the floor and slipped the dashiki over his head instead.

He finally looked at himself full face in the mirror, a dashing rogue clad in jungle green and midnight black, a herd of elephants thundering across his chest.

With a gleam of recklessness in his eye, he grinned.

Thomas returned to the kitchen and ripped another page off the pad he had used for Moira's note.

"Understand, dearest Meghan, when push comes to shove I find myself incapable –" he wrote in his precise graceful hand, using an Elysée pen that Meghan had bought him the previous Christmas. "– of permitting another man to die in my stead," he continued.

He ripped the sheet from the pad and crumpled it, then started on a fresh page.

"'When I am dead, my dearest / Sing no sad songs for me/ Plant thou no roses –'"

Again, he ripped the page from the sheet and tossed it aside.

At last he gave up trying to pen a note and searched the antiquated Yellow Pages for florists. He dialed one at random.

"Thomas Lockhart here. Can I pay for the entire order when you deliver? . . . Thanks. Now perfect blooms, please. Four white roses, four pink, four red . . . My name on the card; and the following message: 'Sweetest love, I do not go / For weariness of thee, / Nor in hope the world can show, / A fitter love for me. / But since that I must die at last, 'tis best / To use myself in jest / Thus by fain'd deaths to die'. Now read that back, please."

He was about to hang up when he remembered to order a spray of lilies-of-the-valley for Mrs. Carr.

Then he checked listings for car services that advertised Cadillac limousines.

In the tall grass of the backyard, Abe was taking a leak. As he zipped up his pants, he peered intently at the shaded windows, unable to detect any motion inside; nor did he notice Meghan slipping out the front door.

CHAPTER 28.

Sinbad Travel

The wind was whipping the awnings on Madison Avenue, buffeting pedestrians who furled in upon themselves like sea creatures in a storm.

Meghan paced restlessly, wishing she were anywhere but that street corner at that moment, wishing that she were anybody in the world but herself. She felt people giving her second and third looks. Nevertheless, she sensed Murdock's noose tightening around her. Gil was ten minutes late, fifteen. She half prayed that he would not appear but felt sickened at the future if he did not.

A young man, pony-tailed and with a European aspect to his clothes and demeanor, noticed her agitation. "Waiting for someone?" he asked. His accent had a soft Spanish undertone.

"Have you seen him?" Meghan nervously responded. "Tall. Dark, curly hair."

"No, I haven't." The man stared deeply into her eyes, and spoke in a voice that carried more than a hint of invitation. "It would be a real pity if he didn't show."

"Don't say that! I mean, maybe it would be wonderful! No, I – Never mind."

She wanted the stranger to go away, but her contradictory answers only seemed to intrigue him further.

"Excuse me," she mumbled.

The stranger backed away a few steps, his attention still focused upon her.

She entered Sinbad Travel, a bustling establishment furnished with half a dozen desks, bulletin boards and racks so overflowing it appeared that not another brochure could be stuffed into them. Seven agents strove to maintain chipper miens despite the pushy customers and continuously ringing phones.

A young black woman, her impressive corn-rowed hair tied into a shock at the back of her head, hung up the phone and nodded from her desk. "May I help you?"

"Has a young man been here about tickets to Key West?" Megan asked. "Very handsome. Dark curly hair. Doesn't sound like he's from New York."

The woman shook her head.

"If he shows up, just tell him to wait. I'll be back in half an hour.

She hurried out of the agency to hail a cab.

CHAPTER 29.

The Harshness of Second Thoughts

Meghan tossed a few bills at the cab driver and without even waiting for her change, grabbed her carry-on and slammed the door.

She rushed over to Gil's building and pressed the buzzer.

No answer.

Again.

She held the button down, "Gil! It's me. Meghan. Where are you?"

She tried all the buzzers in descending order.

"Who's that?" growled a gruff voice.

"Sorry," murmured Meghan. "Sorry."

She pressed the buzzer to Gil's apartment and held it down.

At last, Gil voice came through the tinny speaker. "Yes?"

"Gil, it's me. Meghan."

"Go ahead without me. I've changed my mind."

"But Gil, after all those arrangements. All the fun that we're going to have."

"Too much stuff to do before I leave. Can't afford to take the time off."

She exhaled, panting, relieved that they had at least made contact.

"At least let me return your wallet."

"What?"

"You dropped it at your audition."

"I'm sure I misplaced it here."

After a few moments of silence, the door buzzed open.

Meghan hurried up the stairs, where Gil stood in the doorway, in short cargo pants and a khaki-colored hemp shirt.

She fished his wallet out of her handbag.

"I went by the audition. To see how you did. Nobody knew anything about it. But the man in the house wondered if I knew you, and when I asked why, he said he found your wallet."

"I thought I'd lost my wallet before that."

"Are you sure?" Her reproving stare made him back down. "Just be thankful it showed up."

She handed it to him. He was about to open it when Meghan took it back from him. "I'll take it. I don't want to lose it again before we go."

He tried to take it back, but Meghan refused to release it.

"I'm not going. I've got too much to do before I leave."

Somewhere nearby Meghan felt the presence of Yearwood and the massive surveillance apparatus guiding an expert assassin towards the man she loved.

"What happened? Did Barbara get inside your head?"

"What happened was a bad night's sleep."

"Huh?" she reached out to stroke his cheek but he jerked his head back. "What does that have to do with us?"

"Ever since I met you, you've tried to change me –"

"I haven't been trying to change you," she protested. "I've been trying to improve you."

"– my life has gotten weirder and weirder. I've never been in trouble with the law since I was a kid. Now, all of a sudden, two cops appeared out of nowhere and start groping me. The more I'm involved with you, the less I recognize myself. But strangers seem to be recognizing me as someone I don't know. It bothers the hell out of me."

"Gil, we're connected on so many levels."

She felt that further lies would not add to the weight of the damage that had already been done. But she could not bring herself to utter the ultimate lie, "I love you."

"Please, just get the hell out of my apartment," Gil snapped. "Just get the hell out of my life."

She clutched his forearm, trying to conceal the anxiety beginning to spin out of control within her. "What are you talking about?"

"Please."

She stepped forward, backing him into the apartment.

"Meghan! Just give me my wallet."

"Please, give me five minutes."

She yanked her carry-on into the apartment and slammed the door.

"Meghan!"

He jerked her by the arm and forced her toward the door, steering her carry-on with her foot.

She twisted in his grip and nestled her head between his shoulder and neck. Desperation squeezed a plea from her. "Oh, Gil, Gil. I want you so much."

When he slowed his progress, she managed to lift herself a bit and press her lips against his.

Startled, he resisted only momentarily to accept her kisses with some perplexity. With her free hand, she held his head closer.

Her normally swirling thoughts refused to swirl, replaced by a numb, throbbing self-condemnation.

She pressed him closer, and felt his arousal as her breasts mashed against his chest.

He pulled himself away, "This is wrong, Meghan," he said without conviction.

"Whether it's right or wrong, I don't know," she whispered. "All I know is that I'm helpless."

"So am I. So am I."

She peeled his fingers from her wrist and began to unbutton his shirt. He pressed her now unresponsive lips to his, but he was so focused on the unexpected bounty of the situation that he did not notice that she did not react to his passionate kiss. He allowed her to unbutton the last button and slide it down his arms. Nor did he resist when she undid his belt, unzipped his short cargo pants and let them drop to his ankles.

He stepped out of his flip-flops and shyly began to unbutton her sundress. Soon it fell in golden ripples on the floor.

She felt herself stiffen, a frozen mass of apprehension and premature regret, and prayed simultaneously that Gil didn't see how torn she was and that he wasn't too sensitive to cease his seduction.

The momentum of desire had him its thrall, and he was aware of nothing but the beautiful woman standing in front of him, clad now only in her bra and panties printed with small pink flowers.

Meghan knew she had crossed the line, but when did she actually realize it? When she first thought up the scheme? When she continued with it despite Thomas's reprimand? When she began to unbutton Gil's shirt?

He drew her close and fumbled with the back of her bra.

She was tempted to ask how long it had been since he had made love but speech was becoming more and more impossible, a phenomenon that she could tell Gil was interpreting as intent and intensity.

When he fumbled for a clasp that wasn't there, she gently pushed him back with her finger, unhooked the cups of her bra, and allowed it to fall beside her sundress.

He kissed the side of her neck and then the junction at her shoulder. She stood, eyes closed as he stroked her right breast. He delicately ran his tongue around it, her nipples rigid as they refused to heed the shame and reluctance that coursed through her, more astringent and powerful than her blood itself.

He guided her towards the futon and eased her down.

Gil loomed above her, hovering above her with adolescent giddiness as he slid out of his jockey shorts. He was too focused on her body to notice her wig.

Flashbacks of Sister Mary Alberta and black-garbed widows chastised her without mercy. Chaos engulfed her thoughts, as recrimination cascaded upon recrimination.

Gil lay beside her, lips pressed against hers, which remained firmly unresponsive despite her feeble attempts to signal at least a flicker of desire to his flagrant kisses.

He slid his head down to kiss her breast in a slow, alternating rhythm.

She struggled to convince herself of the magnitude and expertise of the forces determined to destroy Thomas, and thus justify the morally unacceptable but inescapable course she had taken.

Only when she felt Gil tug on her panties did she realize that her legs remained tightly crossed. She reluctantly unclenched them and permitted him to slide them past her ankles.

He grasped her between her legs, rubbing her tentatively, almost as if in awe. Perhaps he was.

She tried desperately to disassociate herself from her body, to suspend herself in some far distant galaxy as Gil savored the pleasures of a body that did not belong to her.

"Meghan," he whispered, "Oh, Meghan."

Echoes of Thomas's more poetic endearments triggered disconcerting memories. As Gil entered her, she thought of the first time she and Thomas had made love in the most lavish apartment she'd ever seen. Disbelief and apprehension that she was a one-night stand soon to be discarded had rendered her almost frigid.

At she felt Gil within her, she realized she was powerless to rationalize or persuade or convince herself that she was not the most unredeemable sinner ever born.

He reached his hands under her bottom, drawing her closer. His athletic enthusiasm almost made her overlook his obvious inexperience. But Gil did not notice that he was making love to Meghan's form, while the essence of Meghan struggled to flee, to escape to some sanctuary where self-respect might still linger.

As Gil purred her name over and over, Megan realized her only salvation was to pretend that it was Thomas reciting her name almost like a poem.

She allowed herself to succumb to guilt-ravaged ecstasy. Gil, now panting like a stallion, increased the power of his thrusts.

Although she had no knowledge of covert actions, she knew they often occurred in situations of great disarray and unexpectedness, and no matter how hard she had tried to convince herself that Yearwood would recognize the substitution, there was a strong chance that in the chaos of the moment, Gil might actually be shot.

She determined to try to be present enough to please Gil, so if things went haywire, he would have at least experienced the most pleasure he had ever had on the final day of his life.

At last, in series of seismic convulsions, Meghan's body consummated the betrayal of the two people closest to her world.

With a contented sigh, Gil withdrew. He leaned one leg over hers, but she turned away, curling in upon herself.

She tried to suppress her crying, but tears seeped out of her of their own accord. She rubbed her eyes, feeling the make-up smearing.

"You okay?" Gil, his voice softened by afterglow.

She nodded, her back still to him.

"I suppose I could take a few days off. Might do me good to work New York out of my system."

She turned to him, trying to uncrumple her smile, and nodded.

"Meghan, you're crying."

"I'm okay. We better go."

He attempted to kiss her but she averted her face. He handed her panties to her but she shook her head.

"I need to take a quick shower first," she said. "You go ahead and pack."

●

After twenty minutes of scrubbing in near-scalding water and endless squeezes of a sports body wash, the surface of her body was the cleanest it had ever been while her soul felt more than equally soiled. She wondered if she would ever redeem herself from betraying the man she had most loved and another who was almost as naïve and innocent as she had once been herself.

A knock on the door. "You okay in there?" asked Gil's concerned voice.

"Out in a sec."

●

When she emerged, wrapped in a towel, Gil was standing there, his carry-on bag on the floor beside him. On the counter was a hemp sack in which he was placing a plastic container.

She pointed to the shopping bag. "What's in there?"

"I fixed us lunch. A melon salad, vegetable croquettes."

"Scrumptious," said Meghan, forcing a smile.

Despite her lack of inflection, Gil seemed pleased as he peered into the sack. "Nowadays they don't serve you anything unless you're flying to Antarctica or somewhere. Everybody is gonna to be so envious when we they see what we're eating."

"I'm sure they will," Meghan automatically replied.

CHAPTER 30.

Sinbad Travel Redux

Meghan and Gil entered the travel agency, Meghan on edge as she attempted to feign the role of eager lover. From a store entrance far down the block, Barbara, wearing a blue hoodie, fedora and dark sunglasses made careful note of their entrance. Her outfit did not succeed in disguising her but merely rendered her genderless.

"You look even more beautiful than I remembered," Gil whispered to her. "I was wondering if I had dreamed you."

He bent toward her. She evaded his kiss.

"Well, here I am and in person. Almost forgot. I have a present for you."

"Really?" said Gil.

"Let's sit down first."

They settled into chairs in the tiny waiting area. Meghan fished a tissue-wrapped package from her handbag and presented it to Gil. He accepted it reverently and carefully opened the paper, his eyes lighting up when he glimpsed the dashiki. He stood back up and unfurled the garment. "Fantastic! Thank you."

Oblivious to the sideways glances of the other customers, he removed his shirt and slid into the dashiki.

He stood and did his Thomas-walk.

The other customers looked more openly now, smiling.

Meghan bit on her knuckles, and when Gil laid his hands on her shoulders, she shrunk back.

"What's wrong, Meghan? Did it belong to him?"

"Oh, no way. It's brand new."

"And you went out and bought it for me?"

She roused herself to a pallid smile, her gaze see-sawing around the room, as she strove to keep it from intersecting Gil's.

"You're different. Have you changed your mind about going?"

"Of course not. It's just , . . ." Meghan trailed off.

"Level with me."

"I don't know. Maybe my horoscope is out of whack or something. Maybe I'm still haunted."

"You're such a mystery," he said. "I never know what to expect from you. We're going on vacation. You can't be like this the entire week."

"I'm so confused. Like . . . you're him, and he's you."

The corn-rowed woman bid a customer good-bye then turned to Meghan and Gil.

"Come on," said Meghan as she rose. "Let's get this over with."

She recklessly paid for the tickets with her credit card, knowing that even if they had filed an alert on it, they would look for her to be flying from LaGuardia to Key West.

•

Barbara, her expression forlorn but tenacious, crossed to the northeast corner of 77th against traffic. She entered the computer software store on the corner. Extracting a brochure from a display rack at the front, she thumbed through it without interest, her attention focused on the travel agency diagonally across the street.

•

In the darkened conference room adjacent to Murdock's office, the only illumination came from the glow of a television screen. Murdock sat on the edge of his chair, leaning forward and licking his lips.

Briefcase in hand, Yearwood entered, wearing a tropical shirt, sunglasses and Panama hat. "Ready, boss?"

Murdock started. "This'll make your mouth water."

Yearwood peered closely at the screen but was forced to remove his sunglasses. "Wait a minute."

Murdock had played back the video in ultra-slow motion. Onscreen, Meghan was tilting her head in tiny staccato jerks as she peered upward to stare at the teddy bear in Murdock's suite, his legs visible in the background.

"Something else, isn't she?" said Murdock. "Claimed her name was Brigitte Budica, but obviously that's an alias. She's from Queens. We'll find out who she really is soon enough."

The screenglow exaggerated Murdock's and Yearwood's features with lurid intensity.

"How do you like my collection?" asked the onscreen Murdock. He pointed to Jobim's simulacrum and added, "That's my newest addition."

"You did good, Yearwood," Murdock said.

"What are they?" Meghan asked on the screen.

"Plaster casts."

Yearwood leaned forward. "Pause it."

Murdock paused the recording as Meghan asked "What about the space in the middle?"

"That's her!" Yearwood exclaimed as he took a step back. "Shelley Clementine. Excellent work, boss."

"What do you mean?"

"That's Shelley Clementine."

"The one with Lockhart? No way," snapped Murdock. "You said she had red hair. That woman has black hair and glasses."

He grabbed Yearwood by the shoulder and shoved him closer to the screen. "Can't you see?"

"Maybe she dyed it," Yearwood said lamely.

On the screen Meghan had turned, the beginnings of terror on her face as she looked towards Murdock's trophy shelf.

Murdock released the assassin. "Are you absolutely positive this is the woman you saw in Lockhart's apartment?"

"I'm certain. But how in the hell did you track her down? Was it a lead from that TV show?"

"So Lockhart's her boyfriend. That's what she was up to last night! Damn that conniving little bitch!" Murdock slammed his fist on the table. "My intuition said that she was up to something. But I assumed it was blackmail."

Yearwood was about to make a wisecrack but thought better of it.

"By god she's going to pay. And pay. And pay. When you delete Thomas, you make sure she's watching. Let her know who's responsible. I warned her about people who take advantage of me. And she's gonna learn the cost of treachery the hard way."

"So where is she?" Yearwood asked.

Murdock pressed a key to bring up Moira's address. "And the son-of-a-bitch has to be hiding there also. Unless she's two timing him, which wouldn't surprise me."

Yearwood's lips moved as he memorized the address. "Abe's got it staked out."

"Queens! Of all places," said Yearwood. "Let me check with Ilsa, and I'll get right out there."

He flipped open his briefcase to insure that his space-age gun was in place.

"Just Lockhart. Don't hurt the woman. It's crucial that she sees what happens but remains safe," said Murdock. "Any suffering she does in the future is under my jurisdiction."

"She's gonna be sore no matter what I do," Yearwood replied.

CHAPTER 31.

Pursuit, as It Were

As Abe returned to the grey Chevy, a white Cadillac limousine, driven by an Asian chauffeur, pulled up to the curb in front of Moira's house. The chauffeur dialed a number on his phone and an instant later, Thomas leaned out from the bedroom window.

Abe looked up, shocked, as their eyes met.

"Father Abraham," Thomas merrily called out.

"Doubting Thomas!"

The chauffeur rolled down the passenger window.

"Down in a jif," Thomas said to him.

He pocketed the wallet from the dresser and picked up his briefcase.

He dashed down the stairs, and after a wistful glance at the pinball machines, loped out to the stoop. Abe interposed himself between Thomas and the limousine.

"Hold on, *havair*, I have the Chevy. I'll drive you," said Abe.

Thomas responded with an airy chuckle.

"You can go on, I'll take care of him," Abe told the chauffeur.

Protected by the opened door, Thomas called over to Abe. "Cadillac's more to my taste. But follow on, Abe, as I'm certain you will."

He scooted in and signaled to the chauffeur. The Cadillac took off.

Abe dashed over to the Chevy, the phone ringing in the passenger seat He tried to answer it as he started the Chevy and whipped away from the curb. But his fingers fumbled on the button and he disconnected the call. He held the phone in his lap as the two vehicles headed toward Northern Boulevard.

The phone rang again when Abe pulled onto the Queens-Midtown Tunnel approach. The traffic was heavy, and the limousine managed to pull two cars ahead.

"Yearwood! I'm tailing Lockhart. He's in a white Caddy limo. We're right at the Queens-Midtown Tunnel."

"So am I," said Yearwood. "On the Manhattan side."

His Buick reached the tollbooth.

"Can't turn around."

He dropped the phone into the console.

To make it more difficult to track their movements, his vehicle and Ilsa's had never been provided E-Z Passes. Normally, this was a good precaution, but, in this particular situation, it complicated things immeasurably..

He flung a ten-dollar bill at the toll taker. There was absolutely no way he could turn around. The phone fuzzed with static. The line went dead.

"Heading where? Abe! Talk to me."

Yearwood shouted into the phone. He pounded the steering wheel in frustration and screeched into the tunnel.

Heading into Manhattan, deep in the innards of the tunnel, Abe flung his own phone down. He was trapped behind a slow-moving Man-with-a-Van, and because of cars zipping past him, could not change lanes. No telling how many cars between his and Thomas's.

"Chalk one up for his Lordship," Abe muttered

Yearwood emerged into Long Island City and swerved through traffic till he reached Northern Boulevard.

A battered green van tried to crowd into his lane. Yearwood leaned into his horn and gave the driver a blood-chilling look. The driver backed off, apologizing so fervently that his lips could be easily read through the window.

Yearwood speed-dialed his phone. "Abe, you screwy bastard. Whadya mean he's in Manhattan? . . . . Of course I didn't hear you! I was in the tunnel."

He hung up, muttering, "Pain in the ass."

There was no way to make a legal U-turn, so Yearwood whipped the Buick into the opposite lane. Half-a-dozen drivers honked their horns; two gave him the one-finger salute. He ran a red light. A station wagon slammed on its brakes, narrowly missing him. A young mother swore at Yearwood with the fluency of a longshoreman. Her daughter, strapped in the kiddie seat beside her, watched her mother's performance, fascinated.

CHAPTER 32.

Park Avenue Revisited

Meghan and Gil, wearing his dashiki, walked east on 77ᵗʰ and rounded the corner. Even glimpsed through the buses and taxis on Fifth Avenue, Meghan cut a striking figure in her amber sundress. The old men sitting on the benches by Central Park craned forward to peer appreciatively at her. The trees above the loungers stirred and shivered like a single unit as storm clouds massed above in grey battlements.

"If we start for Kennedy at noon, we'll be there in plenty of time," said Meghan. "Let's go somewhere. Be alone for a few hours. You know we're right near the apartment."

"The one he left you?" Gil asked.

"Shall we?" Meghan threaded her arm through Gil's and did her best to appear enticing.

Gil could not disguise his reluctance. "I guess we will end up there, won't we?"

"If we make love there –" Meghan offered.

"– the ghost will get laid too," Gil finished. "Sorry. I know it's lame."

"You might well be right," said Meghan, eking a wan smile out of her torment.

"And you might well be insatiable." He smiled back at her.

They were midway down the block between 78ᵗʰ and 79ᵗʰ when Barbara peered around the corner of the Indian Embassy on 77ᵗʰ. She darted across Fifth Avenue and followed cautiously, a block behind.

Meghan and Gil did not speak as they continued up Fifth Avenue, each wrapped in their own dreads and anticipations. Flags and canopies whipped in the wind, marking time as rhythmically as African drums. Only when they crossed 84th did Meghan say to Gil, "We're almost there."

"He lived in one hell of a neighborhood, didn't he?"

"Come on, Gil. You're slouching again. Walk tall. I want to be proud of you."

She stopped and placed her hand on his arm.

"Gil, do you think you could do one last favor. Would you . . . walk like he did?"

"You want me to go in like him?" said Gil.

"And come out like yourself."

•

From her vantage point in the Temple of Dendur room, Greta saw Gil Thomas-walk into the apartment, followed by Meghan. She threw her binoculars into her knapsack and pulled out her and speed-dialed the ops coordinator. "His Lordship has just landed in Location Alpha. Looks like he has Lady Clementine in tow. They've got bags."

By that moment, Barbara had reached the Metropolitan Museum plaza and mingled among a group of Dutch tourists. When Meghan paused under the canopy and scrutinized the area around the apartment, Barbara ducked behind a man reading a map.

Yearwood fretted in the slow traffic approaching the Queens-Midtown Tunnel tollbooth, phone held to his ear while the ops coordinator patched Greta through. He listened attentively as the surveillance woman made her report.

"Hey, buddy," said the toll clerk, with nary a single personal item to distinguish her from all the other legions of toll clerks. "Three points for talking on your phone while driving."

"Good stuff, Greta. Call me back in five," Yearwood said into the phone, and then, to the toll clerk, "Yeah. I got it. Receipt please."

He handed the woman a few bills.

"How, the hell did he get there already?" Yearwood muttered as he waited for his change and receipt. "He go through a wormhole or something?"

•

Meghan, on edge, and Gil, his jaw set, crossed the lobby by the elevator. Julio poked his head out from the rear as the elevator doors opened. "*Hola, amigo.*"

Meghan quickly pushed Gil inside the elevator, into the corner.

"The cops been here, *la policía*," Julio stage-whispered in a hoarse voice. "Many kinds of *hombres siniestros*. I didn't tell them *nada*."

Meghan smiled at him as the doors closed.

"Bless you, Julio."

Gil seated himself on Meghan's carry-on. "Police? He took me for somebody else."

"That Julio. He's a little cop crazy."

Meghan tried to embrace Gil, but he held her apart.

"This guy. The one who died. Just exactly how much do I look like him?"

"Maybe more than just a little. Please, Gil, I need a hug. I need a kiss."

Gil put his arms around her, but kept his face out of kissing range. "That's the third time in two days. What did this guy to for a living?"

Meghan, on tiptoe, offered her parted lips. Gil remained troubled, his resistance at the point of collapse when the doors slid apart.

CHAPTER 33.

Home Again, Home Again

Meghan felt dislocated and disoriented as she and Gil entered Thomas's apartment.

Everything had been meticulously restored after the forensic team's search, as if it had never taken place. The only hint of the intrusion were the bright spots where fingerprint powder had been scrubbed off, making the surrounding area seem dirty by comparison. The room was at once welcoming and forbidding, simultaneously familiar and awful.

Gil was impressed but puzzled as he set his suitcase down. "He must have been a real prince."

"He was the best. But you are, too."

"Coming back must be so hard."

Meghan did not remove her handbag. "It's, it's – Gil, if you only knew how – but I'm so grateful you –"

She looked up at him, mesmerized by his trusting features, despite herself.

Her voice quavered. "All I want is for you to be so happy. I want to remember you."

"What's to remember? Let's enjoy now. We can remember when we get old."

"That's – that's a good idea. Now, let me make sure I've got everything."

She pulled her purse out of her handbag. "Purse."

The same for sun block. Increasingly frantic, she made a show of searching the bag. At last, she dumped its contents on the sofa and raked through them.

"Oh, no. Gil. I was so busy making sure I had everything. I don't have a driver's license. I overslept and dashed out in such a rush I left my passport at my apartment."

"Let's go get it then."

"No need for that. I'll go. You stay. Meantime, make yourself completely at home."

"What about his ghost? Won't it get jealous?"

"Don't be silly. You're not superstitious. Just imagine us on the beach."

"With your breast against mine."

"Exactly," said Meghan. "If I'm not back by four –"

"What?"

"– head for the airport."

"This is too much, Meghan." He flung his head back in exasperation. Thoroughly annoyed, he paced in front of the sofa.

"Listen, once we reach Key West, we'll do nothing but make love."

"Promise?" He swallowed hard.

"Promise."

She turned towards the door, then turned back. "Oh, I almost forgot."

She removed Gil's wallet from her handbag. He reached for it and began to open it, but she instead shoved it into his pocket. She smiled weakly at him and took his hand to lead her out.

Instead, he drew her towards him. Unable to evade his kiss, she allowed herself to accept the pressure of his lips. She found herself responding with unsuppressed sincerity. At last, she slipped out of his grasp. Before he could say anything further, she exited.

Gil stood for a moment, doubtful and immobile, his arms outstretched.

●

The storm clouds had accumulated into a solid black ceiling as Meghan fled the building. She hurried across Fifth Avenue and headed uptown. Her eyes were wide and burning, her lips fluttering as she repeated again and again in a low voice, "God forgive me. God forgive me."

"Lady Clementine has just left the apartment," Greta relayed to the ops coordinator, who in turned relayed the information to Yearwood and Ilsa.

"Gonna make our job a hell of lot easier," Yearwood observed when he hung up with the ops coordinator.

From the museum plaza, Barbara watched Meghan dash across Fifth Avenue. She studied Thomas's building, then looked uptown to see Meghan pause at the 85th Street entrance to Central Park.

Clearly torn, Barbara began to cross Fifth Avenue in the middle of the block. When a shoal of taxis bore down on her, horns blaring, she retreated to the curb. After a moment of hesitation, she headed uptown, towards the Park entrance.

Greta, binoculars to her eyes, leaned as far forward as she could without falling. Then she polished the lenses against her sleeve and looked again. She let the binoculars dangle as she rubbed her eyes with her fists and then hurriedly picked them up again to squint through the glass.

As the limousine pulled up in front of his building, Thomas leaned forward to speak through the partition.

"Well done!" he told the chauffeur. "How much.

"One-fifty, plus the bonus you promised."

"No problem." Thomas pulled out his the wallet and flipped it open. His jaw dropped when he saw Gil's eyes staring at him from a Washington State driver's license.

"Oh, my god," he whispered. "Oh, my god."

He flipped open the wallet and counted the bills. Sixty-eight dollars.

"Can I pay by card?"

The driver grunted.

Thomas took Gil's credit card and slid it into the reader attached to the partition.

After a few beeps a message came up onscreen. "Transaction Declined."

"Bloody hell," Thomas exclaimed. "There seems to be a problem."

He yanked off his wristwatch and slid it through the opening. "This is an emergency, and I forgot to bring any cash. Take my watch. It's a Vacheron Constatin."

The driver took it and eyed it suspiciously, "What am I supposed to do with this? Get the money back from the Nigerian fake-watch salesman?"

"Sell it. Pawn it. I don't care," Thomas said as he yanked the door open. "I guarantee you'll get at least 10k for it."

He leapt out of the car and dashed onto the sidewalk.

"Hey," called out the limo driver. "Hey!"

Thomas paused a beat under the canopy and looked up toward the Temple of Dendur. He bowed toward it, as if aware of Greta's presence, then dashed into the lobby.

Abe pulled up in time to see Thomas' dashiki through the lobby doors. He parked the Chevy behind the limo and when the limo screeched away, took its place.

Meghan sat down on a park bench. She drew her feet up, clasped her arms around her knees and pressed her face between them. She rocked back and forth, trying to make herself as small as possible, eyes closed to block the sight of something she both anticipated and dreaded.

A puzzled three-way conversation was in progress between Abe, Greta and Yearwood, who was stuck in traffic on East 40th.

"I know he went in," Yearwood snapped. "Ten minutes ago."

"No! He got out just this minute, I'm telling you," insisted Abe. "I've been on his tail."

"Abe's not bullshitting you, Randall," Greta insisted. "He DID go in. Twice."

Yearwood at last managed to speed onto First Avenue.

"Albert didn't see him slip out the back? Where was he anyway? Jerking off? If you goldbricks let his Lordship get away, you're gonna pull a long tour in Iceland."

He dialed Ilsa.

This time she answered. Yearwood spoke urgently, softly. "All systems go. Meet me outside his apartment as arranged. Over."

●

Gil, unhappy, ill at ease, explored the apartment.

He opened the door of the armoire. "Meghan, why are you lying to me? Where are your clothes?"

He returned to the living room and idly turned on the computer monitor.

He froze when he saw Thomas's unmoving image. He ran his fingers through his hair, then stared at them, as if some of the chemical reactions from the permanent impregnated themselves in his flesh.

He clicked PLAY.

The image of Thomas sprang to life and poured the vial of pills into his hand. He raised his glass in a toast.

"Here's to you, Yearwood, old killer. This video is for our beloved boss's trophy shelf. Souvenir of the one that got away."

He took the swig of scotch. Meghan's arm came into view as she jarred Thomas's.

"Thomas, stop it!"

Gil's jaw dropped a fraction of inch with every frame.

"Bloody hell!" shouted Thomas's image. "What are you doing here?"

Her bare leg enlarged to fill the television screen the instant before it went dark.

"Bitch! You lying whore!" Gil shouted with unadulterated fury, the thick rug and velvet curtains barely absorbing the force of his rage.

A movement in the wall mirror caught Gil's eye. He quickly looked upward to see another dashiki-clad figure reflected.

Gil whirled.

Thomas regarded him with half-smiling affection, putting a hand to his own hair.

"Of course you're not dead," said Gil. "Why should you be?"

"Because the warrant has been signed," Thomas gently offered.

"But – But – You're dead. Aren't you're dead?" Gil's expression was indeed as if he were speaking to a ghost.

"I soon shall be," Thomas said. "In a manner of speaking, yes, you are quite right."

"Were you ever in that plane across the Atlantic?"

"A time or two."

"Why don't you have any medical books? Why was she lying to me?"

The rough shape of the truth slowly dawned on Gil, but he was unable to pin down precisely the exact nature of Meghan's betrayal.

"The police, it's you they're after. And she's never coming back."

"Oh, but she will," Thomas replied. "I promise you."

CHAPTER 34.

Contact

Thomas peered through a gap in the velvet curtains. On the street below, Abe was arguing with a traffic cop, Julio gesticulating at the pair. Finally, Abe pulled out a wallet and displayed it to the cop. The officer scrutinized the credentials, hmmphed and continued down the block, unmollified.

No one noticed the Buick heading south down Fifth Avenue.

Curious, Gil came toward the window and peered over Thomas's shoulder.

"Stay back! Out of sight! Take that off!" He yanked the neck of the dashiki; the cloth ripped almost to the navel.

Gil stared down at the hanging shreds and lifted the gaudy folds in disbelief.

Thomas pulled the remnants down off his shoulders.

"Take whatever you like from my closet. Maintain *la bella figura.*"

"They're going to kill you."

His voice somewhere between disbelief and statement of fact, Gil tried to fathom the crisscross of suspicions, dreads, betrayals.

"It would appear."

"They would have killed me instead."

Gil was barely able to utter the words. His shock made him appear much younger, and Thomas's resignation rendered the latter so much older.

"You're safe as long as you stay here, away from the windows," Thomas reassured him. "Word of honor. Relax. Have a drink. I have some Distiller's Edition Lagavulin in the cabinet. A bath. Don't think any more about any of the last few days. Wait till she comes back."

"You're actually going down there?"

"'If 'twere done when 'tis done, then 'twere well / it were done quickly'," Thomas repeated, more to himself than to Gil.

He jockeyed Gil towards the sofa.

Gil recovered, stepping quickly around to block Thomas as he headed toward the door.

"No way I'm going to let you out. We'll call the police. Or go out the back."

Thomas gave him a look as Gil continued stubbornly, "If I let you go and you get killed, then it would be my fault."

Thomas smiled such a deep smile of pity at Gil's naïveté that even Gil realized the ludicrousness of his suggestions.

"Please, sir, don't be one of those bog-standard Americans whose conscience always works overtime. You were innocent before this whole affair commenced. No matter how it ends, your virtue will remain undimmed."

With a flick of his wrist, quicker than the jab of a reptile's tongue, Thomas grabbed Gil's wrist. His thumb gouged a spot between Gil's tendons, bending the younger man's arm sideways. Gil could only offer minimal resistance as Thomas led him to the sofa and forced him down.

Before Gil could massage his throbbing wrist, Thomas shook his hand.

"Pleasure meeting you, old chap."

He started off with his springy lope, the half smile on his lips.

Gil leapt up. "Wait!"

He ran to the door as it closed and fiddled desperately with locks he could not get open.

•

Meghan rose from her bench in Central Park and squared her shoulders. She twisted her hair, psyching herself up. She started back toward Fifth Avenue. A low wind moaned through the trees overhead, soft but chilling as a banshee's cry.

Barbara swung around through the stone-lined gate and found herself face-to-face with Meghan. She grabbed her adversary by the shoulders. "Where's Gil? What have you done with him?"

Meghan was stunned from reverie into reality, both states equally grim. "Why are you here?"

"What are you doing to him?"

"Barbara!"

"Who'd you expect?"

"You love him, don't you?"

"Enough chitchat. What are you up to?"

"Go away!" Meghan begged. "Don't stay here."

"I'm not going away!"

"You never should have followed us."

"What's going to happen?" Barbara pleaded. "You wouldn't hurt him, would you?"

Meghan shook her head, her mouth open.

"You would!" Barbara grabbed Meghan by the shoulders. "Listen, you rotten bitch. If anything happens to Gil. If he even gets scratched, I swear I'll kill you. I swear –"

Tears spilled from Meghan's eyes.

Barbara softened. "You've been in his arms. In his bed, no doubt. You care about him, don't you?"

"Yes," Meghan admitted. "I do."

Barbara pulled her by one arm toward the building entrance, entrance. "Come on then. If he's in some awful danger, let's go. We can help him."

Meghan allowed herself to be pulled along until Barbara, impatient, released her hand and rushed down Fifth Avenue.

Yearwood finished buttoning up the Emergency Medical Service – EMS – tunic as he stepped out of the Buick near East 85th. He surveyed Fifth Avenue, his poise and gaze as feral as a leopard's.

When she spotted him, Meghan shuddered. All her mental preparation did not prepare her for the depth of fear the assassin aroused in her. She felt her throat tightening, her chest constricting so much that even drawing a breath was almost impossible.

Yearwood walked briskly down Fifth Avenue. He slid his hand under his tunic as he crossed East 85th with the light, oblivious to Barbara and Meghan.

Thomas, head high, walked proudly out into the sunlight.

●

In the Queens spotters' basement, in the next-to-last cubicle in the second row, a nervous older woman, with wrinkles that suggested a life spent in the sun and several packs of cigarettes a day, observed the scene unfolding outside Thomas's apartment.

She flicked a switch and the red light above her came on. Almost immediately two black-suited men appeared behind her. She started to rise, but the taller of the pair indicated that she should sit.

The young man beside her watched the exchange, and with a few strokes on his keyboard, he too saw Thomas emerging from his building.

He whispered to the Asian woman beside him, and she, too, switched to the scene of Thomas surveying the street.

Within moments, every single monitor was displaying the scene as Thomas spoke to Julio, who was putting a cloth and bag of brass polish into a bucket.

●

Meghan was too far away to discern that it was the man she loved. Having no reason to think otherwise, when she glimpsed the dashiki, she assumed the man was Gil. She tried to speak, but no sounds came from her mouth. She covered her eyes, a sob already swelling up in her throat.

Barbara, not looking back, impulsively darted through the honking traffic.

Julio had gone back inside and the traffic cop had continued south on his rounds. Abe had pulled out to circle the block and was not in sight.

Barbara sprinted towards Yearwood as he manipulated his gun inside his tunic to draw a bead.

Thomas spotted the assassin and waved cheerfully, stepping forward to make himself a better target. He looked Yearwood dead straight in the eye.

"GIL!" Barbara screamed. WATCH OUT!"

Yearwood, distracted, lost his aim.

Thomas paused in his moment of sacrifice and stared past Yearwood to try to determine the identity of the young woman.

Hearing the exchange, Meghan squinched her eyes and covered her ears with her hands.

Yearwood aimed again.

Barbara leapt and bowled him over with a flying tackle. The gun fired, its peculiar hiss almost inaudible. Yearwood's tunic flared outward, a charred hole torn through the fabric.

Thomas fell backward, wounded and unconscious.

Yearwood struggled to rise but Barbara pinned him down. Passersby paused, uncertain of the connection between the scuffling pair at the end of the block and Thomas, fallen beneath the canopy.

"Help! Murder! Police!" said Barbara. Turning her head aside, she shouted at Meghan, "I'll get you."

Yearwood seized the opportunity to coldcock her with the pistol. Quickly, gently, he rolled her off and fled to his car. No one intervened, or even knew if they should.

A messenger hopped off his bicycle and allowed it to crash on the sidewalk. He knelt by Barbara's side, gently cradled her head as he reached for his phone.

Julio hurried from the building to stoop by Thomas.

Several passersby rubbernecked around the wounded man and unconscious woman. Most hastened past, pretending not to see.

Greta was running across the street as Abe came panting around the corner.

Meghan stood on a bench across Fifth Avenue. She craned to see the man lying on the sidewalk in the green and white and black dashiki, newly patterned with red.

Like a sleepwalker, she stepped away from the bench, looked down the street and spotted a phone kiosk.

She prayed that it was working and raced towards it, oblivious to the pedestrians who swore at her as she buffeted them aside.

She lifted the receiver to her ear, her finger poised over the dial, uncertain, her eyes glazed.

Beside her, a stout, well-dressed, blue-haired old woman shouted into the receiver that she held at arm's length. "Whadya gotta do to get an ambulance in this town? I tell you 911 doesn't answer."

Meghan at last dialed Moira's number.

The phone rang unanswered on the kitchen table, surrounded by Thomas's crumpled notes, its sound mingling with the chants of the girls jumping rope on the sidewalk outside.

> Cinderella, dressed in yella,
> Went downtown to meet her fella.
> How many kisses did he get?
> One. Two. Three –"

But the skipper stumbled before the fortunate fella had received his fourth kiss.

On the third ring, Meghan hung up.

CHAPTER 35.

Ambulance

In the garage of Lenox Hill Hospital at East 77th and Lexington, two EMS technicians walked along a row of ambulances. One was on jacks.

"Gotta gunshot and an unconscious. We need a honeymoon special," said one of the technicians, a stocky man with a soft-Haitian accent and the "Jean-Baptiste" on his nametag.

"This one," suggested Ernie, the second technician. Wiry, light-footed, his voice was harsh with hints of his native Brooklyn.

"Forget it. Catches fire." Ernie pointed to another one. "Naw, got a busted axle," said Jean-Baptiste.

He proceeded to a third one and climbed into the driver's seat. He started it with difficulty as his partner got into the passenger's seat. The ambulance backed ten feet out of its slot and stalled. Both technicians cursed as Jean-Baptiste struggled with the ignition. At last, he managed to get the engine revving.

He flipped on the lights, and the ambulance lurched out of the garage.

•

Thomas lay amidst a knot of people, his dashiki soaked with blood.

Julio now knelt beside him, pressing against his wound as an old woman hovered, reciting the rosary.

"*No me mueras.* Don't die, *amigo*," Julio begged. Over and over, he repeated the healing children's rhyme. "*Sana, sana, culito de rana. Si no sana hoy, sana mañana.*" ("Heal, heal, little tail of a frog. If you don't heal today, you'll heal tomorrow.")

Sirens blaring, two NYPD patrol cars had raced up, and slammed to a stop beside the cars. Four uniforms, leapt out, guns drawn but held at their sides, and surveyed the scene. Two headed toward Barbara, two toward Thomas.

"What's keeping them?" the old woman grumbled into the phone. "Five blocks already!"

The rain began to fall with leaden drops.

Two blocks east, at 85th and Madison, a car had skidded into another, gridlocking the intersection. The ambulance sat blocked on Madison, siren howling futilely.

The ambulance driver shouted into the microphone. "Clear the intersection! Move to the side!"

Cars squeezed to one side to allow the ambulance to squeak through to East 85th.

Meghan had returned to her bench, indifferent to the rain, her cheek resting on her clasped hands. She barely noticed either the policeman examining Barbara and Thomas nor the ambulance screeching to a stop.

The younger technician hopped out, performed a quick assessment on Barbara, then nodded toward Thomas.

Jean-Baptiste raced over to Thomas, and checked his wound and vitals. His partner hurried over with an intravenous line and bottle, which the Haitian inserted into Thomas's arm.

Ernie slid out the ramp and wheeled a gurney out of the back. With tenderness and caution, the pair hoisted Thomas onto it, and wheeled him into the ambulance.

Next, they retrieved Barbara, still unconscious, from the sidewalk, eased her onto a gurney and wheeled her in beside Thomas.

Ernie hopped out, shut the door and returned to the cab. He started the engine and flipped on the siren.

The cops spread out among the passersby, notepads in hand, as an unmarked car and two sports-jacketed detectives jumped out.

•

Gil peered through the curtains in Thomas's apartment.

Meghan, a pony-tailed man in a suit, and a plump woman with a German accent had all hailed the same cab and were arguing vociferously over it.

Gil struggled to open the window.

Meghan! Wait!" Gil shouted, his voice unheard in the din of the Upper East Side.

Meghan settled the argument by thrusting herself into the cab and slamming the door. It pulled away, leaving the man and German woman to vent their mutual anger at the usurper.

"Where to, lady?" The driver was in his thirties and had a skullcap bobby-pinned to his hair.

"Jamaica Station, Queens." But then almost immediately she said, "No, make that Lenox Hill Hospital. I think."

The driver turned around.

"I've changed my mind. Jamaica Station."

"If you didn't know where you were going, you should have let that other woman take me while you were making up your mind."

Meghan swallowed hard. "I guess I have time to go by Lenox Hill first."

"Thank you," snapped the driver.

"Murderer," Gil, unheard, shouted at the departing cab with Meghan in the back.

●

In the back of the ambulance, Thomas lay on the left-hand stretcher, and Barbara, a moist towel on her head, lay on the right.

Jean-Baptiste sat between them, monitoring Thomas's vitals.

Barbara moaned for a few moments as consciousness returned. The towel fell, revealing a bruise on her temple. She struggled against her restraining strap, groggily trying to get to Thomas. "Oh honey sweetie darling dearest, you're alive! Alive!"

Jean-Baptiste eased her down.

"Lie back now. He's gonna make it, sweetheart. I can tell."

Gratefully closing her eyes, Barbara collapsed back onto the gurney.

●

The ill and injured clustered four deep around the intake desk of the Lenox Hill emergency room.

A black man in khaki uniform, holding his bloodied bandaged hand.

A white-haired woman in a colorful smock, moaning in pain.

A heavyset, Hispanic woman unconscious upon a gurney.

A young woman dressed in black, her nose pierced with a silver ring, thrust a crying baby at the starched, Eastern European LPN standing at the intake desk.

Meghan, hair slick from the rain, pushed her way through.

"This is no city hospital," the nurse snapped at the woman with the nose ring. "You take the kid down to Bellevue."

"Please," begged the young woman. "You got to –"

"You heard me," said the nurse and turned away.

The woman sadly gathered her child and trudged toward the exit.

"There was a victim of a shooting. Over by the Museum," Meghan spoke so quietly the nurse strained to hear her.

"The gunshot? Got no information yet. I'll call you when we know. Until then, will you sit down?"

"You must know something," Meghan said, still softly, but more insistently.

"He's probably on the way to the Trauma Unit," replied the nurse with some irritation.

"Where's that?" asked Meghan.

The nurse, exasperated, ignored her as she turned to the next supplicant.

•

In the hospital laboratory, cluttered with display screens, instruments pumping blood through Tygon tubes, trays full of labeled vials, a young orderly hovered over the lab technician, a woman in her mid-thirties, whose dark hair was heaped beneath a Tyvek cap. A clipboard, forms and blood-donor cards, including the one from Gil's wallet, were laid out before her.

She signed off on a form and flipped it up to the next one on the clipboard.

"Hey, dollface. Let's shake it," said the orderly.

"Get off my case, would ya. I got fifteen crossmatches ahead of ya," the woman responded.

"They're going to be screaming for this in surgery in just a few minutes."

The woman held up two slides. "Gilbert DeLeo. Gabriel Leonard. One's O negative, one's AB positive. Now which one . . . ."

"Here, dopey. Says right there, AB positive." The orderly indicated Gil's insurance plan card.

"It does indeed," the woman admitted.

"Thank heaven's he's a Universal Recipient. The blood bank's running low on just about everything."

•

Meghan continued pacing the emergency room, waiting until the intake desk freed up. She again approached the LPN, who glanced at a form and spoke before Meghan had a chance to phrase her question.

"He's been stabilized downstairs. He should be heading up to surgery soon."

"He's alive," Meghan whispered. She shut her eyes and supported herself on the edge of the desk. Relief and distress battled each other for supremacy over her expression.

"You a relative?" asked the LPN, softening.

Meghan quickly dropped her left hand out of sight. "His wife."

"Okay. Waiting room, tenth floor." Meghan turned toward the elevators as the LPN said, "Follow the arrows, Mrs. DeLeo."

Meghan froze.

The only way they could have gotten the name was from the identification in the wallet.

And Thomas's wallet was now the one with Gil's name.

She swallowed her words. Summoning every smidgen of self-control she possessed, Meghan staggered into the elevator.

CHAPTER 36.

OR #3

In the laboratory, the orderly and technician continued to bicker.

"You're probably right," the woman responded. "But I'm not going to end up like those people at Coney Island Hospital who mixed up the wrong types."

"Yeah, getting fired would be a real drag," admitted the orderly.

"Ending up on the cover of *The Post* because you killed a patient would be a hell of a lot worse," said the technician as she held a slide up to a viewing box. "It would be beyond incompetence; it would make us murderers."

"The guy might be dying. You gotta get his blood down there ASAP," the orderly complained.

"I'm hurrying, I'm hurrying," muttered the technician. "But I'm not about to hurry some poor slob into an early grave."

She ripped the print out from the blood typing-machine. "O positive?"

•

Meghan rushed down the silent corridor, peering through the observation windows into the operating rooms. The first and second were empty. She dashed to the third, where a surgical team labored intensely over their patient. A glimpse of dark curls was visible at the head of the operating table. Meghan gasped, unable to breathe, when she heard the high-pitched warning of a heart monitor.

"Blood pressure's dropping," said the anesthesiologist. His glasses gave his dark face an owlish cast.

"Adrenaline! 500 cc," the surgeon, a pale young man, spoke with urgent authority.

"He's coding!" said the scrub nurse.

"Adrenaline, 500 cc," said the second nurse as she prepared the injection.

"Cardiac arrest," said anesthesiologist.

"Give me the paddles."

The surgeon was pounding on the man's naked chest. The second nurse handed him the defibrillator paddles and the surgeon positioned them. The team was too focused on their procedures to notice Meghan's frantic face flattened against the window.

"One. Two. Three. Now," said the surgeon.

The scrub nurse triggered the defibrillator unit.

Meghan glimpsed a leg convulsing under the sheet. The monitor beeped irregularly, then resumed its warning signal.

Meghan, against the door, her arms wide, pleaded with the universe. "O doctor, O nurse, Please, save him."

In the operating room, the team persevered. "Four. Five. Six. Seven. Again," said the surgeon.

Again the connection, followed by convulsions.

The team waited for the heart monitor to beep, and when it remained mute for a few more minutes, the surgeon said quietly, "He's gone." He removed his cap. "Disconnect him."

Meghan burst through the door. "THOMAS!"

The team halted, staring at the screaming intruder.

"Get her out of here," the surgeon barked.

Meghan flung herself towards the onrushing group.

"He isn't dead! I won't let him be dead."

"Who's Thomas?" the scrub nurse managed to utter.

"He's not Gil!" shouted Meghan as the nurses vainly tried to pinion her.

She broke through to the operating table and stopped. The patient on the table was neither Thomas nor Gil but a young Hispanic man whose curly hair flowed over the edge of the pillow. His eyes were closed, and the expression, at least that part visible beyond the edges of the anesthesia mask, seemed to be puzzlement rather than agony.

•

Ten floors below, an orderly wheeled Thomas, on a gurney, into the elevator. He had turned around to press the button when a voice called out behind him, "Stop!"

He paused as a heavily bandaged patient was guided in on a gurney by another pair in EMS uniforms: Yearwood and Ilsa.

Puzzled by the intrusion, the orderly peered out into the corridor. When he pulled his head back and the doors slid shut, Ilsa pulled the Emergency Stop button.

"There's been a mistake," Yearwood smiled at the orderly. "You have the wrong patient."

"That's impossible."

The orderly was slight and blonde, his accent noticeably Southern. Something about the pair, their uncertainty, some discrepancy in their uniforms and the scorched hole in Yearwood's tunic, made him very nervous.

"Listen, I've got to get him up to the O.R."

"That's not Thomas Lockhart there," said Yearwood.

The orderly relaxed. "Of course not. It's Gil DeLeo."

Yearwood and Ilsa exchanged a puzzled glance, then both studied Thomas's prone form, breathing slowly but steadily.

"That's the problem," Yearwood said smoothly, pointing to the gurney he had just brought in. "This is Gil DeLeo."

The orderly bent over toward the patient the pair had brought in the elevator. "This man is dead."

"The guy's a genius," muttered Ilsa. "Let's get out of here."

She walked around to the head of Thomas's gurney and pushed the orderly aside to grip the handle.

"What are you doing?"

"Mr. DeLeo has an appointment with us."

"He has to get up to surgery," the orderly said with increasing agitation.

"Take him wherever you like. To the Central Park Zoo for all I care. That's not my problem."

"You can't do this. I can't do this."

Yearwood eased his pistol from behind his waistband and held it under the orderly's chin. "I'll bet you can. Just tell 'em Mr. DeLeo expired."

OR #3

Although the weapon was small and its goldenrod color not nearly as intimidating as gunmetal blue, the orderly got Yearwood's point. He flinched; his eyes grew wide, but he did not cower.

"Hurry up, Yearwood," Ilsa chided.

Yearwood glowered at her, then said, "My assistant observed that you're a genius. Even a three-year old knows how to keep his mouth shut. An Einstein like you should find it easy."

"Yeah, well I'm going to alert –"

"Who? The people I work for keep track of things. Particularly people who remember things they should have forgotten and are stupid enough to tell other people."

Ilsa pushed the Emergency Stop knob back in. The doors slid open. After ensuring the corridor was empty, she and Yearwood quickly wheeled Thomas through the swinging doors out onto the loading dock platform.

As they were loading their trophy into an ambulance, Yearwood studied Thomas's expressionless face. "Think we'll be able to get anything out of him?"

Ilsa scrutinized Thomas's shallowly breathing body with a practiced professional eye. She shook her head. "I just don't know."

"Come on," Yearwood. "It's a chance we gotta take."

They wheeled Thomas out to the Intelligence Enhancement ambulance, and Yearwood opened the door.

●

In the hospital ten storeys up, a young African-American intern escorted Meghan down the corridor.

"So where is Thom – Mr. DeLeo? Do you think he's okay?"

At the other end a surgical team – surgeon, anesthesiologist, two nurses – was coming through the swinging doors. They walked on the balls of their feet, tense, confident, expectant. Like a baseball team about to take the field before a crucial pennant game.

"If Dr. Iyer can't save him, nobody can," the intern replied with hopeful encouragement. "Now, I'm afraid you're going to have to go out into the waiting area."

A Filipino nurse hurried past them. Something about her fixed expression filled Meghan with foreboding. She turned around to watch the nurse's progress and felt the intern's hand upon her arm, light but insistent, urging her down the hall.

The nurse spoke quietly to the surgeon, the conversation transferring some of the grim cast of her face to that of the surgeon's coffee-colored one. He removed his cap and shook his hair free as he spoke to the members of his team.

Meghan could see their postures sagging, their tension easing in a way that terrified her.

She broke away from the intern and raced down the hall, the intern pursuing. He caught up to her as she reached the team to address the surgeon.

"Mr. DeLeo. Are you going to operate on Mr. DeLeo?"

The surgeon looked at Meghan, hesitating for a second before he turned to one of the nurses, a tall Nordic woman, with big bones and a no-nonsense face. The surgeon nodded and somehow the nurse instinctively understood the instructions implicit in his glance. Her hands dwarfed Meghan's as she took the latter's into her own.

"We can go outside and talk," the nurse said in a soothing voice.

Meghan jerked her hands free. "No, tell me now. I want to know what's happened."

She glanced from face to face. The team members avoided her look, except for the tall nurse, who again tried to take Meghan's hand.

"It can't be," she implored them. "Are you all such cowards? Can't you tell me straight? Did Gil DeLeo make it or not?"

At last, the surgeon sighed and uncomfortably shook his head: "No."

Meghan shrieked as all the pressure of the last few days vented from her.

She was about to scream again when the intern clasped his hand across her mouth.

"Sorry to bother you folks," he said.

He took Meghan's arm and half led, half dragged the unsteady woman towards the swinging door.

When he removed his hand, she did not scream, but gasped with chesty sobs.

"I'll go with you," the tall nurse called out.

She quickly caught up to them and laid her hand upon Meghan's shoulder. "I know this must be terribly dreadful –"

"Don't make it worse with idiotic platitudes," Meghan snapped through her tears.

This quieted the nurse until they passed through the swinging doors into the waiting room.

"Would you like to see a counselor?" suggested the nurse. "There's one on duty right now. Or a chaplain or a priest. If we can do anything to help you –"

The elevator doors opened and Barbara, her head bandaged, ran out. She immediately took in the tableau of intern, Meghan and nurse and dashed over to confront them.

"It can't be true. The man in the ambulance told me he was going to make it. Gil can't be dead."

She slapped Meghan with a ferocious spontaneity that stunned the intern and nurse more than Meghan.

"It's your fault. You killed him. Why did you do it?"

Barbara drew back her fist for another swing but the intern pounced on her, pinning her arms to her side as Meghan studied her, meek and morose.

"Gil was such a beautiful person. There wasn't anyone like him in the world. He's dead and you killed him!"

"It wasn't Gil," Meghan managed to say. "Gil's alive,"

Barbara did not let her guard down, but seemed less ready to strike. "Are you sure? How do you know?"

Meghan considered the dashikis, the switched wallets, the foolish nobility of Thomas's unannounced sacrifice, and realized she would never be able to explain the complexities of the situation.

"I'm positive." Her lips fluttered weakly as she managed to repeat, "I'm telling you Gil's alive."

The intern and nurse glanced at each other.

"I'm sorry, miss," the nurse insisted softly. "But he deceased downstairs, several minutes ago."

"That wasn't Gil DeLeo," Meghan stated, with matching softness but infinitely more obstinacy.

Barbara glanced at the intern and nurse. Their heads, shaking with subtle sadness, indicated that they thought Meghan, unable to bear the truth, was denying it.

Studying her adversary more closely, Barbara decided that Meghan was indeed telling the truth. Her eyes squeezed shut, her lips parted, Barbara shook her head as though to clear it. Hope reviving, she cupped her hands on Meghan's slapped cheek.

"I believe you." Then, to the intern and nurse. "It's okay. I'll talk to her."

"Are you sure?" said the nurse. "She seems –"

Meghan weakly waved the pair off.

The two left reluctantly, continuing to stare over their shoulders as they passed back through the swinging doors.

"Then tell me what's going on? Where is Gil?"

"Could you get me a glass of water first?"

"Do you promise not to run away?"

Meghan nodded.

Barbara, suspicions still not absolutely quelled, headed towards the back of the waiting room where a small queue gathered around the water cooler near the nurses' station.

The instant Barbara turned to speak to a nurse at the counter, Meghan hurried to the window. The catch was stuck and she had to stand on tiptoe to hammer it loose with the side of her hand. The window itself was stiff and required every ounce of Meghan's strength to force it up. But once she pushed the sash open the first few inches, the window rose easily in its tracks.

A gritty breeze gusted in, carrying with it the bustle of the streets far below, the exhortations and plaints of the vehicle horns and more than a hint of imminent rain.

She peered longingly down ten stories. 77th was clogged with Yellow Cabs and cars dropping off patients and visitors. Nurses and doctors in scrubs and hospital whites threaded their way purposefully among the more leisurely pedestrians. A construction crew was erecting scaffolding across the block; she could almost read the words on their hardhats.

Behind her, the elevator doors were opening. She unsteadily lifted a leg atop the sill, needing a moment to compose her last thoughts, but knowing that if she took that moment, she might lose her opportunity for her aching devastation to cease.

"This is for you, Thomas," she murmured. "I'll see you very soon."

OR #3

She hesitated an instant, the empty air so refreshing, so inviting, but qualms of a greater and overbearing guilt hindering her from jumping. All the moralizing she had preached to Thomas, her revulsion at even the idea of suicide, were overwhelmed by the tragedy that she herself had instigated.

Meghan flung her head back. She closed her eyes and gratefully released her grip from the upper sill to clutch her miraculous medal with the portrait of the Virgin Mary.

CHAPTER 37.

Thwarted

Instead of falling into the inviting air, Meghan found herself jerked back into the waiting room to stare up into Gil's furious face; he again wore his hemp shirt. The torn dashiki was loosely knotted around the strap of his carry-on.

"You just don't give up," he shouted. "Do you, Meghan?"

"Let me go."

She struggled to climb back up on the sill but Gil refused to release her.

"Why did you do it?" snapped Gil. 'I want to know why you tried to kill me."

"It wasn't –" Meghan began.

"Or have me killed or whatever."

"Listen, you've won," said Meghan. "You're alive."

"Downstairs they told me I was dead. Didn't bother to correct them. But your lover was the most honorable man I ever met. He died for you, didn't he? Just marched on down there, brave as could be. A noble man like that deserved a hell of a lot better than a devious bitch like you."

"Love made me a monster. I deserve whatever happens to me. You wouldn't know how I feel because perhaps you've never held anyone in your caring spot, anyone you wanted to protect, shelter from all the crap around you. I've lost the only person who still cared for me. The only man I could trust."

"You?" Gil shook her with fury. "Talking about protecting others? The most deceitful, cold-blooded manipulator I've ever met, daring to mention the word 'trust'. It stinks when it comes out of your mouth."

"Listen, I'm doomed, Gil. You'll never be able to punish me like –"

"That almost looks like remorse on your face," he continued, outraged and uninterruptible. "But I know you. You can slap any look you want on your face and pull out a date-stamped receipt to prove it's genuine. Meghan, I'm not the same sucker you lured into your trap. Quit using those eyes on me."

"These are the only eyes I've got," Meghan protested. "All they're good for now is weeping. So that's what I'll use them exactly for that, if you don't mind, Mr. Gil DeLeo."

Fine lines of rain were slanting through the open window onto the floor. Meghan broke free and reached for the sash. Gil jerked her loose, slapping her.

"Stop it," she wailed, futilely reaching for his hand. "Why don't you just let me go back up on the sill? I'll make all of us happy."

"You know what would make me happy? Smacking some remorse, some feeling, anything, into that beautiful head of yours."

He raised his hand, but before he could strike, Barbara intervened, pulling his hand to his side. Her cup of water fell to the floor and spread across the linoleum.

Gil tried to shove Barbara aside.

"Let me hit her, Barbara. I want to hit her."

"Remember, you're a pacifist," Barbara admonished him.

Gil managed to reach past Barbara to grab Meghan's shoulders and violently shake them. Meghan's head snapped violently back and forth as if it were attached merely by springs as Barbara tried to separate them.

A security guard, a tall and muscular Hispanic, his baby face aged only by a moustache, raced down the corridor and managed to interpose himself. "*Basta*, outside. All of you."

He was younger than the antagonists, and tried to make up for his own uncertainty with a booming voice.

"Sir, let me speak to these two, in private," Barbara said. "I'll make sure they behave."

"Are you certain?" The security guard's dark brown moustache was the same color as his eyes. It fluttered as he studied the trio. "We got a Zero Tolerance Policy here. If you don't calm down, I'm gonna throw you out."

Gil nodded; Meghan continued to gaze yearningly at the open window.

The rain was now a downpour; drops ricocheted off the windowsill, encouraged by restless gusts of wind. The security guard pointedly shut the window and slowly retreated down the corridor, keeping his eyes on the trio.

Barbara took the opportunity to slide between Gil and Meghan.

"Get out of my way," Gil ordered Barbara. "She tried to have me killed. She stole my wallet."

"I beat her up already," Barbara replied. "Honest. For both of us."

"She'd do it again," Gil muttered. "I know she would."

"Gil, she loved him, and now he's dead."

"She's not capable of love."

"She is so," said Barbara as she gently put her arm around her rival's waist.

"Okay. Loved him so much she'd lay down my life for him."

"He died in your place," said Meghan softly.

"Because he was too damn decent to go through with that ludicrous scheme," and at Meghan, "Your scheme."

"I wish there were some way we could thank him," Barbara said. "I know it seems premature, but he deserves some sort of memorial service."

Meghan untied the dashiki from Gil's carry-on and buried her face in it.

"I'm sorry. I'm sorry. I'm sorry. I know you can't forgive me," she whispered hoarsely through the dashiki.

"No kidding," Gil responded.

"You will forgive her though," said Barbara, "for your own sake."

"Will I?"

He refused to meet her gaze.

"I warned you and warned you," Barbara continued, her tone that of a disapproving high school principal. "You had it coming. Even you have to admit that."

"Maybe I will," he grudgingly conceded. "I guess I always knew there were some things you don't gamble with."

He turned to Meghan. "But you. You made me reckless."

"No, she didn't." Barbara reminded him. "Your own gullibility sucked you in."

"Dammit, the trouble with you, Barbara, is that you're always right."

"I am, amn't I."

She happily embraced him.

For the first time, Gil seemed to notice the bandage on her head and gingerly touched it. "What's that?"

"Oh, it's only my head."

Meghan looked at Gil, her expression shattered and vulnerable, devoid of intrigue. She tried to speak, but her lips merely separated without emitting any sound.

At last, she gently twisted the hem of Gil's T-shirt.

"Thomas left me something. I know it can't be undone. I got nothing to equal your pain, but maybe it will alleviate it somewhat."

She undid the dashiki and rummaged through her carry-on to pull out the manila envelope. She slid out the sheet of legal paper and unfolded it to show Gil the instructions in Thomas's meticulous handwriting.

"What is that?" he asked scornfully.

"Instructions on how to redeem these things called bearer bonds. They're negotiable. As good as cash and virtually untraceable."

Gil snorted indignantly.

"Cash! How much cash?" Barbara asked skeptically.

"I don't know. Sixteen or seventeen million dollars."

The two were staggered, Gil recovering first. "I won't touch it."

"Wait a minute, Gil. Think about it." Barbara grew more pragmatically calm by the instant. "The Revolutionary Cuisine. Kiss Slater good-bye. Your own laboratory."

"Blood money," said Gil.

"Believe me, I paid for it with everything I've ever held dear and sacred. It's free and clear," said Meghan with primal mournfulness. She felt ancient, and could not bear to imagine how much the tragedy had ravaged her features.

"Keep some. For whatever you've always wanted to do," offered Barbara. "You can join us." She nestled into Gil's side. "I'll even consider sharing him."

"Barbara!" said Gil.

"You've lost your mind!" Meghan snapped simultaneously.

"It was just a suggestion, you square pair." Barbara touched her bandage. "May we never have a day like this one again."

She threaded her fingers through Meghan's.

"Do you want to go with us? It's going to be horrible to spend the next few hours by yourself."

"I might as well get used to it. There are plenty more where these came from."

"And you're sure about this?" Barbara asked, indicating the instructions.

Meghan waved her hand in a dismissive gesture, having already reneged on all sense of ownership. She met Gil's eyes for an instant, then both their gazes slid away.

"Take care, Gil." She spoke to the floor. "And never let any wretch even think about trying to change you."

"How long will it stay like this?" Gil touched his shorn hair.

"It'll grow out fast."

Barbara pulled a railroad watch from her pocket.

"Come on, Gil. It's not even two o'clock. There's so much we must do. Cash the bonds. Get you shampooed. Find you a new apartment –"

Gil lay his finger on her lips. "Us. Except that we're not going to find –"

Barbara had built up the momentum of her checklist, and it took a second for Gil's statement to derail her. When it registered, her eyes brightened. She lifted her face hopefully, happily, to his. "We?"

The pangs of envy were too much for Meghan. She flinched, then turned her head away to conceal her glistening eyes as Gil nodded his affirmation to Barbara. She bent to pick up the dashiki.

"We're not going to find a new apartment. We're going to buy a car and drive back to Seattle. We are going to be out of this city by six o'clock tonight if we have to walk."

"Are you sure you don't want to come with us?" said Barbara.

Meghan shook her head.

"Promise not to try and kill yourself?"

Meghan grunted.

"Look me in the eye and swear that you won't even think about it," Barbara persisted.

"I promise," she muttered.

"You're at least going down to the ground floor." Gil took her arm and guided her towards her the elevator. But when they reached the lobby, Meghan remained inside. "Don't worry," she reassured them, "I'm going downstairs. I want to see –"

"I understand," Gil said with genuine pity, his expression a gentle, devastating doppelganger of Thomas as the doors slid shut.

•

Meghan wandered the narrow basement corridor, past the laundry carts and deliverymen with hand trucks turning corner after corner until she reached the morgue.

The young blond orderly stood outside the door, not exactly on guard, but preventing anyone else from entering. "Please," she said, clutching the dashiki like a talisman, "may I see Gil DeLeo."

The request seemed to catch the man by surprise. He glanced at his pocket as Meghan reached for the door, then grabbed her wrist. "Afraid you can't go in, ma'am," he said with his gentle Southern accent.

"Isn't he in there?"

"Well, yes."

"Then why can't I see him?"

The man looked nervously around and cleared his throat. "Y'all have to come back in a couple of hours."

"Why?"

"Hospital regulations."

Even after Thomas's death, the system was determined to torment her with as much petty misery as it was capable.

She stuffed the dashiki into her carry-on. Her head weighted with sorrow, she plodded toward the ambulance loading dock and out the swinging doors.

CHAPTER 38.

Consolidated Resources – Reprisal

Yearwood had parked Ilsa's specialized ambulance on a deserted street in Red Hook, just beyond the fringes of gentrification. Decrepit brick buildings were festooned with for-sale signs designed to entice developers that were nowhere to be seen. Whatever fragments of sunlight managed to slash through the thickening clouds rendered them momentarily appealing before the clouds overwhelmed the beams and gloominess returned.

Yearwood and Ilsa sat in the cab smoking, Camels for Yearwood and an apple-flavored vape for Ilsa. Each occasionally directed hostile glances in the other's direction.

At last Yearwood rolled down his window and flicked the remains of his cigarette into the gutter.

"What if we can't track the bitch down?" grumbled Ilsa. "We got until noon tomorrow. Then what? Kiss the bonds good-bye? I don't know how much more useful information we're going to be able to get out of his Lordship."

"Let him sleep," muttered Yearwood.

He phoned the Ops Coordinator. "Any news on Lady Clementine?"

He irritably hung up when there was none.

"You're not getting sentimental, are you?" demanded Ilsa.

"Chill out, Ilsa. Murdock wanted a corpse and a mask. He got both. Right? Isn't eight million dollars worth chilling out for a few hours?"

•

At the Consolidated Resources plaza, Brigitte Budica, also known as Lady Clementine, also known as Meghan Joyce, stood defiantly as the first fingers of the hurricane thrashed the skies above Brooklyn. The plaza was almost deserted. The surrounding skyscrapers concentrated wind to near gale force. Litter spiraled in eddies. Her head tilted back, she silently issued a challenge to the grim skyscraper. The wind whipped a strand of her now raven-colored hair across her face and pasted it against her pale brow. Something ancient and Celtic stirred in her soul, an icy courage granting her the power of imagining and executing legendary feats. She felt herself capable of summoning lightning, of invoking chaos for her personal bidding.

She marched steadfastly across the plaza and through the revolving doors.

The vast dark lobby was charged with the sense of crisis. People shuttled about on urgent missions, their visages dark and preoccupied. The few conversations were low and terse.

A dozen scowling executives and military people, including Colonel Judd and Marwari, emerged from the elevator, irritably slammed their passes onto the tray on the console and stalked out.

Harry studied Meghan for a beat, trying to recall where he might have seen her. Then she leaned her lovely bosom over the console, and he lost his train of thought.

"Brigitte Budica. I have an appointment with Mr. Murdock."

Harry scanned the visitor's log, then looked up. "Afraid your name's not on the log."

"He's expecting me."

Harry picked up the phone and dialed a few numbers, "Mrs. Carr? There's a Brigitte Budica down here. Says that she's here to see Mr. Murdock."

He snapped to attention as Murdock himself came on the phone.

"Send her up by my private elevator."

"Yes, sir. Would you like –"

But Murdock had already hung up. Harry's rosy face flushed towards crimson.

He signed her in and handed her a red security pass. He buzzed the turnstile for her and when Meghan passed through, he nodded toward the only elevator in the wall opposite to the half-a-dozen others from which employees came and went. Murdock's elevator had no floor indicator, no signage of any kind.

She pressed her pass against the reader and entered. The elevator had only three buttons: P, L and B.

She pressed B.

•

The crackling of the Ops Coordinator came over the scanner mounted on the ambulance dashboard. "Lady Clementine spotted –"

Yearwood had already turned the ignition key and was gunning the accelerator. "– in the lobby of Black Rock South."

Yearwood and Ilsa looked at each other, dumbfounded. In the instant Yearwood paused, the engine died. He was so angry at the malfunction that it took him three tries before he had to go through the process all over again.

•

Five minutes later, Meghan still had not arrived at Murdock's office.

Murdock, unshaven, his jacket off, his tie loosened, paced irritably by the doors to his private elevator.

Mrs. Carr sat at her desk, her face puffy, her eyes red, a spray of lilies-of-the-valley before her.

The conference room table was covered with papers. The map of the Indian Ocean on an easel had been heavily annotated with Magic Markers.

"So where the hell is she?" demanded Murdock.

•

Murdock's private elevator had only three unmarked buttons, the light going from the one in the middle to the one on the bottom.

Meghan entered, and when the doors in the basement slid open, she pulled out the EMERGENCY knob, insuring no one would be able to summon the elevator upwards. She hurried down the stark fluorescent-lit corridor, past the bins filled with cans and bottles, carts overflowing with shredded paper, the secrets which tomorrow would be worthless but for which today people died. The hum of water pumps, the creak of elevator cables echoed off the white walls.

A white-haired man in a green uniform glanced at her questioningly. She glared at him, and he scuttled down a side corridor. There were no amenities in the grim catacomb. It was the realm of expendable workers, those who toiled anonymously to sustain the glamour of the people in the skyscraper above. It was also the universe from which she emerged and into which, if she survived, she would not doubt soon plummet. The thought of her impending fate did not depress her but instead filled her with resolution.

She tried various doors along the corridor until she found a utility closet, where she filled a mop bucket with water. Reluctantly, she left her carry-on beside the sink as she came out.

She tried to look as much like a cleaning woman as she could – hunched over, purposeful, unobtrusive – as she wheeled the mop bucket into the service elevator and rode up to unmarked forty-second floor.

The door remained firmly shut until she quickly pressed the red pass against the reader as Thomas had done.

On an overhead monitor, Harry spotted Meghan marching the bucket down the corridor. He stared at her uncertainly, wanting to be positive. He snatched his phone.

"Red alert! Red alert! Forty-second floor," he shouted.

At the computer room's frosted glass door, Meghan held the red pass into the reader. The door buzzed open, and she shoved the bucket inside.

"Main corridor. Intruder. Forty-second floor. Red alert! Red Alert!" Harry's voice boomed over the emergency speakers.

Meghan hoisted the bucket to her chest and hurried through the towering black devices.

Franklin was running to intercept her. Three other staff members were heading there from the back. Outside in the corridor, two guards were struggling with the door.

"No you don't!" shouted Franklin.

With superhuman strength Meghan hurled the water on the power unit upon which she and Thomas had consummated their connection.

Alarms shrieked. Monitors went black. Two terminals exploded, their faces blowing outward. Sparks shot in all directions. Clouds of steam, tinged with a burnt electrical smell, issued from sizzling units. The water cascaded off the computers and streamed through the white floor tiles. Several tiles lifted off the frame as the cables underneath shorted out. Fire suppressant systems exploded in the ceiling. IG55 gas hissed out of nozzles, spreading in ghastly white whorls throughout the room. The lights went off.

A second later the emergency lights came up. An incandescent brilliance stroboscoped through the clouds of gas, smoke and steam.

"You see, my love, just like you said. Water not glue," Meghan whispered as she collapsed beside the power unit.

Franklin yanked her up and grabbed her by the throat. Two analysts struggled to pull their rabid boss's arms down.

A siren down the hall joined the clamoring alarms.

Murdock, clutching a small blue velvet pouch, broke through the crowd.

"Let her go!"

Franklin angrily but obediently released her. The men restraining him redoubled as Meghan's coughs gradually subsided.

"That's an order," snapped Murdock.

Reluctantly, the men released their grip on Franklin.

Meghan swiftly knelt and lay her cheek on the power unit. Raw smoke enveloped her face, coating it with a thin layer of soot.

Murdock yanked her to her feet. She tried to spit in his face. He ducked, spun her around, and held her from behind.

"He can't hear you. He's a corpse, your dashing Don Juan."

Meghan wailed, an ancient and consonantless sound.

"A common thief," Murdock hissed. "A traitor."

Franklin's cursing was so uninterrupted that all stopped paying it any attention.

Members of the computer staff were ripping up the floor panels. Others were throwing paper towels, sweaters, anything that might absorb the rogue water. A few were frantically punching keyboards, trying to bring the system to a safe shutdown. Everyone was shouting at the top of their lungs, contradictory orders and demands.

"Everybody out. Off this floor," Murdock snapped.

He had a softer voice than everyone else, but filled with such fury and authority that the staff, even Franklin, immediately stopped speaking.

"Let us handle this, Mr. Murdock," one of the security guards suggested.

The dozen or so men resumed muttering among themselves.

"I'll kill her," Franklin struggled in the grip of his subordinates. "Let me kill her. Once and for all."

"Get him out of here," ordered Murdock.

"But Mr. Murdock, if we don't try to salvage –"

"Look at this," Murdock gestured with the velvet pouch. "You're not going to salvage anything. Prepare to go to hot site immediately."

Reluctantly, the men exited, dragging Franklin with them. Several paused outside the glass door until Murdock's glare sent them scurrying.

He released Meghan.

She whirled to face him, her fists clenched.

"Murderer. Pig. Scumbucket. Filth. Bully. Slime. Worm. You worthless piece of crap."

Murdock's smile increased like clockwork with each decreasing insult.

"But I'm alive and he's dead. He can't help you. He can't even hear you. He never will."

His words struck her like body blows, but at least restored her anger.

"We brought you to a screeching halt, though. Ha."

Murdock lifted his hand to slap her, but then controlled himself. "You don't think we have complete backup system? A contingency site? One week, at the most two, this outfit will be back in business."

"And you'll be out on your big naked butt."

"You're very naïve, aren't you? You have no idea how protected someone at my level is." He looked at her with profound pity. "I'll have a new position within a few weeks. Perhaps one with even more money and more privileges."

"I'm going to tell. All of them out there. Your wife. About you tied to a rack, begging and drooling."

"You wouldn't dare."

"Wouldn't I?"

Murdock did not seem shaken in the least. "You're no whistleblower."

"You wish. I'll phone *The Times*. McGee O'Hanahan at *Channel Two News*."

"And what makes you think that they aren't already bought? Check the clips. You won't find a single harsh word against this company. In fact, you'll never even find a single word ABOUT the company."

"You'll never rest easy, will you?" Meghan laughed bitterly. "Unless you throw me in jail. Or shoot me."

"I want you alive and free, Meghan Brigitte Budica Shelley Clementine Joyce."

"You're letting me go?"

Meghan could not believe it. She studied his face, his expression, his air of assurance still unmarred.

"You're not calling the cops? Not having me shot?"

"Like I told you, you got a lot of potential for an amateur," Murdock said softly. "You have to get ready for our date. Thursday night. Six p.m. Sharp."

Meghan fell to the power unit, gripping the edge. "I won't! I won't! I won't."

He smiled with a gentle omnipotence. He drew his finger through the dusting of soot on her face.

"Oh, but you will."

"Noooo," said Meghan.

She was surprised that instead of being repulsed by his touch, it tingled with a strange power.

"You think you can run away? You don't think we can find you and bring you in no matter where you try to hide? Be sure to wear that miniskirt. Now, allow me to escort you out."

He pulled her to her feet and dragged her out of the computer room, into the corridor and down the emergency stairs. He seemed obsessively protective of his velvet pouch. The evacuation announcement continued to play in an endless loop, the colorless official tone echoing off the drab green walls. Several employees descending from the upper floors spotted Murdock and hurried down the steps to catch up. Their ID badges flew in nervous arcs at the end of their chains.

"What's going on? Is it . . . ." A chunky African-American woman in a bright orange pantsuit swallowed hard. ". . . like the World Trade Center?"

Murdock flashed his politician's smile at the woman and she relaxed visibly. Meghan stumbled downward at her own stubborn pace.

"We're not in any danger," Murdock reassured the employee in avuncular tones. "The evacuation's only a precaution. Let's continue going down in an orderly fashion, shall we?"

He gestured toward the steps. The group of employees hurried toward the bottom, parting as they passed by Meghan. Murdock sped up briefly to catch up to her and took her arm. Meghan neither conceded nor resisted.

They finally reached the bottom and went through the grey doors into the stormy late afternoon.

•

The cloud-created murk was counteracted by the flashing lights of fire trucks and ambulances. Crowds were gathering across the streets. Tourists had surged from the entrance of the South Street Seaport. Many were filming the pandemonium with their phones, more than a few taking selfies. The windows of the skyscrapers adjacent were crowded with gawkers.

Meghan cast a spiteful glance at the darkened Consolidated Resources building, now more than ever resembling a black tombstone.

Evacuated employees clustered around Murdock, all talking at once. He raised a hand for silence, then summoned the fire chief. His subordinates settled into a ring around him, their positions in the circle almost identical to their rank in the corporate hierarchy. They awaited instructions while their boss and the fire chief conferred.

Murdock reminded Meghan of nothing more than a barracuda surrounded by a school of sycophantic remora. He was in congenial command, almost regal in his mastery of the catastrophe. Meghan was astounded (though she should not have been) that he was treating the evacuation as his moment of personal triumph, instead of the chaos that would hurl him down from his personal Olympus.

The last thing Meghan saw as she threaded her way through the gathering was the kiss Murdock surreptitiously blew at her. She jerked her head to the left, hoping it would fly past her. She thought it did, but she could not be certain.

She broke away from the knot of employees.

"Oh, Meghan," Murdock called her over. "I almost forgot."

He, too, had broken away from his subordinates. He opened the drawstring of the blue velvet bag. He withdrew a white plaster oval and held it up. "I have something you might like to see."

Despite herself, Meghan turned toward him.

Murdock held the object in such a way that she could not fathom what she was looking at. She bent closer. Murdock turned it at an angle to catch the sun.

The pale features leapt into focus: Thomas's face, his lips creased in pain, his eyes closed.

Meghan gasped, then screamed, disconcerting the crowd and causing Murdock's entourage to step closer to him protectively.

She reached out for one last connection to the death mask, a trophy to the monster before her, to Meghan a memorial of the man she loved.

Murdock wagged a reproving finger at her.

"Mustn't touch. He's still damp."

She buckled to her knees. Air came in and out of her throat without lingering in her lungs; half moans wheezed from deep within her chest. The employees looked on, but they were more concerned with their boss's wishes than Meghan's anguish.

Murdock gazed at the death mask for a moment, then slid it lovingly into the velvet pouch.

"Remember? I told you he would be the pride of my collection."

He laughed a deep jolly laugh.

The knot of employees trailing behind him dutifully echoed his mirth without understanding its provenance.

Meghan managed to drag herself to a planter and leaned against it, lowering her head towards her knees.

Several men and a few women asked if she was okay, but she waved them away.

At last she managed to stagger unsteadily up Water Street.

She desperately studied the expressions of the people who walked by, wondering how they could remain casual, even happy, in the face of such overwhelming tragedy. Though they might be escaping personal devastation at the moment, did they not sense the doom that awaited them around the corner?

At last she passed by the tiny lighthouse at the entrance to Seaport Plaza. The scent of freshly cooked seafood blew in from an outdoor restaurant. A jaunty Dixieland tune wafted from a band on the stage near the river.

For a moment she considered walking over and continuing walking until she nestled in the permanent sanctuary of the East River. But she had promised Barbara otherwise and besides, there were too many people around. Not only would she not achieve her aim, but she would end up providing yet another tawdry momentary spectacle for people she despised.

She desperately needed human touch, a shoulder to cry out her misery upon. Someone to share her loss. But there was no one in the world, other than her cousin Moira, with whom she could share the events of the recent few days. Simultaneously, she wanted to crawl in some deep burrow to find the comfort that darkness and insensibility would offer.

The crowd's jolliness, the bright synthetic merriment of Seaport Plaza, was suffocating her.

She stumbled from the tourist glare to the comforting darkness between the gentrified warehouses. Perhaps she would have a drink at the bars starting to fill up with Wall Street workers. Or several drinks, and see if liquor would provide an escape, no matter how fleeting.

She reached Peck Slip and realized that she only had another block before the bars and restaurants ran out. She stood on the corner, uncertainly looking around.

Unwelcome pragmatic questions nipped at her. Who would notify Thomas's family? How would she even track them down? Would the state allow her to claim Thomas's body? Why had they never allowed themselves to discuss what to do if he were actually assassinated? Where did he want to be buried? Did he want to be buried at all?

A stooped woman approached Meghan, the woman's posture so bowed that she could not lift her head up. Her raincoat dragged along the sidewalk.

"Please, ma'am, can you spare a quarter so an old lady can get a cup of coffee?"

Meghan studied the scarf covering the woman's grey hair. Incongruously, it was fine silk, Hermes or Balenciaga, and Meghan wondered from which discard pile or thrift shop the woman had obtained it.

"I can do better than that," Meghan said sadly. She was rummaging through her handbag for a few coins when she felt a sharp stinging at the base of her neck.

"Ow!" she cried and slapped herself.

"Are you okay, ma'am?" the old woman inquired anxiously.

"I don't know. Got stung by something. Wasp. Or hornet."

"You're not allergic, are you?"

The woman graciously extended her hands.

"I don't think so."

Meghan resumed searching in her handbag. She felt queasy, and when she looked up, the buildings were whirling around her. She staggered a few steps toward a doorway.

The woman followed after, her posture miraculously straightening, her features rejuvenating, as she sought to catch the careening Meghan.

The last thing Meghan saw before the world went black was the gloating expression of Ilsa.

CHAPTER 39.

Escape from New York

"First things first," said Barbara, as she entered a stationery store, where she purchased a pair of scissors.

"Okay, yeah," said Gil.

"Let's get a cup of coffee first."

They paused in front of a coffee shop, and Gil hesitated. "I know they're not from Seattle, and I should be supporting the local team . . . ."

Barbara took him by the arm. "One hour ago you almost got killed. Don't you think being this persnickety is a little trivial?"

He allowed himself to be led inside. He barely had time to sip his double espresso and turn up his nose when Barbara said, "Come on. The coast's clear."

She punched the code to the toilet door, and making sure no one was watching, yanked Gil inside and shut the door. She sat him in the front of the toilet and holding his head back, snipped off his permanent as close as she dared. Short shiny black ringlets cascaded into the bowl.

She tilted his head, making tiny adjustments here and there, then flushed the toilet.

Someone was knocking on the toilet door.

"Whaddya think?" Barbara asked.

Gil rose to study himself in the mirror.

"I think I looked better as a poodle."

"You didn't look like a poodle. You looked like a target. Now come on."

When they opened the door, a blue-haired woman with an enormous designer handbag stood there, scowling.

Barbara beamed at her, then turned to Gil as the woman stepped past them.

"Daaaahling, you were wonderful!" Barbara said to Gil. "And I always thought I was insatiable."

The woman's expression spiraled from scowling to aghast.

"What?" Gil exclaimed. "Wait a minute –"

He turned to explain Barbara's joke to the woman, but the toilet door had already slammed shut.

"What are you doing?" Gil demanded.

"Something I've always wanted to do." Barbara smiled. "Didn't you see her expression? I wanted to give her something to tut-tut to her trophy grandkids."

"I thought we were trying to be inconspicuous."

Barbara studied Gil from head to foot.

"You're right. We can never go into a Park Avenue private bank dressed like this."

•

They realized their quest for new outfits might not go as smoothly as they anticipated when the first consignment shop they found had a sign in the window reading, "$500 off your first $1,000 purchase."

Gil and Barbara glanced at each other and decided to head north to more familiar territory.

They got lucky at the Housing Works shop on East 64th.

When they emerged, Gil wore a crisp new seersucker suit and shiny wingtips; Barbara a skirt suit and white shoes (in which she almost felt comfortable). A demure violet hat with a veil covered her bandaged bruise and she carried a glossy handbag of similar hue. Gil carried a carrier bag containing their old clothes.

"You know, you look pretty good in purple," said Gil.

"It's not purple, it's mauve," Barbara corrected him.

"And even better in a skirt."

"What are food revolutionary farm women supposed to wear? Other than bibs and braces?"

•

Doing their best not to act apprehensive, Gil and Barbara ascended the portico steps of a Park Avenue skyscraper between East 48th and East 49th.

With deep exhales and a brief handclasp for luck, they entered the bank's lobby. Marble walls, discreetly covered with brass screens, soared to the lofty ceilings. The walls, the security console, the escalators to the mezzanine gave the space the profundity of an Egyptian temple, although the god worshipped was Almighty Commerce not some lesser deity.

"I sure hope Meghan wasn't lying," Gil remarked. "I'd hate to think we just spent your life savings on clothes we're only going to wear once."

"She was telling the truth," answered Barbara. "Woman's intuition. Now, do you remember all the things you're supposed to say?"

Gil nodded as they crossed the solemn granite distance to the security console.

•

The 35th floor office of the Private Banking department was even sleeker and more intimidating than the one on the ground floor. The receptionist, behind a desk almost as austere as she was herself, had cheekbones that would cut glass.

"May I help you?" she asked with an Eastern European accent."

"We're here to see Mr. Sebastiano Briones," Gil told her.

With a deferential smile, the austere woman escorted the nervous pair through the heavy walnut doors to Briones's office overlooking Park Avenue. The banker could not have been much older than Gil, but his snug designer clothes and the grave self-assurance that mantled him endowed Briones with the authority of many decades in the banking industry.

"Thomas Catherton told us that you would be expecting us," Gil said after they shook hands.

Briones studied Barbara carefully. "I thought Mr. Catherton said you were a redhead."

"I was. But even redheads get tired of stereotypes," Barbara smiled.

"We're here to redeem these," Gil said. He opened the envelope and handed the instructions over to Briones.

Briones read it carefully. "Can you give me a few seconds?"

He unlocked a drawer in a sideboard and removed a small file box which he also unlocked. With a magnifying glass Briones had taken from his desk drawer. he scrutinized the signatures on the legal sheet and the file card.

He lay the magnifying glass down and looked up.

"It's genuine."

Below the level of the desk, Gil and Barbara squeezed hands.

"If you'll just wait here. Thank you. Give me a few minutes."

Gil and Barbara exchanged a glance, daring not allow any expression of relief to escape lest it jinx their impending good fortune.

Briones went through the doors and returned five minutes later with a fat Redweld. "Everything seems to be in order."

He turned the Redweld upside down and dumped the bearer bonds upon his desk. Their gilt edges gleamed upon the dark mahogany. Briones's expression was unreadable as he rapidly thumbed through the ornate certificates.

"You know that Mr. Catherton's wishes were to set up an anonymous custodial account with Credito Aurelio in Nassau," Gil said.

"He indeed mentioned that possibility." Briones tamped the bonds against the desk until all their edges were aligned. "Have you selected your access code?"

"Uh, yes, the access code."

"So he can get the money wired to him," Barbara added helpfully.

"PLANKTON1," suggested Gil. "All caps and a number one at the end."

"Usually we recommend a more random mixture of numbers and letters."

"In that case," said Gil, "make the first P lower case."

"As you insist, sir," sighed Briones. "And policy dictates that once the money goes into the custodial account, we will no longer have any control over it nor any method to even trace where the money went. There will be absolutely no chance of clawback."

"He's quite aware of that."

"Let me fill out the requisite forms," said Briones as he rose. "Allow twenty-four hours for the transfer to take effect."

•

When they emerged from the bank, Gil was so tense he could barely breathe. With the information to retrieve the money discretely tucked in her new handbag, Barbara found that only deep gulps of the humid air allowed her to surface from her dazed astonishment.

The pair walked west on East 49th, their expressions of awestruck wonder distinguished them from the mass of similarly clad young executives hurrying out of the towering buildings.

The minute they crossed Fifth Avenue, Gil let out a whoop of delight. "Can you believe it! We pulled it off!"

A few passers-by turned to look, though only the tourists expended more than a quick glance at the couple.

"Shh," admonished Barbara. "Do I have to remind you? A man died so that we could have that money. It's not something to celebrate. It's something we should always remember with regret and respect."

"You're right," replied a chastened Gil. "I'm just a little wound up. I can't believe that this morning I was going to die by proxy and this afternoon I'm a millionaire. Now what are we going to do about getting out of this mad-house? How are we going to buy a car, get insurance and replace your driver's license? Especially since it's almost five, and the money won't be available for twenty-four hours."

"Well, she did give us all that money," replied Barbara. "I suppose we could use it to take a bus to Chicago and stay with my friends."

"We're millionaires, Barbara. Millionaires don't travel by bus."

"No, we're not. Not until the day after tomorrow."

Gil laughed, the first expression of relief he had made the entire day. "Just kidding. I'm still Gil. Believe me, after the last week, I always will be. Now come on."

He dragged her a few steps towards Sixth Avenue.

"Where are we going?" Barbara asked suspiciously.

"Where else?" Gil replied. "Port Authority to catch our bus."

CHAPTER 40.

Ambulance – Again

When Meghan awoke, she felt as if she had been traveling for hours, though she could not explain why.

In her mind she knew that Gil and Barbara had forgiven her, but in her soul she wondered if she would ever be capable of forgiving herself, knowing the depths to which she had so willingly plunged.

A roaring headache prevented her from opening her eyes more than a slit. What she glimpsed made her shut them immediately: Ilsa's face looming over her, her tongue flicking with anticipation, traces of saliva glinting on the borders of her lips, like a reptile anticipating its helpless victim.

Meghan tried to struggle away and realized that her chest and legs were bound to the bed. She sensed that she was reclining upon some sort of mattress or futon but dared not peek.

Ilsa gripped Meghan's chin between her thumb and forefinger; her strength was demonic.

Meghan grimaced from the additional pain, but refused to open her eyes.

"I know you're awake. Don't try to fool me." The woman's breath was warm and minty. "All I want is the money, and I'll let you go."

"It's in my handbag. All my credit cards have been shredded."

Meghan felt a slight pinprick in her earlobe and her head exploded. She cried out in pain. The sound echoed back upon her almost immediately. She could sense that she was in a confined, almost claustrophobic space.

"I warned you, Ilsa," said a voice that she almost recognized. "Nothing esoteric on the woman."

Meghan felt the needle being yanked out of her ear. The pain diminished in blessed waves.

"Jesus, Mary and Joseph," she said despite herself.

"Acupuncture's not esoteric," the woman muttered.

Meghan sensed the woman shifting her weight to allow someone much larger to take her place. A man whose voice was silky, but whose unstated threats were far more terrifying.

"Yearwood!" she exclaimed.

Her eyes flew open. The assassin was hovering above her, still wearing his EMS tunic, now with a scorched hole at the waist.

Meghan peered down through blurry eyes, swiveling her head as far as she was able and found herself strapped into the right-hand gurney of an ambulance.

A plastic curtain hung from the ceiling, draped over both Ilsa and Yearwood. On it hung stainless steel implements that bore an ominous resemblance to torture devices in Murdock's bolthole.

Whenever Yearwood or Ilsa stirred, the instruments clanked against each other, a sound that penetrated her hearing like an ice pick. Meghan shuddered as she considered the instruments' purpose and history and tried to put her speculation as far back in her mind as possible. She did not succeed.

"Would you care for a glass of water?" Yearwood asked.

There was so little room in the ambulance that she could sense the corded muscles of his legs through his uniform. She tried to shrink away from his contact, but she could compress her body no further.

"That stuff really dries you out," Yearwood sympathized.

Meghan nodded.

Yearwood gestured to Ilsa, who fiddled with a cooler against the driver's compartment. She handed Yearwood a paper cup.

"It's no use lying, Meghan," Yearwood said as he tipped the cup to allow her to drink.

A few drops dribbled down her chin, and Yearwood gently wiped them off with a tissue.

"We know you left the house with a manila envelope with instructions on cashing in seventeen million dollars worth of bearer bonds."

"How do you know that?" Meghan asked.

"What did you do with them after you and the kid came to his Lordship's apartment."

"I gave them away."

She gave Yearwood her most defiant smile.

"You WHAT?" exclaimed Yearwood.

His dark eyes blazed; he thrust his face into hers, but Meghan maintained her defiant gaze.

"The woman's an inveterate liar," snapped Ilsa. "Please, Yearwood, give me five minutes with her."

Ilsa held up a syringe and squeezed the plunger. A single drop glistened on the silver needle tip.

Meghan eyes widened. She tried to shrink back but the straps prevented her.

"I had this bradykinin custom-synthesized," Ilsa bragged to Yearwood. "I tell you, just a few micrograms. Not only will I find out where the bonds are, but I'll get you their denominations and serial numbers. I promise I won't do anything esoteric. I'll get the information out of her the old-fashioned way."

"Go ahead, kill me," said Meghan. "It just means that I'll rejoin the man I love that much sooner."

Yearwood and Ilsa exchanged a look, then Yearwood said, "Always the Irish romantic, Lady Clementine. If we kill you, we'll never find out where those bonds are. Now, we can get the information very quickly."

"Or very slowly," said Ilsa, indicating the syringe. Her delighted eagerness was almost erotic.

Meghan defiantly closed her eyes. She was starting to cry, not at the thought of impending torture, but at how horribly wrong everything had gone: the loss of Thomas, the suffering she had inflicted upon an innocent young couple. The great emptiness that she would face in the unlikely event she survived.

Her tears obviously discomfited Yearwood. "Now who are these alleged beneficiaries?"

Meghan continued, sniffling.

"Yearwood, get a hold of yourself," Ilsa growled. "Women cry on cue. We've been trained to do it since birth. Her tears mean nothing."

"Let me take care of this," Yearwood retorted. "If I don't get anything out of her, I'll let you take over."

He leaned into to Meghan's face. "Somewhere between the time you left Thomas's apartment and arrived at the computer room, you hid that envelope. Now tell us where you concealed it, and you'll be a free woman."

"I'll never be a free woman. Not after today."

"Sweetheart, your repartee is less and less entertaining."

"I told you, I gave it away. I didn't have any need for it."

"Listen, if you don't tell me soon, I will unleash my colleague. Trust me, you don't want that."

Yearwood's gracious façade was starting to crumble.

"Go ahead and tell them, Meghan, dearest," croaked a voice from the other side of the curtain.

"Damn!" said Ilsa. "I told you we should have gagged the son-of-a-bitch."

"I thought he would be out until morning," said Yearwood. "He must have the constitution of a horse."

"Thomas?" whispered Meghan, not daring to believe.

She opened her eyes and craned her head as far as the strap across her chest would allow. She saw only the expanse of the white curtain.

"Is it true? Is it you? Are you really alive? Or is it some sick trick to find their bloody money?"

"Both," Yearwood replied.

He drew the curtain back; it bunched at the back of the narrow aisle; several of the instruments clunking to the floor.

Thomas was strapped in the left hand gurney. His dashiki was ripped; the first graze still bandaged. Tape held down a wad of gauze on his shoulder wound and an IV bag dripped into his arm. In the dim, garish light cast by the bulb in the ambulance's roof, Thomas looked haggard, as if he had aged a decade in a day. His face had an oily sheen that was flecked with whitish bits of a rubbery substance.

"As you can see, I'm very much alive. Well, alive in any case."

He attempted to smile.

"Oh, Thomas, oh, Jesus."

Her emotions collapsed. She wept openly. In gratitude, in the realization that the second lease on happiness she had just been granted would probably soon be taken away from her.

"What did they do to your face?"

"I guess I'm the only person in history who modeled their death mask and lived to tell about it."

He laughed, but even that slight effort was agonizing.

"The histrionics are cute, but what about the bonds?" Ilsa reminded the group.

"Just tell Yearwood what you did with them," Thomas urged her.

"Why? So they can kill us? Or torture us and then kill us?"

"Would you stop this chit-chat," Ilsa exploded.

She laid the syringe upon the cooler, then unhooked an implement from the rack.

"If you insist, we can start simply."

She pressed a lever upon the instrument over and over. Its severe metal click penetrated to Meghan's very marrow.

"Tell them what you did with the instructions, Meghan," Yearwood ordered.

"I gave it to the chef and his girlfriend. To repent for the fact I almost had him killed. I mean, it wasn't exactly something for which I could say an Act of Contrition, was it?"

"Why would anyone just give away seventeen million dollars?" Yearwood asked, not believing a word she said.

"I thought Thomas was dead," she snapped. "Whose fault was that?"

"Did you really, dearest?" Thomas whispered.

Even he was skeptical.

"What's this jerk's address?" Ilsa said. She took one step to the left, one step to the right, clicking her implement.

Meghan studied the three faces: Ilsa's anxious to the point of apoplexy, Yearwood's dubious and unreadable, and Thomas summoning astonishment despite his suffering.

Meghan stonily returned the stares of the group.

"They were going to cash in the bonds, buy a car," Meghan continued, "and drive out to Seattle. They intended to be out of the city by six o'clock tonight. So I guess now their address is New Jersey or Pennsylvania."

Yearwood studied her with a chilling analytic gaze. "Okay, we're going to start from the beginning. We know you brought the patsy to his Lordship's apartment."

Ilsa brought the instrument close to Meghan's ear, clicking it remorselessly. Yearwood did not restrain her.

"His name is Gil. He was a drama major at the University of Washington. He worked at Restaurant X but he quit. His girlfriend is named Barbara. I don't know where she's from."

"You expect me to believe that's all you know?"

"Oh, I forgot one thing. Gil's very good-hearted, and he didn't deserve what I put him through."

"Damn," said Ilsa. "Damn. Please, Randall, just give me five minutes alone with her. And let his Lordship listen. I've really been practicing since the last time we went out on our botched joint mission."

Yearwood did not speak; his face was inscrutable as he considered alternatives.

Ilsa's voice grew cold, a tone far more intimidating than her heated fury. "If you're not going to let me question her, let's stop wasting time on these two. They're utterly useless to us. I know a bridge about twenty miles outside of Albany. We'll just park the ambulance —"

"Thomas, I'm sorry I brought this upon you," Meghan managed to say between sobs. "I didn't realize how much over my head I was in. Anything I did was because I loved you."

Thomas reached across the gap between the two gurneys.

Meghan tilted her body towards him, as far as her bonds would allow.

Ilsa smacked Thomas's arm down. He grimaced in agony as the impact rippled up his arm to his shoulder.

"Stop it," cautioned Yearwood.

"Well, what do we do with them?" said Ilsa. "We can't take them back to New York."

"'O my God, I am heartily sorry for having offended Thee.'" Meghan whispered to herself, her lips barely moving as she resigned herself to the diabolical ingenuity about to be unleashed upon her. She tried to convince herself that she deserved whatever was about to happen, but she did not succeed.

Partial images flooded her imagination, senselessly and in no particular sequence.

The time she and Thomas went to the Greenwich Village Halloween parade, her amusement at the bank employees who costumed themselves as a cow herd.

A basket of cheer that had been her prize at a parish bingo game, the only thing she'd ever won in her life.

The smell of City Island during a winter storm, her father frantically scurrying about the boat landing as he performed his futile experiments.

But particularly vivid were the sculptures of the damned suffering the torments of Hell in Fatima dioramas.

She wondered at what point, what decisions made or unmade she could have chosen that would have averted such a horrible ending.

Allowing Thomas to throw himself into the Hudson?

Recognizing that he was light years out of her league, she should have squelched any possibilities of involvement from the time they first met.

Those black-clad widows and their relish of disaster had been absolutely right about life being nothing but a catalogue of misery and suffering. Distress and despair had always been her birthright. Thomas had bestowed on her the one brief year of happiness she had been granted, and she chastised herself even more fervently for her ingratitude.

As she resumed another Act of Contrition, her inner prayer was that the two assassins would be quick and extend whatever mercy they were capable of to her, and especially to Thomas.

"Look, Mr. Yearwood –" Meghan began.

Both Yearwood and Ilsa tensed.

"There's only one chance you and Lover Boy," Ilsa said, "have getting out of here alive."

She brandished her shiny little toy and clicked it several times for emphasis.

"If you tell us exactly what happened to the money. And that bullshit story about giving it to some stranger off the street doesn't count."

The air was growing fetid with their shared breath.

"I know that. So I'm not going to try and convince you. Even though it's the truth. I'm not even going to ask you to spare our lives, because you're going to do what you intended to do all along. I mean why should I beg for mercy, when I didn't show any to poor Gil?"

"Remember, Yearwood, your promise," Thomas's voice was growing hoarse. "You promised to look me in the eye."

"But before . . . before you do whatever, could we have a few moments alone?" Meghan asked. Resigned to anything that might befall her, her tone was unruffled, unsharpened by whimper or plea.

"No," said Ilsa.

"Yes," said Yearwood, though not as quickly.

"I knew it!" Ilsa stamped her foot. "I knew you were getting sentimental on me."

"One last request," Meghan pleaded. "Is my miraculous medal still around my neck?"

"We're killers," Ilsa snapped, "not thieves."

Yearwood seemed startled by the question and peered at the pale field of Meghan's upper chest. He nodded.

"I know it shouldn't, but it means a lot to me," Meghan continued. "I'd feel a lot better if it were still hanging around my neck."

Yearwood lifted up the medal and studied the embossed figure of the Savior's mother. Meghan could see the sparkle of reflection from the ceiling light track across his salt-and-pepper beard into his eye.

"We'll dump these two in that ravine near Albany, then head for Seattle," snapped Ilsa. "We'll use the spotters to find that chef, then have our little pleasure with the thieves."

Click. Click. Click.

"Then split the money."

"You don't think Murdock will blow a gasket if we don't show up for a couple Mondays?"

Furrows on Ilsa's bland face grooved more deeply with her rising anger. "Why are you hesitating? The boss is right. You're losing your resolve."

"You think so?"

"I know so."

Randall whipped out his pistol and fired three times, the shots clustering directly above Ilsa's heart. The impact of the bullets propelled her sprawling out the doors into the highway darkness.

The shiny instrument in her hand fell to the floor, and it, too, bounced outside.

Meghan screamed as rain mist drifted inside to mingle with gun smoke.

"Why should I split the money?" Randall shrugged as he slid his pistol back into his holster.

When he glimpsed Meghan's stricken expression, he said, "Oh, dear. I just accidentally killed my colleague. Perhaps Ilsa was right. Maybe I AM losing my edge. "

He patted Meghan's wrist. "Anyway, this world and the one wherever she ended up are both better places."

"What . . . what are you going to . . ." Meghan asked.

"What else? Drop you off somewhere safe."

"The St. Regis Indian reservation," Thomas spoke. "There's a casino there, and I'm sure with a little of investigation, we can find someone to smuggle us across the St. Laurence into Canada."

"Canada?" Meghan replied.

"Tell me, would you feel bored in a ranch outside Saskatoon?"

"Listen, I have earned every bit of my boredom. But why?"

"I have a sister whose husband died a few years back. She still owns the ranch, but I've been sending her money from time to time to help her out and some to stash away for me. Meghan, my sweet Meghan, there should be enough to see us through till I've healed."

The three exchanged glances as Meghan took it all in. At last she spoke. "But what about the bullet that's still in Thomas? I know it would be risky to take him to a hospital, but –"

Randall reached into his pants pocket and pulled out a small plastic envelope with an fragment of irregularly shaped metal. He handed it to Meghan.

"What's this?" she asked.

"The bullet," Randall replied, and at Meghan's puzzled expression. "Because of, uh, her line of work, Ilsa became quite an expert into sticking bits of metal into people. Thomas's impromptu surgery was just a collateral benefit."

Meghan closed her eyes under the weight of accumulating gratitude. And when she opened them, "But what about Gil and Barbara? You'll let them keep the money, won't you?"

Averting his gaze as his fingers brushed the necklace on her pale bosom, Yearwood undid the buckle of the strap restraining her.

"At least some of it?" continued Meghan.

"Don't stand up too quickly," he instructed her.

"Please, don't hurt them," Meghan begged.

Yearwood shrugged. "That's gonna be up to them."

"I'm sorry about the money," said Thomas.

Yearwood paused, framed in the door. Headlights from overtaking cars and trucks cast fleeting rainbows through the gentle drizzle.

"I never thought she'd give it away to a total stranger," Thomas continued, "but I'm proud of her."

"It was bullshit for someone like me to hope to even glimpse a whiff of the money without a struggle."

"There's a small painting by an English artist, J.M.W. Turner, in my apartment. It won't fetch seventeen million, but you're welcome to flog it for a few bob."

"I don't think there's enough money to compensate me for the risk I've put myself in. You ever consider what Murdock's replacement's gonna do to me if he ever find's out you're still alive and Ilsa's dead by my hand? Even if we sell that painting, you still owe me, Thomas. I don't know how you'll ever repay me, but you'll still owe me."

"As you Americans are so fond of saying," Thomas smiled, "deal."

Yearwood pushed the back door all the way open.

Smells of ripe earth, of corn about to be harvested, the rich overwhelming ripeness of life itself gently overcame the clinically ominous pungency of the ambulance.

"Please don't harm Gil and Barbara," Meghan repeated. "They didn't do anything except encounter me."

Yearwood did not respond, but slid the curtain all the way to the front of the compartment.

"The late Ilsa Hagel can ride up front with me. As far as her favorite ravine," Yearwood said.

He stepped outside, then paused and turned. "Know what they call this type of ambulance?"

"Torturemobile?" Thomas volunteered.

"Nope. 'Honeymoon Special'." He smiled. "Enjoy your ride, lovebirds."

He closed the door.

●

The ambulance lurched forward, wheels crunching the gravel on the shoulders. Several thumps as the vehicle gained the pavement, and then the whirr of the accelerating tires as Yearwood steered the ambulance West.

The instruments clanked softly in their nests in the curtains bunched at the front of the compartment.

Meghan unbuckled the gurney strap and rose unsteadily. She staggered with the sway of the truck to cross the gap between herself and Thomas. She clasped his hand, their eyes absorbing each other in pulses of disbelief and gratitude.

"Will they really let us go?" Meghan asked, unable to accept that Fate, which grants no one a reprieve, had spared her.

"Yearwood's always been a man of his word," Thomas assured her. "And I suspect he's gloating that somehow he has tweaked Murdock's tail."

He patted the gurney, and Meghan slid in beside him. She snuggled against him, and when she leaned against the pillow, her head felt an irregular lump. Curious, she reached underneath it to extract a bundle wrapped in a rayon scarf.

She undid the scarf and allowed her grandmother's rosary to spill out.

Grateful and astonished, she ran the beads through her fingers. "These were my grandmother's! 'Hail Mary, full of grace . . .'."

She lay the beads aside to examine the other object in the bundle. "Budica!" she exclaimed, and squeezed the picture book to her breast.

"I made them go by your apartment," Thomas said. "I thought it would be the least you deserved if you gave up the money."

She happily flipped a few pages – Budica standing up to the Romans, Budica exhorting her troops.

Nestling against Thomas, she held up the book so he could study the colorful pictures. He used his good hand to peel the black wig away.

When she saw his discomfort, she reached up to assist him. "Let me help."

"No, I want to do this myself."

She tilted her head to allow him freer access. After a little more struggle by Thomas, her tawny hair had been freed. She shook her head to unfurl it to its full glory, and at last it tumbled down upon her shoulders.

Thomas took a handful of strands and inhaled their natural fragrance.

"Meghan, I'm glad that we survived, if only because I have something to confess," Thomas sighed. "I'm not an aristocrat. I didn't grow up on an estate."

"What?"

"I wasn't raised by a nanny. Hell, I'm not even British. I'm an American. Old man was a bricklayer from Gary, Indiana, named Robert Watts. My real name is Robert Watts, Jr."

"Your poetry. Your accent. Your entire being."

Meghan had almost lost the capability of being shocked, but her face creased with what little astonishment she was able to muster upon hearing this latest bombshell. She could tell that the act of speaking was causing him pain, but somehow she knew that he might never again lay down his guard as he did at this moment. "But how?" she managed to utters.

His crisp enunciation softened, as with every word the rounder tones of the Midwest eased through. "Ah, in my wild and misspent youth, I was bumming around Europe. Applied to Oxford as a lark. Some how I got it into Keble, the most impoverished college of all."

"And . . . did you graduate?"

"Only went one semester. Then some people from an organization on the lookout for people who could 'live by their wits'," His speech slowed. "Being a chameleon with a gift for mimicry, they thought I might have some 'potential'."

Her jaw dropped in stunned disbelief, as she tried to come to grips with the force and circumstance that resulted in her being stuck in an ambulance in the middle of nowhere, the risky flight to sanctuary ahead of them, and now, stripped of most resources. She could not help but pray that somehow his calculated deception had somehow cancelled a betrayal instigated by the noblest of intentions.

"They repapered me. Crafted my legend. I worked in the City of London for a couple of years as an ersatz merchant banker."

Concerned by the toll the exertion his confession was taking on him, Meghan interrupted. "You can tell me all this later."

Waning energy would not halt him, and Thomas continued. "My dad fell ill, so I went back to the States to look after him. When I returned to the U.K., the organization had vanished without a trace. I decided to do the same."

His words in Restaurant X, which now seemed to have been uttered centuries ago, came back to her, his earnestness as he tried to warn her. "I say this not to deceive you, but to protect you."

"So everything you told me is a lie?"

"Maybe about my past. But never about my feelings." He reached out his hand with seemingly his last bit of energy. "Come here."

She tilted her head, softening in the awareness of his unfathomable and unwavering concern for her.

Meghan allowed him to thread his fingers through hers, and close to tears, managed to say. "Darling, I'm so sorry about – about –"

"Shh," he whispered.

"And the fact I gave away all your money. I didn't know you were still alive. Please, don't hate me."

"Hate you?' Thomas tried to smile. "Your generosity just makes me cherish you all the more."

"Yeah, but once you recover and come to your right mind, how long is that gonna last?"

He turned to her as much the IV tube would allow, his face now a visage of pure honesty. Then he murmured, in a voice not much louder than a whisper. "Forever."

Yearwood swerved, the motion of the ambulance throwing her into an embrace with Thomas for which Meghan needed no excuse.

SPECIAL THANKS...

Windswept has had a life history almost as convoluted as my own. So many people have influenced the development of both myself and the novel, that if I have omitted anyone who helped along the way, please forgive me. I will recognize you in subsequent editions.

I'd like to thank Kay Ellen Rahmlow, who introduced me to Brooklyn and all the wonderful people living there and to whom I first told the story one bright spring morning on Henry Street between Remsen and Joralemon in Brooklyn Heights.

If the novel is a smooth read, it is due in no small part to a quartet of talented editors: Michael Simpson, my long-time friend from the old days at the Playwright's Forum in Charlotte, North Carolina; former *Vanity Fair* Copy Editor Alison Merrill; academic author Marcy Manning; and another longtime friend from our Midtown/Wall Street investment banking days, author, biographer, essayist and Spanish-English literary translator Kevin Brown.

I also want to thank my team of readers for their constructive "wait-a-minutes!": Marti Cooney, Karen Erani, Nancy Taggart, Kate and Stan at Whitman House, and especially Sandra Drew, whose time treading the boards provided great insight into depths of drama and emotion.

My gratitude to friends and family, who have put up with a lot over the years: David and Georgia Sawyer-Classey, Leigh & Jim Paulsen Maddox, Ray & Irene Maddox and Lisa & Tom Goldring. And to Jennie Griffiths for her support and on-target marketing expertise.

Thanks to Tremayne Miller for opening my eyes to so much.

I'd also like to give a nod to my long-time screenwriting partner, Frank Hickey, author of the unique Dancing Max Royster Mystery Series for his support and imagination along the way.

Finally kudos to all the actors who took part in the reading of a screenplay adaptation at the Looking Glass Theatre, W. 57th Street, Manhattan: Joshua Berg, Virgil Goya (Guitierrez), Robin Hussa, William Kirksey, Anne-Marie Lindbloom, James Kentish, Letitia Raines, Monica Russell, Josh Spafford and James Weber.

Any errors that remain are my fault alone.

Shiva Sawyer was born a vagabond spirit and has yet to learn the meaning of "comfort zone."

After earning a degree in organic chemistry at Florida's experimental New College, he was an editor of the underground paper, *The Charlotte Inquisition.* He also wrote "The Tattered Rose" (*Ellery Queen's Mystery Magazine 500th First Story*), lyrics for Wombat Productions bands The Mongolords and Moose Magic & the Spoilsports as well as the First Light Stage Company misfire, *December Never Yields.* He also wrote the cult classic, *Space Avenger*, one of the world's last true Technicolor films.

Founder and publisher emeritus of Pigtown Books and Hidden Pearl Books, Sawyer currently writes screenplays for Norwich-based EQ Films.

•

If you enjoyed *Windswept*, you'll also enjoy Sawyer's other book (co-written with Frances Witlin), *An Uncertain Currency* [trade paper-back], a.k.a. *Other Arms, Other Eyes* [eBook]:

Itinerant psychic performer Mario Castigliani and police chief Beaufort Tyler join forces in Floraville, Georgia, to investigate a suspicious death.

An elderly Black Civil Rights activist supposedly committed suicide, but Tyler has his doubts – especially since Tyler's predecessor recently died the same way. Castigliani's authentic ability to read minds (which Tyler never doubts) proves invaluable both to the plot and to the narrative, which includes frequent "unspoken" clues.

The authors enrich the action with references to Castigliani's Italian past in the Umbrian city of Perugia, local textile mill unrest, personal entanglements, and believable characters.

An excellent read.

~ Library Journal